*Praise for two-time IPPY Award-winning novelist*

# Darden North

"North's visually acute, action-packed style ... is likely headed for the silver screen."

~George Halas
*New York Journal of Books*

"Darden North once again writes the prescription for a perfect thriller ... a dose of current events mixed in an engaging story. Need a great book to read? *Party Favors* is just what the doctor ordered."

~Marshall Ramsey, Emmy Award-winning Cartoonist
Two time Pulitzer Award Finalist

"North's stories are intense, well-crafted, engaging, and fast paced."

~*Mississippi Business Journal*

"Darden North is one of those writers who pays meticulous attention to getting the detail right in the course of his riveting thrillers and *Wiggle Room* is no exception."

~*Mason's Bookshelf*
*MBR Bookwatch*

"*Wiggle Room* is a suspense-chocked, mature, medical/military mystery with smarts to boot. The end was a surprising—but exceptionally satisfying—conclusion to a shivering ride of deception and murder."

~*BookFetish*

"*The 5 Manners of Death* is a satisfying mystery that brings those five manners of death—natural, accidental, suicidal, homicidal and undetermined—to light in a new and unusual way."

~Ellen Feld
*Feathered Quill Book Reviews*

"If you like plot twists and surprises, you'll love Darden North's fifth novel, a fast-moving story of crime and deception in the modern South."

~John M. Floyd
*Edgar Award nominee*

"*Fresh Frozen* is no quick-and-easy 'beach' read, but instead makes the reader pause, look deep inside, and question his own ethical and moral standards. North is a talented writer."

~Susan O'Bryan
*The Clarion-Ledger*

"*Fresh Frozen* should come with a warning label: Insomnia and repetitive motion disorder caused by rapid page turning may result."

~Kathy Spurlock
*Executive Editor, The News-Star*

"*Points of Origin*... heart-stopping, spellbinding ending ... haunted me for days after closing the cover."

~Reader Views

"tension-filled story ... surprising conclusion ... *House Call* is a murder mystery from the 'get-go.' Darden North, MD, may become to the medical mystery genre what Grisham is to the legal thriller."

~Mary Emrick
*Bluffs and Bayous Magazine*

# ROOFTOP

Also by Darden North

*House Call*
*Points of Origin*
*Fresh Frozen*
*Wiggle Room*
*The 5 Manners of Death*
*Party Favors*

# ROOFTOP

a novel

## DARDEN NORTH

WordCrafts Press

*Rooftop* is a work of fiction. The author has endeavored to be as accurate as possible with regard to the times in which the events of this novel are set. Still, this is a novel, and all references to persons, places, and events are fictitious or are used fictitiously.

**Rooftop**
Copyright © 2025
Darden North, MD

Hardback ISBN: 978-1-967649-07-5
Paperback ISBN: 978-1-967649-08-2

Cover concept and design by Mike Parker.



Published by WordCrafts Press
Cody, Wyoming 82414
www.wordcrafts.net

*If you tell the truth, you don't have to remember anything.*
~Mark Twain
*Notebook*, 1894

# Chapter 1

Diana Bratton snapped the laptop closed and tucked it under her left arm to shake hands with the man. He sat dressed in clean white boxers, bare-chested except for the matching muscle-man tee. "Sorry about the hour wait, Mr. Garnett," she said. "Hate to make a bad impression."

She moved Roy Garnett's blue jeans and plaid shirt from her desk chair to a metal bench at the end of the examination table. A pair of Western boots stood in the corner.

"Morning was empty for me anyway," Garnett said. "No business appointments. Besides, your other patients in the lobby said you're worth the wait."

Diana opened the laptop and highlighted the icon in the upper left corner of the screen. *Cummins–Bratton Surgical Center* spun from the center like a pinwheel in bright blue font to expand and fill the empty space. A few more commands replaced the image with the first page of an electronic medical file. "My PA is out on maternity leave. She usually fills out this new patient stuff for me," she said. "Please bear with me a little longer."

The name *Roy Allen Garnett* topped the page with the image of a driver's license in the upper left-hand corner. The stone-cold expression on the license matched the vacant stare of the man in the room. Garnett appeared his age, fifty-eight. A grey, receding hairline topped a round face and flabby chest with pot belly, obvious under the tight tee shirt.

Birthdate and mailing address information copied from the

license and entered by the clerk at the front desk occupied the space below and *Real Estate Development/Multifamily Unit Management* completed the occupation section.

The rest of the pages remained blank.

"No problem about the wait, Doc." Garnett pulled against the neck of his tee. "I've been sitting here half-naked, thinkin' about what kind of man murders his own sister."

Her fingers poised over the keys, Diana turned away from the screen and the missing information in the *Reason for Appointment* and *Past Medical History*. "What's going on here, Mr. Garnett? Is there something medical I can help you with?"

"I told the reception lady up front that I work in commercial real estate. I guess you can see that on your computer."

"That's about the only thing I have here," Diana said. She thought about pushing the nurse-assistance button on the wall and making an exit.

"People call me a slum lord. Slummy or not, I'm a self-made millionaire."

Before Diana caught herself, she entered *slum lord millionaire* and *a murdered sister* in the *Reason For Appointment* space. She closed the laptop and stood. "Mr. Garnett, this clinic is very busy, and I'm happy to help if you need the services of a general surgeon. If you need the police or a financial planner, then that's another matter."

"Don't give up on me, Dr. Bratton," Garnett laughed. "And call me Roy. I really need your help, Doc. Besides, everybody has family problems."

"I'm legally and ethically obligated to report if a patient feels threatened or seems in physical danger or threatens someone else or—"

"Forget what I said about the sister thing." He tugged at the thin, white paper covering the surface of the examination table. "Got a new lady friend and need to get rid of this hernia and the turkey neck. Thank the Lord my plumbing still works."

Garnett ran his hand up and down his chest and over his

protruding abdomen, then massaged his neck. He stretched out and stared at the ceiling, still pulling at the sagging skin under his chin. "Need to get all this jiggly stuff taken care of, Doc. Lady friend likes the beach. Can you help me?"

Diana stepped to the examination table. "I can fix an abdominal hernia, and I have plastic surgeon buddies who can do the rest. Let's see what we're talking about. You'll need to slide that tee shirt off."

"Will do, Doc." Roy Garnett slipped off the shirt and tossed it to his boots. "This new lady friend, Doc. A real godsend. Takes my mind off the other family crap."

Diana palpated the patient's abdomen. "You've got what we call diastasis recti. Your abdominal muscles have separated."

"I got two adult kids, Doc. Their mother's been dead ten years. One of my kids, the youngest, is twenty-eight and can't hold a job. In and out of rehab. Guess he's counting on his inheritance, and he'll probably come out on top. My line of business has been good to me."

"Seems it's not the police you need. I need to call social work for you instead, Mr. Garnett."

"Then there's my nephew. He's my sorry inheritance, thanks to the deceased sister."

Diana pressed her fingertips against the significant herniated bulge in the midline of his lower torso. She next palpated the thick layer of fat in each of the four quadrants of Garnett's abdomen. "Don't find any masses or enlarged internal organs here," Diana said, "as far as I can tell." She continued to the pelvic region. Her findings there came up negative.

"The nephew—he's the kid who thinks I killed my sister, his mom. He showed up at her house, if you can call it that, and found her dead. She lived in a trailer park west of the interstate, near County Line Road."

Diana took a deep breath and reopened the computer to enter the physical findings. "I can handle your surgery. However, I'm not the person to discuss family situations. You need a therapist."

She continued to type on the keyboard. "My secretary can make the referral."

"I'll keep that in mind."

"I hope you will." Diana made more notes. "When you're ready to schedule the procedure, I can arrange one of the plastic surgeons on staff to address your cosmetic concerns, and you'll need a pre-op consult with them too—plus medical clearance for major surgery from an internist, make that a cardiologist."

"You seem to play by the book, Doc."

Another deep breath. Diana fought a sigh. "You exercise any? Exercise can lower the risk of surgery." She noticed his athletic wrist band and pointed. "And you can keep up with your steps on that thing."

"There's this group of neighborhood guys I walk with most nights after supper—for at least an hour. This hernia in my stomach," he patted himself, "it's been bothering me so much I sometimes beg off from the walks. Besides, the new lady friend's been taking up a lot of my time."

Garnett sat up and reached for his clothes before Diana could close her laptop and exit the room to give him privacy. He stepped behind the curtain in the corner and began to redress.

"Dr. Bratton, I just wanted you to know more about me and my situation. I'm not a crazy old fool in midlife crisis. And I've got money—plenty of it—to take care of what I need from you guys."

"Once you get clearance from cardiology, the scheduling clerk will post your surgery."

"What about the plastics stuff. Remember?" Garnett zipped his pants, the sound easily heard past the curtain and across the room. "My lady friend wants me in shape fast."

"Again, you'll need a pre-op with plastics if you want to go through with body sculpting under the same anesthesia and after I finish my procedure." Diana pulled several pamphlets from a display on the wall and placed them on the chair. "Please read through this information and give me a call if you have any questions. We'll go over the abdominal herniorrhaphy, the hernia repair procedure, in detail at your pre-op with me. You'll sign consents then."

Roy Garnett pushed the curtain away. "Thanks for your help, Dr. Bratton."

Fully clothed and wearing the cowboy boots, Garnett appeared much taller than Diana expected. "Sure. See you in a few weeks."

Diana closed the laptop and stepped toward Garnett. He returned the handshake and walked past her toward the door into the hall. "Touch base with the appointment secretary up front in case she needs any more information," Diana said, "and she can make the referral appointments to cardiology and to plastics if you like." She watched from the hall as Garnett worked his way to the front area of the clinic building.

"Interesting fella," she muttered. "Guys in plastics gonna get a kick out of him." Diana took a deep breath and tried to shake off the interaction with the unhealthy time bomb named Roy Allen Garnett. She popped open the laptop and stared at the rest of the day's packed patient schedule.

"You got a minute?" A female voice from behind startled her.

"Voncelle? I thought you were off this afternoon."

"It's Chuck, my husband. He needs to see you."

"As a patient? Sure, anytime. I remember Chuck from the clinic Christmas party. A true joker."

"That he is—most days."

"He even dressed the part." Diana laughed. "I remember a four-inch-wide Santa Clause tie with reindeer print slacks. His shirt was red and green horizontal stripes and hung over his belt."

"My husband's not joking much now due to his gallbladder, but stomach pain hasn't kept him away from the barbeque—or the fried chicken—or from traveling for work. You might be surprised to learn that Chuck is a wheeler-dealer."

Diana turned and referred again to the patient schedule. "Has he had an abdominal sono?"

"Chuck hasn't seen a doctor since they locked up John Haynes for murder. I suggested he see Haynes, and he'll never listen to me again."

"I remember that Chuck took credit at the party for getting you to sign on with us. Said you would have changed practices even if they hadn't put your old partner in prison."

"All that seems like ancient history," Voncelle said. "My Chuck Wallace might have been one of that bastard's last patients." She stepped to another computer and signed into the Metropolitan Hospital radiology files, then entered her husband's birthdate and social security number. "Haynes ordered this sono for Chuck and never discussed the results with him. His gallbladder's full of stones."

"If Haynes had been released on bail, Chuck would likely be absent a gallbladder."

Both women chuckled, then lowered their eyes embarrassed when a nurse passed them in the hall.

"Stubborn Chuck only sat on the problem. I almost had to take him to the ED last night for the abdominal pain."

"Of course, I'll be happy to see him." Diana reconsidered her full schedule and swallowed hard. "Even this afternoon—if he wants."

"Thank you, Diana. A lot's been going on at home." A thin tear ran down Voncelle's cheek, marring her light makeup. "I'm not sure that I have ever thanked you enough. You've been a real friend."

"Voncelle, you don't have to—"

"I was practically out of a job." She shook her head. "No, I *was* out of a job. No practice can survive what happened to my old clinic."

"None of that was your fault. Brad saw through your old boss when they were deployed together in Iraq. John Haynes left you and the others in Mississippi to work your butts off while he was overseas screwing a nurse and killing her boyfriend."

"John wasn't so bad to work for, but when he was convicted for the murder, the practice dissolved. One day the waiting room of the Haynes Surgical Clinic was jammed pack with patients. The next you could hear a pin drop. And you went to bat for me when I called begging."

"Please! I didn't take it that way. Neither did Brad. We needed you in our practice."

"I know you feel that way, but I'm not so sure about Brad. There's no *warm and fuzzy* when I'm around your hubby," Voncelle said. "He knew John Haynes over there, and I'm glad Brad made it home safe."

"You are a great surgeon, and Brad has always admired your work. We were almost desperate for help in the practice. Your timing was perfect." Diana fought a grimace. "I didn't mean to say *desperate*. Why don't we bury that history. Now, what can I do to help?"

Voncelle took a couple of steps forward. "Chuck's an ornery sonnavabitch, and he's let his health slide for way too long. I really don't know what's going on in his head. I hope you can deal with him."

"I can work Chuck in this afternoon. My nurse or secretary will set things up. You want us to call him?"

Voncelle smiled and slid her cell from the back pocket of her scrubs. "I'll text him to call your appointment secretary. He felt too bad to go to the office today, so his schedule is wide open." She stepped out of earshot, the tone of her voice transformed into an almost sarcastic singsong. "You've come to the rescue again, Diana. Proud of yourself?"

# Chapter 2

Diana's search for Roy Garnett in the patient EMR revealed a scheduled consultation with a therapist. "No way," she said and shook her head. "He went through with it. Can't wait to read what the shrink has to say about that joker." She scanned the next few pages in the computer.

"An appointment with a plastic surgeon too? That Garnett guy moves fast."

She pecked and clicked through the keyboard until she completed the remainder of her medical records and found nothing as interesting as the Garnett case, then slid the laptop into her bag. "I dread seeing Chuck Wallace with Voncelle peering over my shoulder."

Her cell phone rang. The caller ID lit: *Aunt Phoebe*, and Diana answered.

"What's up?" Diana tossed the laptop bag over her shoulder and left her office for the hall to the rear exit.

"Are you kidding me, Diana? I can tell from your tone you're still at work. You need to cut back those hours," Phoebe said. "You've got a gorgeous husband and a lovely daughter. Explore the world and enjoy life!"

"That *gorgeous* husband had the afternoon off and is playing golf," Diana said, walking quickly down the hall, "and left me with a slammed clinic and a lot of work-ins—many were his patients. Not an empty chair in the waiting room. And I was the only doctor working this afternoon."

"Golf? That explains it," Phoebe said.

"Explains what?"

"Brad finally answered my text. Guess he was having drinks in the Nineteenth Hole. Said he's up for dinner at my place tonight and said it's your call."

Diana considered the contents of the Cummins-Bratton refrigerator: cottage cheese and a half pack of deli meat, waxy and brown at the edges, and no milk for the one box of cereal in the pantry. Her meager homemaker skills never took hold and stalled completely after her divorce. Even marriage to Dr. Brad Cummins, which marked the end to her single mom life, brought no improvement.

"Dinner's good," she said before her aunt's change of mind. "Thank you. And I know Kelsey will be excited. No way Brad would turn down the invitation."

Diana dropped her phone into her bag and turned into a hall leading to a separate section of offices as well as patient exam rooms. Brad called it The West Wing, absent the politics. She heard a voice from inside the second office and stopped at the doorway to see Voncelle place her cell phone face down on her desk. Diana took a quick assessment of her newest partner's office. Despite square footage identical to her own space, Voncelle's office appeared more spacious. Perhaps, the neatly organized bookcase and slimly designed, contemporary furniture made the difference.

"Voncelle? You're off this afternoon. What are you still doing here?"

"I, uh, needed to review a case coming up next week." She reached across the desk for her laptop and flipped it open. "This pancreatic cancer case, candidate for a Whipple. Nice lady, only sixty-two."

"That's a tough situation."

"Been a patient of mine for a while. Stuck with me after the old clinic went under. The procedure has got to go well."

"Do yourself and that lady a favor." Diana tilted her head in the direction of Voncelle's laptop. "Get whatever paperwork—or computer work—you need done on that case and get the hell out of here. Make yourself scarce around here when you can. Go home and take care of that funny husband of yours with the gallbladder issues and get some rest."

"Got it," Voncelle said and tapped a few keys on her laptop. "Will do."

Diana passed up the elevator to continue down the hall for the rear stairs. Her phone rang and she fished it out of her purse. *Phoebe again.* Diana answered.

"I forgot to tell you that Kelsey's already over here and upstairs doing her homework," Aunt Phoebe said. "I picked her up after cheerleader practice."

"I guess she called you … because I forgot. You're the greatest—though you know that already." Diana popped open the metal door and began to descend the stairs to the physicians' parking area under the building. "Kelsey will be driving before we know it, and that will cut the chauffer service." She pushed open the door into the dimly lit garage, vacant except for her SUV and a tall stack of boxes that once held medical supplies and waited for the janitorial service to discard. "Not sure I'm ready to let her go."

"You better be, and don't forget—I know a few things about teenagers."

Diana passed by the boxes and walked toward her vehicle. It snapped to attention courtesy of the key fob in her bag. "You molded me into perfection. Plus, I made it through med school."

"I hear all about everyone's grandchildren at bridge club, the good and the bad. The good mostly makes me nauseated, but I could write a book about the bad stuff. You'd be surprised what old ladies share after a couple of glasses of wine."

Diana opened the driver's door and laughed. The interior detail of her BMW SUV lit in bright blue. "Sounds like a wonderfully talented and sincere group. Let me know if I can ever put on some make-up, take a few bridge lessons, and join the merry crowd. Gotta go. Bye." She dropped her phone into the pocket of her coat and slid behind the wheel. As she turned away to toss her bag into the front passenger seat, a figure jumped from behind the stack of boxes, pushed the driver's door control to unlock the left rear door, and sprang into the back seat.

"Stay still and let's talk a minute," the man said. Cold metal pressed deep into the right side of Diana's neck. He sounded young, maybe early twenties. "Go ahead and start the engine and leave the car running. This expensive baby has got to run quiet. Leave it in park and just relax."

"My wallet is inside that bag on the seat next to me." Diana gestured to her right, then gripped the steering wheel even tighter. "I don't have any drugs on me, only cash and my credit cards. Take the bag and this never happened."

"I slipped by your receptionist late this afternoon and checked out your private office. I've already searched your bag. This sweet X-5 ain't nothing to sneeze at, but I'm not interested in the car."

Diana stole a glance in the rearview mirror. He was Caucasian. Thick blond eyebrows peaked out of a 3-hole ski mask.

"Like what you see, doctor?" He laughed. "We could take a go at it in the back of this baby. I hate to disappoint you, but that's not what I'm here for." He relaxed the pressure of the gun barrel against her neck and leaned back slightly in his seat.

Diana dropped her eyes to the right and leaned her head toward the console between the front seats. The Smith and Wesson Brad gave her was inside.

The man reached between the seats and opened the console. A pronounced click jerked her back to attention. She stared into the brick wall ahead of her parking space, one over from husband Brad's. "You thinkin' about this sweet thing, Doc?" The man exchanged the original gun for hers and briefly waved it in the rearview mirror. "I'll put this new one to good use. Sort of tired of mine. Besides, ain't you worried that daughter of yours could get ahold of it? She almost driving age?"

Diana thought about the tiny can of mace dangling from her

key chain. "What is it you want? We don't keep narcotics in the building either."

"Don't want any of that shit."

"And the janitorial service will be here any minute, so you better—"

"And I thought you medical people was smart. How do you think I got down to the garage? Slipped right past those suckers when they pulled up to the front door an hour ago. They ain't interested in you. They want to empty the garbage cans and get the freak outta here."

Her heart pounding and mouth dry, Diana forced slower breaths. *I should have paid more attention at that personal protection seminar Phoebe dragged me to,* she decided. "My family will be wondering what's happened to me. I should be home by now."

He laid Diana's gun on the rear seat beside him and returned the original weapon to her neck. He pressed the tip even deeper. "You get that line from a TV show?"

"I'm going to ask you again," Diana said, her breathing labored. "What is it that you want?"

"Now, slow down a bit. You ain't in no position to order me or anybody else around." He kept the gun barrel steady. " You saw a patient earlier today by the name of Roy Garnett. He's my uncle, and he's one crazy sonnavabitch."

"What? Come on, what's this about?" Diana said and tried to twist her neck free. He only followed the motion. "Doctors don't give out patient information."

"Maybe not. Except in this case, it don't matter," the man said. "Snobs like you think a person like me ain't educated. That's where you're wrong."

"Get out of my car, and we'll forget this happened."

The man snickered. "You watch too much TV, Doc. Stay focused on business."

Diana darted her eyes to the left and right. *Is Voncelle still upstairs?* Voncelle parked on the other side of the parking garage, out of sight of Diana's vehicle. If she had taken Diana's suggestion and left for home, she must have chosen the other set of stairs and not the elevator a few steps from where Diana parked. She felt her breathing quicken again.

"You're wrong if you think I'm an ignorant, low life. I'm good at computers. But don't ever call me a hacker."

Somehow the guy managed to dig the barrel of the gun deeper into Diana's neck. She winced and tightened her grip on the steering wheel.

"I hate that name *hacker*. Besides, I didn't know that Uncle Roy was your patient until today."

Diana remembered the empty Family History section in Garnett's medical history.

"What is it you want from me?"

"I have my laptop right here and read your notes about Uncle Roy's medical problems and what he said about killing a sister. You did the right thing sending him to a shrink."

"You hacked into our medical records system?"

A deep sigh of annoyance erupted from the back seat. "Ughh … remember, I don't like *hacker*."

"Sorry." Diana fidgeted and stole a glance from side-to-side. She felt the barrel of the gun follow her. *Housekeeping will come back down to the garage. I know they will.*

"That stuff is easy-peasy. If Uncle Roy is online, I know it. And stop trying to turn your head."

"Can't help it. My back's starting to get stiff."

The door from the stairs swung open and a heavy-set man with a faded navy-blue uniform embroidered with *Jackson Janitorial Service* stepped into the garage. Diana stopped short of blowing her horn. Deeper, firmer pressure against her neck from the gun took care of that.

The janitor shuffled his feet and seemed to make a quick survey of the area for any missed trash. Finding none, he disappeared into the stairwell.

"Another favor for me, Doctor Bratton. Certify my uncle Roy a wacko. He makes up lies about me."

"Our clinic therapist is just that—a therapist. She's not a psychiatrist."

The young man stroked the back of Diana's head and the right side of her neck, this time with a gloved hand that felt like leather. "You can make it happen, Doc. I know you can. And if you do, you'll never see me again."

"I can't. I won't falsify medical records," Diana said, "for any reason."

"You ain't no different from anybody else. You don't know what you'll do till you have to." He ran the tip of the barrel across the back of Diana's neck and popped her between the shoulders with his fist.

She jerked forward toward the steering column. The shoulder strap of the seat belt caught her.

"This afternoon in your office with no one around, I saw all the pictures on your desk of that cute girl. Nice cheerleader outfit … fits snug. She's fillin' out good."

"Get away from me." Diana reached for the door handle. "You're not getting near my daughter."

The man lunged forward with a chokehold. He wore long sleeves. Diana could see the tips of the leather gloves. "You do what I say. But if you don't, I'll be back, and it will hurt—a lot."

He released the chokehold and bolted from the car. In seconds, he jumped the barrier arm gate at the entrance and exit to the garage and vanished into the thick shrubbery bordering the property.

Diana grabbed her neck, coughed and sputtered for a few seconds, and grabbed the cell from her purse. She called 911 for the police, then she called Brad.

"Brad, this crazy lunatic attacked me in the clinic garage. He was waiting for me."

# Chapter 3

"I told them he wore gloves, although the police still dusted my car for prints," Diana said. "There're going through the servers for security camera footage—outside the front of the building and in the garage."

Phoebe pulled back Diana's collar and scrutinized her neck. "Thank God you weren't bruised. A chokehold? I never heard of such a thing." She set the pan of lasagna in the center of the table. "Was that policeman there? Now, what was his name?" She turned to the kitchen counter for the bowl of salad. "That guy who used to follow you around? What a pest."

"That pest saved your life and put my worthless ex in prison. Key Martin is Police Chief now."

"Must not have had much competition downtown," Phoebe said and tossed the Caesar salad with a long sterling silver fork and spoon set.

"I suspect Key is beating himself up over not being first on the scene in the clinic garage," Diana said.

"Don't doubt he was disappointed," Phoebe said. "You two on a first name basis?"

"I'm not worried if Diana gives up formalities after the last caper." Brad patted his stomach. "Martin has kept both of us on his radar over the last few years—more so my wife."

Diana frowned in annoyed disapproval. "He'll get involved in the case sooner or later. And I don't want Kelsey to know anything about this until she has to. I'm glad she finished her homework early. Thanks for suggesting she spend the night out with a friend."

Phoebe pulled another large spoon from a drawer and plopped two helpings of pasta on Brad's plate, then filled the rest of the well with salad. She slid a generous slice of buttered French bread onto the lip of the plate, hiding it under a large leaf of romaine lettuce.

"What happened to ladies first?" Brad stared at the heap of food before him.

Diana reached under the table and squeezed his love handles. "Wanna keep these as long as I can. You know what they say about finding stuff under the sheets."

"Too corny, Diana, and if Aunt Phoebe keeps up this pace, those love handles and I will need a bed by ourselves. Regardless, if you can't find me, I'll find you."

Phoebe and Diana joined Brad's laugh as Phoebe finished serving the main course.

"Oh, I almost forgot the dessert." Phoebe turned away from the table, grabbed mitts from a drawer, and removed a tall pie from the oven. She set it on the counter and took her seat. "It's apple. If somebody doesn't like apple, well … that's un-American."

"I'll get the wine." Brad pulled an open bottle of chardonnay from the refrigerator and poured. "After the day you've had, Diana, you might want a couple of glasses. I expect Phoebe's got more in the cellar."

Diana took a long sip. "One of Key's underlings told me they recovered my pistol in the drainage ditch across from the clinic."

"That's nice, I guess," Phoebe said and finished the dregs of the glass poured earlier while she cooked. "I never liked that you carried that thing around. And a lot of good a gun did you today."

"For Diana to carry sounded like a good idea at the time, considering the late hours we work." Brad swallowed his chewed lasagna.

"Made a great Christmas present. And the private shooting lessons at that indoor firing range? Very thoughtful." Diana smiled and chose a small bite of her serving of lasagna, but a larger sampling of the wine. "They're keeping my pistol for evidence, at least for a few weeks."

"Fingerprints?" Brad speared salad with his fork and chewed. "Oh, I guess not. You said the thug was wearing gloves."

"Gloves or not, there were no fingerprints," Diana said. Phoebe and Brad both raised an eyebrow. "I've already heard from Key."

"No real surprise on that," Phoebe said.

"Tell your boyfriend I just hired 24-hour security: three off duty cops at eight-hour shifts, the chief's finest. I wouldn't be surprised if he signs up for a shift himself."

"So far, nothing on the news, and I hope it stays that way. Word will get around anyway, and our patients and staff will be glad to see the new security," Diana said. "And, Brad, you know that I've never encouraged Key Martin—professionally or otherwise—not from the minute I first met him as a detective when your brother was shot."

"Wouldn't take much more than a nod for a loser like Martin," Brad said. "And that guy fumbled through the investigation into Brian's murder. I agree with Phoebe. How has he lasted this long, and how in the world did he make chief?"

Phoebe opened the freezer and removed a carton of vanilla ice cream. "How about a change of subject," she said.

"Good idea." Diana dabbed her lips with a napkin and stared at her meal. A grisly flashback of cold metal pressed deep into her flesh overcame her. She forced herself to shake her head clear and think of anything else. "Let's see. Oh, I know. Voncelle Wallace wants me to take care of her husband's gallbladder."

"That wasn't what I had in mind," Phoebe said and speared some salad.

"Glad she didn't ask me," Brad said. "Chuck Wallace is a ticking, medical-disaster time bomb. Flabby, overweight—the guy can barely climb a flight of stairs before giving out. I saw him struggle up the steps from the garage one afternoon when he dropped by to see Voncelle." Brad took another helping of lasagna.

"Need to loosen that belt, Brad? Don't be so quick to judge," Diana said and chewed slowly.

"We should be having a nice Chianti with this." Phoebe sipped her third glass of chardonnay. "Sadly, this chardonnay is all I had."

Brad put down his loaded fork. "I'll grab myself a water, and google personal trainers later."

Diana grinned. "Remember, leave my love handles alone."

"I don't think you have anything to worry about," Brad said.

"I'm going to do Voncelle a favor and fit Chuck in this week." "The mastectomy posted for Thursday got rescheduled."

"What happened?" Brad asked, untwisting the plastic water bottle and sliding back into his chair.

"The patient wants two brand new ones, and the plastics guy she prefers for the breast reconstruction isn't available until next week. The lady wants a triple *D*."

"Better gig than operating on Chuck Wallace," Brad said. "I wouldn't touch that guy without medical clearance. Chuck hit the chips and dip hard at our Christmas party. Lots of trips to the bar too."

"Was that before or after he started with the jokes?" Diana said.

"The one he told in the Cajun accent was downright raunchy. Even made me blush," Phoebe said. "By the way, thanks for letting me tag along, Diana. Too bad no single guys my age were there … at any age, for that matter."

"I must've left before the jokes, I guess," Diana said. "I got called to the ED early. A vascular shunt clotted off."

"ED?" Phoebe peered up from her plate.

"That's what we call the ER these days. It's not Emergency Room anymore. It's Emergency Department," Diana said.

"I don't care what you call the place," Phoebe said. "Keep me out of it."

"Will do." Brad smirked at Diana. "As far as Chuck is concerned, the guy was over the top at the clinic party—working the crowd, typical of someone in corporate sales. He outlasted Voncelle and took an Uber home."

"I'll get him checked out before he goes under," Diana muttered. "He might could use a full cardiology work-up."

"Gotta give the guy credit. He seems to have a lot of energy despite his size," Brad continued. "Told me about a group of neighborhood guys who walk for about an hour, every night no matter the weather, and put in almost four miles in an hour."

"Every night?" Diana asked.

"Except Friday and Saturday, unless there's a tornado warning or hailstorm." He regretted tonight's dinner plate, once filled with meat and cheese and garlic bread. "I could use a regular workout like that."

"Sounds like torture to me," Phoebe said and opened another bottle of wine.

"You want me to get Chuck's cell from Voncelle?" Diana asked. "Make a call and see if the walking group will let you in?"

Brad put down his fork and pushed the plate of food away. "The meet-up spot is about ten minutes from here. Yeah, please get me his number."

# Chapter 4

Chuck listened to the coffee machine come to life with a sputter and hiss as water pushed through the pod of flavored coffee grounds. No matter the season, he liked pumpkin spice. His employees could use the coffee maker and eat or drink anything out of the break room refrigerator. But if they used the last pumpkin spice flavored pod, they were at HR's mercy.

"That's it." Chuck smelled the spicy, delicious aroma and sipped from the ceramic coffee cup, a present from his wife, the successful general surgeon with tons of devoted patients who adored her—if you believed the constant stream of glowing Instagram posts. *It's no telling what that clinic pays its marketing firm to keep that up*, he decided. Chuck read the inscription across the face of his cup:

*Greatest Boss In The World.*

"I'm nowhere near the level of Dr. Voncelle Wallace."

A voice crept closely from behind. "Mr. Wallace?"

Chuck stirred in a half packet of artificial sweetener and stared into the swirling coffee until it dissipated. His stomach hurt.

"Uhh, Mr. Wallace?"

"Sorry, Libby." He looked up. "Whatyu need?"

"It's nearly six, and I was supposed to leave at five. My family expects me to make it home in time for church."

"Church?" Chuck slurped from the cup. "It's only Wednesday."

"It's Wednesday night service, and my son sings in the children's choir."

"Those spreadsheets I asked for taken care of?"

"I'll finish up in the morning," Libby said. "I can't miss tonight. My son has a solo."

"Wouldn't want you to miss that one for sure." Chuck slurped some more and massaged the area under his lower right ribs. "Problem is, those guys overseas are not very patient. The report was due an hour ago."

"I can get my husband to run carpool tomorrow, so I can come in early." She gawked at the stacks of paper folders, off limits to the janitorial service, and the piles of empty candy wrappers, ignored by the janitors. "I'll complete the file and email the spreadsheet first thing."

More coffee noise and Chuck returned to the papers on his desk. "That'll work. You go ahead and enjoy the solo. Why don't you take a video and show me tomorrow." He set the mug on the leather coaster on his desk, inscribed with another *Best Boss* message. "That is if the preacher will let you."

Libby turned for the door, then stopped. "Mr. Wallace? You all right? You're rubbing your stomach and chest again."

"Yeah. It's my gallbladder. Need to get it taken care of."

"You want me to call someone tomorrow for you about an appointment? Your wife—she's a doctor, isn't she? So, could she—?

"Don't worry about me getting a doctor. Get that stuff emailed out early tomorrow. See ya then."

"Yes, sir." Libby shut the door behind her.

Chuck peeled an antacid from a roll stashed in a top desk drawer and chased it down with the last of the coffee. He thought about the near empty bottle of vodka waiting in the bottom right drawer. Instead, he swallowed two more tablets dry.

"Could've met the midnight deadline if Libby had finished that report." He jerked open the drawer, grabbed the Tito's, and erased the coffee taste.

"That's not the first time Libby has skipped out on me," he said to the now empty bottle. "Voncelle would have been that kind of mother." Chuck slid the empty back into the drawer instead of using the waste can. "No, probably not. She'd get tied up with an emergency patient and miss the solo. Leave me sitting by a vacant seat."

He noted the time and opened the encrypted file on his desktop computer. It was a few minutes after six. "They're seven hours ahead and wanted the figures by midnight. What's an hour or two or three late to those European guys."

Chuck scanned Libby's spreadsheet. A smattering of incomplete tabulations spoiled her handiwork. Each empty blank screamed at Chuck. "Damned children's choir. No! Those Spaniards won't be happy with this—or the delay."

He unlocked a different desk drawer with a key from his pocket and found another bottle of vodka, this one Belvedere, along with a different coffee cup. Chuck planted the bottle and fresh cup on his desk. Pouring with his right hand, he managed to type a few numbers with his left into a desktop calculator. $1,257,000 seemed a reasonable annual accounts receivable for a six-person internal medical group. "Those numbers should work, but could actually test a bit low."

He revised the amount to $3,257,000 then contemplated the gamut of ancillary services offered by the internal medicine group to their patients: the medical spa and massage center, the facial neurotoxins and cosmetic fillers, the hormone treatments. Chuck added another million dollars to the ledger.

He tapped a few more keys on the calculator and adjusted Libby's entries in other columns, then moved the cup of vodka to his left hand to speed up the process. After a few more tabulations and entries to fill in the blanks, the numbers were flush. As he hit *SEND*, his cell phone rang as though to celebrate successful completion of the spreadsheet and delivery through the internet.

A heavy voice filled his ear. *"Una hora tarde, Chuck. Asumi lo mismo."*

"Lose the tongue, Garcia. I already told you. I dropped freshman Spanish at Ole Miss," Chuck said. He imagined Hernando

Garcia dressed in pajamas, sitting at a desk in his den with a lit cigar and a glass of sangria, and already salivating over the final, revised financials of the Belmont Internal Medicine Clinic and Wellness Enhancement Spa.

"Okay, okay," followed in a thick Spanish accent. "It's been a long day. Stayed at the office twiddling my thumbs, waiting on your delayed email. You pay your staff to get work out on time?"

"You manage your people, and I'll manage mine."

"Settle down, *amigo*. We are together on this."

Chuck envisioned cigar smoke circle Garcia's head. Several seconds of silence passed until Chuck was sure he heard papers shuffle across an expensive mahogany desk.

"Our clients are very excited about the American Medical Investment Fund that I am putting together," Garcia said. "Medical workers in Spain get a fixed hourly wage that depends on the level of service. What's the word? Uhh … uhh … *complexity*. Yes, *complexity*. Unlike most systems in the U.S., no incentives exist to improve profitability."

"This group of American doctors is ready to sell out. They've got a herd of patients, a waiting list for new patients, and new docs fresh out of training ready to push the old guys out to pasture."

"*Pasture*? Oh, I see. You mean *retirement*."

"These guys are busy and offer a lot of patient services to clients willing to pay."

"And from the guts of these financials, those medicos are doing well. I can see the BMWs in the parking lot or one Mercedes after the other. *El infierno*! I bet the secretaries drive Cadillacs."

Chuck made no comment. He envisioned a freshly lit Garcia cigar, a Cuban.

"My clients like the mutual funds based on American firms, ones that show profit like these Belmont guys. Profits roll back into the funds in Spain, no annual capital gains tax like the U.S. I'm happy you pitched this one to me, *compañero*. I like it. Like it a lot."

"Happy to hear that. You know, the doctors highly value themselves and what they do. There's no argument to that." Chuck scrolled up and down the spreadsheet. He could have tweaked the numbers even further, made things present even better. "You should move fast on this, Garcia. The president of the medical group tells me that he gets a couple of emails and phone calls a week from firms wanting to buy them out."

"My board meets next week, early next week. I believe we will move forward."

"One thing in our favor, my wife is buds—"

"Buds?"

"That means *friends*. She plays in a Mahjong group with the wife of the president of the Belmont group—once a week," Chuck said. "My wife's a doctor too."

"I don't remember a Wallace on the list of doctors, or is she like most new age Americano women—or do you Americans call them *progressive*—and uses her maiden name?"

"My wife, Voncelle, is not in this medical group, but she practices surgery through another clinic. She's sort of traditional—goes by the surname *Wallace*."

"Your wife works with you on these deals?"

"No, she does her thing, and I do mine. Keeps the marriage fresh."

"In my opinion, Chuck, you might be wasting a good resource, an inside perspective?" Garcia said. "Inside scoop that could play in your favor."

Chuck again imagined a fresh cigar, smoke swirling about Garcia's head and a foot propped on his desk. He might still be in an expensive suit and tie.

"What I'm saying is we don't discuss business at home—don't mix business with pleasure," Chuck said.

"Might want to reconsider, Mr. Wallace. You might be wasting a wonderful resource. So, are these Mississippi doctors ready to make a decision?"

"Most of the members of the group want to sell the practice."

"Most?"

"There're a few holdouts. A small group of newer physicians. Even a sister."

"Sister?"

"Dr. Ellis Belmont recently took over as Chairman of the Board of Directors from his sister, Sidney. There's some type of officer rotation system, although I understand Ellis wants to end that. He's a big thinker, dreamed up the idea for a leveraged buyout of the practice before he approached me to broker the deal. The practice is the largest medical group around. Patient parking lot stays full."

"I found all of them on the web. Goggle is my friend," Garcia said. "Almost as valuable a friend as you."

"Since Ellis Belmont is the most senior and experienced partner, he would likely be the first to see the value of the business piece of the clinic practice. Not only are the accounts receivable and the physical plant and property of value, but the community goodwill built by the Belmonts over the last sixty-plus years is tremendous. Ellis Belmont figured it was time to cash out and that an outside entity group might be eager to buy."

"Interesting. From my experience, these types of physicians, any medical doctors for that matter, are not always the best businessmen."

"My legal team requested and reviewed the bylaws of the Belmont medical practice. The bylaws call for a two-thirds vote of the stockholder physicians to approve any deal to sell the practice. Ellis Belmont will push it through—even after his father, the elder Ellis Belmont, passed away unexpectedly, and they lost a *yes* vote.

"Unexpectedly? I still see his photograph on the website."

"He was ninety-two, to be exact. Fellow died on the golf course," Chuck answered.

"I see," Garcia said.

"That leaves Ellis and his younger brother, Miles Belmont, around as the next two in line as senior partners not counting the sister Sidney—with plenty of other Belmont cheerleaders to carry on and garner the votes to sell: two nephews, a daughter-in-law, and a niece or two—all internists or subspecialty fellows. A few cousins work as nurses and lab techs."

"*Todo un asunto familiar* … quite a family affair," Garcia said.

"Ellis Belmont lobbied the other docs hard to move forward with the sale."

"I would hope these American doctors see the value of international involvement and investment in what they are trying to do for their community and their state. Mother Theresa! For their country," Garcia said. "Is there a problem here, amigo?"

"I've met with these guys several times. Made lots of presentations. Shown them lots of PowerPoint." Chuck took a deep breath and reached for his most convincing voice.

"They're all on board now."

"I certainly hope that's the case, Sénior Wallace, because that's what I have told my people over here."

"This new president of the clinic, Ellis Belmont, is hitting seventy, but he's not talking retirement. You've got plenty of years of productivity in every one of the physicians on staff," Chuck said, "including Miles Belmont, right behind Ellis in age. Both men are likely to keep practicing until they drop dead—as did their father—and both put almost a million on the books every year."

"I am confident that everyone in the Belmont group will be pleased in the long run," Garcia said. "Financial guarantees exist that should make everyone feel at ease—guarantees that work both ways."

"The prospect of a big, fat buyout is staring them in the face. All of the Belmont physicians and related medical personnel will be tickled pink when this finally goes through and they see their already inflated bank accounts go through the roof," Chuck said. "Paid-off mortgages, new and more expensive cars and boats, trips to Europe to please the spouses and boyfriends/girlfriends, worries over college and private school tuition gone with the influx of cash. They'll be no hard feelings, even from last minute minority nay-sayers who might make trouble at the final vote. I'm certain of it."

A few seconds of silence passed before Garcia responded. "This is on you, Mr. Wallace. Push this deal through and everybody's happy."

Chuck scanned the fabricated spreadsheet and was pleased with the altered entries. "The numbers add up and frankly, Garcia, there's no reason you should not be impressed—and no reason the Belmonts should not make good on the deal."

"These people would not be where they are if they were not smart."

"Obviously," Chuck said.

"The Belmonts must realize that much of the doctor stress will fly out the window when Garcia International Enterprises and its management resources acquire them. And it's with all due respect that I say this. This deal is what those physicians want, whether or not all of the primadonnas know it."

"Absolutely," Chuck said.

"GIE will grow. Become what you Americans call the *nuts and bolts* of a *bigger picture*. The Belmont organization is only the beginning."

"The Belmonts and the other doctors brought on board through the years should welcome the off-load of management stress," Chuck said, "as well as the financial return."

"I cannot wait to see their smiling faces. No more day-to-day haggling over salaries with administrative and other staff, no more employee whining. The people on the ground at Garcia International Enterprises will relieve the duties of many of the current employees and eradicate those bloated ancillary salaries. The toil of day-to-day clinic operations will disappear, as will much of the mundane paperwork. More time for the Belmonts and their buddies to take care of patients."

Chuck took a deep breath. He didn't want to lose this deal. "A few of the docs will get crosswise with any decision to let long-time employees go without cause. No, more than that—really pissed-off if you say goodbye to their trusted people when your guys take over."

"Now, Mr. Wallace, I'm not entirely familiar with the expression *crosswise*, but I know what *pissed off* means. Those frowns, those red faces of doctor anger, will vanish into big, wide smiles at the swollen bank accounts when the transaction is completed, and GIE is in control. The surviving support staff will get raises after we make cuts in other departments—modest raises, yes, that's true, but raises, nonetheless. So, happy doctors and happy staff make happy and healthy patients."

Chuck imagined another drag on Garcia's cigar, a call girl waiting in the wings.

"Not to mention the wide grin on your face from your hefty commission," Garcia added.

Chuck poured more vodka.

"Send me anything else you have on the financials. Let's get the signatures completed, then all that's left for your people to do is business as usual—continue to work hard and take care of patients," Garcia said. "Good outcomes for the sick and infirmed. You Americans can do it. You like to be heroes."

Chuck downed more of his drink.

"And if the Belmonts and their underlings don't cut the mustard—you see, I do know your American expressions—we cut their salaries like the rest of the employees."

"It's all in the contracts," Chuck said. He found a few more useful financials in the file during the call, linked them to Garcia's email, and hit *SEND* as his cell buzzed. While a number he did not recognize, it was without a telemarketer warning. "Check your email. It's gonna be a winner for everyone."

"Counting on it, Mr. Wallace."

"For sure, so let's talk later. I gotta another call."

Chuck hung up the desktop receiver and answered his cell. "Chuck Wallace."

"Hey, Chuck. Brad Cummins here. If you've got a sec, tell me more about your walking group."

Garcia hung up the phone, finished his cigar, and flipped open the leather box on his desk. Celebration over potential consummation of another deal called for another smoke. His promise to Lucinda to give it up was only one day old and was not the first lie to his wife—or the first disappointment. The lie would also not be the last. He lit the cigar, pivoted in his chair toward the window behind him, and swung a foot on top of the windowsill.

His office in central Madrid overlooked the Prado Museum, its exterior bathed in much more than standard security lighting. A rainbow-colored sequence of rotating beams of light draped the building, more grand than anything Garcia had seen in his fifteen years of association with the company. He studied the illuminated, nearly two-story vertical banner that draped the front of a wing, an announcement of the curator's next exhibit.

"Surely Lucinda will join me at the opening," Garcia said. He reached back for the museum brochure on his desk and flipped through it. "She danced along the edge of Neptune's Fountain in celebration of the Titan opening at the Prada, or was it for Raffaello Sanzio?" *No, it was after the El Greco pieces and the open bar*, he decided. He remembered dinner afterward at Cicero and what came later back at their apartment.

"Yes, she will not want to miss it—or the wine and caviar reception before the unveiling."

He tossed the brochure back to the desk and reached for the silver-framed photo of his wife.

"Oh, my *esposa*. My beautiful Lucinda, my wife. You and I will dance the night away when I score with this American deal. We can enjoy a new life, a better life. Say goodbye to our cramped apartment for a sprawling villa."

He returned the photograph to his desk and shuffled through other papers until he found the property disclosure. Eight full bedrooms—ten including the pool house—and as many bathrooms, plus a powder room near the grand stairs in the foyer. A close-up photo of the miniature, gold-enameled fixtures mounted to the water basin of the powder room topped one page.

"Yes, it will be Boadilla del Monte. Our permanent place—exquisite—and the envy of our friends. And, of course, a home for our family." Garcia turned the other pages of the property disclosure, an elaborate multipage document complete with color photographs of every other room and bath. The wine cellar, laundry room with adjacent servants' quarters, and four-car garage were detailed along with the pool house, pool and spa, and the rose and tree garden.

However, he had work to do.

"This will no longer be a dream; this will all be reality. The *Americanos*—the medicos americanos—they will make sure of it."

"Make sure of what, Hernando?" A tall, slender woman with black hair to the shoulders appeared at the front of Garcia's desk. He spun around in his chair, dropping the Belmont prospectus and nearly knocking his desk lamp to the floor. "I thought you were going to give up those nasty things," she said.

"My darling, Lucinda. You agreed—*we* agreed. My limit is one per day," Garcia said as he rubbed out the cigar in the ceramic ashtray on his desk and pushed the butt of the first cigar to the side.

They both stared at the ashtray, the company logo barely visible at the bottom. Lucinda raised her eyes to stare at her husband. Hernando Garcia remained fixed on the remnants of his two expensive two cigars.

"That was yesterday's smoke. I promise, my *hermosa esposa*," he said.

"I don't believe you, Hernando. I will let it go. There are much bigger fish to fry," Lucinda said.

"What do you mean, and why are you here at the office so late?"

"You fired your sales analyst last month. What else are we going to do? You forced me back to work."

"No, no. That was your choice. After I proposed, and the priest blessed our union at the Cathedral of Almudena, I told you that you no longer needed to work in the accounting department."

Lucinda moved around the desk to face the window. She noticed the information about the Boadilla del Monte property and other printed materials scattered on the floor. She kicked away a sheet of the Belmont property disclosure with the tip of her right high heel. "I know you are expecting big things from this medical real estate venture in the States."

"I just hung up the phone with the broker in Mississippi. He is on top of the matter," Garcia said. "My associate is very optimistic."

"You may not think much of my online university degree in accounting and finance from Rey Juan Carlos, but even I can read a spreadsheet. I went through our account and the email files that Wallace sent. The numbers don't add up."

"Nonsense, nonsense, my Lucinda." Garcia slid his arm around his wife's waist and pulled her onto his lap. The desk chair wobbled under the added weight. He rubbed his face against her neck and bust. "The American Medical Investment Fund is a sure winner. This Wallace fellow knows his stuff. Besides, his wife is a physician herself."

"Listen to me. The Belmont financial projections appear inflated. And from what I understand, those health insurance companies in America don't always pay the doctors well. In the blink of an eye, uppity doctors like the Belmonts are left out in the cold."

"Lucinda, Lucinda, you are always so negative. I thought you were only here to see me." Garcia gently grabbed her calf and slowly ran his hand up her leg.

"Don't be foolish. It's all about the bottom line." She pushed his hand away and jumped from his lap. "I knew you were working late and expecting that call from Wallace." She flexed the middle finger of her right hand around the forefinger in a twist. "Your appointment secretary and I are just like that. And you can forget about that insanely expensive villa for us. That deal on the floor is trash, a ridiculous dream, as far as I am concerned."

"Lucinda be reasonable." His tone was a mix of disbelief and aggravation.

"I hope we can continue to afford our current apartment in the city, much less purchase a larger, more luxurious home. The landlord may toss us to the streets after what you have gotten us into with the Americans."

Garcia jumped from his chair, sending it to roll hard against the window. "This deal will be a good one. This new venture will make good of the past. A new house and more galas for us. That means more gowns and dresses for you. A step forward—I will make sure of it."

# Chapter 5

Mid-January weather in Mississippi requires a thick jacket and winter boots one week and shorts and flip-flops the next. Sometimes choosing an ensemble for the next day can become an overnight dilemma. Tonight's evening weather forecast: high 50s to low 60s.

Chuck Wallace made the case, indirectly, that Brad should measure up to the dress code of the neighborhood men's walking group. For his first night out with the guys, Brad chose a pair of hiking pants taken on vacation with Diana to the Canadian Rockies the year before and sported a new pair of tennis shoes, the kind the kid in the sports gear shop said was best for long treks. The guy clinched the sale with news that a local high school cross country track team wore the same footwear.

Brad found a fitted souvenir tee-shirt from the same trip to Canada and a light blue hoodie to coordinate and complete his outfit. He tried to play it simple so as not to arrive as an over-prepared or over-dressed nerd standout. Chuck had not mentioned outdoor reflective gear, but probably not a bad idea for walking residential streets after sunset.

Diana withstood a brief modeling exposé of Brad's outdoor athletic outfit, put together for the big premiere. He made a closer study of the finished product in the master bedroom mirror. After a head-to-toe examination of his expensive, color-coordinated athletic garb, Brad decided that regardless how anybody saw it, he was a nerd. Yet, drip or not, the full body profile view in the mirror, mainly the flabby sideview, made joining the men's exercise group mandatory.

"I'll text Chuck today after my last case to make sure of the time and place to meet."

"Good plan. You seem excited about this." Diana removed the last hot roller, combed out her hair, and topped the style with hairspray. She reached for her make-up drawer and grabbed mascara. All of this for daughter Kelsey, to keep up with the other mothers.

"Trying to get into going every night," Brad answered. "I'm the latest rookie. I guess they can toss me or vote me out if I don't measure up." He undressed and placed the neatly folded hiking pants and tee shirt on a shelf closet next to his new tennis shoes and pair of white, low-rise socks—also recommended by the teenage salesman at the sporting goods store.

His surgical scrub suits hung nicely in the next section of his closet, monogrammed in white with the appealing logo of the surgery practice. After his brother Brian died, Brad exchanged black for navy-colored material, as did Diana and anyone else associated with the clinic. The slim fit of the surgical scrubs was another reason to get in shape and stay that way.

The following day Brad parked next to Diana in the section of the Jackson Metropolitan Hospital reserved for physicians. Gone was the gaudy *Doctors Parking Lot* sign, replaced by white block letters painted across the pavement at the top of each slot: DOCTOR PARKING ONLY. Usually the first physician to arrive in the morning on surgery days, Diana always chose the parking space to the left nearest the landscaping and pulled the driver's side against the curb, positioning her vehicle clearly away from the next lined spot.

Brad took the space next to Diana's car, made a note of her intentional parking, and chuckled at his beautiful wife's paranoia. How many times had she ranted over getting nailed by the door of a car parked too near? He left enough room between his vehicle and Diana's BMW to squeeze out without chipping the paint job.

The tight effort reinforced his decision to join the walking group and not miss a night.

"I'll probably hear about this," Brad said. He eased his car door closed before swinging the overnight bag across his shoulder. Tonight was on-call hospital duty, and he kept a fresh change of clothes and toiletries in the soft leather bag. "Diana will scream when she sees my car before she realizes it's me. She needs to learn how to take a joke."

Brad smiled at their vehicles as he walked toward the hospital. "Just like we sleep in bed, tight and personal."

He rode the staff elevator to the med-surg unit on the fourth floor where most of his postoperative patients were hospitalized and walked past his least favorite room, the one down the hall and around the corner from the nurses' station and now filled by one of Diana's post-ops. Brad spent four days there once, recovering from an attack by a former patient who followed him back from Iraq and murdered his twin brother.

*Seems like a lifetime ago.* Brad slid into the cramped enclave off the main hall designated as the doctors' medical records workroom.

"Cummins?" A gruff voice in a heavy, yet authentic, southern drawl brought Brad to attention. He sprang from the vinyl roller chair positioned in front of a computer.

"Dr. Belmont, what can I do for you?"

Ellis Belmont stood at the entrance from the hall, hands buried deep in his coat pockets. Dressed in white, traditional doctor's garb, his hands gave the impression of being trapped in the heavily starched cotton fabric. He stood six feet—six foot two twenty years ago—his bald scalp reflecting the fluorescent light overhead. The thick grey eyebrows and frowned forehead demanded attention.

"The gentleman in twenty-five, the guy with the Whipple—why in God's name did you operate on him, son?"

"Well, the tumor was accessible in the head of the pancreas, and he opted for the procedure. Besides, he's always had trouble with his gallbladder. CT scan IDed the location of the malignancy, and we went for it. Intra-op findings supported the decision."

"What's that old saying? *Surgery was a success, but the patient died?*" Belmont said.

"No sir. Mr. York stayed less than twenty-four hours post-op in intensive care. He's out on the floor, a few doors down from here."

"For God's sake, of course I know that. I've got his chart right here." Dr. Belmont gestured to the stack of thin metal charts held against his chest. "And as you will see, I have fought all that electronic medical crap your age seems to love. The nurses know I hate it. They work around it for me."

"I was on my way to see Mr. York. He's only post-op day two, and the nurses haven't called me about any unexpected problems."

"Where have you been? The man's sats are in the low eighties, and his urine output is almost below measurable. He begged me to take out his catheter, but I explained that strict I&O is required. You surgeons never tell these poor patients what to expect."

"We spent a good while in the clinic talking about—"

"Don't believe it, Cummins, not one iota. I sat down on the side of the bed and explained respiration and adequate intake and output to York and his daughter—the things that are important before and after surgery. Thank God the daughter was there to take it all in since York's wife has dementia. I'm told she has a year or two of nursing school," Belmont said. "Her mom, Suzanne, has never been right in the head, anyway. I helped get her into that swanky, new Alzheimer's unit in the nursing home."

Brad straightened his posture and footing and managed to interject, "I had cardiology and pulmonary assess Mr. York pre-op. He got the greenlight for surgery."

"I don't give a flip about what those pencil pushers say even if they are part of my medical group. I've been the man's doctor for thirty years or longer. He's a medical time bomb, a ticking time bomb."

Brad took a deep breath and stepped out of the small space into the hall. Dr. Belmont moved a few steps out of the way. "Anything you can do with Mr. York's post-op care will take a lot off me, Dr. Belmont. Thanks."

"I've told you Millennials or people in the Generation Z to call me *Ellis*. I expect that of you too, Cummins."

"Then along those lines of familiarity, why don't you go for *Brad*. And I'd like to go along with the younger age and timeline thing, but the older Millennials claim me."

"It's all about labels, isn't it?" Belmont said with a smirk. "Of course, no problem. It's *Brad* from now on. And why don't you try *Ellis*?"

"I've got a couple of other post-ops that might need tending to. You up for more consults, Dr. Belmont? Sorry … Ellis?"

"Possibly one or two. I'm short on time—have a lunch meeting. Of course, there's always the hospitalist to lean on today, and a fairly good one, some import from Mayo. Unlike the teenybopper crew in my practice, I continue to carry a full load, and I'm including all the Belmont clan in that reference. I can only do so much to take up the slack around here."

*Hanging around in the hall, bullshitting, is a great use of time.* Brad swallowed his smile.

"And all the new computer work that I cannot avoid. Takes time away from patients. Fortunately, my PA does most of it."

"I've worked with guys from Mayo before," Brad said and lowered his voice. "A few do a great job. Others …"

"Wave of the future, Brad! Similar to all this computer crap." Belmont stepped closer and patted him on the back. "You *older millennials*, as you say, should be all about that." He then peered around the hospital ward and lowered his voice. "Speaking of what's up and coming—there's this out-of-state investment group that wants to buy the equity value in our practice. You might want to talk with them. They'd jump at your outfit."

"My brother Brian and I promised ourselves we'd stay private. No outsiders. The surgeons who have joined our group since he died like the fact that we run the medical and business aspect of things our way."

"The buy-out money's good, Brad. These people saw our bottom line, and—no surprise—they liked it. Even a less mature practice like yours, a general surgery practice, should be appealing to these venture capitalists."

A nurse appeared dressed in scrubs with a festive *Happy New Year* badge hanging by a lanyard around his neck. "Dr. Cummins, sorry to interrupt. The man in twenty-four wants solid food for breakfast. He kept down liquids last night, is walking the halls—"

"Yes, that's fine, Jake. Go ahead and advance his diet."

"Thank you. I'll take care of it, Doc."

As the nurse walked away, Belmont said, "I've always believed that after January fifteenth, it's time to let the new year greeting go."

"Never thought about that." Brad took a few steps from Belmont and smiled at a couple of patient visitors several yards away. "Thanks for your help with Mr. York. His family's ready for him to get home."

"Certainly they are." Belmont again lowered his voice to a whisper. "You're bound to have some business sense, Cummins—I mean—Brad. It's obvious. Think about that monstrous building you've got."

"That facility was all my brother's idea. Brian had big dreams."

"I've chaired hospital credentials for the last seven or eight years, my third stint in service, you know, and I've seen the new surgeons, PAs, and nurse practitioners you and Bratton have added to your payroll."

"I appreciate the information." Brad took a couple of more steps down the hall. "Diana's been a full partner for several years now, and no question our practice is growing. That means more hospital rounds to finish, so—"

"Don't put this business stuff off. Don't ignore corporate America. It's sucking up the medical profession." Dr. Belmont scanned the area, the hospital corridor empty of visitors and medical staff for the moment. He withdrew a business card from his jacket pocket and handed it to Brad. "Give this guy a call. Likely your paths have crossed since you practice with his wife, Voncelle."

Brad glanced at the card and dropped it in a side pocket. "I know Chuck—socially, and we're glad to have Voncelle practice with us. Diana and I currently make most of the business decisions for the practice, and we're all set."

Diana appeared from around the corner. "All set with what?"

"I'm trying to educate your husband about the economics of modern medicine." Belmont darted his eyes between Diana and Brad. "Or should I say, your business partner?"

"I was explaining to Dr. Belmont that we aren't interested in selling our surgical practice."

"Agreed," Diana glanced around to see no one else within ear shot. "Our clinic patient numbers are growing, and we've got an awesome administrator and accountant. The doctors are making good decisions about how major money is utilized in our practice."

Belmont shook his head and chuckled. "Imagine, a man about twice your age knows more than either of you about the changing world around them. The medical insurance companies screw us on payments more and more every day. It's atrocious!" He gestured to the lower pocket of Brad's jacket. "You've got Chuck Wallace's card, plus an inside track to reach him through his wife. You and your wife are obviously the major producers in your clinic, and it's time to cash in before it's too late."

"Excuse me, Dr. Belmont. If you believe the appointment schedule on my phone, I got a full clinic waiting on me," Diana said and walked away.

Brad slipped back into the cramped computer workstation and dropped into the chair nearest the door, intentionally blocking further entrance into the space. "Sorry, Ellis," he called out into the hall. "I'm sorta swamped too."

Belmont tailed him to the door. "You gotta man-up on this one, Brad. Take the lead and give Chuck Wallace a call."

Brad forced a smile as he waved his hospital badge across the terminal near the computer, then entered his password. An alphabetized list of his hospitalized patients populated the screen.

David York anchored the bottom of the list.

Belmont's cell rang just as Brad noticed a new text on his own phone. Belmont offered a half-hearted smile and stepped out into the hall to answer the call. "Yes, this is Dr. Belmont. What? No, I'm afraid you're mistaken. Those orders on Mr. Kellum were sent in hours ago. Learn to read, won't you?" he said loud enough for anyone in the hall to hear. Brad thought he heard Belmont reporting the caller to a head nurse as he left.

Brad check the text message from Diana.

> Is the old guy getting a sales commission from Chuck Wallace?

Brad laughed and texted back.

> Wouldn't be surprised. 
>
> Pizza tonight? New place in District.
>
> Walking Group. Chuck's group. Remember?
>
> You serious?
>
> Gonna shower after. Wanna join me?
>
> Need pizza. Not shower. 😃

"The walk around Chuck's neighborhood is all the sweating I'll be doing tonight," Brad said. He thought about the last time he and Diana had showered together, managed to shake away the steamy image, and began to click and scroll through the medical records on the computer screen.

~

Ellis Belmont finished his verbal thrashing of the travel nurse from New Jersey, the clumsy new graduate assigned to staff the medicine unit on second and who confused his orders for Mr. David York. He made a mental note of the name with plans to speak to the Director of Nursing about the downward slide in the hospital's staffing policies. He stepped into the unoccupied patient room adjacent to the elevator and took the next call on his cell.

"Miles? I thought you had clinic today. Aren't you knee deep in vials and syringes of neurotoxin?"

"Cut the crap, Ellis. The PAs give all the injections. Besides, you're getting your share."

"And glad to get it. You gotta make sure your staff is pushing the max on those units and not pocketing product for their own parties."

"Can you turn it off for a second? Just let it go?" Miles asked.

"Better sign those vain, paying clients up for more skin peels and facials too. I pulled up last quarter's numbers—down twelve percent. And don't forget to charge for that expensive laser." Belmont dropped into the visitor chair of the recently refurbished patient room, actually a suite four times the hospital standard—compliments of the Belmont Healthcare Foundation.

The Belmont clan or their designated friends got first dibs of the pricey and much sought-after accommodations when they needed hospitalization. Fortunately for other high-end, but less notable donors of Jackson Metropolitan Hospital, the Belmonts and their close, wealthy friends and family were rarely ill. This morning the room remained empty after Ellis Belmont's pickle ball partner recovered from ankle surgery and was discharged yesterday.

"What's the problem, Little Brother?"

"I hate it when you call me your little brother. We're only three years apart, and Jesus, Ellis, we're both nearly seventy years old!"

"You're getting all worked up over probably nothing. What is it this time?"

"This Wallace guy, Chuck Wallace. He brought over all these papers for me to sign. No, it wasn't him. It was a secretary or administrative assistant or whoever the damn she is."

"That's right, and I'm headed over to the clinic in a few to sign my copy. Somebody must see and care for the hospitalized patients over here. You certainly can't count on surgeons to do the right thing, like the two I ran into this morning."

"Ellis, I'm not signing this crap for Wallace."

"Now, Miles, or whatever you want me to call you." Belmont stood from the cushioned chair and gazed out the window. From this angle, the view of the Christine Belmont Commemorative

Garden was spectacular, even in bleak January. The hollies had kept their bright red berries through Christmas, and the variegated Silver Queen euonymous remained beautiful in bright sun nearly year-round. Fortunately, the glass and steel monstrosity next door called a bank building and designed by an expensive Alabama architect did not obstruct Belmont's study of the landscaping.

He envisioned the inviting, six-story art deco hotel, which once gleamed on the site of the gaudy, contemporary building that soared fifteen floors before him. Belmont's smile turned sour at his failure, one of only few he could remember. The fight to block the hotel demolition ended with his fruitless effort to mount a counter pur-chase and designate the building a national landmark. Big money from an out-of-state financial outfit bought the stunning 1930s hotel, razed it, and left Belmont more than bitter. Nonetheless, his late mother had to be proud that he tried, even if she were looking up from below instead of smiling down from above.

*No matter where she is, she's probably shaking her head: 'My son, the loser.'*

The flop to save an architectural wonder continued to burn a hole in Belmont's gut. He wrestled with defeat by auditing a local college night class on cooperate real estate. Despite no grade or credit, he knew he could have aced the exam after all he absorbed from the lectures and required reading. A guest course lecturer introduced the idea of investing not only in brick-and-mortar corporate real estate but also in the sweat equity of the people who built and ran the operation within the walls.

Quick to understand and accept the medical practice value concept, Ellis Belmont decided to cash in on his years of back-breaking work required to build a patient base, take after-hours calls at night and on weekends, and render perfect medical care. *They call it goodwill.*

Selling that goodwill for the financial gain of the Belmont family had consumed Ellis Belmont.

"Ellis? Hey, Ellis. You still there?"

Belmont turned away from the window and back to the phone conversation with his younger brother. "We voted, Miles. You were there. We were all there. Almost every Belmont is on board to move forward with this sale of the practice. Most of the others in the practice also said *yes*. We need little sister Sidney to see the light, and it's a go."

"Sorry to break it to you, but I've reconsidered. I wanted to tell you in person, except there's no need to put it off."

"Dammit, Miles. What are you saying?"

"It's wrong to sell everything we've worked for, everything we've built, to these foreign corporate thugs. I was wrong. You were wrong. We're all wrong," Miles said.

Several Canadian geese swooped into the hospital garden and caught Ellis's attention. The birds began to pick at the mulch in the planting beds. "What pests. Mother hated those things and their mess. Nasty," Ellis said.

"What? Who are you talking to?"

"We've gone around and around on this. Selling the medical practice and spa is the right thing to do. And, if it will make you happier, I will drop the *Little Brother*. Return to your senses. It's the right time, and it's a financial windfall for us considering our age."

"There's grumbling from the other guys. Even a few of the ones who voted to sell to Chuck Wallace want to back out. They're avoiding a confrontation with you."

"First of all, we're not selling to Wallace. Think of him as a broker. He found the best opportunity, and we're getting top dollar." The geese flew off. Several stopped to walk atop the metal picnic tables belonging to the bank and relieved themselves in murky, messy goop. Ellis grinned in satisfaction.

"You don't get it. The senior guys like us can't keep making up the rules. Others in the practice think as much of themselves as you do, if you can believe that."

"I'm a big boy, Miles. Bring on the verbal abuse. I can take it, and I don't run from an argument," Ellis growled. The Canadian geese grew tired of the bank and flew away. Someone would need to rinse off the employee picnic tables with a garden hose, if those corporate guys cared to bother. "This is nonsense about objecting to the sale. Those ingrates need to come to their senses. I'll talk to them."

"A group is going above your head. They're going to call Chuck Wallace," Miles said. "They don't want to sign and will stop the sale. They plan to get their own attorney if they have to."

"It's gone too far. We've had many, many conversations about this. Wallace's investment group will sue if we back out now. But there's no reason to back out—too much money on the table. You've let the whiners get to you. Those screw-ups!"

"Ellis, they're gonna try to stop this. They're really pissed. My opinion doesn't even matter, and for once you're—"

"For once I'm *what*, Little Brother?"

"You have pushed and pushed your whole life. I've always admired you, respected you. I even went to med school because you did and played basketball and sang in the high school choir because you did."

"Cut the crap." Ellis Belmont stormed out the empty hospital suite with his cell phone tight to his ear and into the path of the hospital cleaning service. "My God, man, get out of my way," he said to the employee who pushed the cleaning cart. A plastic bottle of floor cleaner bounced to the floor, followed by a broom that teetered off the pushcart. It barely missed Belmont's left leg and foot.

"You've always landed upright, Ellis. But for once, you're going to lose," Miles said.

# Chapter 6

Brad pulled against the curb of a two-story brick home located on a corner in Chuck Wallace's neighborhood, the reported twelve-year rendezvous location and starting point of the walking group. The house number matched Chuck's information stored in Brad's phone. Had he walked and not driven, tonight's scheduled four-mile trek for Brad would have been six, almost seven.

The garage doors were lowered, the house lights dimmed. No other cars stood in the driveway or in front of the house. Brad checked the notes on his phone and reconfirmed the address. He was four minutes early. "Chuck said they took off at eight, no earlier, no later. *You snooze, you lose,*" he said aloud. "Maybe they called tonight's walk off. I'll come back tomorrow."

Instead, Brad turned off the ignition and stepped from his car. He tightened his shoelaces and dropped his key fob into the tight pocket of his Nike pants, leaving his wallet locked in the front seat console. The air felt chilly and breezy. Pants, not shorts, had been the better choice. Brad shivered and regretted the tee shirt. Even a long-sleeved tee-shirt would have been better. He glanced into the rear seat and hoped to see a half zip or hoodie left behind but came up empty and shrugged. About mid-way through the walk, he would likely want to shed clothing anyway.

Headlights suddenly draped the rear of Brad's vehicle before another Ford F-150 pick-up pulled into the driveway. The truck stopped short of entering the garage as the door rose to swallow it. A man jumped out and jogged toward Brad just before several other vehicles appeared and parked behind and in front of Brad's truck. Others filled the driveway single file behind the Ford. Men began to congregate in the street in front of the house.

"Hey, you must be Brad," the excited driver of the Ford truck and apparent owner of the two-story said. "Chuck told us you might be coming tonight. Glad to have you. I'm Ralph Anderson." After a quick handshake, Ralph motioned to his driveway and lowered the garage door with a control on his key chain. "It's fine to park in the driveway, but don't block my wife's side. She always parks to the right, closest to the kitchen. She's at bunko tonight."

"Got it," Brad said. He scanned the men gathered in the sparse streetlight and again referred to the time. Two minutes to lift off, and no one resembling Chuck Wallace. "Chuck made it clear to be ready at eight. The group doesn't hold back for stragglers, he said."

"You snooze, you lose," Frank said.

Brad responded, "So I've heard."

A sedan rounded the corner and parked across the entrance to the driveway, leaving enough space for Mrs. Anderson to squeeze through, provided she drove nothing larger than a golf cart. A man in a white baseball cap with light-colored tee shirt and shorts jumped from a Volvo. Brad compared the tennis shoes trimmed in orange reflector tape to his own navy shoes and socks. Considering the sparse street lighting, he decided reflector tape and lighter clothing would have been a better idea. He should have followed his earlier concerns about nighttime safety.

"Now that Chuck's here, so we can go ahead and start!" A voice boomed over the light conversations among the waiting men.

Someone toward the rear of the dozen said, "Yeah, it's all about Chuck."

Chuck seemed to be adjusting his phone as he approached. "I've got the PaceKeeper app set. Let's try to do under fourteen tonight."

The men pushed ahead at a brisk pace. Surprised, but grateful, that Chuck did not lead the pack, Brad fell in line beside him. "What did you mean by, *under fourteen?*"

Chuck popped the cell phone from his pocket and flashed Brad with the screen. *14:15 min/mi* displayed prominently in the lower righthand corner. "We hit *13:46* last night for an average. This thing tracks the pace." He returned the phone to his pocket.

"Got it. I hope y'all aren't counting on me for the extra speed," Brad said and forced a light chuckle.

"Like we talked before, this group's got all kinds. You'll fit in fine," Chuck said.

"Fairly large group of guys tonight?" Brad felt the laces of his right shoe give and wanted to retie them, but he remembered Chuck's prep talk. As far as anyone could remember, the group had only stopped their stride once. One night a member, who had since moved away, tripped on a pothole and broke an ankle—and even with that, only a couple of guys stayed behind with him to call 911. No way anyone would wait for newbie Brad Cummins to tighten his shoelaces.

"Last fall we had seventeen show up—even on a Monday. Cool night, low humidity. Good night to walk."

Brad's other shoe seemed to loosen under the strain of the pace and matched the right. The balance of pressure against his feet somehow felt better now. The men entered the next street with the climb of a low hill.

At mention of the final score of the recent Ole Miss bowl game, Chuck turned to the guy at his left. "Roy, no way any decent team could have missed that field goal. Crap like that screws up recruiting. Anyway, I've about decided to give up my season tickets. My wife's too busy to go up to Oxford with me, and besides she's all about LSU football and—"

Chuck's ringing cell phone interrupted the light rant. He jerked the phone from his pocket and studied the screen. "Thought it might be Voncelle, but she knows better than to call me during a walk." The phone kept ringing. Chuck almost tripped on a section of uneven asphalt. "Sorry, guys. I gotta take this."

Brad slowed his pace to follow Chuck.

"No, man. Stay with the group," Chuck said. "I'll catch up. Remember? We gotta make the low thirteens."

Brad nodded and continued the brisk step.

"So, you decided you're up for this torture," the tall, lanky man to Brad's right said. "They say I'm the oldest member, not in years of participation, but in age. Hell, I can walk circles around most of the guys under fifty!" The man laughed and increased his speed. Brad took it up a notch.

He tilted his head back toward Chuck, visible on the side of the street near a light pole and deep in conversation on his cell. "Yeah, my wife works with Chuck's. He's been on me to hit the pavement. I'm bad outta shape."

"Chuck's not so toned himself," the man snickered and stumbled on the uneven walkway. He quickly righted himself.

"One of us is going down hard," Brad said.

"Hazard of city living. Name's Peter Mitchell, but *Pete* works best, and don't worry about your friend. Chuck's a longtime veteran of this group. He'll catch up."

"Fine. *Pete*, it is," Brad said. Despite the moderate temperature, Brad felt sweat run down his back and sensed the makings of a cramp in his right foot. He fought to ignore both. "Chuck told me that tonight's what y'all call the hills course, not the flat track around the lake. I should've probably started on that one."

"Yep, the hills course every Tuesday and Thursday—my favorite. The guys in the group who don't have what it takes skip for the easy Monday and Wednesday route around the lake. This is an ambitious initiation tonight," Pete said. "You'll find the scenery interesting—lots of nice two-story houses up on the ridge." He motioned to a large home that sprawled over what appeared to be two lots. "Like that bloated place. Wow, those people must've blown a bundle on landscape lighting and on interior lighting too."

Brad did his best to work the muscles inside his tennis shoe while maintaining the pace. The muscle cramp began to subside.

"Sometimes the owners forget to draw the shades or close the curtains, particularly in the bedrooms." Pete erupted in thunderous laughter before almost tripping over another pothole in the street.

Another man came up from behind to Brad's left. "Don't listen to anything Pete says. Name's Matt Batson. Glad you made it. Chuck mentioned he was trying to recruit you."

"I hope I can keep up," Brad said. More sweat trickled down his back into his shorts. The key fob in his right pocket felt heavy.

They turned the corner to a gradual incline.

"Sunday night is sort of a combined course. A rough hill or two, but mostly smooth," Matt said, "except at the end."

Brad breathed heavier. "Can't wait." He wondered if Chuck would be offended if this was his first and last walk. He needed to hit the gym or get a personal trainer before trying to keep abreast with a group like this.

"You'll adapt. I got a feeling you're gonna fit right in," Matt said. "It's *Brad*, isn't it?"

Brad nodded and turned his head to the rear for a second, then remembered the potholes. "Do we need to keep an eye out for Chuck?"

"He knows the course, same route since we started this elite organization years ago." Matt snickered. "Once he's finished with his call, I expect he'll take a shortcut and meet us up ahead."

"That's the unique thing about this group," Pete said. "Most aren't late to start the walk or drop off to take a call like Chuck did unless it's urgent, but the routes and times are so consistent it's easy to rendezvous."

The gradual incline became a steep hill. As Brad leaned forward into the change of terrain, a black cat sprang from a bush near the curb, barely missing him before it ran across the street. The cat stopped and glared at Brad before bounding into another shrub.

Brad leaned further into the sharp ascent. His feet and legs ached. His breathing deepened. He wanted to be home glued to TV and drinking a beer. There were at least two cold cans in the refrigerator at home. When Diana drank, it was always wine, so the beer was safe. Brad wanted to binge another episode of that new show on the British TV channel.

"This is a tie for worst hill. But don't worry; you'll be numb to the pain by the time we reach its twin," Matt said.

"Especially if Matt starts in with his Cajun jokes," Ralph Anderson said, coming up from the rear.

"Stuff it, Ralphie Boy," Matt said. "Chuck Wallace is the real joke of this group. He can barely keep up. Chuck, the human sloth."

The group topped the hill to a gradual decline into a neighborhood of expensive brick homes with high-pitched and flat roofs and even more elaborate landscape lighting. Scattered residences had not yet removed the exterior Christmas lights and other holiday decorations. They passed one house on the right with a **For Sale** sign.

A figure walked through the intersection at the bottom of the hill.

"Hey, that's Chuck. Knew he'd find us," Peter said.

"Will he stop and let us catch-up?" Brad said. Matt was right; his feet were going numb. They didn't hurt anymore.

"Chuck's not that great on speed," Matt Batson said. "Sweats like a pig. We'll have no problem catching up with him. No problem at all."

"Which is it, Matt?" Pete asked. "Sloth or pig?"

All the men within earshot laughed.

"Don't get us wrong," Ralph said. "We all love Chuck, and he gives it back to us. When we catch up to him, you'll see."

"Yeah, Ralph's right. Chuck's a longtime friend," Matt said.

"Sure is," Pete agreed.

Despite the reassurance, Brad found himself picking up the pace, and strangely the alternating pain and numbness in his feet continued to ease. All these guys seemed jovial—friendly and welcoming, true jokesters in fact. However, his connection was with Chuck, and he wanted to catch up with him.

Chuck kept moving forward without even a glance back at the others, his advance steady, as though he were deep in thought and could care less if the others gained on him. No one called out. They knew they would catch him in a matter of minutes or less.

Brad wanted to yell, "Hey, Chuck, wait up!" but knew that would be taboo and sophomoric.

The walking group remained silent as the men approached Chuck, silent except for the rhythmic, almost military, movement of tennis shoes against asphalt. A single dog barked from somewhere in the distance—no more cats anywhere.

Suddenly, a piercing thud erupted from the right. The barking halted and Chuck stumbled. His left shoulder sank.

"What the eff was that?" Matt said, all eyes on Chuck Wallace.

The sound repeated, more like a popping balloon this time, originating from a house somewhere on the right side of the street, high—from the roof. The house with the **For Sale** sign.

Chuck Wallace fell hard to the pavement, his body rolling past a mailbox into a drainage ditch between two driveways. A stereo of barking dogs exploded out of nowhere.

Brad jerked his head toward the roof and nearly stumbled, seeing no movement related to the house. It remained dark.

The men ran down the hill and reached Chuck in seconds. A few from behind the front line overtook the others.

"Chuck's not moving!" the guy to reach him first yelled, someone whom Brad had not met. The guy pointed the flashlight from his cell phone at Chuck. "There's blood. God! He's been shot."

Brad glanced again in the direction of the two-story house—still all quiet, no one around. "Somebody call 911." He pushed through the men in front of him. "Who knows CPR? If you do, get down here and help me. And keep that light on us."

The guy with the cell phone complied, and Brad felt Chuck's carotid pulse. Nothing. He started chest compressions while a burnt-brown, crimson stain blossomed from under Chuck Wallace's chest.

"I'm no good at medical stuff," Mark Batson blurted, "but I got 911 on the phone now. And Justin, keep that light steady."

Brad continued the CPR, then checked Chuck's neck again. "I got a pulse. But tell the EMTs to hurry."

# Chapter 7

Diana's heart raced. She loved this.

Four years of college and the same in med school followed by a five-year general surgery residency paid her share of the bills, but this stuff tonight brought excitement. Not the thrill she felt in watching her daughter mature and find her own place in life—not the thrill of her husband's hot, sensuous touch when he pressed himself against her, but an out-of-the-box, living-on-the-edge adventure. She *liked* solving crimes. No, she *loved* it.

Diana steadied the side of the aluminum ladder with her right hand and stepped off the last rung onto the roof. The evening temperature was mild, not uncommon for late January in Mississippi. She brushed the light dirt and green moss from the thighs of her new surgical scrubs, fresh from an online retailer and the monogram shop.

"I thought a dark color would hide dirt better."

"Sorry, Doctor Bratton, my detective found the ladder tossed away in an old flower bed on the other side of the house," Key Martin said. "We dusted it for prints—nothing fresh. A cast off from the previous owners, I suppose. Been there for a while—covered with leaves and that moss."

Diana picked a partially decayed oak tree leaf from her shoulder. "Wasn't there another way up here besides climbing a ladder?"

"The house is a suspected crime scene, at least the roof is. We have full reign of the place, but I didn't want to get all tied up with the real estate agent about getting a key to the interior."

"The agent's his ex-wife," the detective chuckled.

"Which one?" Diana said. "If I remember correctly, Chief Martin has several."

Martin glared at Detective Thomas. "The first one, Dr. Bratton. The one that's making more money than me."

"Wouldn't be too hard to do that, judging from what the department pays me," Thomas muttered as he walked the span of the flat-surface roof above the over-sized breakfast room. More months of decaying leaves littered the space. The home had been vacant for months. Near the rear edge of the roof and opposite the ladder, the yellow outline of a footprint stood out in the mess. "Seems the shooter was a real Boy Scout." He gestured to the markings made in the flower bed below, typical of the base footing of a ladder.

Diana tread lightly across the roof in her tennis shoes and glanced at the street. "What are we canvassing for? Gun shell casings? More footprints?"

"You never know what you'll find, what you'll stumble across," Chief Martin answered.

"Is that how your department is investigating the creep who broke into my car and held me at gunpoint?" Diana felt a vibration from her phone, a text from the post-op unit. "I'd like to get an update on that sometime."

"Not much we could do with no fingerprints or facial recognition," Martin said.

"I gave you the name of Roy Allen Garnett after I got it cleared with the state medical board, only because the guy mentioned that Garnett was his uncle, and he wanted me to falsify Garnett's medical records. That put me in the middle of a strange doctor-patient confidentiality issue."

"We couldn't locate Mr. Garnett. We believe he's out of the country at the moment," the detective said.

"And there are no grounds to detain him otherwise," Martin said.

"I'm sure your department is on top of it." Diana read a new message. "Can't stay long. It's getting late. I need to get back to the hospital and put the patients to bed."

Martin looked from Diana to the murder scene across the street. "I knew my luck when the detective told me your hubby was a witness."

"By *luck*, I guess you mean you had good excuse to drag me into another case," Diana said.

"The bonus was the ID of the victim," Martin said.

"Bonus?" Diana began to move back toward the ladder. "Not a big plus for poor Chuck Wallace."

"It's a nice coincidence Dr. Cummins was around, and the victim is the spouse of one of the other surgeons." Martin shrugged. "You're right. I knew you'd get involved in solving this thing."

"I know you wear a badge somewhere under that suit, and there's a soul in there too, but my husband still feels uneasy around you. And you're not helping the situation."

Martin lowered his head a second. "Only doing my job, Doc."

"Sure, Chief," Diana said. "Great comeback."

"So—what about the coincidence—your husband and Chuck Wallace?"

"Brad and Chuck were friends." Diana said. "Well, not exactly friends, but acquaintances through our surgical practice. They met at the Christmas party."

Martin walked to the edge of the roof and faced the direction down the street where Chuck Wallace fell. "Over the past few years of my career, even before I was chief, you and Dr. Cummins have been at the center of my most interesting cases—guess the big boy word for 'em is *challenging*."

"I can see why you called me in to help on this case, but not so much for the kid abducted a few months ago or the woman who murdered her meddlesome mother-in-law last year."

"That MD behind your name's got to stand for something. You always add to the investigations, provide a common-sense approach."

Diana's cell buzzed again. "I've got to go, Martin."

More text messages from nurses:

```
Need orders for new patient sent up
from the ED
Post-op in 426 spiked temp, 103. New
antibiotics?
Alexander in 438 wants more pain meds.
```

"I don't know anything about ballistics. Or why anyone would want to shoot Chuck Wallace." She walked to the yellow footprint. "All Brad does is work—no tennis, sometimes a little golf. For weeks he's been talking about getting more exercise. That night, he tried."

"Your spouse is not a suspect here, and you've already busted me. It's obvious I used Dr. Brad Cummins to pull you into another investigation. Oh, and I need to update you on that girl who stole the dismembered limbs from a path lab."

"Rather not know," Diana said and looked off toward the street. "I've been nothing but a sounding board for you on most of the other cases, someone to bounce ideas off."

Martin gestured to his detective. "This guy's not so bad to work with, but sometimes I need another prospective—sort of an outsider's take on things. And most of the time, Dr. Diana Bratton, you're on the mark. You're good."

Detective Thomas frowned. "Hey, what's this about?"

"You do good work, no doubt about it," Martin said. "I count on Dr. Bratton to bring a new prospective."

Diana smiled at the detective and gestured toward the bulge in the pocket of his suit jacket. "You're the one who's carrying, I suspect, so I yield to you when it comes down to it."

"Thanks, Dr. Bratton." Thomas grinned an *I-told-you-so* at Martin.

"I'll talk to Brad. Go over his last conversations with Chuck. See if he remembers anything that could suggest trouble at work—or at home," Diana said, addressing both men. "They weren't good friends, I don't think, but I suppose men talk among themselves. Brad's been closed mouth about the whole thing. I'll see what I can find out."

"This has bound to have been quite a shock to Dr. Cummins. For the other guys, too. Just out for a nighttime walk," Martin said, "to get exercise."

"We have no motive against the victim. For all we know, it could have been a random shooting," the detective said. "Some psycho."

"You two guys are the police here, but from what I understand, Chuck Wallace was separated from the other men. If a deranged person wanted target practice, he—or she—would have taken out several, made multiple scores. Chuck was the intended victim."

Diana stared down at the outline of the footprint that resembled a larger-sized tennis shoe. "Yes, a male shooter, don't you two think?"

"He could have picked Wallace out since he was ahead of the others on the street—an easy, single target," Thomas said.

"Do you know of others familiar with this group of men and the scheduled walks?" Martin asked.

"No idea, except I remember an article in the newspaper a year or so ago—big headline: *The Walking Group* with a picture identifying everyone standing together on a porch. I don't remember any specifics about time or location. But then, I really wasn't that interested."

"Thomas, get that article," Martin said.

"Sure thing, Chief. Probably can pull it up on the internet." He began to search his cell phone.

"We'll need to talk to Wallace's wife. Since you work with her at your clinic, Dr. Bratton, can you help with that?"

Diana read the next text on her phone. "You guys need to be a bit more sensitive. Voncelle Wallace just lost her husband, and the poor woman continues to try to work, to take emergency calls, even. In fact, that was a message from her about one of my patients."

"I would hope she wants to know why her husband was shot—and who did it." Martin stared down at the large footprint. "Know much about how they were getting along?"

Diana stepped away from the footprint and walked closer to the edge of the roof, remaining several feet away. She faced the street in the direction of Chuck's fall. "From what I know, since Dr. Voncelle Wallace joined our practice, she and Chuck seemed to have a good marriage. No kids," Diana said. "She mentioned Chuck often—and talked about what they planned to do together, like on the weekends. Yeah—stuff like that. But then …" Diana's voice trailed off as her mind drifted to a recent conversation with Voncelle.

"Dr. Bratton?" Chief Martin stepped around Diana to face her.

"Yes, uhh, their marriage—their relationship seemed stable," she said, jerking her head away from the spot of Brad's attempt to resuscitate Chuck Wallace. She stared into Key Martin's eyes. "Actually, I don't know anything about their relationship—except that they were married."

Martin tilted his head. "Sure about that?"

"Hey, I'm due back at the hospital. Gotta go." Diana nearly sprinted for the ladder left propped against the corner edge of the roof. She almost slipped on the many damp leaves littering the flat rooftop.

"Steady there, Doc," Detective Thomas said. "Let me hold the ladder for you."

Diana began her descent down the extension ladder as Thomas steadied the top against the edge of the roof. She felt the phone buzz again. "I should have already left, and it's getting late."

"I'll be in touch, Dr. Bratton," Martin called out.

Diana lifted her head and yelled back while fighting sarcasm, "Counting on it!"

"We're not far behind you," Martin answered.

When her foot missed a rung, Diana slipped but caught herself before falling from the ladder. "That was a close one, you guys," she said, again tilting her head up. "Next time, might need to collect workman's comp from JPD." She reached ground, released the ladder, and thought she heard a twig snap.

"You got it, Doc?" Detective Thomas called down to her as she disappeared into the shadows.

"Yep, made it."

A hand jerked her shoulder around the corner into a thicket of overgrown foundation shrubbery. She pushed a limb away from her face. "Hey, what's going on?"

"You say something, Dr. Bratton?" Thomas called again.

A man's voice whispered, "Quiet, bitch. I'm here to finish what we started the other night in the garage. You let me down."

Diana again felt cold metal against her neck.

"Stay quiet and walk with me around to the garage. We'll slip into your car and drive away. Stupid cops won't suspect a thing." His heavy breath smelt of bourbon. She recognized the voice from the backseat of her car. He pushed closer to her, still behind her. She was taller than he.

"All I have to do is scream," Diana said, "and the police up on that roof will get you, get you quick."

"You scream, and I'll drop you right here," he whispered and pressed harder with the barrel of the gun. "How's that work for ya?"

Diana's back stiffened. She clinched her fists.

"Now, let's move around to the back before those stupid cops come down that ladder, and I shoot them in the butt. That is, after I blow your brains out. I've been waiting almost thirty minutes for you, bitch. Tracked you here."

The man pushed even closer and tugged at Diana's waist. She sensed his foot slip on the rotting leaves around the base of the shrubbery. An incident in the bedroom with her abusive ex-husband when Kelsey was a baby flashed before her. Diana dropped her head to swing around and deliver a hard kick to the guy's groin.

After what sounded like the groan of a wounded animal, the gun fired in a split second, exploding one of the bedroom windows. Diana's second kick nailed the man's arm and the weapon flew into the bushes.

Both Thomas and Martin were down the ladder and around the corner in seconds with weapons drawn. The ladder had tumbled from the side of the house as Martin jumped to the ground from the second rung. He winced and stayed close behind Detective Thomas.

"This is the same guy that threatened me in my car that night in the clinic garage," Diana said. "I never saw his face, but the voice, the voice—it's the same." She rubbed the ache in her right hip and noticed Martin favored his right foot and ankle.

The assailant continued to hold his groin and writhe in the leaves. "All I wanted to do was talk to you," he moaned.

"How about making an appointment with the Doc in her office, you asshole, like everybody else," Thomas said as he bent to cuff the man behind his back. "Now, stand up."

Martin called for back-up and managed to retrieve the assailant's weapon from the shrubbery, sliding it into a bag to preserve fingerprints.

# Chapter 8

Chief Martin shifted in his office chair at the Jackson Police Department. The boot bracing his lower right leg, ankle, and foot banged against the inside of his desk. *Jumping off the lower rung of that ladder—stupid, stupid thing to do,* Martin decided again.

The orthopedic clinic provided the gray walking boot when the doctor diagnosed Martin's ankle fracture. "You're a lucky guy, Chief. No surgery needed, only ankle immobility for six to eight weeks. We'll x-ray it again and see. The older you are, the longer it takes sometimes."

"Thanks for that, Doc," Martin had said. The boot again hit the inside of his wooden desk with a loud thump as Thomas entered with an opened laptop.

"You wanted to see the old newspaper article about that group of guys Wallace was walking with," Thomas said. After a few clicks, he positioned the computer in front of Martin on top of a messy stack of paper files.

A group of fourteen men stood smiling and loosely positioned in two rows on what appeared to be the front porch of a residential home. A Christmas wreath hung at the entrance. Most were dressed in tee shirts and shorts, comfortable outdoor attire much of the time during winter in the Deep South. A few wore light jackets or sweatshirts.

The reporter included a brief history of the long-established organization's activities and their five-night a week gathering. For an hour or so they walked in a North Jackson neighborhood along established routes with no specific street names or courses detailed. The men pictured were identified by name in the byline. Chuck Wallace stood between Matt Batson and Pete Mitchell.

"Looks like a congenial bunch of guys," Martin said. Judging by the porch furniture and decorations and the front door entrance, the residence was high-dollar, not unusual for that section of the city. "I wonder what's the total net worth of these gentlemen."

"Dunno. Likely high. We might could find out," Thomas answered.

"The only one that really matters is Mr. Chuck Wallace," Martin said. "His wife's an MD, so we know she's sitting pretty."

"Didn't Doc Bratton say that Wallace's wife was kind of new to her practice?"

"When we convicted John Haynes, Dr. Voncelle Wallace's old practice sort of dissolved, and she needed a job. As physician surgeons go, she might have been in a slump."

"I'll verify Wallace's life insurance policy, coverage, and date of issue," Detective Thomas said.

"Diana—Dr. Bratton—said the Wallaces had no kids. Find out about any favorite nieces or nephews, any beneficiaries to rain on Dr. Wallace's parade."

"Will do," Thomas said.

Martin moved his leg. The side of his desk shook. "This temporary setback might sideline me on this investigation."

"If I know you, Chief," Detective Thomas said and winked, "you'll find a way to keep your nose in this case. Especially if Dr. Diana Bratton is involved."

"It's strictly professional between us," Martin said.

"Boss, the *between us* is what they call *a bit of a stretch*."

Martin slid Thomas's computer to the side and tapped a few keys on his own laptop to pull up the Charles "Chuck" Wallace file. After several misguided clicks, he found the correct information. "In the old days, my secretary would have typed this all up and brought in a paper folder. If you held it under your nose, you could smell her perfume. A brand from Belk, I remember. My ex-wife used to wear the same thing."

"Which one? And I don't mean the perfume."

"Tired joke, Thomas. Move on."

The headshot of a smiling Wallace perched in an upper corner oversaw the material on the rest of the screen.

"I pulled that information from his firm's website. Wasn't much on social media," Thomas said.

"Nice job. When I started out as a detective, we went door-to-door enquiring. None of this surfing the web with our feet up."

"Times have changed, Chief. If it makes you feel any better about your team's energy output, I do great detective work on my laptop while on the treadmill and stationary bike in the fitness room."

Details about Wallace's medical acquisitions company filled the rest of the page below the face shot. Scant personal information other than cell number and email was included with no mention of family other than his wife, Voncelle. Most of the copy touted years of success closing corporate real estate deals until more recent endeavors focused on private venture capital investments, rising through the business ranks as a go-to for high yield investment opportunities. Several blurbs of praise for the successes of Wallace's firm were extracted from *Global Private Equity* magazine.

Martin skimmed until he reached the last paragraph. Recent successfully closed transactions were listed with several acquisitions pending, including the Belmont Comprehensive Medical Clinic and Wellness Enhancement Spa.

"Belmont Clinic—that's local," Martin said. "Went there for a while with high blood pressure. Old guy, bald—Ellis Belmont—tried me on two or three different pills." Martin darted his eyes at Detective Thomas. "I finally got cured after tossing an ex-wife and flushing that darn medicine."

Both men laughed.

Thomas walked to the opposite side of the office and stood at the window. "My pressure was up for other reasons too. My mortgage and other bills were out of control. I couldn't get in with that doctor you saw." He cleared his throat. "From what you say, maybe that was for the best."

"I remember a slew of Belmonts listed on the sign out front—and on the paperwork they gave me to pay on the way out."

"A younger doc, a son or a nephew, in an office down the hall on the far side of the clinic building," Thomas said. "Did a good job, yeah, he did—got my blood sugar and pressure down. Problem was—that freaking medicine gave me the runs."

"Spare the details, Detective."

"I stopped the meds and that took care of the stomach situation—that, and downsizing to a smaller house and giving up doughnuts at the café down the street."

Martin stared up from the laptop. "With that belly, Detective, you need to stay away from the café all together."

"Hey, come on, Chief. The wife picks on me enough." Thomas struggled to straighten his posture and suck in his stomach.

"Sorry, an easy punch for me since exercise is out for a while," Martin said. "I gotta stay clear of that café too."

Thomas observed his whole-body profile in the window's reflection and frowned, then shook off the concern. "We need to confirm the list of deals Wallace has closed over the last five years as well as his active clients. There could be unhappy campers out there."

"That includes the Belmont outfit. Hope that doesn't make it awkward with you and your young doc," Martin said.

"No problem. I never started back on the pills."

# Chapter 9

"They don't print much in the obituaries these days." Ellis Belmont folded the newspaper and tossed it to the couch in the Jackson Metropolitan Doctors' Lounge. "You have to punch in letters on your phone to get any information." He removed the cell phone from inside his jacket and scrolled across the screen with his forefinger until he landed on a page of *The Clarion Ledger* and read through it. "Doesn't mention cause of death."

Sidney Eleanor Belmont pivoted in her swivel chair away from the computer cubicle and two hours of catching up on medical charting. "The shooting was all over the front page a few days ago. Besides the family pays for an obituary pub, by the line or the word. The longer it is, the more they pay. What was Voncelle Wallace going to say? My dearly departed husband was assassinated in a Jackson neighborhood one night while walking with guy friends?" She giggled and turned the chair back toward the computer. "Holy hell, I took a second off, and now this freaking thing wants a new password: at least eight characters, a capital letter or two, and a symbol of some sort. Let's see, what about *CWallaceDead!*"

"Tacky, tacky, Lil Sis. Makes it seem like you're happy about the situation."

"Maybe I am. Maybe I'm not."

"I would suppose that our brother Miles got to you. At first, you were in favor of selling the practice to that outfit in Spain, then turned tables on me. And after all I've done for you."

"And how would you know how I voted, Ellis?" Sidney remained focused on the screen and continued to follow the sign in prompts. "Any fingerprints on those cheap paper ballots the CEO printed up? Or the scent of my perfume?"

She entered *CWallaceDead!* in the space provided and confirmed the new password. The hospital electronic medical records software came to attention with an updated list of hospitalized patients belonging to the Belmont Comprehensive Medical Clinic. The spa patients were listed in a different private computer program unassociated with the hospital. Despite the fact she worked more hours covering the clinic and the medical spa and seemed to spend the most time taking care of patients after hours, the majority of the patients were assigned to her two older brothers, the senior members of the firm.

"As you know, the practice's attorney and I stood behind the CEO as she counted your *cheap paper votes.* You are the only member of the Belmont Medical Clinic who writes in blue ink. And you're left-handed, so the check mark was reversed."

"We should've passed a box around the room and dropped a tiny black ball in the slot for a *No,* like I hear they do in fraternities—way back in the day. Like when you and Miles were in your prime."

"Why our parents waited almost twenty years to procreate for another time after Miles came along, I'll never know," Ellis said. "Obviously an *Oops.*"

"Glad to have you around too, Big Bro Number One," Sidney said and pulled up another medical record, a delinquent discharge summary document. She tapped a few keys and standard verbiage populated the screen, satisfying the blanks with the required information. "Now with Wallace out of the picture, what's next for our organization?"

"I still believe we should sell. It's in the cards, Sidney. Time to go."

"You might be ready to retire, but not me. I'm not sitting on a dozen nest eggs like you. I'm ready to travel, and that's expensive." She pushed back in her chair and grinned. "India, South Africa, possibly Southeast Asia. I get slick travel brochures in the mail three or four times a week, and I must be on every travel agent's email list."

"Spam—it's ridiculous," Ellis said.

"No, I signed up for several travel websites. For every email I delete, two or three appear in their place."

"You'll get a cash bonanza when the practice sells, plenty of money to travel."

"Travel will be a moot point," Sidney said. "I doubt our new employer will give me that much time off."

"Nonsense. Physician vacation time is defined in the contract and guaranteed."

Sidney spun around again in her chair. "There's really no reason to discuss this any further. Chuck Wallace is dead. The deal is over."

"Charles Wallace was only an agent, a go-between. Negotiations with that Spanish outfit were very firm and near completion." Ellis retrieved the newspaper from the couch. "Wallace's death, his murder, is purely a ripple in the negotiations. I expect a call soon from Garcia or one of his associates."

"You still don't have my vote. And Miles *has* talked to me. We went over the pros and cons of selling the practice. Sorry to tell you, but he's coming over to my side. A *No!*" Sidney struck one of the computer keys hard in emphasis.

Ellis opened the newspaper. "There's got to be something of interest in here: college sports or even high school playoff stuff. I read this same crap on the front page two days ago on my phone." He flipped through the paper and tossed it to the coffee table with the other seldom read periodicals. "And I'm tired of you and this negative discussion, Sidney. If you were closer to Miles's and my ages, you'd understand—and he will come around."

"Come around to what?" Miles entered from around the corner. "No need to discuss the sale anymore since Chuck Wallace is out of the picture."

"Sometimes you're as dense as the silly schoolgirl with her nose in the computer," Ellis said. "Think Charles Wallace is—was—our only option? You are so naïve, Miles. We've had many offers to buy the practice. Wallace brought that Spanish firm and the best price, the best profit-sharing options, the best retirement plan—even included opt-in investment options for the employees. Don't forget, Wallace was simply a go-between."

"You've got to let this drop, Ellis. Can't you see the writing on the wall?"

"Terrible cliché, but often a good one. The *writing on the wall*, as you say, is that it's time to cash in. All the hours rounding at the hospital till after ten at night or much later and getting called to the ER or the ED or whatever they call it now. Not to mention hours in the ICU dealing with Mr. or Mrs. Jones and their out-of-control diabetes, MI, or renal failure—when they won't stand for anyone other than a Belmont to see them …"

Beads of sweat erupted on Sidney's forehead. She pushed the keyboard away and jumped from the cubicle. The swivel rolled hard against the low table behind her. "I've had it with this discussion. I'll never vote to sell the practice. Never!" Undaunted, Ellis Belmont remained seated on the couch as she stormed out of the Doctors' Lounge.

Miles stepped closer. "We're in this too deep because you have pushed the practice to do everything, to offer patients everything. Clearly to make an extra buck."

"That reminds me." Ellis slid his cell from the front pocket of his jacket and scrolled through his email. "I received this offer for a training course at Martha's Vineyard. It's on sclerotherapy. Nearly every patient I see over the age of sixty complains of varicose veins. Thought I'd fly up on Wednesday and do a little sailing, take in a few restaurants. Course starts Friday morning with good old fashion vein stripping. It wraps up Monday at noon after the last session on injecting veins to ablate varicosities, the newest techniques."

"What? You want to do vein stripping too? With only a residency in internal medicine? All you were trained to do is write prescriptions."

"Nonsense, I wouldn't be doing the procedures," Ellis said. He took another empty chair at the computer bank. "We'll hire a nurse practioner or PA to do the vein procedures and then sign off as medical directors. Same model we put in place for the neurotoxins, facial filler injections, and other stuff in the spa."

Miles pulled against his collar. It felt tighter and tighter.

"I've already talked to the course director. It's a simple process to set up the service and get practice certification—like we've done before for the other ancillary procedures," Ellis said. "We've got space on the third floor—a couple of empty offices and exam rooms up there gathering dust."

"Our malpractice company won't cover anything else—at least they shouldn't if those jokers running it had any sense," Miles said. "Don't get me wrong. I like the extra cash all that stuff brings in, and Frances and I don't mind the free shots to get rid of wrinkles. But we as a group of board-certified, upstanding physicians in the community don't have any business offering some of the services we already do for our patients—much less add to them."

"You mentioned the free shots. You're the biggest hypocrite, Miles. I've heard you boast countless times of friends who refer to you and Frances as the most youthful-appearing married couple their age."

"Yes, I know." Miles hesitated. "I-I appreciate the information about the vein stripping program. I just don't think we should expand."

"All we have to do is designate one of us to serve as clinical director. Call the new program a name like The Vein Relief Center. The director would then simply sign off charts after the nurse prac we've hired does the vein procedures, same model as our other ancillary programs. We send her or him to the three-week technician training course."

Ellis pulled a slick, multicolored brochure from his jacket pocket and tossed it toward Miles. It landed on the coffee table atop the pile of newspapers and magazines.

"You've lost your mind, Ellis!" Miles stared down at the brochure a few seconds before retrieving it. He absentmindedly rifled through it.

"Might even be a full month of employee training on our dime, although in a cheap, hellhole location—like this other one offered in New Jersey." Ellis slid another brochure from his jacket pocket and likewise pitched it toward Miles. "The education presented is quality and thorough, since the training is certified by the Academy of Dermatology."

"We can't be all things to all people," Miles said. "We already do more than any other internal medicine in the state."

"All that *more* as you put it, dear Miles, has kept us in the black—month after month—and allowed you and wife Frances to continue galivanting around the globe. You think your listening to someone's chest or doing a rectal exam or pushing antibiotics or blood pressure medicine is going to pay the bills for your wife's exorbitant lifestyle much longer? Do you? Or pay for the exorbitant dinners you charge to the practice in the guise of marketing?"

Miles remained silent.

"When I got sick and tired of all the bellyaching at administrative board meetings about the cost and stress required to keep us afloat, I made the decision to pursue and promote the sale of the practice."

"What bellyaching?"

"Where have you been?"

"Here. Doing the work," Miles answered.

"And it's time to cash out for that work. Get away from the micromanaging of this practice."

"I'm saying we need to hold steady—continue what we're doing," Miles said.

"The more we do, the more services we provide, the more the practice is worth," Ellis said. "Not to mention that you get to keep that new Porsche."

"I have to admit—I thought you were full of it when you pushed the board to provide those botulinum neurotoxin injections in the office," Miles said. He opened the door to the men's room and admired his face in the mirror for a few seconds—not a frown line anywhere on his forehead, the cleft between his eyebrows long gone.

"And the cash infusion from the health spa—that's another reason investors find our accounts attractive."

"Then why are we selling out?" Miles took another study in the mirror and ran his forefinger along his vanishing crow's feet, first the right then the left. He turned his face side-to-side in comparison and attempted unsuccessfully to wrinkle his forehead. "Perhaps we *should* expand that spa, Ellis. Those girls you hired do a great job. Face stings a bit during the treatments, but what price is beauty? Frances likes me to look good." He gave a short laugh. "In fact, she's having a hard time keeping up."

"They need to be treating and doing procedures on paying customers, Miles. The practice cannot turn a profit with pro bono work, even if it's our own physicians."

"You've got the knack for dealing with the business world. Find another way to cut overhead, besides trashing the free samples. I'm a walking advertisement for what this internal medicine clinic and its spa can do. And all thanks go to Ellis Belmont, MD—my big brother—my smartest big brother."

Miles stepped into the nearby men's room and propped the door open so Ellis could hear. "I'm a living, breathing success story, but I wouldn't let Sidney touch me. I went to the nurse prac who runs the assistants. Those girls took fifteen years off my face with injections, then I lost fifty, more like sixty, pounds on our other treatments. Not bad for a clinic that's supposed to be nothing more than a pill mill for cholesterol and hypertension meds," he said.

Miles continued to admire himself. He tightened his belt a notch and adjusted the wrinkled shirt at the waist.

"That's correct," Ellis said. "You really do see the big picture. If we don't think out of the box, we'll end up with a patient list of grandmas and grandpas on hyperglycemic and cholesterol medications." He settled on a collection of pre-op cardiology reports to sort through, all scheduled for surgery by the Cummins-Bratton clinic. "And as far as those spa employees you love so much who keep you propped up and tightened, it's the financial success of those good employees trained under my—under our—direction that makes corporate guys interested in us."

"Yes, I can see that," Miles said.

"An employee is an employee; they all want higher salaries and more benefits," Ellis said. "If someone buys the practice and takes over the administrative aspect, that problem disappears for us. No more dealing with greedy and complaining employees—a big part of the reason to sell—even if the ingrates are otherwise doing a good job. By the way, we keep the physician pro bono cosmetic treatments in the buy-out contract."

Miles sought more affirmation in the mirror. "That could be a game changer. And what's the other part of the reason to sell, big brother?"

"A bundle of cash, little brother. A big bundle for you and me."

# Chapter 10

The circulating nurse leaned against the door frame outside the operating room and broke the news to Diana. "I know you don't want to hear this, since we finished a big case a minute ago, but there's an MVA in the ED. They need you now, Dr. Bratton."

As the scrub team and anesthesiologist finished with the now post-op patient, Diana hit *Enter* on the computer and peeled the disposable blue covers off her tennis shoes. One landed in the small trashcan near the scrub sink, the other on the linoleum floor. "Why are you telling me? Call Ortho." She removed the index card with printed sticker from the inside pocket of her scrub suit. It contained her patient's name and room number. "I need to talk to the family. The Whipple didn't go so well. Pancreatic tumor was more widespread than CT showed."

The OR circulating nurse stepped closer. "Triage nurse says that ortho is tied up in that big osteosarcoma case in four, and the ED docs are running a code on an accountant from one of those big firms downtown."

"What about the nurse prac assigned to ED? Everyone thinks he's great." Diana picked up the microphone from the cradle beside the computer monitor and typed on the keyboard.

"Heard he called in sick with the flu. And there's no back-up, no one on call to fill in."

"Why are you frontline on a message that's gonna piss a doctor off! Hey? Aren't you up for OR director?" She scrolled through the choice of patients on the screen until she found hers.

"Don't blame the messenger, Dr. Bratton." The nurse let the door to the operating room close hard behind her. "My supervisor called in sick this morning, and with all the hospital cutbacks I'm next in line to deliver bad news."

"My husband, not me, is the trauma surgeon. Today he's working at our satellite clinic in Oxford," Diana said. The information for her fresh post-op patient populated the screen, and Diana clicked on the prompts to begin an operative procedure note.

"ED's down to a unit secretary running emergency triage, a pissed-off guy who's got two years of college after high school. And the schedule says your practice is on unreferred call. Hate it for ya."

"Got it. Any drop-ins are all mine."

The nurse referred again to her messages. "The ED unit secretary is threatening to walk out if somebody doesn't come down and take over. You know, talking about *above his pay grade*. The patient is raisin' all kinda commotion, he says."

Diana picked up her pace on the keyboard. The spell-correct software that included medical terminology took care of most of her typos. "If I don't enter these post-op orders correctly, those PACU nurses won't lift a finger."

The nurse glanced down to her phone and read another text from the unit secretary. "He says the patient blames her wreck on the shots she got in her face at the Belmont Spa yesterday."

"What?" Diana said. "That's a first."

"Right side paralyzed from her face down to her chest and arm. Everybody noticed when the EMTs rolled her in. She lost control of the car."

Diana retrieved the small microphone from the cradle at the left of the computer screen, pressed the tiny icon near the tip, and dictated the rest of the surgical procedure information into the electronic medical record. When she finished the dictation and returned the microphone to the cradle, it failed to snap in place and popped loose to drop to the floor. "I'm coming, though I could call the back-up from West Jackson Memorial to come over and see her."

"Oh, and I forgot to tell you. The patient is also complaining of right lower quadrant pain. You might get an appendectomy out of it."

"Geeze," Diana said. "This day couldn't get better." She signed out of the computer, leaving the microphone where it landed near the shoe cover. She grabbed her jacket from the wall rack outside the operating room and walked briskly to the ED. "Unreferred, emergency call coverage," she muttered in disgust. "Why can't the guys who own Metro hire other physicians to handle these patients who don't have an established doctor."

Diana pushed the elevator button for the ED and imagined a much simpler life. Had she taken the soccer scholarship to junior college instead of pushing through pre-med at Ole Miss—who knows? The door opened to a tall, bald, though distinguished, man dressed in a stiff, white cotton coat with stethoscope draped sideways around the back of his neck. *Ellis D. Belmont, MD* was monogrammed in black above the upper left pocket of the jacket. Diana stepped into the elevator.

A laundry-fresh, white shirt peaked out at the collar with a tiny *EDB* monogram on the left tip. Diana found her eyes drifting downward to his pressed grey trousers and low-healed black leather shoes. Diana remembered him from the other day with Brad in the hall trying to make rounds. An oval-shaped, gold-colored metal ring topped each of his shoes. "Italian," she said and felt somewhat self-conscious in her wrinkled scrubs and matching thin, waist-length jacket, also wrinkled and ordered from a healthcare apparel website.

"Beg your pardon," Dr. Ellis Belmont said.

Diana shook her heard slightly. "Oh, sorry. Mind was somewhere else." She glanced around the bland walls of the elevator. How long could it take to descend three floors.

"Ellis Belmont." He extended his hand.

"Diana Bratton," she returned.

"Oh, yes. Dr. Bratton."

"In fact, I'm on the way to see one of your patients, I'm told. Emergency Department is hectic today and short on staff."

"That's all we hear these days. Not enough medical and hospital staff to go around. Where will it all end? When will it all end? Somebody's got to take charge."

"Triage, if you can call it that, suspects appendicitis. The patient also has unilateral facial and upper body paralysis. She got neurotoxin injections this past week at your spa."

The elevator reached the first-floor wing of the hospital and opened to light foot traffic in the hall. Diana and Belmont stepped out and parted in opposite directions. "All of our patients sign a treatment consent. We counsel them thoroughly regarding benefits and risks of therapy," he said loud enough for only Diana to hear.

"I hope you do, Dr. Belmont," Diana said.

"Call me *Ellis*. My brother, Miles, and sister, Sidney, and I, or anyone on our team, will be happy to help in any way we can."

"You may have done enough already, Dr. Belmont," Diana said and rounded the corner for the hall to the Emergency Department. Floor to ceiling windows lined the corridor interspersed with giant potted plants and sections of faux-marbleized wall paneling. Visitors occupied the occasional upholstered chair arranged between the windows and scrolled or tapped on cell phones.

"Yes! Made it to level eight," a man screamed into the screen of his cell phone and clenched his fist in the air. "Give me nine, baby!" He jumped from his chair in excitement, driving it backwards, hard against the wall. "Five more triple stars and I'm there!" The chair bounced away to collide with the table beside him. An open can of Diet Coke sitting atop it flew to the floor and rolled away in a messy stream of brown fluid. "And Marge said I'd never do it!"

Diana grinned with a touch of embarrassed audacity and rolled her eyes. She walked past the man, whose eyes never left his phone.

"Marge won't be able to live with that guy if he makes it to freaking ten," she said and pushed through the doors into the

Emergency Department, the area quiet compared to the corridor outside. Diana remembered the details about the waiting patient and turned toward bay eleven.

A woman in her late forties or early fifties, wearing a long, white lab coat and facing the entrance, bent over the bed and examined the patient's head. She glanced up. "Oh, Dr. Bratton. Triage said you would be coming."

The patient's distorted expression due to paralysis of the left side of her face was obvious even from a few feet away, her opposite arm in a sling. Diana moved close enough to read the name embroidered above the physician's coat pocket and nodded: *Sidney Eleanor Belmont, MD—easy to spot a Belmont with the heavy starch.*

"Dr. Belmont."

"Please call me Sidney. My parents added Eleanor as a middle name to make the feminine designation obvious on legal documents."

"Makes sense," Diana said and smiled in the patient's direction. The woman had turned her head away.

"Friends call me *Sid* and so do most of my neurology patients. And I kept Belmont as my professional name. My husband—now ex-husband—didn't mind."

Diana smiled again, forced, and responded quickly with: "I recently spoke with your brother in the hall."

"Which one? There're two of them, both physicians on staff here."

"Ellis. He the oldest?"

"And the smartest. Just ask him."

Diana moved closer to the patient's bed and read the information on the computer suspended from the nearby wall. The name matched the information passed along to her outside the OR.

"Mrs. Gerard, can you tell me what happened?"

The woman struggled to turn her head slowly in Diana's direction, the wince of pain from her shoulder and arm obvious. "They told me I could have up to a hundred units, so I went with that." She shook her head as though to escape the facial weakness, although her speech remained slurred and garbled. "Those facials and chemical peels weren't helping my wrinkles anymore. Couldn't stand myself in the mirror. I was frantic."

"I've … uhhh, essentially finished my examination, Dr. Bratton. I'll leave Mrs. Gerard to you."

Diana found more information on the computer. A series of images from the radiology department populated the screen. "Thank you, Dr. Belmont." Diana tilted her head in that direction.

"Oh, sure thing. And remember, *Sidney* is fine—or even *Sid*."

Diana remained with her back to the door and assumed Sidney Belmont had left the area. She brought more digitalized images up on the screen and studied them for a minute or two.

"Mrs. Gerard, this is reassuring news, good news. Your head CT is normal."

"That's correct," Sidney Belmont said.

Startled, Diana nearly jumped at the interruption.

"Like I explained to our patient before you arrived, paralysis associated with neurotoxin injections is a seldom reported complication—and should be temporary," Belmont said. "Regarding the arm, the nurse told me there's no fracture, only a sprained shoulder, so the sling should be all that's needed."

Diana left the keyboard and the computer monitor. She moved closer to the patient, gently pushing the other physician to the side. "Yes, I reviewed the x-rays myself—no broken bones. She tossed a sharp goodbye grin to Belmont. "Thanks again. I'll give you a call later to discuss if needed." Diana touched the patient's shoulder and arm. "Hurt anywhere else, Mrs. Gerard?"

"You were notified about the patient's complaints of abdominal pain in the right lower quadrant," Belmont said, moving closer. "It's been a while since I was a third-year medical student, nevertheless that could mean appendicitis."

The ED nurse returned to the room. "Lab says the CBC results wouldn't upload to the computer, so I printed 'em out for you, Dr. Bratton. And here's a printout of the abdominal CT report too."

Diana took the papers as a quick study and glanced over to the patient. "Radiologist describes the appendix as thick-walled and dilated. That's classic for appendicitis." She referred to the patient's name again. "May I call you *Jennifer*?"

Jennifer Gerard nodded, her head skewed to one side.

"If Dr. Belmont believes you are neurologically stable, then we should prepare you for an appendectomy, although we don't have much choice. We can do it using a laparoscope and a surgical stapler. As far as general surgery is concerned, you'll be able to go home a few hours post-op."

"Do you think your abdominal pain caused you to lose control of your car?" the nurse asked.

Diana noticed the Belmont Medical Clinic personnel tag hanging from the nurse's pocket under other suspended tags, one designating her *Metropolitan Nurse of the Month*. "Jennifer, let's get you consented for surgery. Your nurse will get you to sign on an iPad. Any family with you?"

"I would like for Jennifer to answer the nurse's question. It's important," Sidney Belmont said. She now stood nearly shoulder-to-shoulder with Diana.

"It's important if you're trying to cast blame away from the neurotoxin injections she received," Diana said.

The nurse darted her eyes at Dr. Belmont. "I'll get the consent. Be back in a sec."

Jennifer struggled to straighten herself in the hospital bed and sit up more. She spoke slowly in broken phrases, still mostly slurred. "My tummy's been hurting on and off—for a few days. Got worse after—breakfast—a lot worse—but—I still drove to work. This is a real crappy situation. Just—look at my—face. Girl in the ambulance—let me see in a—mirror. And I—don't have—medical leave for surgery."

"What kind of work do you?" Diana asked.

"Scan records and do filing at the courthouse. 'Bout halfway to work, I felt weak—lost control of—the car—"

She fell back into the pillow just as the ED nurse, who worked part-time in the Belmont practice, returned with the electronic tablet and a stylus pen for the touch screen. "Here you go. Sign here and then we'll move you to OR holding. It's been at least six or more hours since breakfast, so anesthesia says we don't have to wait."

Jennifer Gerard winced, groaned, and tried to move her limp arm and hand in an effort to grab her stomach. The last shade of color drained from her face. The nurse dropped the iPad on the bed, too late to handle the situation with the emesis basin from a side table. Jennifer hurled the remnants of her breakfast and last night's supper on the sheets. "My—stomach still hurts. Even more now."

Sidney Belmont screamed and pushed away from the patient's bed. Diana and the nurse gawked as the neurologist ran from the room, face buried in her hands.

Belmont stumbled against a short stool by the door and knocked it on its side in a loud clang before losing a high heel. She grabbed the stool clumsily and groped her way into the hall in grand exit.

"Wow," Diana said, staring at the aftermath around the door to the hall before nodding in half-hearted sympathy to the nurse about the mess on the bed and the clean-up ahead. "Anesthesia will be glad this happened in here instead of in the OR. But don't worry, Jennifer, we'll get that bad appendix out, and you won't hurt anyone. And that upset stomach should be fixed too."

Diana turned for the door. "As far as the other issues related to what's going on with you, we'll let Dr. Belmont and her spa figure out what to advise next."

# Chapter 11

Sidney Belmont sat in the doctors' parking lot outside of Metropolitan Hospital, sandwiched between two full-size SUVs, and glanced around for any foot traffic. She repaired her scant eye make-up and lipstick in the rearview mirror. The unexpected incident with Jennifer Gerard getting sick in the emergency department had taken a lot out of her, reminding her why she had gone into neurology. She loved her medical practice. With her profession, the only time you ever touched a patient was to check reflexes with a hammer.

All quiet around her parking space, she slid her smart phone from the bottom pocket of her jacket and brought up the search engine. A couple of clicks later and *Diana Bratton, MD* filled the screen. Sidney scrolled through references to Diana's community health awareness presentations at various local clubs and civic organizations. Most were women's groups and the majority of comments about Diana's presentations earned her five stars—the same rankings from patients through her surgery clinic website.

"How nice," Sidney said and thought about her own 3.8 ranking on the Belmont site. She lowered the driver's window of her Porsche, adjusted the seat back, knocked her right high heel shoe loose, all while enlarging the website photo of Diana. Comparing it to her mental image of a busy Dr. Diana Bratton with the wrinkled clothing who joined her in the Emergency Department several minutes ago, she laughed softly and mumbled, "This retouched pic must be from a better day."

"What's so funny, Sis?"

Startled, Sidney straightened herself in the seat. She dropped her phone back into her pocket. "Diana Bratton is not our friend."

Miles Belmont leaned into the opened window and propped his elbow on the door ledge. The tip of an expensive shirt cuff peaked out the sleeve of his tailored jacket, the initials *MB* embroidered in tiny, bold print. "I saw you feeling her out on your phone. Good-looking girl, wouldn't you say?"

"Not interested in that, Miles," Sidney said. "And how long have you been standing there?"

"Long enough," he said. A couple of other physicians passed by in a hurry, a man and a woman. Miles smiled at them both. "I think she's married—and has a kid. Teenager, a girl."

"You ran the injection clinic these last couple of weeks. Isn't that correct?"

"Sure, Sid. You know that. You make out the schedule."

"Bratton thinks a patient wrecked her car because of the injections. The woman wanted rid of her wrinkles. Instead, she wound up in the ED with her arm in a sling and half her body limp as a dish rag."

"You couldn't stick a pin in her and knock the lady out of it." Miles laughed and slapped the hood of Sidney's car with his palm. "You're losing your touch, little sister."

"She also messed up her shoulder," Sidney said. "I smell a malpractice suit—and even worse, a lot of bad PR. One nasty article in the newspaper or if one of those awful influencers on social media gets wind of this, we'll be stuck with a lot of unused vials of neurotoxin. That stuff has a short shelf life."

"Nobody reads the newspaper," Miles said.

"It's not the newspaper or even TV I worry about. It's what the woman might post herself on social media," Sidney said. "One or two vicious social media rants or bad reviews on the Belmont Clinic website and—"

"Who is this patient?" Miles asked. "Give me her name. I'll investigate and see what I can do."

"See what you can do?"

"I know the hospital CFO fairly well. We play golf every Thursday. I've gotten him a few dates. Guy's a loser."

"That could help the situation if the hospital bill would go away," Sidney said. "Jackson Metropolitan Hospital can afford it."

Miles sensed two people step up behind him. "Hate to bother you but do y'all know where Dr. Bratton's clinic is?" a woman's voice asked. "We figured you were doctors and you'd know."

"Yeah, I'm late for my appointment," the man beside her said. "Never seen the lady before."

Miles turned around to face them and scanned their appearance. The woman's frizzled grey hair hung to the shoulders. She held a thick manila folder to her chest as though a treasure map. The man stood with a cane; his shoulders caved forward into his chest. Each breath seemed a great effort.

"We've heard good things about that lady surgeon," the woman said, "and that her clinic is real nice."

"You're over by the hospital and not near the clinic." Miles motioned toward the front of the building. "Best if you go inside and ask for directions at the information counter. The woman in charge will give Dr. Bratton's office a call, and they'll send a limo for you."

Miles flipped his face back toward Sidney, buried his chin, and swallowed hard to hide his snigger—with no success.

"We might just do that. Come on," the woman said and led her husband away from the parking lot. They stopped and spoke to a security guard who pointed them to a shuttle golf cart driven by a boy perhaps old enough for a driver's license.

"That was rather mean, Miles," Sidney said. "Even for you."

"I was serious." He smiled. "Bratton's clinic is minting cash. That couple's government insurance is as good as anyone else's, and that ol' codger has got at least two or three potential operations in him—that is if Bratton can get Pulmonary to tune him up."

"Too bad someone in the Belmont family didn't do surgery.

We wouldn't have to be running all this other stuff on the side," Sidney said.

Miles straightened his back and wiped his palm over the hood of his sister's car. "Your baby could use a wash." He flashed his dirty palm at Sidney. "Speaking of *other stuff*, you're on the schedule to run the vein clinic for a week, starting tomorrow. Your first time—finally putting you to work in there."

"I'd like to get as far away from that as I can."

"Come on. All we do is sign off on the charts," Miles said. "And if Ellis gets his way, we'll soon have less of the administrative crap to put up with."

"If you're talking about that practice buy-out from the discussion in the lounge awhile back, I'm totally against it. And I'm going to talk it down to the others."

"Might want to reconsider. I felt that way at first. On the other hand, after hashing it out again with Ellis, selling the medical practice is the way to go, particularly at our age."

"No way, Miles. Not gonna vote for it. Ever."

"Ellis won't be happy. He might stick you with heading up the new vein stripping department."

"When was I ever trained to do vein stripping? I barely know enough to answer patients' questions about procedures like that," Sidney said. "Then there's Miles Belmont. Always quick to learn new stuff. You're a specialist."

"Huh?" Miles surveyed the parking lot. Only rows of quieted vehicles and shrubbery lined the perimeter of the striped pavement—no foot traffic. The area was clean, free of discarded food wrappers or soft drink cans. He pulled at his sleeves and smoothed his hair.

"Have you ever admired our clinic's website?"

"Why would I ever pull up my own website?" he asked. He removed a handkerchief from his pocket and wiped his hands. "We toss a ton of cash at some social media gurus to manage that mess—no more than housewives who work part-time and call themselves webmasters. Ellis makes all those worthless decisions."

"Those *webmasters* have included lots of retouched pictures of the lobby and an empty treatment room. You'd think the place was a country club."

Miles tweaked his collar. "That's about right."

"There's a paragraph quoting you, Miles."

"Me?"

"You come across as an international expert, discussing the causes of varicose veins, why they develop for certain patients, and the procedures we offer to correct them. Don't you remember making the video?"

"Yeah, I guess so. I read off a teleprompter. The girl took the video with a small camera."

"You go on and on trying to explain blood vessel insufficiency and how that leads to varicose veins. You're all about stamping out the discomfort of varicose veins, not purely the awful cosmetic aspects," Sidney said. "What an actor!"

"If you think I'm familiar enough with the procedure actually to do it by myself in the treatment center, you're nuts."

Sidney took a deep breath and rolled her eyes. "Your Academy Award performance would have fooled me."

"The nurse practitioners or PA will do the whole thing. They're back from a week in Atlanta, all expenses paid. No telling how much that training course cost. If we had already sold the practice, the expense would have been on someone else's back."

"Still a *no* from me, Miles."

"Those vein-trained girls will consent the patient, take care of those god-awful swollen blood vessels, do the chart work, and most importantly—take the payment," Miles said and chuckled. "Great time for the doctor in charge to hideout in the back office and catch up on email and texts until it's time to close out the patient charts. Might even listen to a podcast or an audiobook."

"I don't want to hear anything else about that or the proposed buy-out." Sidney noted the time on her cell phone and started the engine. "You'll never change my mind about selling the practice. I need to go. I'm in charge of the injection clinic today."

Sidney slipped the Porsche into reverse and quickly backed away, without waiting for her brother to step away from the car.

"What the heck?" Miles said and stumbled clear. He straightened his jacket and brushed his pants with his hand to smooth them. No one seemed to have noticed. "Girl's a witch," he said and walked to his Range Rover.

Phoebe pulled into the nearest parking lot. It surrounded a newly built convenience store in a high traffic area with red brick façade and lines of gas pump islands arranged in the center. Neon signs offering Thai cuisine ready in minutes for takeout were posted in the windows to the left side of the building complex, and fried chicken and pizza were available opposite. The choice of Thai food sparked her interest for a return visit, so she snapped a photo of the building to jog her memory later.

She idled her vehicle and again found the Belmont Clinic website in her phone, verified the address, and reentered the information into her vehicle's GPS software. "Must have typed in something wrong the first time. It's not that far from Diana's office. I should have known."

Fifteen minutes later Phoebe reached the Belmont compound. Laid out in similar fashion to the convenience store and gas station complex, except for the pumps, the main entrance directed patients toward the new Varicose Vein Center. Other directions prompted anyone interested in spa services to turn left instead. The Center for Wellness and Enhanced Longevity, or the internal medicine clinic itself, was dead ahead. *Where's the ladies' room*, she wondered. *Surely up here close to the lobby.*

Phoebe spotted a bank of mahogany stained doors each labeled with both the silhouette of a man and women holding hands and joined by a figure meant to represent a toddler or a diapered infant. She picked the nearest one designated *Unoccupied* on the door. Inside, the diaper changing station was in a far corner, to the right of the mirrors. "Glad I don't have need for that thing. Got enough of that with Diana's Kelsey." A pang of guilt briefly passed through her. "I should have been around to help out more."

A glance in a mirror lead to a more thorough study. "Not all that bad for over fifty ... or sixty ... plus ... plus." She massaged her crow's feet with a forefinger and then gently ran the tip of the nail along and inside the ridges of the shallow skin creases. With minimum effort she wrinkled her forehead and squinted and smiled to exaggerate her imperfections. She considered the sign outside that directed clients down the hall to the left to the Belmont Rejuvenation Spa.

"Girl at bridge said you can get facials in that spa. Injections too."

The receptionist for the newly opened Belmont Varicose Vein Center handed Phoebe an electronic tablet at the sign-in desk. She stared into the screen, flipped it over to examine the back, and again studied the opaque glass. The overhead lighting caught her blurred shadow in the center of the screen. "What's this thing?"

"You're a new patient. We need you to fill out your medical history."

"Why?" Phoebe lowered her voice to a whisper. "I'm only here to get the atrocious veins on my legs taken care of. I'm tired of slacks and long dresses."

"Yes, ma'am. We sent an email at the early part of the week. You were supposed to enter your medical history on our website through our patient portal." The receptionist glanced at her desktop computer and then back up at Phoebe. "Yes, ma'am. We did. We sent you the email."

Phoebe ran her finger up and down the screen. The machine did not respond in scroll fashion like her smartphone. She shook her head and noticed the electronic prompts scattered over the device. "Guess your email wound up in my spam?"

"Could have," the receptionist said. "Please have a seat in the lobby waiting area and complete the requested information on that tablet."

Forty minutes later Phoebe returned to the reception desk with the electronic tablet. Gone was the girl with the short blonde bob and bangs bent over the computer. Instead, a receptionist sporting a flowing collection of Havana Twist braids greeted her.

Phoebe placed the tablet on the desk. "I'm afraid I can't do anything else with this contraption. I tapped and clicked my way through the fool thing until I'm blue in the face."

The braids swung away to a youthful woman scrolling fiercely on a cell phone.

"Perhaps I would have better luck with an iPhone, like yours," Phoebe said.

"Thank you. I'll take that tablet. All we want you to do is try. Makes the nurses' job easier if they don't have to fill in all that stuff." The Belmont employee took the electronic tablet and placed it in a recharging cradle. "I'm LaToya, by the way," LaToya said and smiled. "Fillin' in while Felecia's on break. She needed to talk to her boyfriend outside in the back. I'm usually over in the injection spa."

Phoebe sensed LaToya's quick study of her own appearance: the wrinkling neck, slightly baggy arms, and manicured fingernails. She straightened the collar of her short-sleeved blouse and dropped her hands to the side.

LaToya slowly lost her smile and set her phone face down on the desk. She scanned Phoebe's sketchy information in the computer, pausing at the periodically skipped areas of social and health data. "Thank you for inputting your information. Most of our clients struggle with our new electronic medical records system—especially the ones your—"

"Age?" Phoebe said. She glanced around the lobby. A few people were scattered about in the waiting room, one or two absorbed with their phones, another read a magazine. She removed the make-up mirror from her purse and repeated her study of the lines and creases marring her complexion. A ping from the phone deep in her purse demanded attention, and she exchanged the mirror for her cell.

"I see you offer some specials."

"Ma'am?" LaToya said. She had returned to her cell.

"I chose to sign up for your firm's text alerts, and guess what? I just got a text from you Belmont people about a special you're running: *Get Rid of Your Wrinkles Week?*"

LaToya popped the phone back down and redirected attention to the desktop computer. "Let me refer to my email. We get updates every morning from marketing."

"I can fill you in." Phoebe read from the advertisement. "Seems your chemical peels, facials, and injectables are on sale—only the rejuvenation products and services, whatever that means."

Phoebe pointed to her phone. "It says here with an exclamation point: 'Restore your youth. Schedule your very own dream skincare package now!' That sounds good to me." Phoebe turned her phone screen toward LaToya. "Here, see? Sign me up."

"Yes, ma'am. Dr. Belmont got that package up."

Phoebe tapped the link on the text and the clinic website appeared. She scrolled through the list of physicians. "Which Dr. Belmont? There're several."

LaToya giggled. "Oh, yes ma'am. I meant Dr. Miles. Dr. Miles Belmont."

Phoebe returned to the photograph of a smiling Miles Belmont, which gobbled up nearly half the screen. This time she ran her fingertip over his smooth, white, perfectly aligned teeth and the sides of his face—no wrinkles anywhere, at least none allowed by the professional photographer. *I think he's about my age. I wonder how many times a week he visits this spa.*

"Your Dr. Miles Belmont doesn't seem the type to know much about computers," Phoebe said and continued to examine the color photograph. He wore a crisp white shirt with no tie under a tailored navy sports jacket with a tight print design of lighter blue in the fabric. A striped, yet tasteful, pocket square peeked out the front pocket. Phoebe tilted her head and admired his full head of blond hair, stylishly cut short with no fault anywhere along the hairline.

*Amazing. An expensive toupee?* She opened the link that offered a complete list of the clinic physician staff and associates. Individual, although much smaller, photographs of the entire Belmont Clinic and Spa support staff filled the screen. In addition to the physician assistants and nurse practitioners, were the clerical and reception team. She recognized LaToya and Felicia.

Phoebe then scrolled to a group photo of the physicians, standing in rows in front of an enormous fountain with Greek statues in the center. She studied the legend under the photograph and noted only a few doctors outside the Belmont clan. She again admired the youthful image of Miles Belmont in front row center and wondered who at the spa treated him.

"Slipping up, Miles," Phoebe mumbled. "Identical jacket to the one in your portrait."

"I'm sorry. Were you speaking to me?" LaToya asked.

"I need to know what you people can do for women—like me."

"Info about available services is online, like on your phone, and I've got printed brochures available. Look around the corner in that rack on the wall." LaToya pointed. "Felicia's supposed to keep that rack filled."

Phoebe grabbed one of the several-page brochures from the first row. Its cover seemed to be another version of a physician group photo, this one taken in front of an enormous indoor fireplace. The few female physicians relaxed in upholstered antique furniture. The men stood casually in front of the fire. Phoebe judged this photo an earlier version of the group seen on the website, since handsome Miles appeared even younger.

She opened the brochure and went through the choices of physicians, all pictured individually and dressed informally, unlike that shown on the cover. She noticed Sidney E. Belmont. Assuming a printer's error, Phoebe flipped back and forth through the brochure. No mistake—the same woman, the group picture on the cover a much, much better day for her. *A cousin? Surely not a sister to attractive Miles.* "That hair and no make-up. Should be a law against it!"

"Miss Phoebe, is something wrong?" LaToya called out as she once again set her cell phone face down and addressed the patient.

Phoebe stood at the window, dropping the brochure in a nearby waste can. "I would assume you have lots of female patients my age?"

"Oh, yes, ma'am we have lots of older—I mean …"

"Never mind. I guess interpersonal social skills don't come with the job, so I'm not going to report you. Sign me up for the works. Here's my card."

Phoebe handed LaToya her platinum AmEx. "And I've got a very high limit."

# Chapter 12

*What do you do for a surgeon when her husband is murdered?*

Diana wondered if she should wait and do something later for Voncelle Wallace. In a few months maybe treat her to a fancy girls' night out with food, drinks, and pseudo-Magic Mike dancers or go all out with a long weekend girl trip to Florida: Destin, Watercolor, or even Alys Beach—Voncelle's choice. Diana was not sure of Voncelle's friends outside of work, but she could fill in the gaps of an invitation list with one or two of the female nurses and a couple of appointment secretaries. Brad would agree with her using the clinic credit card to pay for the event—at least she hoped so.

*I could be doing this all wrong.* Diana reconsidered. *Make it simple, unique, very nice. That would be more appropriate.* Show that she and Brad cared and were sorry for Voncelle's loss. Offer a week or two free of after-hours call?

To Diana's relief, her clinic secretary volunteered as chairman of the newly formed clinic bereavement committee. "I organize all the home meals for anyone at church who's had surgery, been sick, or had a death in the family. I first started doing it for my Sunday School class."

"Guess you did too good a job," Diana said. "Now you do it for the whole church?"

"Guess so." The secretary laughed. She pushed a thumbtack into a sign-up sheet on the bulletin board in the staff break room. *Meal Sign-Up For Dr. Wallace* headed the 8 x 10 sheet. "I didn't do it by email. That seems too impersonal. We do it like this in church the old-fashioned way," she said and hesitated. "I guess it's not so old-fashioned since I saved this form on my computer—in case we need it again."

"Good idea," Diana said. "Let's hope not anytime soon." The secretary stepped aside, and Diana moved closer to the bulletin board. "I better go with an appetizer." She withdrew a pen from her scrub suit top and filled in the slot for Wednesday. "I'll also do a dessert."

Brad's office nurse and two of the women from the business department entered the room. Their noisy discussion centered on childcare. "Awesome. Already got the sign-up sheet posted for Dr. Wallace," said Brad's nurse.

Diana slid her pen back into her pocket and got out of the way.

"Dr. Bratton, you've got Wednesday started," said one of the women, the new girl hired to do insurance claims and whom Diana did not know well. "I'll do the meat—make my mom's chicken casserole recipe. My grandmother handed it down to her." She filled in the appropriate spot.

"Let me have a peek at that." Brad's nurse wedged her broad shoulders and hips up to the list. The other two women parted to make way. "Dr. Bratton, I didn't know Boss married you for your home cooking. I thought you were into take-out."

"You don't know everything that goes on around my house, now, do you, Shelley?" Diana grinned, gave a thumbs-up, ran her fingers through her hair, and skirted out of the break room for the elevator. One flight down, the doors opened into the underground parking garage.

The motion detector kicked in, flooding the area with fluorescent light as Diana focused on the path to her vehicle. The additional garage lighting was an upgrade after the murder of Brad's identical twin brother in the elevator several years before. Her own recent horror dulled the visual of Brian Cummins's blood and brain matter splattered across the elevator walls. While her partner—and ownership status in the surgical firm ranked one of the parking spaces nearer the elevator, ample walking distance afforded time to let her heart quicken—the consequence of being held at gunpoint twice. She still felt the young man's hands around the back of her neck and the pressure of the barrel of a gun against her skin.

*Come on. Shake it away.* She should breathe easier now that the police had arrested her assailant. *Let it go*, Diana resolved and walked calmly to her car.

A gourmet bakery and food catering shop lined one of the streets on her route home. Diana slowed in front to study the window display and pulled into the parking lot of the business next door. She removed her phone from the dashboard charging station and quickly entered *easy appetizers* into the search engine browser. "I shouldn't have signed up for an appetizer and a dessert. Why make this so hard?"

She darted her eyes over to the gourmet shop. A woman wearing a hairclip with two small children tagging behind, one with a pacifier, emerged through the exit carrying a large, round card-board box. Diana guessed a cake, probably birthday. The woman pointed her keys at the full-size BMW SUV a few vehicles down and cordoned her kids in that direction. Diana imagined the tumultuous feat of juggling the box without marring the icing before strapping two children into car seats.

A rendition of Captain Rodney's Cheese Dip popped onto Diana's cell screen, the headline over the photo: *Easiest Appetizer Ever. Makes In Minutes and Perfect Anytime.* The picture of the final project screamed delicious. A video followed featuring perfectly manicured, slender feminine fingers arranging an assortment of crackers along the edges of the serving dish.

*Click Here to Grab This Fantastic Ovenproof Pottery & Serving Container to Wow Your Guests! 50% Off!* streamed repeatedly across the bottom of the screen.

"That's perfect," Diana sighed. After a long surgery day, Brad would gobble up a fourth of the pan. "Can't say I wouldn't either."

The slender fingers scooped up a generous serving of the dip with one of the crackers and teased it into a male mouth with light stubble on the lower cheeks and chin. His lips somehow smiled as the guy chewed.

"Yes, that's Brad," Diana said. The video ended, and the website post included the recipe. Diana remembered the added promise of a dessert and reconsidered the food shop. Another girl in her late twenties entered the store, this one carried shopping bags with a figure that would never allow even a taste of Captain Rodney's dip, much less eat a whole cracker nor sample anything inside that shop.

Brad's nurse, Shelley, had ribbed her over her lack of success at home cooking once Brad shared the infamous Thanksgiving dinner story. Diana cooked the entire meal and Brad, Kelsey, and Aunt Phoebe all complained of stomach cramps later and spent a day in bed. They politely claimed a "stomach virus."

"I ate the same food, and I didn't get sick," Diana said with a sigh and slid the phone into her purse. "Better not chance it." She found a parking space and followed the slim girl into the gourmet bakery and food shop. "I hope they can help me."

An eager teenage salesclerk greeted Diana inside. She decided the young girl must work on commission, since by the time she made it to the register to pay, her cart was full. A frozen, pre-made appetizer similar to Captain Rodney's Cheese Dip (microwaveable after thawing), a variety of decadent crackers, and a box of petit fours and assorted homemade dessert cookies would fill the glass serving tray the girl also persuaded her to purchase. The tray cost more than Diana's monthly take home salary as a fifth-year general surgery resident.

The lady at the register suggested that Diana add fresh fruit to the culinary display, such as plump, juicy grapes—both purple and green—available at the natural foods store nearby. Diana charged it all to her clinic personal expense account.

"I guess I'll have to leave the expensive tray with Voncelle," she said and arranged the purchases carefully on the floor of the backseat. *Not bad*, Diana decided after standing back from the opened car door and judging her purchases. *Not bad at all.* Another skinny girl meandered into the bakery shop as she shut the door.

"Wouldn't be right to ask for the tray back." She remembered a heavy wooden tray at home won as a guest at a clinic secretary-nurse Dirty Santa party. "I don't remember Voncelle from the party that night. She'll never know. I'll switch it out before I go by her house."

She locked the car and ran into the grocery store for the fresh grapes, then returned to set the bag of fruit next to the other purchases. Diana suddenly remembered the long day ahead tomorrow in the OR and clinic. *I signed up for Wednesday, but it won't hurt to be a day or so early. This food will keep in Voncelle's fridge until she needs it. She'll enjoy the cookies no matter when.*

After a quick exchange of the expensive, just-purchased serving tray for the simple tray on hand in her own kitchen, she rearranged the grapes around the bakery-bought dip and drove toward Voncelle's home.

*Should I text Voncelle before dropping by?* Diana glanced at the back seat. Her prized purchases safe and sound. *Too late now.*

An unrecognized vehicle pulled away from the Wallace residence as Diana approached. Voncelle stood at the front door waving, a handkerchief clutched in her left hand. Even from the curb, the widow's weeping was obvious.

"That was our—my—minister's wife. Such a lovely, lovely, God-fearing woman," Voncelle said at the door. Diana stood balancing the wooden tray against her right hip for support, the tray laden with high-caloric cheese dip surrounded by pricey crackers. With her left hand, she held the handle of the wicker basket found in a quick search of her kitchen. The bakery dessert purchased earlier waited inside.

"I brought this—a little something from Brad and me."

Voncelle continued to gaze in the direction of the departing vehicle. "Oh, Diana, I'm sorry, so ... so ... scattered. Please, yes, please come in. Let me help you with that." She took the tray, leaving Diana to follow with the basket.

"The place was such a mess when Chuck—passed away. It had been my week on call, and my husband was never much of a housekeeper. Fortunate for me, several church ladies came over and cleaned the place up, even wiped out the refrigerator and oven—more like scrubbed the oven. The woman who just left organized all that."

"How nice," Diana said.

"What would I ever do without my church? You and Brad should go with me one Sunday or even try the Wednesday night service."

"Sure, we'd like that. I won't stay long. You've gotta be worn out." Entering Voncelle's kitchen, Diana set the dessert basket on the counter. A pang of guilt shot through her over her substitution of the expensive glass tray for the re-gifted wooden one.

"God knows, I've worked many a long day in the OR and lots of all-nighters on call. You have too," Voncelle said. "But then again, wow—the visitors who've dropped by after Chuck's funeral service. Lots of chit chat and reminiscing although we haven't lived around here all that long. I did take a nap yesterday afternoon." Voncelle laughed softly. "When was the last time I took a nap?!"

Diana nearly bit her lip. Every physician had personal time off built into the contractual partnership agreement, while most surgeons never exercised the option—or had to. In Voncelle's over weeklong absence most every other physician's schedule in the clinic was double-booked, even triple-booked in a few spots. Diana caught her reflection in the glass of a nearby china cabinet and fought the comparison to Voncelle Wallace. Diana came across exhausted; Voncelle did not have a wrinkle or bag under an eye.

"Diana, your coming by is so very special." Voncelle took a peek inside the basket. "Petit fours, my favorite! And the dip. You really out did yourself. Who knew you were such a cook?"

Voncelle picked one of the petit fours, the one with a tiny red flower in the center of the thick white icing, and took a bite. "Hard to choose where to start with these goodies. Dessert, always my weakness." She finished the confection. "Where are my manners. Can I pour you a glass of wine? Oh, you might be on call. A Coke instead?"

At the mention of something to drink, Diana thought of the restroom. She had not gone since before lunch. "I could use the ladies' room," Diana answered. "Sorry, in a gorgeous house like this—the powder room. Down the hall?"

"The closest one is on the left, through the library. I'll pour the wine. We can get into the cheese when you get back." Voncelle opened a drawer for the wine opener. "This is definitely what I need."

Diana entered the hall. Photographs of Voncelle and Chuck lined the walls, no children, only dogs of various size and breed appeared now and then with a white tip-eared, orange and black cat propped in Voncelle's lap. Diana guessed from the scenic background of most of the pictures that the Wallaces traveled often and took their pets. However, she did not remember any food bowls in the kitchen.

"You findin' your way, Diana?" Voncelle called down the hall as Diana disappeared into the library. She took another sip of wine and sunk back into the kitchen.

When Voncelle mentioned library, Diana envisioned a cramped home office off the master bedroom, similar to the Cummins-Bratton home. Instead, this room was spacious. Diana spotted a door in the far corner, set back a half foot or so from the line of crowded bookcases and beyond a mahogany desk near the center of the room. Her lower stomach cramped. "The potty, yes. Thank goodness."

In her rush toward the restroom, Diana's thigh collided hard with a corner of the desk. She grabbed her leg, chewed her lip, and somehow kept from wetting herself in a twisted grimace. A quick glance up from the sharp pain, she spotted a glass cabinet directly across from her in the opposite corner, set against the main wall. Suddenly the urge in her bladder eased, then disappeared.

Diana carefully approached the cabinet. Two rows of rifles and shot guns filled the cabinet except for a display of handguns that lined the lower section. The key was missing from the escutcheon in the center of the double cabinet doors.

She finished in the restroom and returned to the kitchen.

Voncelle poured another glass of wine. "Sorry, I'm a tiny bit ahead of you. And I started on that awesome cheese dip you brought. Really, really good, Diana. Nice texture ... delicious." She skimmed the surface of the dish with a fresh cracker. "Where'd you say you got the recipe for this appetizer?"

"I didn't," Diana said. She wanted to mention the gun cabinet. "I'm a lot of things, but I have no secrets and am certainly no cook. Ask Brad. I picked everything up from that bakery and food shop in Fondren, the dessert too."

"Good choice." Voncelle took another swipe, choosing one of the larger crackers and scoring more dip. "I'm in that place all the time."

Diana accepted the glass of wine. "I noticed the gun cabinet in the library. No way to miss it."

# Chapter 13

A deep-tissue massage preceded the chemical peel, followed by neurotoxin injections to the face. *I want to get the most out of this stuff and the special pricing*, Phoebe thought. *I'll do the vein thing later.*

Meeting and being treated by Dr. Sidney Belmont had been unexpected. The physician assistant assigned to Phoebe's case was called away due to a sick child, and the doctor herself had to step in. Phoebe judged the Belmont woman's live, unretouched appearance somewhere between the good and bad photographs she had seen before in the brochures. *Closer to the bad ones.*

She obeyed Belmont's instructions after the injections and exercised her facial muscles throughout the soak in a mineral bath, the next offering on the one-day facial rejuvenation package and part of the optional whole-body relaxation experience. Courtesy of the female attendant who helped her dress, Phoebe emerged from her coconut oil-laced, oatmeal mineral bath clad in a kaftan, a Turkish piping robe constructed of tightly woven cotton with cuffed sleeves, rolled back a few inches. Although she saved nearly $200 after choosing the all-in-one day package, Phoebe decided that for the total amount levied on her credit card the robe should have been monogrammed.

"My face stings and my eyes burn," Phoebe said.

"Perfectly normal," the attendant purred. "Is all part of being beautiful."

Phoebe judged the women to be late thirties to early forties—no older than forty-five. The eyelashes were fake, much too long and thick for her face, nonetheless the current fashion in certain circles. Her face was perfectly tanned—and not a wrinkle anywhere.

Although she had a twenty for the girl, she giggled to herself that had a talented, buff male attendant with roving fingers been in charge she would not have had the appropriate tip.

"Did you do your facial exercises like Dr. Sidney said?" The attendant lowered her voice to a whisper. "Her PA gives the best injections of anybody around here. I'm sorry she had to leave."

The attendant's smooth teeth beamed wide and white; her eyebrows and forehead remained frozen. "I only let the PA do my shots, but Dr. Sid is fine. Let's go ahead and sign you up for a three-month follow-up appointment. Wouldn't put it off any longer than four. Three is best in the long run. See you then!"

She led Phoebe to a private dressing room, more spacious and better appointed than the previous one. A miniature box of Godiva chocolates sat near a hand-written thank-you note signed by the attendant, wishing Phoebe much beauty and well-being until her next visit to the Belmont Wellness Enhancement Spa. *And thanks for the nice tip!* was written at the bottom surrounded by Valentine heart-shaped symbols. Phoebe's clothes hung in the corner on a padded-satin hanger above a short, richly upholstered stool not far from the note and the Godiva chocolates. Her eyes stung a bit more. The image in her mirror a horrific surprise.

*I look exhausted. The red face and eyes don't help.* Phoebe dressed, then remembered her purse. A soft knock came from the door, then a slow turn of the handle.

"Oh, Miss Phoebe, you forgot your locker key in the bath suite. I found it and got your purse for you since it was getting late. Here ya go." The attendant handed Phoebe the purse through the cracked-open door and eased it shut.

*Must be ready for me to hit the road. Quittin' time? Or perhaps another client needs the space.* "I'll be out and gone in a minute," Phoebe called out. She took another glance in the mirror at the red face. "It's binging TV for me for a while and no bridge club," she mumbled and dressed. "In my opinion it's worth it."

Three clients stood waiting at reception when Phoebe emerged into the lobby and stood in the opened door. A man with generous, wavy grey hair stood first in line. He seemed impatient, insistent.

"Sir, I pulled you up on the computer. It's been barely two months since your last injections," said Felecia, back from her break and again at her post.

*I wonder what went down in the parking lot with her boyfriend?* Phoebe thought.

"I need more than a roller job on my face, miss. Dr. Sidney promised me. And I don't care what your stinking computer says. See these creases?" The man ran his fingers over his face. "You people have got to take care of this. I paid for sixty units last time, but I look horrid now." He turned around to grimace to the two patients in line behind him and exaggerated the imperfections in his complexion. Several people remained in the waiting room. The woman nearest the far corner seemed the most alarmed at the commotion.

"I've liked all your videos on Quik Snap. You guys promised me better results—that you could take twenty years off my face without surgery!"

The door banged closed behind Phoebe, breaking the man's rant. Everyone stared at her, the disgruntled man's eyes the most penetrating.

"Sorry," Phoebe said and tried to shield her face.

Felecia swallowed hard. "Let's get you to a private room to see Dr. Belmont."

The man snapped his head away from Phoebe and back toward the receptionist.

"The doctor will know what to do," Felicia said.

He gathered his leather bag and cell phone. "I certainly hope so. I've dropped enough cash around here already." Felecia motioned for the man to enter the spa through a side entrance. The same female attendant emerged to greet him and lead the way. The two clients left in line moved toward the reception window.

"I've known Sidney Belmont for years," the man said. "She better fix this, or I'm going to ..."

The man's voice trailed off behind the closed door, and Phoebe stepped toward the front exit of the spa building. "Oh, ma'am. Ma'am?" Felecia called out. "Don't you want to make your next appointment?"

Phoebe gave a weak wave at the receptionist as she pushed open the door and called back toward her. "I need to check my calendar."

She stopped for a minute outside in the parking lot. *I guess Diana—and Brad—deal with crazies like that all the time. What a spectacle!* She found her car and grabbed the rearview mirror. Scattered needle puncture marks broke the beet red surface of her face. At least her muscles felt relaxed and the skin of her arms, hands, and legs soft. *The massage and the oatmeal bath ... I'm ready for that again any time.*

Diana found Kelsey upstairs in her bedroom. She wore earbuds and was in the midst of doing homework on a laptop—or at least it appeared that way. Without opened books and pencil or pen and paper, it was hard to know. Nonetheless, Kelsey's grades were good at private school; teachers reported that she seemed popular and well-adjusted; and the expected parent-teenager clashes at home were at a minimum—even with a stepfather around. Kelsey came short of calling him awesome one day, but the descriptor *cool* slipped out once or twice, even a weak: *I'm happy for you, Mom.*

The den was off the back stairway, the family room dedicated to TV. Diana and Brad tried to contain paying household bills and working on patient electronic medical records at home to the library off the master bedroom. "There you are," Diana said.

Brad lay on the couch enjoying a football game, the lower half of his body covered with a soft brown, king-sized blanket, which Diana picked up at a local discount store. Brad still wore his scrub suit.

"What'd y'all do for dinner?" Diana sat at the end of the couch and pulled a section of the blanket over her.

"Ordered pizza. Free coupon for frequent customers popped up on the app," Brad answered. "Ordered two, and got your favorite, the California veggie. What's left is in the fridge."

Diana inched closer. "What about dessert."

"Didn't order any. No specials on the cinnamon twists or fried pies." The opponent scored a touchdown, and Brad voiced his disappointment with a strong expletive. "I hope Kelsey's got her earbuds in upstairs."

Diana removed her tennis shoes and socks and slipped deeper under the blanket. Next went her scrub suit, bra, and panties. "Sounds corny, I know, but I'm dessert." She moved closer to Brad and pressed her naked breasts against him. Her hands slipped to his inner thighs and moved toward his groin. She loosened the ties to his scrubs and felt him.

"Kelsey's upstairs," Brad managed to say and took a deep breath.

"Yes, her earbuds are in. She won't hear a thing." Diana darted her eyes toward the television. "It's halftime, and I'll be quick."

Hernando Garcia bent over his desk and perused the spreadsheet again. He took a hard draw on his cigar and scrolled through the pages on the computer screen.

"It's the same old figures arranged or rearranged on different spreadsheets," Lucinda said.

"At least, that's what I saw."

"These follow-up numbers don't add up. The initial figures were in the black," Garcia said.

"Don't be so hard on yourself." Lucinda moved behind Garcia's desk chair and massaged the back of his neck and shoulders. "You listened to Mr. Wallace, that American from Mississippi. You trusted him."

"And easy to do. Commercial real estate, predominantly in the U.S., has been such a sure bet for me—for us—until now."

Lucinda dug deeper into her husband's shoulders. "Spain's own commercial real estate market is the fifth largest on the continent. Growth expectations are in the trillions. Foreign investors are knocking on our door," she said. "I do more than sit at the reception desk out front and smile and answer the phone. I read the financial news."

"You are not only a beautiful woman, Lucinda, you are intelligent. No one understands that better than I. We must remember that Garcia International Enterprises needs a niche. That's why I was working with Charles Wallace. For Christ's sake, we were going nowhere worldwide."

Garcia winced at the pressure of his wife's fingers. He could feel her nails through his suit jacket. "I had such faith in Wallace. The patient numbers and the wide range of ancillary services all geared toward servicing those self-absorbed American patients. The physicians on staff were well-respected—I offered top dollar for that medical practice on behalf of the new equity fund."

"The board of directors is not going to be happy about this, specifically Pérez." Lucinda stopped the massage and popped him with a hand to the mid-upper back. "Tell me about that last phone call with Wallace and how deep we are into this transaction."

Garcia took three puffs on his cigar, the first two short but strong, the third longer—and deeper. "That guy, Charles Wallace, God rest his soul, a remarkable salesman. I hate to think I was duped. He justified every financial entry made by that Belmont outfit over the past five years."

"We did our own due diligence on the Belmont medical practice. Didn't we?"

"Due diligence? Looked them up on the internet, then I flew to Mississippi for an onsite visit. Fancy set-up. Lots of smiling faces in the patient lobby and nice-looking secretaries and nurses everywhere. I pored over the onsite financial records myself, all except these last ledgers sent shortly before his death."

"And Pérez questioned your expense account for that trip: the first-class seat, the fancy meals out."

"Federico Lorca-Pérez is nothing but a hypocrite. He uses every excuse he can to travel and charge expenses to the GIE corporate account."

"Blame your father. He appointed Pérez as chairman of the board for life." Lucinda walked to the window and the view of the museum.

Garcia knew she cared nothing for the museum or the arts. She was in deep thought. She cared about money.

"With Wallace gone, who is in charge of that medical practice deal?" Lucinda asked.

"The most senior physician, Ellis Belmont." Garcia continued to work the cigar.

"Maybe the family has changed their mind and doesn't want to sell any longer. Maybe they see the murder of their agent as an omen."

"I do not see that happening. My understanding from Wallace was that Dr. Ellis Belmont is the real champion of the sale. He pulls the strings around the practice. From what I saw during my visit, I believe it."

Lucinda returned to her husband's desk and gently pushed him aside to pivot his opened laptop toward her. She entered *Belmont Medical Mississippi* in the search engine bar. The link to the website for the Belmont Comprehensive Medical Clinic and Wellness Enhancement Spa appeared first in the results. Various healthcare professionals with the surname Belmont followed. She brought up the clinic website and chose the *Physician Staff* link.

"Most of them are Belmonts," Lucinda said. "Brothers, sisters, nieces, nephews, cousins? Nepotism reigns in America, it seems."

"And most of the doctors photograph well, although photoshop can only do so much," Garcia said and winked. "I should travel again to Mississippi. This time for their medical services. I need to look good next to my beautiful Lucinda."

Lucinda laughed. "Hernando, my dear, when I say that might be like throwing good money after bad, I don't mean your appearance because I like you the way you are. I mean that this Belmont deal may already be sunk with Wallace no longer around to mediate. Besides, with more travel expense, I can see more criticism from Pérez and others on the board of directors."

"I'm going to stare those Belmonts in the eyes." Garcia moved the laptop away from Lucinda and returned to his study of the financial spreadsheets. "There are many lies on this page and others. I can see that now. I want to know who started theses lies, who jumbled these figures."

Lucinda pushed against the back of Garcia's chair and stormed to the hall door. "Our financial future is on the line. Your father is no longer around to clean things up, *mi amor*. I enjoy my lifestyle, and I don't want to lose it. Wallace is the one who lied to you. He made up those numbers. You better fix this mess."

The office door slammed hard behind her. "I will work this out, Cariño. I promise," he called out to Lucinda.

# Chapter 14

Phoebe groaned with her head sunk to her breasts and swung her legs to the floor, finding slippers on the third try. Her face and eyes felt on fire. She straightened her posture the best she could and glanced at the clock on the nightstand. Somehow, she managed to read the numbers through the stinging haze. The alarm was set at thirty minutes away, about the time a late morning Ambien hangover usually wore off and brunch would be delivered.

"I need the bathroom." She wanted the mirror above the bathroom sink even more. The glass begged for what should be the new and improved Phoebe. But would the bathroom mirror recognize her? She pushed an arm against the mattress to steady herself and grappled for her cell phone. In a few stumbles she reached the bathroom.

"Oh my God!" she slurred and rubbed her bloodshot eyes in the mirror. Her left eyelid fell to cover half the eye, and the left side of her mouth drooped toward the chin. Blistering skin beamed at her. She managed to pull up Diana's cell phone number under her Favorites menu and make the call.

"Take a deep breath. And what's this all about?" Diana asked, interrupting Phoebe's garbled comments. "I didn't know anything about your appointment with those Belmont people. Can you do FaceTime, so I can see?"

Fumbling through the prompts on her cell phone, Phoebe produced Diana's image in the lower righthand corner of the screen. "Just look at me!" She moved her phone across her face and scrutinized Diana's reaction the best she could. "Tell me what you think."

"What all did you have done, and did they tell you what could go wrong?" Diana walked from her car. The image on the screen bobbled up and down. "You're a grown woman. You obviously gave your consent. Why didn't you call me before the appointment to talk about this?"

Phoebe dropped the phone to her side for a few seconds and studied her cherry red face again in the mirror, turning her head from side to side. She struggled to speak so that Diana could understand. "They made it sound so easy—that girl at the reception window was a great salesman. I guess she works on commission."

"The blistering on your face, that will resolve," Diana said. "They must have given you a full-blown chemical peel and overdid it. Your skin is thinner since—"

"Since I got old, Diana? Damn right, I'm old. That's what everybody thinks. Even the Belmonts!" Phoebe shook her head and pulled her bangs across her forehead to no improvement. "Not wanting to be ancient is what this is all about. Thank you for rubbing it in."

"I'm trying to help you, Phoebe. Remember, you called me," Diana said. "Let me see your eyes again."

Horrified, Phoebe again gawked at herself in the mirror and flipped the phone setting to give Diana another study.

Diana breathed deeply, moved her head a speck, and said, "You have conjunctivitis; that's the redness you're seeing in your eyes. It should resolve in a few days."

"My eyelids—the drooping. Have I had a stroke?" Phoebe groaned.

"It will take time for those complications to resolve," Diana said. "Be patient. You have not had a stroke."

"You've got to help me, Diana. You always do."

"I've finished morning surgery, but a few patients are waiting in the clinic. Look, I'll have somebody from my office come and pick you up, someone in the medical records department. First thing is to get you to a neurologist, someone other than a Belmont."

"Neurologist? One of my bridge partners went to see a neurologist. His son and daughter-in-law thought he had a stroke." Phoebe continued to stare at her distorted reflection. She turned her head side-to-side, doing her best to show Diana her face and skin via her phone. From every angle she appeared the same—awful. "And they were correct! My bridge partner did have a stroke. Now he's recovered and back at the bridge center."

"Get dressed. Somebody will be there to pick you up in about half an hour. I'll meet you at the neurology office. On the way, I'll call Ellis Belmont."

"You're scaring me, Diana." Phoebe's voice broke. "I'm going to be okay. Tell me I'm going to be okay."

"You should have gone to someone who specializes in facial plastics or at least a cosmetic spa affiliated with that department."

"You're making me feel as awful as I look, Diana, and totally stupid. I just wanted to be more youthful, and that spa made it seem so easy."

Diana took the elevator up to the floor of patient exam rooms and her private office. The elevator doors shut hard behind her, and she walked down the hall. "Nothing's ever as easy as it seems. You know that."

"But they gave me a couple of brochures and a video with all kinds of before and after pictures: people my age—even older—all beautiful now. The list of treatment side effects—print was so small, almost impossible to read." She fought back tears and tried to lift her eyelid back in place with her fingers. "One thing those people didn't show me were photos of monsters."

Phoebe felt as though her eyes would explode. The make-up lights over the sink shot spears through her eye sockets.

"Try to calm down. I don't believe you have had a stroke, and I think the neurologist will tell us this is all temporary," Diana said. "I saw a lady in the ED with appendicitis the other day who didn't want wrinkles either. Her facial weakness from those shots is nearly resolved."

"I hope you're right that this will all go away, Diana."

"It will. You can lay low for a few days, wear extra makeup to cover the redness."

Phoebe took a deep breath. She pressed her trembling hands palms down against the veined marble counter surrounding the sink. "How long do I have to get dressed before somebody picks me up?"

"Like I said, about thirty minutes. I've already texted someone to come and get you. I'll call in a few favors, but you'll still be a work-in at the neurologist's office."

"Thank you, Diana. Without you, I wouldn't get in at all on such short notice."

"Was a doctor inside the spa, what we call *onsite*, when you got your injections? My guess is that a PA or nurse practioner actually gives the shots."

"The physician assistant had to leave, something about a family emergency. A lady doctor treated me," Phoebe answered. "One of the Belmonts."

"Which Belmont?"

"Diana, you won't believe how terrible the woman, the doctor, came across in one of the clinic pictures in their brochure."

"Phoebe, which Dr. Belmont?" Diana dreaded the answer.

"Sidney. Yes, Sidney Belmont. She did the injections."

"Sidney Belmont," Diana repeated and shook her head. As she paced the room, she pulled the phone away from her ear and swallowed hard to hide the anger and frustration. She thought again about Sidney Belmont in the Emergency Department, hovering over the partially paralyzed woman with appendicitis.

"Hey, isn't Dr. Belmont a neurologist? I thought I heard someone say that today in the spa. I sure as hell don't want to see her again after what she did!"

"You'll be seeing someone else, but I need to hurry and get dressed. Bye, bye."

Phoebe's beaming red, distorted face disappeared from Diana's screen, and Diana promptly called the head of the Metropolitan Neurology Clinic.

"Sure, we'll be happy to see your aunt. Bring her right over. We'll get her in today," was the answer.

Diana did not have time at the moment to call Ellis Belmont about Phoebe's predicament, nor was he likely to care. *Come on, what good would that do, Diana, to criticize his sister, accuse her of incompetence?* She signed into the office computer and pulled up her morning clinic schedule. *Calling the patriarch of the Belmont dynasty only makes you a tattletale, Diana, a medical community tattletale.*

She scanned the day's appointment schedule. "Good, one patient cancelled. That frees me up a little." She scanned the rest of the names and the reasons for the office visits. All seemed straight-forward—a couple of post-ops, one new patient who wanted to discuss thyroid surgery, a short office procedure to remove a skin mole for another, and a woman worried about her gallbladder. Diana printed a copy of the short patient list and noted one more name added at the bottom of the roster—*Roy Allen Garnett*.

"Not him again. Just what I needed," Diana said.

# Chapter 15

Phoebe's text message to Diana read:

```
At neurologist. Nurse says doctor run-
ning behind.
```

Diana's text back was a stretch.

```
One left to see. Be there in a few.
```

She was uncertain about the next appointment.

Phoebe shot back:

```
Nurse let me wait in empty room where
nobody can see me. 😞
```

Diana read through her notes from Garnett's last visit and his surgical care since. She noted her several references to comments about Garnett's nephew and the nephew's suspicion about the death of his mother at Roy Garnett's hands. That patient visit spiraled into two physical attacks against Diana. She decided against a call to Key Martin before she entered the room to see Garnett again.

*The nephew's the one to worry about, and he's locked up.* Diana pushed through the door into the examination room.

"Mr. Garnett, good to see you again today."

"Doubt you really mean that, Doc. Not after all that's happened." Garnett wore the same boots Diana remembered. Her nurse had suggested he remain dressed, and he sat in the middle of the examination table.

Diana forced a concerned, professional demeanor. "My surgery scheduler never heard back from you about your hernia, though from the records here I see that Dr. Cummins fixed you up. We could have prevented that trip to the ED and the emergency procedure."

"You surprised I didn't call you back? After what my nut-case nephew did the first time I was in here? And then what he did to you after Chuck was killed?" Garnett's downturned face turned crimson.

Heavy beads of sweat erupted from his forehead.

"I understand the police believe he may have shot Chuck Wallace," Diana said. She set her iPad on the exam room desk and decided to sit on the stool next to it. She read through the rest of the medical record from the last visit.

"No way my nephew's a murderer," Garnett said. "My nephew is all talk."

"Before we discuss your medical problems, I've got to respond to that." She closed the program and the iPad went blank. "When your nephew stuck a gun into my neck and back, it wasn't all talk. He meant it."

"He denies all that."

"Police got DNA from the backseat of my car. It matched the sample your nephew gave when they arrested him the second time he showed up."

"The police are wrong about my nephew. Chuck Wallace was a friend. Why would my nephew want to kill him?"

No missed calls or texts appeared on Diana's phone. The neurologist was bound to have gotten to Phoebe by now. She touched the iPad control, and the screen came back to life. "Your nephew told me he hacked into your computer and had seen your medical records. He read the *murdered sister* comment and was trying to force me to send you to a psychiatrist."

"The *murdered sister* was his mother," Garnett said, "and he found her strangled in her mobile home. She lived in a trailer park in northwest Jackson off I-220."

Diana studied her more detailed notes made in reference to

Garnett's surgical issues. "You'll need to partially undress so I can examine you."

"What I said before about murdering my sister—that was hypothetical. Truth is, I set her up, put her in the situation," Garnett said as he unbuckled his belt and pulled out the shirttail. "I fired her from her secretary job at my office when she kept drinking at work. She lost her house. All she could afford was that stinkin' trailer in a bad part of town." He unbuttoned his shirt and started to drop his trousers.

"No that's far enough," Diana said, sliding the iPad to the desk and approaching the exam table. "I just need to check your incision."

"My nephew moved out after graduating high school. He's done odd jobs for me and my business, mostly minor repairs at my less important rental properties. Actually, Dillon has been a decent employee." He grimaced as Diana palpated his abdomen and checked the site of the surgery. "I was going to increase his responsibilities, give him a slight raise, until he started pulling these stunts."

"That hurt? Or did I catch you off guard." Diana removed a stethoscope from a drawer, placed the bell against the skin of Garnett's abdominal wall, and listened to the normal rumblings of a moderately obese male's colon. She pulled the instrument away and returned it to a drawer. I'm glad you're not in any post-op pain."

"No physical pain, Doc. Only mental."

Diana recalled from Key Martin that the sister's body was found by her son, Dillon Garnett, strangled in the living room of the mobile home with no sign of forced entry and no prints on the body. Nearby neighbors saw or heard nothing the evening of the murder. They answered most of the police questions with a shrug. Mr. Garnett and his nephew, the victim's son, both had alibis.

"I'm sorry about your family dilemma," Diana stepped back from the exam table, "and sorry I got drawn into it."

"Bet you are, Doc."

"I remember explaining at your first office visit that you should not put off getting your hernia repaired, so it's good Dr. Cummins took care of it. You're healing well, but just don't lift anything heavy for another month."

"I can handle that, Doc."

"However, I'm sure you can understand that considering the situation with your nephew and moving forward, I'm not the doctor for you, nor is anyone else in my practice."

"Why, Dr. Bratton? You're the best. That's why I came to see you."

"Under the circumstances, I don't believe it's ethical for me or anyone else in this practice to continue to care for you, Mr. Garnett. And, frankly, I'm uncomfortable with the whole situation. Your nephew has involved me in your personal affairs in a big way, in fact endangered my life twice."

Garnett sat up on the exam table, perplexed.

"If I knew you'd be back as a patient, I would have sent you to another doctor after your nephew attacked me downstairs. Seeing your name on my clinic schedule today was a real surprise."

"My nephew—always screwing things up," Garnett said.

"I'll be happy to refer you to Capital Surgery Associates, a nice clinic across town."

Garnett sat up on the table quickly and began to button his shirt. "Hold on a second, Doc. I don't want to go anywhere else."

"If you have anything against the other surgery clinic, my front office will send your chart notes anywhere you want to go for follow-up after you sign the medical records release."

"One more thing, Doc. I know you're interested in police work, like solving murder cases. Why else would you have been on a roof with a couple of cops?" Garnett continued to dress. "I know this because my nephew told me. I've been to see him while he's been locked up. Hope to get him out on bail."

"You need to get your nephew help, a therapist or even a psychiatrist. Someone who will see him in jail." Diana retrieved the iPad and moved toward the door in the hall. "Stop at the first secretary you see at the windows up front. She'll make the referral."

"You got up on that roof to help the cops figure out who shot

Chuck." Garnett reached for his boots. "I sure hope they catch her."

Diana wanted free of Garnett's health issues and what he planned to do for or with a girlfriend. She wanted no more of him and his demented, confused, and unstable nephew, who had threatened her life twice. Nonetheless, she stopped in the doorway and turned toward Garnett.

"Catch her?"

Garnett leaned sideways against the edge of the exam table, facing Diana. She took a deep breath, lost the battle with her curiosity, and stepped back into the room. Her informal criminal investigative work with Key Martin and the Jackson Police Department tugged at her.

"Why did you say, catch *her*?" she repeated.

"I knew Chuck Wallace when we both lived in New Orleans and reconnected with him after I moved to Jackson. He invited me to his neighborhood men's group. I know you practice with Voncelle Wallace. She was married when she met Chuck in New Orleans. They had an affair, and he felt guilty."

"What's this about, Mr. Garnett?"

"I never thought much about all that history until he died—was shot."

"Thought about what history? The affair?"

"No, that Voncelle's first husband died too. She was a new doctor, working in a surgery clinic near the French Quarter and out of training only a few years. Married the guy when they were in med school. Took his name—*Peters*."

From her time serving on the hospital credentials committee, Diana remembered a few things about Voncelle's formal education and employment history prior to the Haynes clinic. She completed general surgery residency at Tulane, then landed a job with a private surgery clinic nearby. Voncelle had active hospital privileges in New Orleans and was in good standing before relocating to Jackson. There had been no references to family.

"The first husband was a radiologist in some type of fellowship training with more left to do. Chuck said Voncelle doubted the guy could pass the certification exams."

"You and Chuck talked a lot?" Diana asked.

"Chuck and I used to meet at LeFleur's Bluff and play nine holes, then go for a quick drink. Golf is a slow game most of the time, lots of time to talk."

To Diana's relief, Brad had minimal interest in golf, playing only occasionally. Her first husband played any chance he could, often when she needed him to babysit their daughter, Kelsey. A corporate golf membership at the county club was one of the perks of the big law firm downtown, and he claimed the partners expected him to play with clients to drum up more legal business and make partner.

"Chuck first met Voncelle in a coffee shop when they lived in New Orleans. She had been on call all weekend, he said. He was doing well selling commercial and residential real estate in Louisiana and was brokering the sale of that coffee shop. Voncelle was struggling to pay off student loans for herself and her husband."

"Unfortunately, not all marriages work out, Mr. Garnett," Diana said, the relationship with her ex-husband and the physical and emotional abuse a prime example. "Sometimes it's time to move on."

"That's just it. Chuck said he and Voncelle—I guess it's all right to call Dr. Wallace *Voncelle*. But I'm rattling on, and you have patients to see."

"My other patients will have to wait. I want to hear what you have to say. So, please …"

"Sorry." Garnett stood away from the exam table and took a step toward Diana. She shifted her feet.

"Chuck told me Voncelle found plenty of time to meet up with him back then and, you know, get together," Garnett said. "Sometimes she showed up dressed like she was just out of surgery. Then, one night she broke a date—called and told him her husband was in the hospital."

"Is that when he died?"

"The guy had surgery. Appendix taken out, or gallbladder, or some dang thing, and he didn't make it. I'm surprised you don't already know this."

Diana turned away. She almost wanted to agree. "Voncelle—Dr. Wallace—and I stay fairly busy around here. Not much time for chitchat."

"Seems like she would have shared information that important, especially since you're both surgeons," Garnett said. "Now the lady has lost two husbands."

"That she says. Now about the secretary out front. She'll give you the name of a couple of other surgery clinics." Before Diana could reach for the door latch, the door popped open toward her.

"Dr. Bratton, hate to interrupt." Her secretary darted her eyes between Dr. Bratton and the patient. She forced a smile. "There's a neurologist on the phone for you, a Dr. Stewart? Says he's calling about your aunt?"

# Chapter 16

Voncelle slid the box off the second shelf of her refrigerator. She recognized the name of a local restaurant printed on the top. "Yum," she said.

The note taped to the cover offered condolence for her loss in flowery, cursive black ink script from the PACU nurses at Metropolitan Hospital. She tossed the message aside and ignored its flutter to the kitchen floor. Voncelle opened the box to an Oreo chocolate pie, covered in whipped cream and chocolate shavings.

"Not bad. These big babies run twenty-five to thirty dollars—maybe more."

She placed the box on the kitchen island, pulled up a stool, and grabbed a dessert plate and fork, then thought better of it and ate straight from the box. *It's just me, anyway.*

Halfway through what would have been a second slice of chocolate pie, Voncelle pushed the box to the side and opened the laptop she discovered in Chuck's downtown office. Chuck Wallace had always been predictable—predictable about what he ordered at a restaurant, what nights (or days) of the week he wanted sex, and how he wanted it. Thus, figuring out a password was not a problem since he kept a list in the *Notes* app of his cell phone. Problem was, up until now, the phone had been in police custody.

"Now, what was that nice detective's last name? *Thomas.* Thank you, Detective Thomas for returning my husband's cell to me. Chuck was never without it." She knew the code to unlock the phone and had shared it with JPD. Voncelle checked Chuck's notes. "Yes, here it is."

She reached back toward the pie with her fork, took another taste, lifted the cover of Chuck's laptop, typed in *BigDaddy100$*, and the computer came to life. The file belonging to the Belmonts was the first place she went. As Voncelle scrolled through the numbers, a thick Spanish accent came up from behind.

"My beautiful sexy, now *senorita*. Can I have a bite?"

At Voncelle's startle, the laptop slammed shut, and the fork flew across the counter. Hernando Garcia jumped for the utensil before it struck the floor.

"Lucinda thinks I'm staying at the Marriott, the one a block off the interstate. I registered at the front desk, got a room key, and didn't unpack. Hope I can stay here instead." Garcia licked away the remnants of whipped cream from the fork. "Not bad. Might try a full piece. And thanks for leaving your side door unlocked."

"It wasn't intentional. Chuck was always on me about leaving the garage door up and the door to the mud room open," Voncelle said. "Besides, I thought you were coming tomorrow. I wanted time to review what financials Chuck submitted to your board of directors."

Garcia slid an arm around Voncelle's waist and stabbed at the center of the untouched half of the pie. "My board was skeptical about the deal in the first place, and now with Chuck out of the way—or should I say now that he has *passed* away—the board is nervous. He was the driving force to make this Belmont thing happen."

With Garcia peering over her shoulder, Voncelle skipped through several pages of tables and graphs. One page listed the physician members of the Belmont family, interspersed with the few physicians, physician assistants, and nurse practitioners not part of the clan. Each healthcare provider was credited with a running twenty-four-month total of cash receipts collected from assigned patients or their insurance companies, representing their individual monetary productivity.

She stopped at the EBITDA calculation page.

"That figure allowed us to assess the operating activities, the financial health of the Belmonts, not personally, of course, only their medical business. EBITDA is an important key figure used to compare companies financially, particularly on an international basis. Think of it as net cash flow."

"Of course, Chuck wanted this sale to go through. He talked about it all the time. It was supposed to be a career changer for him."

Garcia touched a column on the computer screen. "This value shows high annual net profit and a high profitability for the medical organization as long as the doctors continue to produce."

Voncelle reached for the pie and pushed him gently aside. "You make this—us—the medical profession seem like another simple commodity, a buy and sell product." She took the fork from his hand and scooped up a mouthful, then slid it between his lips.

"You whispered to me during your first trip to Madrid with your late husband, that you hoped this deal would go through, that a big win economically for Chuck would lessen your financial load."

Voncelle wiped the overflow of whipped cream and chocolate from Garcia's lips with a finger and sucked the finger clean. "I'm tired, Hernado. Tired of the early hours in surgery, tired of the late hours in the emergency department, tired of being called out of bed at all hours." She kissed him.

"Bed. Interesting subject," Hernando said.

Voncelle ignored the idea. "I guess you've been in contact with the Belmonts. That's why you made the trip, to try to salvage the deal now that Chuck's gone."

"Mixing business with pleasure—that's how you Americans put it." He slipped his arm back around her waist and pulled her closer.

"Ellis Belmont is a classic ass. He's the one Chuck talked the most about," Voncelle said as she rubbed Garcia's back. "Next in line is Brother Miles, an almost prissy *yes* man who's too well put together for his age. With all his tennis and pickle ball games and cocktail parties, Miles might be one doctor-employee not to hold up his end of the bargain. Every time I go to my salon, I see Miles getting his nails done and hair colored and cut."

Voncelle let out a long sign. "Then there's Sidney Belmont—the little sister. She's another story. Hate to say it, extremely weak as a physician. Not very productive, I hear, and a ticking time bomb as far as potential malpractice cases."

"I have an appointment with Dr. Ellis Belmont tomorrow at ten," Garcia said, "to resume negotiations with Chuck gone. Now, what about tonight? Should I call an Uber to take me back to the hotel? Or stay here?"

"You've got to go back and get your luggage anyway, so why not stay at the hotel. I've already thrown out all of Chuck's things."

Garcia stepped around the corner and retrieved his carry-on. "I didn't leave my luggage at the hotel. You still have the Italian cotton and silk sheets?" he asked and headed toward the master bedroom.

# Chapter 17



*Fifteen years ago—New Orleans, Louisiana*

Dr. Voncelle Peters pushed open the door to OR Suite 4. "How much longer before I can cut."

The circulating nurse tugged at the arm board extension on the patient's surgical bed. "Fella's stocky, so we're still changing a few things. Should have put him in room four on one of the newer beds."

"Pre-op didn't record his BMI?" Voncelle asked. She glanced up at the wall clock and shrugged her shoulders at the surgical tech. Fully gowned in sterile garb, he stood bored under the clock mounted inside a wall of shiny, grey tiles. He returned the shrug and leaned against the back table covered with sterilized surgical instruments.

"I'm already an hour behind from the last case," Voncelle said. "Come on guys, speed it up."

"Sorry for the delay, Dr. Peters. It took a while for anesthesia to put this big guy to sleep. I've about got it." The circulating nurse reached under the arm board and moved the small lever connecting it to the OR bed. The tension on the obese man's shoulder relaxed and the nurse stepped back. "Yep, got it," he said and whipped around to the opposite side of the patient. He worked the same maneuver, and the other side of the patient jerked.

The anesthesiologist peeked up from her cell phone to study the cardiac monitor and the series of vital signs. "Voncelle, this isn't your thing—but if you could give me a hand, it might speed things along so we can get to your other cases," she said. "My anesthesia tech is on another late morning break. Girl must have an overactive bladder."

"Sure, Ava. Anything to push this along." Ava Trabeaux finished her residency several years ahead of Voncelle's trek through training in general surgery. Voncelle liked Ava. She always did a good job with her patients, today's slow turnaround time between cases not her fault.

"Please look over in that extra-supply cabinet in the corner and grab me another vial of Neo," Ava said. "You wouldn't think it. Your patient is having trouble keeping his blood pressure up."

Voncelle raised her surgical mask over her mouth and nose and entered the room. She walked toward the cabinet and realized she still wore her lightweight, long sleeve jacket. "I guess the stuff is labeled? Been a long time since I took biochem."

"Yeah. Neo-Synephrine or Phenylephrine. Only need a couple of the hundred microgram syringes," Ava said. "Have to be careful with the dosing. Don't take much."

With her back turned to the others in the room, Voncelle thumbed through the plastic tray inside the cabinet. She spotted the phenylephrine, the medication designed to constrict blood vessels, with brand name Neo-Synephrine marked in miniscule print on syringes and vials. "I see the tray marked *Neo* with several syringes, and it comes in vials of powder too?"

"Need two of the syringes. And quick." The blood pressure reading for Voncelle's surgical patient remained low.

Voncelle hesitated a second, turned her body to the left to obstruct others' view of the cabinet, and slipped one powdered vial representing a hundred standard doses of NeoSynephrine into her jacket. She then grabbed two smooth individual syringes and in a few quick steps delivered them to the anesthesiologist.

The anesthesia tech burst into the room, chewing the last of a doughnut lifted from the doctors' lounge. "Got your text, Dr. Trabeaux," he said. "Came as quick as I could."

"Sure, Theo," Ava said frowning, pushing the first of the syringes into the IV port. She noted the blood pressure reading on the monitor and gave the patient a second dose. "Dr. Peters filled in for you. Maybe we don't need a tech after all."

"Hey, Dr. Peters. What gives? Whatchu trying to do to me! I need this job."

Voncelle brushed past Theo toward the scrub sink. "Saved your worthless anesthesia tech ass. That's what I did. Oh, and thanks for the easy-to-read med labels in your cabinet over there. Might try larger print next time."

"Need another bag of LR, Theo," Ava called out. "Man, you gotta restock this place if the hospital wants me to keep these paying patients."

"Got it," Theo said. He closed the door to the disheveled contents in the medication supply cabinet. "I'll straighten up later and go over inventory."

"Patient's good, everyone. You can start prepping," Ava said. "Dr. Peters has waited long enough."

Voncelle offered a weak grin and slipped out of the room. She skipped the surgical scrub sink for her private locker adjacent to the Doctors' Lounge. Alone in the cramped room, Voncelle spun the lock on the cheap metal door and jerked open her empty locker. She felt for the vial of phenylephrine in her lower right jacket pocket and considered transferring it to a pocket in her scrub suit.

*No, it will be safe in here.* She hung her jacket on the hook inside and eased the door shut.

*Dr. Peters, ready in OR Four,* burst from the overhead speaker. Voncelle spun the combination lock on the door and hustled to the operating room.

"I pre-heated the oven for a pizza. Pick whichever one you want out of the freezer," Voncelle said. "If you want my opinion, I'd get the meat lovers, thick crust."

Dressed in flip flops and gold and black boxer briefs with the

New Orleans Saints *fleur de lis* logo centered over the crotch, Aaron Peters headed past the sink filled with dirty dishes and opened the freezer to the pizzas stacked about a foot high on the top shelf. Several boxes toppled to the kitchen floor including the variety suggested by his wife. That box spun to a stop near a corner. Aaron gathered the others and returned them to the freezer. "What did you do? Buy out Rouses?"

"I'm on call every other night now, so if I get a chance to go to the grocery store, I gotta take advantage. You radiologist slugs don't know what it's like."

Aaron saw the *April 2009* expiration date, quickly read the instructions on the back of the box, and tore open one end of the package. He peeled away the clear plastic wrapper from the pizza, placed the pie on the center rack of the oven, and took another perusal through the cooking directions. He set the oven timer to eighteen minutes and grabbed Voncelle by the waist before she made it out of the kitchen. "Can't you hang around for at least a half-hour or so and eat with me. Fool around too? It's no wonder you're not pregnant yet."

He pressed the now swollen fleur-de-lis against her as she squirmed clear of her five-nine, 240-pound husband of six years. "Told you, I'm on call again tonight. Only reason I got to come home for a few minutes and shower was three of my afternoon patients cancelled. I bribed the appointment clerk not to fill the empty slots. If the clinic manager doesn't hire another surgeon to give me break, I'm outta there."

Aaron tugged at his underwear to stretch the front, shrugged his shoulders, and turned on the oven light for a glimpse at the pizza. The frozen cheese around the edges had begun to melt. "Tulane should be graduating a new crop of surgeons in June. Can't they hire one of those?"

Voncelle pulled her backpack off the rack by the door. "Won't pay 'em enough. I was willing to work for less since we were stuck here while you finished your radiology fellowship."

Aaron glanced back at the oven and moved closer. The rear exit door to their apartment off Magazine Street was not far from the kitchen sink and oven. Voncelle picked the apartment because of the flower garden and blooming bushes left by previous tenants. Her non-stop surgery practice kept her from enjoying the outdoor area—no time to pull weeds or water the flowers.

"Come on, Von, don't bring that up again. Radiology fellowships aren't easy to come by. I couldn't help that it took a few years to get in after we finished med school, and you were nearly finished with your surgery residency. I've got two years left here in New Orleans with interventional training, then we can see what's out there."

Voncelle stood with her back to the door. "What's out there? I'll tell you what's out there. If I hadn't been stuck here, I could have named my price in lots of other places."

"I know. I know. Female surgeons like you. Everybody wants diversity in their practice."

"The NOLA Surgery Clinic couldn't give a flip. All they care about is bodies who will sign low-paying physician contracts and fill up the ORs with paying patients. They knew I wasn't going anywhere else because my spouse couldn't leave."

Aaron glanced at the oven timer. "Because your spouse was holding you back from a better opportunity while he finishes his own medical training. I get it." The smell of pizza filled the cramped kitchen. The clock said six more minutes before ready, but he peeked inside the oven to be sure. A plume of smoke from burned crust rose almost to cover the ceiling. "Crappy thing never has cooked even."

"I don't have time for this." Her phone screamed more messages, and she slid the backpack on. "Two are waiting for me in the ER, and a couple of ambulances are working their way out of the French Quarter. No way I'll make it back home tonight. I'll sleep in the hospital call room."

"Want me to slip up there and join you? We can try again for a hospital baby. I'll be real quiet."

Voncelle pushed past Aaron for the fridge and grabbed a bottled water. "The triage nurse almost called security on you last time."

"Couldn't help it. The red ambulance lights piercing through the window blinds are an incredible turn on. I get with the rhythm." He glanced back at the oven, popped the elastic on his boxers, and grabbed his crotch again. "Besides, the freaking walls in that hospital are too thin."

"Having you slobber all over me is the last thing on my mind, Aaron. Especially when I can't feel anything between my legs," she muttered. Voncelle turned the doorknob and disappeared.

"Crap," Aaron said as the apartment door slammed shut. He opened the oven to a billow of smoke that covered the ceiling. Half the pizza was on fire. He yanked a stainless-steel spatula from the drawer and removed the pizza from the oven, covering the short flames with a dishrag. "I'll eat half and put the rest in the fridge for Von."

He put the partially burned pizza on a plate and cut away the torched area, then sliced the rest. Next, he grabbed a cold, long-neck beer from the refrigerator. "Not bad, not bad at all," Aaron said and chewed his first piece with mouth opened. He guzzled a large portion of the beer and rubbed his hand against the sharp pain in his stomach.

"Third time today and only after I eat. I'll get the tech to sonogram my gallbladder tomorrow." Aaron let out a loud burp and ate another mouthful of pizza.

Voncelle propped the clipboard against her waist and scribbled orders on the standard patient history form used in the Emergency Room. Rumors were rampant of eventual and total conversion to electronic patient medical records by the hospital. "One more headache to deal with," she said when the hospital and clinic administration discussed the issue at a recent staff meeting.

Despite the even heavier than expected emergency patient traffic that greeted her when she clocked in for her shift six hours ago, Voncelle found fifteen minutes to stretch out between the drop-in

MVA and the surgical wound abscess belonging to a patient of one of the other surgeons. She lay on the bed in the doctors' call room and stared at the ceiling. The revolving lights from the police cars and ambulances in the parking lot outside pushed through the blinds onto the opposite wall. She thought about what Aaron said earlier and the association of the pulsating lights with his sexual performance. *Disgusting.*

She thought more about Aaron lying on top of her and grunting and moaning as she referred to the time. "Yes, he would have had thirteen minutes to spare."

A bright light beside the bed also broke the stillness in the room. Voncelle pushed the lit acrylic square at the base of the phone and picked up the receiver. "Yeah, what you got?"

"White male, age thirty-one, weight about 250. Says he's your husband. I tried your cell, no answer."

"What? Aaron?" Voncelle grabbed her phone and saw the missed calls and texts—several from Aaron and the ER, her ring control set to silent. Voncelle had not left the emergency room since she arrived at the hospital except to steal away to the call room. "My nap yesterday afternoon at home—I forgot to change the ringer. I'll be right there!"

Voncelle scrambled to put on her tennis shoes and tie the laces. She glanced at her face in the mirror above the sink in the corner and considered splashing water in her face. What remained of her eyeliner would run, so instead she ran cold over her fingertips and pressed them against her closed eyelids. The bloodshot was better. *Oh god, my breath.*

The bedside phone lit up again. This time via speakerphone. "Triage says he needs surgery bad. You coming, Dr. Peters?"

"Get the second call doc to see him," Voncelle yelled across the space and bolted from the room. The swinging door into the hall barely missed a lab courier with a cart full of body fluid specimens labeled *Medical Hazards.*

"I can't operate on my own husband. What are they thinking?"

"Say what?" the courier said. "Slow down, lady. I don't care who you are."

Voncelle shot him the finger and turned the corner to the Emergency Room. Once through the double-doored entrance, the triage nurse spotted her. "Dr. Peters, you're here."

"Yeah, Montrese. Where's my husband?"

"I didn't have to page second call. Dr. Guidry showed up. Said something about doing a favor for a next-door neighbor. He walked through the ER, and I grabbed him."

"Is Guidry gonna take care of Aaron? Hope so. You know—this is sorta awkward."

"He's over there in the corner bay with your husband."

Another text appeared on Voncelle's cell. A post-op patient from last week's surgery schedule needed a call back for more pain medication. She read past that message and realized she had missed several others while her phone was set to silent and in the confusion over Aaron's arrival in the ER. "Geeze, why won't they leave me alone? I gotta get out of this place."

The triage nurse appeared behind her and grinned. "Uhh—Dr. Peters, your husband is asking for you." The nurse motioned toward the bay in the corner. "You gotta a second to talk to him?"

Voncelle's cell buzzed again—another message to call a patient who thought he should come to the emergency room. Voncelle held the phone and read the text in plain sight of the triage nurse.

"Oh, your phone is working. Dr. Peters said he tried to get you several times," the nurse quipped.

Voncelle popped her phone back into her pocket. "Been a busy night. Don't you worry your pretty head about my husband."

She shoved past the triage nurse for the bay in the corner. Aaron winced against the pressure of Dr. Guidry's hands against his abdomen. A loose print of her husband's lab results lay on top of a clipboard.

"Hey, Von," Aaron said, struggling to lift the oxygen mask from his face enough to speak. "Guess I should've picked the margarita pizza instead of anchovy." He coughed in a weak laugh and grabbed the upper right side of his abdomen.

"Even though it's obvious, Voncelle, I ordered a bedside gallbladder sono," Guidry said, tossing his right hand toward the bed. "That gallbladder needs to come out. You wanna do it?"

Voncelle pushed past the other surgeon. "Give me a minute with my husband."

"No problem." George Guidry backed away and began writing orders. "I'm afraid he's sick as shit," he whispered. "Likely be in ICU a couple of days or more post-op."

Voncelle bent over the bed as Aaron struggled to speak. She helped loosened the oxygen mask covering his nose and mouth and lifted it an inch. "I texted you a couple of times, and my call went straight to voicemail," Aaron managed.

"Oh, baby, I'm so sorry. Call has been terrible," she said. She glanced back at Guidry. He had finished with his notes and talked with the OR transporter who stood next to a gurney.

"Don't you want to do the surgery yourself?" Aaron coughed and fidgeted with the sheet. "Is this Guidry guy any good. Don't know much about him."

"Haven't heard anything bad about him. He practices with the other surgery group." Voncelle lowered the oxygen mask back in place while she spoke. Aaron's breathing seemed to relax with the improved air flow. "A lap chole is a routine procedure these days. Any new surgeon coming out of an approved residency would have done at least a hundred, and Guidry's been in practice longer than I have. It's a minimally invasive laparoscopic procedure," Voncelle said. "You should already know that."

She noted Aaron's elevated temp on the monitor as he struggled to speak. He pushed the mask to the side. "I'm screwed, Von."

"No, no. You'll be fine. A wife shouldn't operate on her husband. And the rest of my call tonight has been so crazy like I said and ..."

"Not what I mean. I'm screwed because my radiology boards are next week. I need to be studying."

"You can get a medical extension," Voncelle said. "Take temporary medical leave."

"No, I'm totally screwed." Another cough and a long wince in pain. "I didn't tell you. I've already put off the retake two times. Since it's interventional radiology, they'll make me repeat a year of my residency and fellowship if I don't go ahead and pass this step."

Voncelle passed her own boards in the top five percent of scores.

Aaron retched and pulled completely away from the mask, turning the best he could to the side. The effort was too late. He sprayed the top of Voncelle's scrub suit with vomit before a nurse trotted over with an emesis basin.

"Shit!" Voncelle jerked away from the bed. She grabbed several paper towels from the beside sink dispenser and fervently wiped at her shirt. She regretted the profanity but wanted to scream in total despair and anguish over her situation in life.

"I'm sorry, Von." Aaron again struggled to talk before he vomited again into the basin. "I—didn't—mean to. I'm sorry I ..."

Dr. Guidry interrupted. "My buddy Demitri is going to roll you up to OR, Aaron. You've already signed consents, so I can give you some Phenergan, and the Versed won't be long behind." The same nurse with the basin reappeared. She secured Aaron's IV tubing and injected the anti-nausea medicine into the plastic port.

"There ya go: Phenergan, 12.5 mg," she said. "Pre-op upstairs will give the Versed. We call it happy juice. Then you're going feel much, much better." She flashed an awkward smile at Voncelle. "Dr. Peters, you want to try another goodbye before the other Dr. Peters heads up to surgery?"

Demetri, the patient transport, stabilized the gurney with a foot brake and maneuvered Aaron from the ER bed onto clean sheets. Somehow Aaron's hospital gown had been spared.

Demetri retrieved a clean emesis basin from a cabinet and wedged it to the side of Aaron's face.

Her scrub suit top wet and smelly, Voncelle returned a similar smile to the nurse and joined Demetri at Aaron's gurney to roll toward the elevator. Aaron groaned in and out of lucidity, no longer thrashing in pain or vomiting. Voncelle glared back at the nurse, busy stripping the bed in the treatment bay, and felt relieved she did not have to do it. Her own queasiness set in.

"Hubby's going be fine, Dr. Peters. Dr. Guidry'll take real good care of him." They approached the elevator and Demetri pushed the call button. "You headed up too?"

Her husband's eyes shut, his breathing steady, Voncelle said, "No thanks, I'm good. Tell Guidry to text me when it's over."

"Sure thing, Dr. Peters." Demetri and Aaron disappeared alone into the elevator.

The queasiness passed and Voncelle thought about a cup of coffee. She needed coffee more than a shower and a change of clothes. The coffee shop two blocks away remained her favorite getaway with Chuck. Possibly it was luck or written in the stars, but she never ran into anyone she knew in there—definitely no one from the hospital or her neighborhood who would recognize her and wonder why she was not with Aaron.

She wanted Chuck now. She wanted the usual—to slip him through one of the back entrances to the hospital from the alley where small trucks and vans delivered supplies. In minutes they could be in the sleep room. With all the posted security at the front and side entrances to New Orleans Medical Center, this door was seldom if ever locked, like that morning about five-thirty when Chuck worked his way in by himself. Voncelle's heart raced at the thought.

Her shift was over at seven that particular night, and her last patient was already admitted to the cardiac unit. The elderly woman was set for discharge to step-down the following morning and then back to the nursing home if she continued to improve post-op. When an intern spotted a bed sore in the middle of the night and consulted general surgery, it fell to her.

Voncelle had called Chuck and enticed him to come through the alley entrance by himself. Her gamble that the door remained unlocked worked, and he made it inside—barely escaping sight of a sleepy security guard on patrol. Unnerved, he ducked into a janitor's closet, texted her his whereabouts, and she met him there. They had sex up against the concrete wall between two mops hung to dry.

They even skipped the call room the next week for a return to the janitor's closet since it spiced things up.

A buzz and a message on her cell stopped the memory and fantasy of more stolen minutes with Chuck Wallace. Two patients needed her, one bounced her way courtesy of Dr. Guidry, the neighbor he promised to meet earlier in the ER. He was now too busy operating on her sick husband.

*My sick husband. My sick life.*

Voncelle studied her smelly, stained clothes and ran for her locker in the call room. She spun the combination lock, reached in for a fresh pair of scrubs, and noticed the forgotten jacket hanging on a side hook. She remembered the Neo grabbed in the OR the other day before her delayed case and hidden in the pocket.

*The Neo.*

Voncelle reached deep into her jacket pocket and fingered the vial of powder. She remembered the moment she decided secretly to lift it from the OR anesthesia supply cabinet without understanding why—until now. "Oh my God. Voncelle, no!"

She dropped the vial back into the jacket and slammed the locker shut. She flipped around and fell against the closed locker.

*No. I can't do that.*

A member of the cardiology staff burst into the room breaking the quiet. She rambled into a cell phone pressed against the side of her face, threw a quick acknowledgment at Voncelle with a toss of the head, and disappeared around the corner toward the stalls.

Voncelle ignored the interruption. The rancid smell of her husband's puke rose from her scrub suit top and seemed to fill the room. A toilet flushed from around the corner.

*The Neo.*

*My sick husband. My slow, lazy, dumb husband. My sick life.*

In seconds she again popped open the locker; changed into clean scrubs, this pair an odd shade of blue; put on the jacket; and once again felt the medication vial in the pocket. "Ava used this stuff to raise my patient's low blood pressure. 'Have to be careful with the dosing,' Ava said. Doesn't take much," she mumbled.

"You say something, hon?" the cardiologist asked, the cell phone pulled away from her face only far enough to speak outside of microphone range.

Voncelle waved her off. She patted and twirled the vial in her pocket.

*Ava wanted the Neo quick.*

"This Neo," she said as she left the room for the ER, "is mine."

*My sick husband. My sick life.*

# Chapter 18

Voncelle walked straight to the Emergency Room and into the triage nurse.

"Dr. Peters, you changed scrubs. Good," the nurse said. "You come across a lot fresher."

"Probably smell better too," Voncelle said.

"Any word from surgery about your hubby?"

Voncelle noticed the bay vacated by her sick husband had already been turned by housekeeping and restocked with another patient. "No, the circulating nurse texted me when they cut. Nothing since. I'm trying to put the surgery out of my mind. Stay busy and out of the way until Dr. Guidry shoots me an update."

"Keeping you busy won't be a problem."

Voncelle darted her eyes at the new ER patient.

"Yep, that's the first one we paged you about. Twenty-six-year-old bartender with abdominal pain. Says she has appendicitis. You're the expert. You decide." The triage nurse walked with Voncelle to the patient's bedside.

Voncelle grabbed the clipboard from the metal slot attached to the bed and thumbed through the information scribbled by hand on the standard-issue hospital forms. Other sheets of printed paper were copies of treatment disclaimers. The patient appeared to be asleep.

"Where's the other one you texted me about, the eighty-two-year-old man with abdominal pain who hasn't been to the bathroom in two weeks? A problem with constipation, I assume."

"Over there." The triage nurse pointed and smirked. "My assistant,

Roxanne, is in charge of that one. My pay grade is above impactions." A nurse with dark-brown hair arranged in wispy curls with orange-dyed tips hovered over the elderly patient. The man read a newspaper.

"Neither of the two new patients are going to surgery tonight or likely in the near future," Voncelle said. "Thank God." She decided to tackle work-up of the bartender first. "Tell Roxanne to give the old guy an enema and move him closer to the corner bathroom. Let nature take its course."

"Will do," the triage nurse said. "Let me know if you need help with the bartender chick." The nurse worked her way across the busy space to Roxanne and the elderly man to deliver Dr. Wallace's instructions. Voncelle peered through the crisscross movement of bodies in the central area of the ER to catch the brief exchange. Roxanne shook her black and orange hair dramatically from side-to-side, visibly unhappy with the assignment.

Nevertheless, she began the process of moving her patient closer to the bathroom.

"We'll see how that goes. Hopefully, it takes care of the problem," Voncelle said and turned to question the patient behind her. "You gotta wake up now." At no response, she raised her voice. "You think you got appendicitis?"

The twenty-five-year-old bartender stirred and attempted to sit up in bed. She grabbed her stomach while Voncelle palpated the girl's soft, flat abdomen. "I'm going to order a CT scan, and we'll see what's going on in here."

The radiological study would confirm no suspicion of appendicitis or any other surgical problem, granting the girl a wide smile as she left the ER. The naptime and a cocktail-type mixture of GI relaxants relieved her abdominal spasms. The old man moved across the room was fixed up too, and Voncelle signed the discharge papers for both patients.

One more patient later, she saw Guidry's text:

```
Right up there with the worst. Almost
gangrene. Fraid he's sick as shit—Sorry.
```

Needs ICU.

"Bad news?" Roxanne also managed this patient. She accepted the clipboard from Voncelle.

"Decide for yourself." Voncelle handed her cell and Guidry's update about Aaron's condition to Nurse Roxanne. The nurse's frown at the text vanished into utter surprise and shock, and she quickly handed the phone back to Voncelle.

"The other Dr. Peters will be fine. Guidry's good." Roxanne gauged the slow of activity in the ER. "Quiet before the storm? Good chance for you to head up to ICU and visit with your husband. He's what's important now." She pivoted for the nurses' station and did not look back.

Voncelle glanced at the second text, just read by Roxanne. It was from Chuck.

You good? Want me up there? Slip in through the back? ♥♥

"Oh, damn," Voncelle said—thinking worse. *Glad he didn't shoot me another picture of his dick.* She dropped the phone in her pocket and headed to the elevator and Surgical ICU.

George Guidry stood propped against a waist high counter, oblivious to the harried-appearing medical staff mulling behind it. He spoke into a phone receiver in what appeared to be clipped sentences. Voncelle admired the persona projected by his blue surgeon's cap folded up carelessly at the edges with thick grey hair that flipped and peeked out around the cap.

She felt Guidry's eyes on her as she walked toward him, eyes lowered. Guidry shot a weak smile. In seconds he completed the dictation of the operative report and returned the receiver to its base. "Don't like to get behind on dictation—or orders."

"You got me beat there, George. How's Aaron?"

"Not much more to say than what's in my text. The best hospitalist we got is all over him."

Guidry tossed a metal clipboard into a waiting basket. "Hate to say it. I'm beat."

"Not sure what I could have done different."

"Let's face the situation, Voncelle. You're a grown woman, married, and your husband is equally as educated as you and I are about what's healthy and what's not. We guys and girls in medicine are not immune. Carbs and booze are killers."

"Jeez, George. Stop the lecture."

Dr. George Guidry grabbed his white coat from the hook on the rack. "Just doing my job."

"I should have pushed him to see somebody, even a nutritionist. All I did was buy the junk food, every week—the Friday night ritual. Anything I could do to keep from cooking, and Aaron was right there, ready to crank up the grill or the deep fryer."

"Your hubby won't be eating any fried shrimp or crawfish for a while. It's hard to chew intubated in ICU."

"You trying to be funny now?"

"Truth hurts." Guidry stepped into the nurses' break room behind the workstation and grabbed a piece of fruit from a basket by the mini refrigerator. The chomp on a large apple cracked from the room. He emerged holding the last of the fruit and chewing with his mouth open.

The nurse in charge of the area peeped up from a patient's chart and playfully frowned at Dr. Guidry. "Care to drop a couple of bucks in the kitty jar by the fridge, Doc? Goes for a snack run."

"Put in on my tab, Janet. I'll send several pizzas up here this weekend from that new place on the highway. You like pepperoni?"

Guidry finished the apple. The nurse shook her head.

"I need to go see Aaron," Voncelle said.

"Your badge will get you past the visiting hours restriction," Guidry laughed. "I guess you already know that."

# Chapter 19

Voncelle stepped out of the elevator, the entrance to the Adult ICU directly ahead. A row of chairs lined the wall of each side of the hall, the drab upholstery barely enough to cover the metal frames. A couple sat to the right, the girl's head deep into the guy's shoulder. She raised a crumpled tissue to her eye and ignored Voncelle. The guy shifted in his chair and pulled his arm from the girl's waist to wrap it tightly around her shoulder. Voncelle lowered her eyes and pushed through the double doors into the unit.

A harried nurse inside moved frantically between the medicine cart and the desktop computer and one of the patients closest to the nurses' station. Like the couple outside, she ignored Voncelle until she stepped in her path. Voncelle scanned the series of windowed bays occupied by sick patients, most with the screens drawn. Rhythmic beeping noises popped from behind the nearest units.

"Aaron Peters? I'm here to see Aaron Peters."

Arms filled with rolled packages of white gauze bandage and surgical tape to secure the wrap, the nurse appeared to be in her mid- to late-twenties and wore thick-soled, white tennis shoes. Her cell phone peeked from a front pocket of her scrub pants. "I hope all that material isn't for Aaron Peters," Voncelle said.

"No, uhh, this is for Dr. Guidry's surgery patient from early last week. Incision popped open."

"We call that a wound dehiscence."

"Yeah, sure. Of course, I know that." The young woman dropped a package of the supplies. The bandages rolled toward the desk, bumping against the base. She balanced the remaining supplies in her arm, retrieved the errant package of Kerlix, and leaned toward one of the computer screens. Her phone nearly slipped from her pants pocket. Somehow, she managed to tap a few keys on the nearest computer without dropping any more of the load. "He's been moved from seven to number eight. Yes ... *eight*. I remember now from report."

Voncelle gazed toward the end of the line of typical ten by twenty-foot patient cubicles. The last one, number eight, was larger—more like 250 square feet—and reserved for the more critically ill patients and the higher-level monitoring that went along with near death.

"My husband is in eight?"

A buzz emanated from the nurse's pants pocket, and she set the supplies she carried on the desk to answer her phone. "Hey. Hang on a sec. Need to take care of something," she said into the phone, returning her attention to Voncelle. She leaned close enough to Voncelle to read her hospital badge. "*Peters*. You family? Oh, Dr. Voncelle Peters."

"Yes, my husband—like I said."

Suddenly, the phone call did not seem important. The ICU area seemed quiet except for the sound of Dr. Aaron Peter's ventilator from cubicle eight. "The respiratory therapist was in here a few minutes ago, adjusting the settings. It's been crazy busy. The other nurse is pregnant and in the restroom half the time."

"Wouldn't know," Voncelle said.

"One of the doctors from the Pulmonary Department came by and gave orders until the hospitalist takes over."

"That's fine. I'm going to go down there and see my husband —Aaron."

The nurse giggled. "It's not visiting hours, but since you're a doctor—"

"You'll make an exception? Thanks." Voncelle left the nurse and her supplies and her cell phone and the person waiting to chat with the nurse over the phone, glad that the patient with the poor-healing, open surgical wound in the nearby cubicle was George Guidry's responsibility and not hers.

Aaron's hands were bound to the siderails of his bed, the lower half of his swollen face covered by a bridge of dense plastic with a round tube erupting from the center and connecting him to a ventilator. Clean white sheets covered him from the chest down—a set-up, an arrangement Voncelle had seen before in her medical training and on occasion with some of her sickest patients. Although when its family, when it's someone you know, it's different. She reached for his hand restraints and touched the one on the left.

"Dr. Peters?" A female voice startled her from behind, not the voice of the nurse at the station, more authoritative.

Voncelle turned with a quick "Yes." Her hand remained on the restraint. "What is it?"

"I'm Amanda Briggs, the new critical care specialist."

"Congratulations, but I bet they continue to pay you as a lowly internist."

"Lowly? Never thought of it that way," Briggs said. "And I suspect the doctor who swaps shifts with me agrees. But we do get the worst patients, a lot of dumps." Aaron's monitored heart rate remained steady, the ventilator perfectly rhythmic. "Sorry about the restraints. They're hospital policy, you know."

"Getting your gallbladder removed isn't supposed to be such a big deal," Voncelle said. "Sometimes we joke that it's a curse to be in the medical profession—what can go wrong will go wrong when it pertains to you." She sank into the chair next to her husband's bed.

"Did your husband, did Dr. Peters, complain of any fever, any chills before his surgery?" Briggs asked.

"He's a grown man, for God's sake, and a doctor. And I'm not his mother; I'm his wife." Voncelle pulled her cell from her pocket and started to scroll.

"George Guidry said your husband's gallbladder had ruptured. He hadn't seen that since residency. Practically gangrene."

"Thank you for that," Voncelle said without leaving her phone. The ventilator and cardiac monitor sounds remained constant. "Any plans to extubate Aaron? A guy his size is a set up for a PTE. He needs to get out of bed post-op before a clot hits his lung."

Briggs flipped away the sheets from the lower half of the bed, exposing Aaron's legs wrapped in compression stockings to prevent venous blood clots. "Guidry's routine post-op orders take care of that. There's a prevention protocol against VTE—lower extremity stockings and anticoagulant injections," Briggs said. "Of course, you would know that."

"Of course." Voncelle jumped from the chair. Both women stared down at Aaron Peters. His chest and upper abdominal area heaved with the sound of the ventilator.

"Has Aaron been taking care of himself, mentioned not feeling well in any other way?"

"What are you trying to say, Briggs? My husband is not your dumb jock who works on an oil rig out in the Gulf. Sure, he's a doctor. However, he's a man too. He eats pizza, fried chicken—eats and drinks anything he wants and doesn't update me daily on how he feels—like I had time to listen."

"You don't cook, don't plan meals?"

The female surgeon stared deep into the eyes of the clueless female internist who landed a shift job as a medical hospitalist. "Are you kidding? With my schedule?"

Briggs raised her eyebrows and shook her head so tightly side-to-side in a *No* response that it almost vibrated.

Voncelle stormed clear of her husband's ICU cubicle. She brushed by the nurse at the entrance desk. The girl stared up from a stack of additional materials gathered from the supply room and intended to dress surgical wounds.

"Dr. Peters, you need anything?"

Voncelle failed to answer until she passed through the exit and clear of the nurse. "What I need is to get out of my life," she said, her neck twisted back toward the ICU and away from the same couple sitting along the exterior wall. She turned down the hall and wanted to run toward the elevator and out the front door of the hospital into the heavy traffic on Poydras. According to her phone, three new patients waited for her in the ER. Voncelle pulled her phone screen away from her study to see the couple both staring up at her, surprised.

"Something wrong, Doctor?" the teary girl managed. The expression on the face of the boy with her asked the same. They both straightened in their seats.

"Yes, something is very wrong," Voncelle said. "And you bet I'm going to fix it."

The doors opened to an empty elevator and no competition from callers on other floors. In minutes Voncelle was standing in front of her locker. She spun the combination lock, and the door popped open to the jacket hanging to the side on a hook. She could almost see the bulge in the right-side pocket, the vial of Neo-synephrine.

Voncelle grabbed the jacket and slid it on as two other female physicians entered the dressing area. Ignoring them, she slammed the locker door shut without bothering to spin the lock and disappeared from the room. The exit door into the hall slammed behind her.

"Wow, what's that bitch's problem?" one of the women said.

"Stress?" came from the other. She took a hair brush out of her miniature backpack and began to use it. "Heard her hubby is critical in ICU. One of Guidry's." She reached deeper in the backpack, produced a plastic clip, and pulled her hair back. "Gallbladder went bad."

# Chapter 20

*Present Day—Jackson, Mississippi*

Diana finished her third surgical case of the day, a bilateral mastectomy for a breast cancer patient following a successful course of chemotherapy. Brad removed one side and she the other.

These co-surgeon cases involving Brad and her were always fodder for the surgical techs and nurses circulating the room, even the male techs. Lots of goodhearted jokes, generally sexual in nature, about romantic dinners for two with expensive wine and dessert that preceded intimate activity that burned calories—all after a long, tedious day in the clinic and operating room. Forget that a teenager was at home, who had lots of homework.

As planned, a plastic surgeon with whom Diana and Brad often worked continued the case as a breast reconstruction procedure. The outcome for a patient cure, totally optimistic.

Diana completed the computer documentation and eyed the couch in the Doctors' Lounge. It was after lunch, and the place was quiet. Most of the other physicians, including Brad, were back in their offices seeing afternoon clinic patients. Diana, to the contrary, had scheduled an entire day of hospital surgery. The plastic surgeon would be tying up the operating room, busy with their patient for at least another hour, leaving time for a nap before her next case.

She sniffed the once decorative pillow on the couch, decided it would pass, fluffed it a tad, and stretched out. The television played on at the mute setting, and she left it undisturbed. The streaming service was unlike the one they used at home, and besides, she never caught on to the remote in the lounge, so she let the TV be. She rolled on her side, away from the ceiling light and toward the back of the couch. The nurse in charge of the operating room would call her when the next case was ready.

Diana closed her eyes and in seconds was somewhere else for what seemed like forever.

Her cell phone rang. The new melody, courtesy of a recent download update from daughter, Kelsey, blended somehow into her dream of dinner at an expensive restaurant on an outside patio with a linen tablecloth and Baccarat crystal wine goblets, on a cliff overlooking thundering ocean waves with seagulls flying overhead. Brad sat across from her, tanned, with his hair blowing in the breeze and dressed in a white linen shirt, unbuttoned to the waist. He ran his fingers up her thigh to places that made her scream and—

"Yes, what? Yes, this is Dr. Bratton." Diana had grappled for her phone in her sleep when it rang. She pushed the pillow behind her back and checked all around her. She remained alone in the lounge, the door closed. The television was on the *Game Show* channel and still muted.

"Hi, Diana. Hope I didn't catch you in the middle of clinic or in surgery."

"No. I, uhh." Diana shook her head clear. "No, this is good. What's up?" She recognized the voice of Aunt Phoebe's neurologist.

"Phoebe is doing great. I thought you would appreciate an update."

Diana straightened her scrub pants, uncertain why they were so wrinkled, and tightened the string tie at the waist. "Yeah, yes." She sat up and pivoted on the couch to lean into the back.

"Thank you. What's going on?"

"The temporary paralysis from the botulism toxin injection was fortunately just that—temporary. She has full sensation to all extremities, and she has regained all motor function. There is tiny asymmetry to the facial muscles. I don't think anyone other than your aunt will notice any difference between the two sides of her face."

"That's good to hear. She has been so concerned."

"She is indeed a beautiful woman, and no way does she appear her age. You're lucky to have such great genes to draw from."

"We're not blood relation, although I appreciate—"

"I asked Phoebe to return to see me in three months and to continue her PT another two weeks. She should beef up a healthy lifestyle. Better stay away from those injections from now on. There're not for everybody."

The neurologist seemed to lower his voice as though he were whispering into the phone. "Let me share some advice. If Phoebe wants to continue with the botulism injections, get somebody who knows what they are doing to administer them, like a plastic surgeon. I guess I shouldn't share this, but I've seen this scenario coming out of the Belmont Spa before." The voice even lower, quieter. "Lots of times."

"Thanks," Diana whispered, not sure why she lowered her own voice since she remained alone in the room. "I'll follow up with Aunt Phoebe. So thankful she's better. You've been great."

"No problem. She's lovely."

The call ended. Diana tossed her cell phone toward the end of the couch, drawing her legs toward her chest. "Lovely? Phoebe?"

The speaker on the wall next to the door buzzed, and a voice seeped from the front. "Dr. Bratton?"

"Yes, here."

"Ready in the OR."

"On the way!" Diana grabbed her phone and her shoes and headed out the door to surgery.

With surgery finished for the day, Diana pulled away from the hospital parking lot and completed her last dictation using her cell phone and the call-in transcription service. Metropolitan Hospital kept the old-school technology in play in case the computer server went down, and Diana knew the phone number by heart.

The lady who listened to and transcribed the dictation needed the work—Diana was certain.

No one in medical records would say anything about her step back from modern technology because she regularly schmoozed with the few holdouts in the dissolving transcription department. Two of them were her patients. Since Diana ran circles around most of the other physicians in the use of the electronic medical records system and kept up to date with her hospital documentation, her conscious was clear.

She slid her phone into the recharging bay of the BMW console as a text appeared on the display screen. "It's Brad," she said and grabbed the phone.

```
At home. Grabbed pizza. Told Kelsey ok
to eat dinner with Nikki. Study over
there too.
```

Kelsey's friend Nikki lived in the same neighborhood, a few blocks over.

"Good. Everything's all set at home. Got time to see about Phoebe." Diana turned at the next corner and fought to keep her speed down. She realized she'd rather be on the couch at home watching TV rather than running an errand for family or otherwise. "My life: it's either Brad or Aunt Phoebe if not Kelsey."

Diana found Phoebe in her bedroom. She stood in front of a full-length mirror, tilted forward into her reflection as she ran her fingers down the sides of her face. Nearer the eyes she stretched the skin upward and outward, the same along the center of her neck, upward toward the chin.

"Planning the next procedure or have you seen the light?" Diana said and entered the bedroom. "Your front door was unlocked. You should be careful about that. And it's good to see you standing upright and not in a wheelchair."

"Thank you. What a nice thing to say." Phoebe turned to the side and straightened her posture, still studying her image in the mirror. She patted her stomach. "I've been thinking about getting some lower body work done. Kelsey showed me how to follow the best doctors on Instagram. Lots of before and after pictures and videos."

Diana admired the spacious bedroom, past a pair of overstuffed chairs upholstered in a floral pattern and positioned in front of three floor-to-ceiling windows. The last of the late afternoon sun filtered through the window drapery. Phoebe's king-sized bed stood at the opposite wall, not a wrinkle in the bedspread or dust ruffle. Satiny, powder-blue pillows overlay the fluffy pillows at the head. A gold-painted sunburst medallion mounted on the wall above the bed stretched the width of the padded, upholstered headboard—also satin. The closet and the adjoining bathroom were off to the left. Phoebe kept her first computer in that closet.

You've redecorated since I was over here last," Diana said. "But then we were at the kitchen table."

"Good eye, Diana. You and Brad might want to take my lead and spruce your place up here and there."

"Our house is fine, thank you. As it is, Brad and I are barely home enough to enjoy it. And Kelsey could care less."

Phoebe turned back into the mirror. She placed her hands on her hips before moving her hands up and down her buttocks, briefly cupping them. "I've got to get rid of this flab."

Diana dropped into one of the chairs in front of the bedroom windows. "You have barely recovered from your trip to the Belmont Spa, and now you're ready to get something else done? Give it a rest, Aunt Phoebe."

"My neurologist says I'm fully recovered from those injections in my face. Dr. Stewart says what happened in my case is uncommon. Let's see." Phoebe bent closer into the mirror.

"'Very rare, in fact,' he said. That was exactly what he said, 'Very rare.'"

"What about exercise to tone things up?"

"Glad you agree that I still need work. All these years, I've doled out enough cash on exercise club memberships and private spin and palates classes—plus all those massages and the tips—to cover more than one surgical procedure," Phoebe countered. "I know I'm right because I've priced lipo and a breast lift."

"You better recheck your math on that," Diana said. She sank lower in the comfortable chair.

Phoebe pivoted from in front of the mirror and in several large steps stood over Diana. "I didn't ask you opinion about going to the Belmont Spa, partly because I'm a grown woman nearly twice your age and didn't think I needed permission and partly because I was afraid you would talk me out of getting the injections in the first place," Phoebe said. "Diana, you have to admit it. My face was horribly wrinkled."

"Admit it? I'll admit that once you get your mind set on something, there's no holding you back." Diana slipped out of the chair and moved around and away from Phoebe.

Phoebe returned to the mirror for another whole-body assessment, then stepped to her closet. "Money's not an issue, Diana. I guess you know that," she called from inside the space. "And I've got to find an outfit to wear."

Diana could hear Phoebe's frantic searching through an infinite string of clothes on hangers, metal hangers screeching against metal rods. "I know what I can get you for Christmas," Diana said loud enough for Phoebe to hear from the closet. "Some of those velvet hangers—a lot quieter."

A new outfit appeared at the opening of Phoebe's closet. "I've decided to return this thing. Makes my arms look fat." She dropped the hanger and garment to her waist and vanished back into the closet.

"If you want, my office will get you an appointment with a plastic surgeon, someone who will shoot straight with you."

Phoebe next emerged from her closet in an outfit Diana remembered from last spring, a classy dress purchased to wear to the final round of a statewide bridge tournament capped off by a cocktail party. At the time, Phoebe somehow persuaded Diana into completing a two-woman local shopping trip that resulted in Diana buying a few things for herself and Kelsey.

"Recycling that old thing?" Diana said. "Or should I say that *pricey* old thing."

Phoebe glided about her bedroom in her bare feet. She worked her way between the two chairs in front of the windows, brushing by Diana, over to the door into the hall before stopping to pose in the opening. "I've never been much on buying what they like to call *timeless outfits*, but the salesperson at Maison Weiss was on her mark. This will work through several seasons."

Phoebe fanned the dress at her thighs and twirled inside the door frame. The fabric pulled at her waist, and she pointed. "Get an eyeful." She stared in Diana's direction. "I know. I know. You don't have to say it. *Disgusting!*"

"You are magnificent. Most women—"

"Most women my age wouldn't even try. Is that what you mean to say?" Phoebe took another twirl and waltzed to the mirror.

"I can only hope for a crumb of that magnificence and that figure," Diana said, "when the time comes."

"Ridiculous, Diana. The time is now." Phoebe said. "I can barely breathe in this thing! What a difference a year can make. Things sag and pop out so."

"Not so for everyone." Diana thought of Voncelle Wallace. Somewhere between Phoebe's and Diana's ages, and unlike Phoebe and Diana, Voncelle Wallace had toned calves and a much tighter waist than either woman. Voncelle, sans surgical scrub suit and Hoka tennis shoes of standard work attire, wore stylish high heels at evening parties and her slim, sculptured arms and legs easily pulled off wearing sleeveless blouses and short skirts.

"She's in awesome shape—must hit the gym every chance she gets. Where does she get the time?" Diana muttered.

"Who are you talking about, Diana?"

"No child at home to cook for. And now no husband."

Phoebe stepped away from the hall toward Diana. "That doctor, the other lady surgeon in your group, she must be the woman you're grumbling about."

Diana thought through the events of the recent Christmas party. "She's more fun to be around outside of the office."

Voncelle spearheaded the recent Christmas party planning committee and personally hired the disc jockey whose trademark was a playlist compiled from texts sent across the room by live partygoers. Diana had observed Voncelle work tirelessly to send '80s titles to the playlist and then moonwalk her way across the dancefloor. After another drink, she led a cluster of lab technicians and nurses through the shuffle—her students, a group more than ten years her junior—and all while her husband told jokes to a receptive group at the bar.

"She got a workout that night," Diana said. "Slammed all the youngsters."

"What's the woman's name? *Rochelle?*"

Phoebe did carry the dress well, and it did not pull at the waist. All she needed was a diamond necklace and good heels. Diana wished she could better scrutinize Wallace's house and her jewelry.

"It's *Voncelle*. Voncelle Wallace. Not *Rochelle*."

Phoebe took the chair next to Diana. "Do you like this Dr. Voncelle Wallace?"

Diana's mind left the Christmas Party and landed in that afternoon at the Wallace home with her holding a culinary sympathy gift. The more grateful than grief-stricken Voncelle seemed to enjoy the food. "Like Voncelle Wallace?" Diana remembered the gun cabinet in the library, spotted on the way to the restroom and attributed by Voncelle to Chuck's collection.

"I thought I liked her," Diana answered. "Now I'm not so sure."

"How can you be sure?"

"That's what I need to find out. I better head home."

Diana backed out of Phoebe's driveway. So much had happened in the last few weeks. Martin needed to make sense of all this for her, starting with the guy in the clinic garage and on that roof. She thought about a text. *No, I'll call.*

Key Martin answered before she turned to straighten her car

toward home. "Come by the department tomorrow if you have time," he said.

# Chapter 21

Key Martin's personal office as JPD chief of police had not changed except for the crutches leaning askew in the corner—one propped against the wall, the other wedged inside the open space near the top of the other. The same dust-covered, sagging bookcases filled the walls, and several empty, coffee-stained Styrofoam cups littered the area. Diana stood before the suspect and arrest board lined with photographs.

She stepped closer and singled out the guy who held a gun on her across the street from where Chuck Wallace was shot, his voice and touch identical to that in the clinic garage. Diana stared into his smug expression and studied the facial features, her first good look at him.

"His name is Dillon Garnett. Not sure when the judge will grant bail," Martin said. "Assault with a deadly weapon won't come cheap."

"Maybe Uncle Roy will come through with the cash," Diana said under her breath, still studying the board while Martin thumbed through papers on his desk.

"You say something, Doctor Bratton?"

She tapped Dillion Garnett's mug shot with her forefinger. She could still feel the gun against her and his hands on her shoulders. "What happens went they let this guy out? Should I be worried?"

"We'll keep tabs on him. You'll be fine. Your daughter too."

"That night in the garage this lunatic told me one of my patients was his uncle and that the uncle was crazy." Diana studied the picture. "You know, I see the resemblance."

Martin fought the clunky orthopedic boot that held his broken ankle in place and stood as though he were twenty years older, bracing himself against the front edge of his desk. "He hasn't said much about why he was hanging around my ex-wife's real estate listing."

"Garnett trailed me there and told me so." Diana shrugged. "I'm not sure what else he wanted out of me. If the guy's so great at hacking into computer programs, he'd know I kept my promise and got his *crazy* uncle into therapy," Diana said. "It's amazing what a person will agree to do at gunpoint."

The coffee maker stared back at Martin. He moved his foot and boot a few inches in that direction, then seemed to think better of it and dropped back into his chair.

Diana said, "Stay put. I'll get the coffee for you and recycle one of these cups."

"'Preciate that," Chief Martin said.

Diana picked the nearest used Styrofoam cup and verified it as empty. "I'll take the last clean cup by the machine for myself."

Martin waited for Diana to pour both cups from his coffee maker. She served his to him along with a packet of sugar and a wooden stirrer.

"No artificial sweetener?"

"Not around here." Martin grinned.

"It's about time I learned to drink it black," Diana said and quietly sipped the hot liquid. It was strong.

Martin ripped open the packet of sugar and stirred in the entire contents. He enjoyed the swirl and dissolve of the granules inside the cup, then drank with a long, loud *slurp*. "We questioned all the guys on the walk that night. Most were helpful, a few standoffish to me and my police unit. They seemed upset that we showed up at their places of business in the middle of the day."

"I can see that," Diana said. "Been there."

Key Martin nodded. "I'll own up to that." His next loud *slurp* topped the first. "Yeah, I know. Around here we just try to do our jobs." He took only a small sip and tilted his head toward the suspect picture board. "Interesting thing is that Dillon Garnett's uncle was on the walk that night. Man's name is Roy Garnett."

"Yep, you said it. I didn't say my patient's name."

"Doc, I don't think you need to worry about HIPPA in this case, not with what you've been through."

"The guy in the garage—Roy Garnett is his uncle. That's what he told me. What's this all about?"

"Trying hard to put it together. I need you to help me figure it out," Martin answered.

Diana pulled the nearest cheap, uncomfortable chair closer, wiped the seat with her hand, and sat. "He told me he broke into the uncle's electronic medical record and that his uncle was crazy. Talked about Garnett murdering his own sister. I think the sister is Dillon Garnett's mother," she said. "I wonder if Uncle Roy Garnett was the target instead of Chuck Wallace?"

"Then from what the men told me about the layout of the stroll that night, the guy was a lousy shot," Martin said. "Roy Garnett was nowhere near Chuck Wallace."

Diana stopped short of sharing his theory that Voncelle Wallace was the shooter.

*No way that's right. Dillon Garnett is on track about one thing. Uncle Roy is mental.* This was not a scheduled day in the OR, and her patient clinic schedule started in about a half hour. "I need to head to work," she said.

"Hold on a minute please, Dr. Bratton. Your buddy in the garage and at the house that night with the ladder doesn't legally own a gun, if you believe the ATF. The one we recovered at the scene had the serial number scratched off. Likely stolen, of course."

"Wonder why he didn't hold on to mine after jumping me in the clinic garage?" Diana asked.

"Might have panicked. Thought the cops were close."

"By the way, I'm glad your guys found it across the street from my office. Thank 'em for me, please."

"Already did," Martin said. "And they said you're welcome."

Diana shot a quick smile and left Martin's office. She dropped her empty coffee cup in the hall trash.

The drive from downtown Jackson north on I-55 to Diana's surgery clinic took no more than fifteen to twenty minutes. Diana was grateful for the light traffic on the interstate and today's shorter drive time. Before her exit, she passed the golf course at Lefleur's Bluff to the right where Garnett claimed he played golf with Voncelle's second deceased husband, Chuck Wallace.

*Claimed?* she thought and shook her head clear. *Martin's starting to rub off on me.*

Diana took the exit and selected her favorite jazz channel on the console. Instead, Brooks & Dunn filled the interior of her car. Brad had driven yesterday to fill her tank at the gas station. "Brad! Thanks for the errand but stop resetting my channels!"

She smiled and thought about Brad lying on the couch the other night in front of the TV and what they did during several commercials. Diana twirled the control knob to the tail end of a Nicole Zuraitis song. The channel shifted into a selection from Miles Davis, and Diana hummed along until Terri Lyne Carrington took over.

The music bounced around Diana's head all afternoon through a full schedule of patients. She fought worry about the guy who stalked her and threatened her life twice and about his uncle, who likely was untrustworthy. She considered the twice widowed Voncelle and her situation and if she could trust Voncelle moving forward. Kelsey would want supper tonight after cheerleading practice, and her husband would want her in bed.

*I need to get away from this. I want to go home.*

Yet the day was not over.

Diana and her assistant scheduled three new surgeries and admitted two elderly women to the hospital. She spent a half hour talking to the ladies' families and an hour inputting the day's documentation into the computer.

"Good night, Mallory," Diana said on her way out the back door.

She ignored any concern about the empty garage, unlocked her car, and streamed more jazz on the way home. The kitchen light was visible from the street. "Kelsey—doing homework. That's good."

"Mom? Home early," her daughter said without glancing up from her laptop. "Got this essay due tomorrow. What's for supper?"

"Didn't call anything into to our personal chef on the way home," Diana answered. "I should have used the app."

"Ha ha." Kelsey kept typing. "If Brad's the personal chef around here, we'll starve. Haven't you've figured that out by now?" The teenager smiled and darted her eyes at her mother as she kept working. "I guess there're other things you like about him."

"You're right, and it's not his help around the kitchen," Diana said. She dropped her bag on the kitchen table.

Kelsey's fingers came to a grinding halt on her laptop keyboard. "We should change the subject. You know I already know about that stuff. Girls at school talk."

"My advice is to stay away from *that stuff*," Diana said, "for as long as you can." She opened the kitchen pantry and scanned the sparse selection: mostly dry cereal, a few jars of homemade jams and jellies given to her by patients, and several varieties of barbeque sauce.

A peek into the freezer found a desirable frozen pizza from a trip to the grocery store a month ago and a chicken casserole dish compliments of another patient. Since the printed label on the covering of the frozen casserole called for thawing and a forty-five-minute bake time in a preheated oven, the pizza won. Diana set the temperature on the oven and tore open the thin cardboard packaging.

"I agree with your choice. I already scoped out the freezer," Kelsey said.

"Could've at least turned on the oven. Don't ya think?" Diana ripped away the plastic covering, withdrew a baking sheet from a cabinet, and set the pie and baking sheet on the kitchen counter before tossing the pizza box in the trash.

"Didn't want to slow progress on this essay any more than I had to," Kelsey answered. "My language arts teacher says once the creative juices start flowing with your masterpiece you can't lose focus. You must block out the distractions and let your heart take over." Her speed on the keyboard picked up.

Once the oven pre-heated to 425 degrees, Diana removed the frozen pizza from its packaging and per cooking instructions placed it directly on the middle rack. She emptied the dishwasher and reloaded it with dirties from the sink and found time to wipe off the kitchen counter and put ice in the water glasses—all before the oven timer set to twenty-two minutes chimed.

Almost simultaneously, Brad appeared in the kitchen. "Smelled this all the way to the den." He put his arms around Diana's waist and stroked his nose near her neck in a pretend sniff.

"If you like sweat, hand scrub sanitizer from surgery, and pepperoni with cheese, I've got it all," Diana said. "Wait five and let the pizza cool. I'm going to get out of these scrubs. Kelsey, mind setting the table? And please show Brad how to help."

Diana slipped free of her husband and headed for the bedroom to change.

"Gee, Brad," Kelsey said. "You need to do something about that. Guys at school say they know how to get chicks to chill."

"Stop listening to what guys say at school."

"You and mom always give the same advice. Like an old married couple."

Brad found a pizza cutter in a drawer and sliced the pie into eight nearly equal-sized pieces. He filled the glasses with cold bottled water. Kelsey added the paper dinner napkins. Brad stood back and admired the finished product. "We make a winning team, Kels."

He dug vanilla ice cream out of the freezer and managed to serve several tablespoons each into glass bowls he found in a cabinet. He grabbed teaspoons at the last minute.

"I finished my essay about the time the pizza was done. Nice job, Mom. And the ice cream was over the top, Brad," Kelsey said as they finished dessert. "I'm gonna head upstairs to my room. Got a ton of math and science homework too." She took her dishes to the sink, except for the water glass. "See y'all in the morning."

Brad helped Diana finish reloading the dishwasher before he returned to the den television. "Cop show? Or are you gettin' enough of that at work," he said.

She sank into the couch, and Brad followed. He grabbed the remote, propped his feet on the coffee table, and scrolled through the channels.

"I should have poured us a glass of wine," Brad said.

"I'm good for now," Diana said. "You go ahead."

"I'll pass too. Ate too much ice cream." Brad swapped to another streaming service and stopped at one of the shows. "Didn't know they had another season out. How about this?"

"I did talk with Key Martin today," Diana said, showing no interest in the modern-day western series. "Had some free time this morning and went by his office."

"Couldn't you find anything more interesting to do with your time off?"

"You mean like shopping or tennis? You knew you weren't getting that when you found me. And, hey! Don't you want to know more about the creep who's threatened your wife twice?" She ribbed Brad hard.

"Hold on!" He coughed and grabbed the side of his chest.

"Martin seemed to enjoy pointing out that you were at the scene of another murder, like you were a common thread to all this."

Brad continued to massage his sore ribs. "That guy's deranged—stumbles through investigations. His detective did question me like he did everyone else out walking that night, but I thought later about something that may or may not be important to the case."

"Since you think I'm all wrapped up in detective work, try it out on me."

"Chuck was directly behind me on the walk and in the middle

of talking football when his cell rang. I remember he told me the guys took the hour walk serious and that meant cell phones cut off or at lease set to silent. So I was surprised he took a call."

"Who was it?"

"Said it must be his wife and acted annoyed. He checked the phone and backed away from the group. Next time we saw Chuck Wallace, we were giving him CPR."

"It was an overseas call—Spain. A medical investment group he was doing business with."

Brad sat up straight on the couch. "How the hell do you know that? There's been nothing on the news."

Diana grinned and tilted her head to the side. "Key Martin."

"The chief of police shared that kind of intel with you?"

Diana moved to backhand Brad again in his side. Though suspected to be much softer this time, he saw it coming and slid quickly out of the way to the far side of the couch. "You said I was deep into cop stuff. In fact, I might start carrying."

Brad scooted back toward Diana. "I'll keep that in mind."

"Cell phone records are central to a murder investigation," Diana said. "That's obvious from all the TV dramas."

Brad gestured toward the television monitor. The actor dressed in chaps, spurs, and cowboy hat pushed another character dressed the same backwards off a cliff. "Cell phone doesn't seem that important on this show," he snickered. "Guy doing the shoving probably ditched the SIM card."

"The Spanish guy was somebody named Garcia. His company was interested in buying the Belmont Medical Group. I guess they still are. Chuck was brokering the deal."

"I'm coming through to get a snack. Please, hands off, guys, while I'm around," Kelsey said, bounding off the bottom of the stairs into the room. "I peeked through the banister before I came down, and it was all clear."

"Smart move," Brad said.

"If I ace the Algebra II test tomorrow, it's smooth sailing from here," Kelsey said. "Y'all hold off for a least five while I raid the fridge. Then I'm out of your hair."

Brad waited a few seconds until Kelsey was deep into the kitchen. "Girl's got sense. You did good, Diana. Now, I'm ready for a glass. Pinot or chardonnay?"

The refrigerator opened and closed several times. Several cabinet doors opened and closed. The faucet ran for a few seconds. Another cabinet door shut. Kelsey ran up the stairs with a sandwich on a small plate and a can of soda in the other hand.

"How can she possibly be hungry?" Diana said. "Those carbs will catch up to her when she's in college. Took me a year and a half to lose The Freshman Fifteen."

"If I'd been around then, I would have worked it off you," Brad said. He ran his hand up her thigh. "Hold that thought while I get the wine. My choice." Brad pushed off the couch and winked at Diana.

"You border on being corny," she said, returning the wink. "Pinot Grigio works for me—a generous pour, as they say, and hurry up."

The glasses arrived in record time and bordered on overflow.

"Thanks," Diana said. She softly kissed Brad on the lips and rubbed his chest. "Sorry about the punches tonight."

"Don't mention it," Brad said and took a sip of his drink. "This Garcia dude—what does Martin know about him?"

"Nothing more than what's out there in cyberspace. Martin sort of tells me what he wants me to know and sometimes plays games with me. I can't see him heading overseas to question some person from Spain."

"Why don't you ask our buddy if he's had any contact at all with the Garcia."

"*Our buddy*? That's a stretch coming from you. You've never been able to stand Martin."

"Don't like his style, never have. He's no Sherlock Holmes. More of a clumsy Columbo—on a good day," Brad said.

"Key Martin must be doing something right. He's worked his up from detective to chief of police."

"No question, he's into you—no matter his pay grade."

"Thanks for the compliment." Diana's cell vibrated a text from face down on the coffee table. She put down her wine and reached for the phone.

"Neither of us is on call. Must be Phoebe," Brad said.

"It's Voncelle," Diana said.

Brad sat up straighter on the couch. "She's not on call either. What's goin' on?"

Diana read the text aloud.

```
I'm outside. Side door. Skipped doorbell.
Know it's late. Can u talk?
```

"Maybe she's having a bad moment about Chuck's death and wants to vent." Diana thought back to the pictures displayed around the Wallace home—no friends or anyone pictured with Chuck and Voncelle that could be family. "I don't think she has anyone around to talk to. I guess the church support played out."

"Why don't you let her into the kitchen. I'll make myself scarce upstairs, start us a bath. Bring your wine up with you." Brad picked up his glass and the bottle. "Oh, and tell Voncelle there are lots of therapists in town. She can afford one."

"You surgeons are all about compassion." Diana winked at Brad as he ascended the stairs. "A long bath sounds nice. I won't be long."

# Chapter 22

Diana left her wine glass on the coffee table to walk the few steps to the kitchen and through to the short hallway linking the house to the garage. She could see a feminine figure standing outside the narrow French doors, which comprised what the Realtor had described as the friend's entry. *The formal front door would have worked fine*, Diana thought. She released the latch and opened the doors.

"Voncelle? Sure. Come in."

A short porch fronted this side entrance, the outdoor security lighting in the area not much brighter than to find one's way and unlock the door. Voncelle Wallace stood out of the light, her head lowered, her face twisted slightly away.

"This is an extreme imposition, taking you away from your family tonight. I'm sure Brad is put out. And you don't get much time, as it is, to spend with Kelsey." Voncelle turned to slip away. "I'm sorry, Diana. I shouldn't have come over. I'll talk to you tomorrow."

Voncelle hesitated long enough for Diana to suggest otherwise.

"Brad's fine and Kelsey's a teenager. She could care less about being around her mother. Please come on in. We'll talk a few minutes in the kitchen."

Voncelle followed Diana through the passageway into the kitchen.

"Can I get you some water?" Diana asked. Voncelle did not answer as Diana reached for the refrigerator door and produced a small plastic bottle of water. The better lighting of the kitchen revealed an angry bruise across the dark complexion of Voncelle's right cheek.

"What happened? Were you in a wreck or something?" Diana motioned for her to sit at the breakfast table. "Want me to take a peek at this? Or get Brad? Maybe we should go to the ED, get an x-ray."

Voncelle spoke in a whisper. "No, please, please don't call Brad. And I don't need one of the interns groping me in the ED. I just need to talk. And I don't have long."

Diana glanced in the direction of the den and the stairs. She imagined Brad sipping the wine and filling the tub in the center of the master bathroom, installed to hold two adults. After about fifteen, perhaps twenty minutes, he would start to wonder.

"Who did this to you?"

Voncelle gently massaged the discolored area on her face and her swollen right eye. "Chuck represented the Belmonts in this medical practice buy-out deal with someone overseas. Ellis Belmont approached Chuck, and Chuck did the work—made the contacts for the Belmont family to cash out. He was so, so very close to closing the deal when he was shot."

Diana did not reveal her conversation with JPD about Chuck Wallace's financial business dealings. "Are you saying that Ellis Belmont did this to you? Why?"

"No, not Belmont. This guy from Spain. Name is Garcia. Hernando Garcia."

"He's here in Mississippi?"

"He showed up at my house and wanted to see some of Chuck's business records. He should have known I didn't have anything to do with that."

"You should have called the police the moment you were free of him."

"I couldn't. He threatened me." Voncelle rubbed her face again. "You see what he can do. I'm afraid, Diana."

The master bedroom was located directly over the kitchen. Diana could hear the bathtub running. Brad's glass of wine was likely empty by now.

"If you think you're good and don't need the ED, I can go along with that. But do you feel safe enough to go home?"

"Garcia drove off fast from my house, and he took Chuck's laptop with him. I hope I never have to see him again."

The faint noise of running water upstairs stopped. Diana expected a tightly towel-wrapped, dripping-wet Brad any minute in the kitchen. "I can get the police to help you. I've got the chief of police's cell."

Voncelle buried her face in her hands and sobbed. "Why has it come to this?"

Diana glanced again toward the stairs. The guest room was on the other side of the house, with a private bath attached and extra coffee maker inside the room. Voncelle would be out of the way, out of Brad's way.

"Stay here tonight. We keep the guest room ready."

"I doubt Brad wants to run a motel, especially for me."

Bringing Voncelle into the practice had been Diana's idea. Brad did not fight the hire since the surgical practice needed help. Tons of transfer patients from the Haynes Surgical Clinic crowded the books. However, from day one, Diana understood that seeing Voncelle reminded him of his nemesis, John Haynes. Brad's back stiffened, and he went quiet whenever she was around.

"Nonsense, we'd love to have you," Diana said.

"Love to have you do what?" Diana jumped at Brad's voice behind her. Voncelle took a deep breath.

Diana turned slowly around to face Brad, fully expecting him to be in the towel. To her relief, he remained fully dressed.

"The bathtub's full and waiting for us, Diana. I turned off the faucet and held off on the bubbles." Brad leaned against the nearest wall. He appeared both bored and annoyed.

Diana ignored him.

"I should go," Voncelle said. "I'm sorry. I shouldn't have interrupted your night."

"We're all one big happy family at the surgery clinic." Diana fought the urge to back away and defer the interaction to Brad. "At least, that's what we always say," she said. "For now, you're staying in the guest room—for as long as you need."

"Is anybody gonna tell me what's going down here. Room and board is not part of our clinic physician employment agreement," Brad said. He shifted his stance and stared at Voncelle and the bruised eye. "Von, what's going on with the new vibe?"

"Brad," Diana said. "Not funny."

"It's fine. I certainly owe an explanation. This guy showed up at my house. He was Chuck's business associate and wanted to see Chuck's office records. He asked me questions about the business that I would have no way of knowing. I was always too busy with my own work."

"I can see that," Brad said. "Even though Diana and I work down the hall from each other, we still go our separate ways during the workday."

"Secrets between us aren't a big deal," Diana said, "at least from my end." She eye-balled Brad. "Any comment, Babe?"

"Open book here, Sweetie, like always." Brad winked at Diana and flashed a wide smile. "It's getting late guys."

Voncelle remained quiet for only seconds. To Diana it seemed much longer.

"I am afraid to go home." Voncelle touched her bruised face. "Garcia got angry when I couldn't tell him what he wanted to know. He might come back."

"We'll do what we can to help," Brad said. "The guest room is all yours, Voncelle. I shouldn't have been such a jerk before." He turned slowly for the stairs. "By the way, from what little I know about Chuck, he would have beat the crap out of any guy who showed up at his house, snooped into his business records, and pushed his wife around."

Voncelle wiped away a tear. "Chuck's bad luck—now my bad luck—is that he's not around to put together the pieces. I don't know whom to trust, except the two or you. I realize I should have called the police tonight, but I didn't want to cause a scene in the neighborhood. There's already been so much."

"You're sure correct about that." Diana searched the kitchen for a box of tissues she knew did not exist and grabbed a paper cocktail napkin from a cabinet. "I'll show you to the guest room down the hall."

"Stay as long as you need to," Brad said and headed toward the stairs. "I got first case tomorrow at Metropolitan, and no telling how many more to follow. I'll calling it a night."

Diana sensed tension behind his smile this time. The miniature potted plant that crowned the base of the banister trembled under Brad's footsteps.

Voncelle whispered, "No matter what Brad says, it's obvious he's not very happy about this. I should go."

"Brad wants you to stay. He said so. We both want you here," Diana said.

"Follow me. It's down the hall."

The seldom used guest room was painted a pale yellow. Rather than crowd the two girls in Kelsey's room, Diana put one of her friends there for a long weekend while the girl's parents took a short wedding anniversary trip. To keep the room fresh, Diana had the housecleaning service change the sheets and towels every month.

"It's quiet on this end of the house. Bathroom is through the door beyond the closet. There's a basket of guest toiletries on the counter by the sink. That expensive decorator a patient recommended suggested it," Diana said.

"I can't tell you how much I appreciate this."

"Forget it, Von. What are partners for? Make yourself at home. The coffee maker in the corner is another extra that decorator recommended. There's bottled water in the cabinet below."

Diana shut the door quietly behind her.

Voncelle slid her cell from her pocket. She decided the power would last until the morning. Besides, asking for a charger would have been a stretch. She closed the door to the bedroom, slipped into the bathroom, and ran the water in the sink.

A male voice answered the call.

"I'm here," Voncelle said. "And they love me. See what you can do about transferring all of Chuck's accounts to me."

"Won't be hard to do," Garcia responded.

Unlike Brad's OR schedule the next morning, Diana was free until clinic started at 8:30. The kitchen remained quiet after Kelsey left at seven for last minute cheerleader practice. From the crumb-and-jelly stained knife on the counter, she had toasted a bagel and dressed it with Georgia-peach and jalapeño jelly, compliments of a thankful patient from last week.

Diana tilted an ear toward the hall leading to the guestroom—all quiet. She doubted Voncelle would use the coffee maker in the room and poured two cups. *Where is that fancy miniature silver tray Phoebe gave me for Christmas last year?*

She found the tray in a cabinet above the refrigerator and set Voncelle's cup of coffee in the center. Instead of Kelsey's lead with bagels and jelly, she decided to go simple, to go easy. *Sweetener? A spoon?* Diana found a pod of creamer and two packets of artificial sweetener in the pantry and set them with a small spoon atop the folded paper napkin displayed on the tray. Diana admired her work and smiled. *Yes. Perfect. Aunt Phoebe would approve.* She picked up the tray by the handles with plans to deliver it to the guestroom.

"Diana, I have been such a nuisance," came from behind her.

Diana jumped and the tray and cup rattled. She managed to return it to the counter without a spill or break. "Voncelle, I was headed in with room service."

Dressed in the same clothes as the night before, though wrinkled,

Voncelle stood slightly bent at the waist with eye make-up smeared and eyes bloodshot. "I tossed and turned all night. My life's a mess."

"Brad and I want to help. We told you so last night."

"And considering all the trouble you went to this morning .... You guys are fantastic. And I've always known that." Voncelle gestured toward the coffee tray. "I took you up on the coffee maker in the guestroom. It works great. I'm good with caffeine."

"You do need to go to the police," Diana said. "I have contacts at JPD who can help you sort this out."

Voncelle moved away a few steps toward the door. "I admit I overacted, pushed our friendship by showing up and putting you and Brad out. Tomorrow I'll call my estate lawyer and get advice about what to do next. I just hope Brad doesn't fire me."

"Believe me," Diana said. "That's not gonna happen." She sipped her coffee. "Has this Garcia guy left town?"

"I have no idea. I'll get the lawyer to figure it out." Voncelle walked toward the side door. "I'm too rattled for work today. I texted my nurse and secretary last night and told them I was under the weather and to clear my patient schedule, first thing. I didn't have surgery posted in the OR, so I'm good there. I promise I'll be back to full speed at the office soon.

"Voncelle, you have more to think about than work."

"I'll call our office manager this morning and straighten out all my schedules. Don't worry. I'll be back on the financial books in no time, paying overhead for the practice—getting those paying patients and surgeries on the books. Please tell Brad not to worry about me."

Diana observed her walk from the door to the car parked at the curb. "I'm going to the police even if you don't," Diana called out.

The driver's door slammed shut and the vehicle pulled away quickly, reaching the intersection and stop sign in mere seconds and turning onto the busy main street.

"Martin's really gonna like this one," Diana said.

# Chapter 23

Phoebe groaned and turned over in bed.

"A heads-up would've been nice, although I guess I saw this coming," Diana said. She examined Phoebe's bandages. "And thank goodness Kelsey passed her driver's test and can get herself to and from school. You're off carpool team while you recover."

"I confess. Giving her the new Jeep was premeditated."

"Not many sixteen-year-olds get that kind of birthday present."

"Nonsense, Diana. I've seen what those girls in the grade above drive—not to mention, the automotive decadence of the older girls in Kelsey's class. I've hung around her school much more than you have."

Diana offered Phoebe a glass of water and an oxycodone tablet. "It's been four hours, almost five."

Phoebe swallowed and offered a weak smile. "I guess you noticed that I sprang for Kelsey's first year of car insurance. Again, glad to do it. That premium was more than my parents paid to send me to Ole Miss in the late sixties."

"Thanks for all of it. Kelsey loves you."

"Don't mention it," Phoebe said. She took another sip of water. "I love her too—and you—and Brad—and I could die for a Coke Zero."

"I'll pick-up some at Kroger. They don't carry that at Whole Foods."

"My cute plastic surgeon told me to walk around every two hours." Phoebe uncrossed her legs. "Totally unrealistic. That's such a chore."

"He wants to prevent complications, like venous blood clots," Diana said. "Since you had surgery to your face, that's unlikely."

"I can always count on you to make it sound simple, Diana. No—I don't mean simple. I mean—make things make sense."

"You're easy to impress."

"Making an impression is what it's all about." Phoebe grabbed her hand mirror. "I thought I would start with the top and move south since injections to blur wrinkles or tighten skin didn't work out well for me. Now I'm injection free."

Diana picked through the plastic pill bottles on the bedside. "Injection free? Possibly. Narcotic free? I don't think so."

"What?" Phoebe said. She reached across the bedside table into the assortment of medications. "Some are for my blood pressure, like these." She fumbled with the pill bottles as they scattered. "Nope—these are antibiotics. And these are vitamins." Another try came up correct. "Good. Here we go."

Phoebe twisted off the cap and tapped another tablet of oxycodone into her palm. "They told me I could take two if needed." She swallowed the extra tablet dry and tried to smile. "And I need two now."

"I'll open the fridge and see what else you need," Diana mumbled. "Food, maybe?" She scrolled through her phone contacts for the number to a grocery delivery service, then noticed the texts from her daughter and the office and shook her head. No word from Brad. "I guess my husband can take care of himself."

"Is Brad here?" Phoebe asked and slowly fell back into her oversized pillow. "I hope he is." Her eyes drifted shut.

"I'll be in the kitchen." Diana began to type in the grocery order on the phone app and walked away. She added Kelsey's favorite breakfast cereal to take back home with her and an order of sushi along with a seasoned baked chicken from the store's deli.

"Don't forget the Coke Zero." Phoebe stood weakly propped against the door frame to the kitchen. "Add an order of California rolls, won't you?"

"I thought you had dozed off, and how can you stand with all the drugs in you?" Diana continued to work on her phone. "And I'm a step ahead with the deli order." She hit *Send* and a dollar amount populated the order total box on the screen. "I've got your credit card stored in my PayFriends account, so it's not a surprise I'm charging everything to you."

"Go ahead. My niece is a doctor. I should be able to afford it."

A text from Brad popped onto Diana's phone.

Call me

She finished the food and beverage purchase and a link to the email receipt came next. "Brad needs me to call him. I'm going to step out on the porch." She punched in Brad's number. "What's up? My fellow in the ICU coding again?"

"Police found Garcia."

"The MO is the same as your buddy Chuck Wallace," Martin said. "Except he was shot twice. A bullet entered his gut and head."

"Trauma and neuro did all they could," Brad said.

"Now that I think about it, this is the first time you've invited us both down to your office, Martin," Diana said.

"Might be your fault, Dr. Bratton. You called me about your friend, your surgical partner. Said she was accosted or threatened by some joker with a Spanish name, a business associate of her deceased husband. And then, low and behold, told me it was Chuck Wallace's widow."

"Then I call Diana about Garcia being shot and she follows-up with you," Brad said and tipped his cup of coffee toward Key Martin. "Nice detective work on my wife's behalf, wouldn't you say? You oughta put her on your payroll. We could use the extra cash." Brad took a long sip. "Have you seen the new decorator she hired for our house?"

Diana smiled and finished the bottled water. "Smart guy. Part of the reason I married him. And I cancelled the appointment with that new decorator."

Chief Martin tapped a few keys on his laptop and an image appeared on the flat screen monitor mounted on the wall opposite his evidence board. "Another improvement since you came downtown, Dr. Bratton."

A concealed weapons permit issued by the state of Mississippi filled the screen, similar to the appearance of a driver's permit. A smiling Voncelle Wallace in a bad-day hairdo appeared in the upper left-hand corner. "Dr. Wallace completed firearms training at a commercial shooting academy out in Rankin County. The outfit helps facilitate getting the license although at this time permits are not required to purchase or carry firearms in Mississippi. Just don't get caught carrying in a school or a private business that does not allow it."

"Big industry. I've encouraged Diana to take one of those courses since we do a lot of work after hours."

"Seems that Dr. Wallace went through with it," Martin said. "And I talked to the instructor. She said Wallace caught on how to handle and shoot a handgun real quick."

Diana stepped closer to the monitor and the image of Voncelle's gun permit. "When did she do all that, the class and the license?"

"About six weeks before her husband's death, and I see no record of a weapon's purchase, not even a background check. Private gun sales are subject to background investigations too."

Brad's thoughts flashed back to the night Chuck Wallace was shot. His on-site CPR, assisted by a group of guys who stood around wringing their hands, established a pulse without ultimately saving Wallace's life. "Is there any way we—I mean you—could talk to Voncelle's instructor and see what she was after? Like was it all about personal protection with a handgun? Any instructions on long-range rifle shooting?"

"Brad? What are you getting at?"

"We never knew much about Voncelle Wallace, Diana. We hired her because she needed a job after they put her criminal surgeon boss away, and we were desperate for another body to take calls.

And I doubt John Haynes vetted her before his hire. He wouldn't have wanted anyone asking questions about his background."

"You think Voncelle climbed up on the roof of an empty house and shot her husband while he was out walking in a neighborhood, then did the same with one of his business associates?"

Brad spotted Martin's grin as though he were enjoying the show. "Come on, Diana. You said that Voncelle acted sort of strange when you went by her house after Chuck was killed. You even mentioned the rifles in the library."

"What rifles?" Martin asked. He sat up straight in his chair. His booted foot hit the inside of his desk again. "I gotta get this sorry thing off!"

"I went by Voncelle's house after Chuck died. Took food over. I had never visited her at home, and I needed to use the restroom. It was off a room down the hall she called Chuck's library. A gun cabinet stood against the wall between the corner and a line of bookcases with medical texts, high school and college yearbooks, and a collection of novels."

"My detective and I were by the house the next day. To interview the grieving widow is standard procedure. We told her we had his cell phone, and she shared his sign-in info. I didn't tell her we had already opened it up with facial recognition."

"You found the rifles?" Brad asked.

"We didn't have a search warrant, no reason to suspect the need for one. We only asked if we could take a tour. I entered the same room you're talking about. I saw no gun cabinet."

"I don't understand. It was there in the corner to the right," Diana said.

"Detective Thomas and I spent several minutes in that room. He's the guy on the roof that night with you and me—over at my ex's real estate listing."

"Got it," Diana said.

"When Dr. Wallace told me it was the library or her late-husband's study, I thought we might get some insight. I flipped through those college yearbooks you mentioned. I guess the doctor thought we were spending too much time in there, so she walked in on us. By then, I had moved onto Chuck Wallace's desk, and she watched me look through the drawers. No personal notes, only pens and writing tablets, things like that. We talked about the art on the wall. A crazy painting hung near the corner—like the artist had flicked a loaded paintbrush toward the canvass and changed colors from time to time."

"Are you talking about the corner of the room after the line of bookcases?" Diana asked.

"Yes."

"That's where the gun cabinet was."

"Makes sense. I thought the picture, the painting, seemed out of place in the room. I guess she moved the gun cabinet after you went over to her house," Martin said.

Brad shook his head and ran his fingers through his hair. "Why did we let this woman into our surgical practice?" He slid slumped into a chair.

"Stay focused, Brad," Diana said. "That gun cabinet was packed full, all solid wood and appeared heavy. Wouldn't have been easy to move." She turned toward Martin. "Did you notice any scuff marks on the floor or faded areas on the wallpaper surrounding the painting?"

"Detective Thomas didn't put anything like that in the report, and nothing comes to mind. No surprise—I'm no interior decorator," Martin answered. "Ask any of my ex-wives. *An interior slob* would be the response, with a few f-bombs thrown in."

Brad and Diana glanced at each other. Diana smirked. "Can you tell us anything about your investigation into Garcia's shooting?" Brad asked. "More than what we'll see in the news?"

"All privileged, Doc. At least for right now. Of course, we made a connection between Garcia and Dr. Voncelle Wallace from what y'all told me. Department investigators are contacting his overseas real estate firm and next-of-kin. There is a wife. She worked with him."

"Then Voncelle knows we've talked to you, that we told you about her coming over to our house, frightened," Diana said.

"Not necessarily unless someone from the overseas outfit has already contacted her."

"I didn't see Voncelle yesterday. She has slowly eased back into full time work after Chuck's death but is not quite there yet."

"I passed her briefly in the hall of the hospital," Brad said. "She didn't mention Garcia. I assumed she knew what I knew—that neuro thought Garcia would survive the head wound, and GI trauma thought the liver laceration repair was a success despite the massive blood loss. He lost fifteen inches of bowel and had a functioning colostomy in place. The team was surprised when he coded in PACU."

"What about the tapes from the hospital security cameras, Brad?" Diana asked.

"Why would I know anything about that?"

"Chuck survived his shooting long enough to undergo surgery, and the same thing happened with Garcia."

"Good point, Dr. Bratton," Martin said. "I'm going to ask the judge in the morning to issue an order blocking the hospital from erasing any of the security tapes. It's standard procedure for most businesses to erase tapes after a month or so and tape over them, so we've got time. I'll do it tomorrow. There's no need to wait."

The door to Martin's office swung open. His secretary spoke out of breath. "There's this Spanish lady in the lobby demanding to see you, Chief. I told her you were with someone. She is very persistent and is disrupting the work in the front office. I tried to—"

An attractive tall slender woman with dark hair and complexion pushed past her into the office. The woman spoke in a thick Spanish accent. "My name is Lucinda Garcia. I have flown all night to get here, and I demand to know what happened to my husband!"

# Chapter 24

Dr. Sidney Eleanor Belmont afternoon off was Wednesday, time to squeeze in personal business, shopping, or trips to the hair salon. Since shopping and getting her hair done were not priorities, and never had been, managing business arrangements were paramount. She smiled over how she handled herself during her freshly completed meeting with Pritchett, Malone, and Tudor.

*Ellis and Miles think I'm a blooming airhead.* Sidney spotted her reflection in the glass of the revolving doors as she exited the four-story stone and mirrored building. *Do I look like an airhead, a cheap bubble head?*

She turned to admire the two-acre or more sized pond that affronted one side of the office building, complete with a bald cypress interlacing the center of the water as though it naturally grew there. *I remember this place as a cow pasture.* Sidney pointed her fob to unlock the door of her Lexus in the adjacent, almost empty parking lot. Her cell phone rang.

"Sidney, it's Benjamin Pritchett. I hope its proper to call you *Sidney* instead of *Dr. Belmont*, since we've met several times. I hope I'm not being too forward."

Sidney stopped at a raised planter constructed of crushed rock and mortar and filled with ornamental fountain grass that moved in the light breeze. Beside her, she set the booklet of printed documents presented to her and discussed at the meeting inside. "Of course, *Sidney* is fine, but we concluded our meeting. Is there a problem?"

"Not to worry. Not a problem at all. I wanted to speak personally to you for a second—without the others. I had hoped to catch you before you made it to the elevators. Is it acceptable that we speak over the phone while the subject is fresh?"

Sidney checked the vacant lobby through the glass doors and studied the parking lot separately. No one approached—all quiet. Her car waited unlocked. Nevertheless, she decided to take a seat on the short wall next to the planter. Only two other cars remained in the lot and from this distance both appeared empty. "Sure, I have a few minutes. You want me to come back inside?"

"Over the phone is good. I'm alone in my office. Are you where you can speak, that is, confidentially?"

"Unless Pritchett, Malone, and Tudor has audio and video surveillance directed at me outside the building and near my car, we're good."

"There's video, of course. I can see you on my monitor. No audio, I can assure you, except over the phone."

Sidney scanned the area for cameras. She spotted one in a corner above the revolving doors and shot a weak smile and wave. She thought again about continuing the conversation in her car although the drive home could distract her. "What's up? I thought we covered everything during the meeting."

"Yes, yes. The meeting was very, very thorough. Our corporate legal team requires such of us. The three big shots were in on the meeting, as you know, the principal partners—of which I am one. The less experienced members of our firm are such—can I say, *fraidy cats?*

"Fraidy cats?"

"Yes. There is certainly nothing wrong with playing by the books, following procedures in striking a deal. Nonetheless, we have to be practical in these matters. Apply common sense, if you will."

"I should come back inside to your office." Sidney stared up into the security camera.

"No. No. Your coming back into the building might attract too much attention. Let's make this quick."

A hummingbird sampled an early blossom on a yellow flowering vine growing up the façade of the building. A redbird landed briefly on the limb of an ornamental tree in another section of the building's foundation plantings. "Is there a problem?"

"Everything is fine. Our firm can negotiate a buy-out deal of your medical practice and spa at a much higher level than what less-experienced partners assume or propose. I've been in this business for thirty years. Granted, the medical practice piece of our corporate buy-and-sell clientele has taken off only in the last ten years. That's the nature of the beast. This is all economy driven."

Sidney again glanced up at the security camera. "I'm sort of confused about why you're calling me."

"I sincerely believe we can sell the Belmont enterprise for much more than my associates—my partners—have proposed. I know you have had other offers, and Chuck Wallace knew the business."

"My brother tells me the offer is still on the table although I remain very skeptical over the terms."

"I know what happened to Chuck Wallace. Who doesn't? It's been all over the news," Pritchard said. "His successor or successors will be eager to continue the negotiations."

Sidney stared at another redbird hopping from one branch of an ornamental magnolia tree to another. She had not heard any updates from the media about Wallace's shooting, and no one discussed it at the office and clinic. Still another redbird appeared.

Pritchard continued. "Wallace is—was—a fine man, certainly very reputable and a hard worker."

"My brothers were ready to sign with him. They were smelling money. I assume a portion of the paperwork has already gone through, waiting for a majority signature." Sidney took her eyes off the tree and focused on the camera.

*I'm the hold out, and you know that*, she wanted to say.

She walked toward her car. "I have probably pushed this alternative idea too far. My brothers won't like that I'm here. Meeting with your group was probably a mistake and a waste of your time."

"No, no, no, no," Pritchard said. "We can strike a much better deal than what we discussed today. You were spot-on to contact us. My immediate goal is to get the others in my firm on board so we can take our proposal to the next level."

Sidney opened the driver's door and slid into her seat. "Please do that, Mr. Pritchard, and get back with me. My brothers are businessmen. They are good doctors, shall I say great doctors, and they like nice things. They like to be appreciated, and they like to make a lot of money."

"Of course. I definitely see that you and I, that you and my firm, are on the same page to land success with this deal," Pritchard said.

Sidney pushed the control to start her car and began to back out of the parking space. "Put together this revised proposal you're talking about, and I'll shred this thick folder you gave me. Wallace's clients have worked too hard to let the buyout of our clinic go. They'll replace him with someone else, now that's he's no longer in the picture." She headed toward the exit from the parking lot. "By the way, Mr. Pritchard, I like to be appreciated too—and make lots of money."

"I can see that you are forward-thinking, Dr. Sidney Belmont."

Sidney secured her cell phone in the console charging station, set it to the speaker phone option, and exited onto Highland Colony Parkway. "I realize that my brothers still think of me as the poor sister they need to protect. You've struck a nerve with me, and you're correct. It's time to *think out of the box* and cut a deal—a better deal."

"We certainly need to go more in depth with our alternative proposal to buy Belmont Medical—really dissect the plan for you and the others. Help you see the future potential of growth for your practice under our leadership and networking."

Sidney slowed at the approaching four-way intersection. To the right and nearest her lane, a gas station under construction with a rich red-brick façade featured a row of car wash units tucked tastefully to the side. A waste dumpster stood near the curb. She pulled over, rolled down the passenger window, and tossed the one-inch thick, bound PM&T proposal hard enough to land it inside the heavy metal dumpster. She heard it strike the bottom. "Farewell to that garbage. I can't wait to see what they come up with next," she said.

Traffic around was heavy, and Sidney pulled off the boulevard onto a side street of new residential construction and stopped her car. She wanted her full concentration on the conversation with Pritchard.

"Sidney, are you still there?"

"Yes, go ahead. I wanted to ease out of this congestion. And I prefer *Dr. Belmont*."

"No problem at all. Is it possible that you could meet again with our group sometime next week? Whatever time is convenient for you."

"I have tossed your initial proposal into the smelly place it belongs," Sidney said. "And I'll be happy to schedule another meeting with you under one condition." She felt tension on the other side.

"And what is that … Dr. Belmont?

"Yes, I do like that better. Let's continue with the *Dr. Belmont*, as long as you know which one of us you're talking to." Sidney thought her remark clever. "Another meeting is fine and worth my time—but only if you're serious about making the sale of the medical practice a reality—a financial windfall reality for the Belmonts."

A few seconds lapsed. "Certainly. I'll put my best team on this to draft an offer that will be equitable to all parties."

"Equitable to all parties? I think not," Sidney said. "From what I remember from freshman English or was it from that accounting elective I took my senior year in college, the word *equitable* means equal. I don't think we're talking about 50–50 here." She spotted another redbird flutter about in the new landscaping. It carried a twig to its own construction project, a petite nest tucked in a cluster of thin branches. "My brothers and I want a deal where we come out on top."

"Our administrative services will make your day-to-day operations in the clinic and spa much smoother. Each physician will be much more productive," Pritchard said. "More productively lends itself to higher profits for all parties."

"Higher profits sound like a good thing," Sidney said. "Nevertheless, you've got to beat the deal Chuck Wallace proposed."

"Sadly, Mr. Wallace is no longer with us. Therefore, here we are, Dr. Belmont."

Sidney scanned the row of zero-lot line townhomes under construction along the street. Other small birds flitted between the branches, building nests in the newly installed landscaping.

"Wallace represented an overseas company, and a back-up plan from that buyer should be in place. But my firm can beat it," Pritchard said.

Sidney held the phone close and grinned at her vision of a panicky Benjamin Pritchard fumbling through a pile of papers or clicking through pages on his laptop for bullet points of a counter proposal.

"I suspect your clients—your patients—will welcome a U.S. company supporting your practice and working to expand your services," Pritchard said.

"My clients, as you first called them, could care less who supports me financially. They come to the Belmont compound to see *me*—or one of my brothers, cousins, nieces, and nephews—or maybe one of the others."

Several men of Latino descent pushed wheelbarrows of broken bricks and scrap lumber from one side of the property to the other. One of them seemed to struggle with the load. He sweated. Sidney wondered how much each man was paid per hour compared to what she made as a physician who never sweated—at least not physically. "I suggest you dig deep for your best offer, Mr. Pritchard. Real deep."

"I can assure you, Dr. Belmont, that our actuaries have done expert due diligence to evaluate the value of your medical practice and all the ancillary services you offer. The firm has pushed the envelope to get the appraisal value to the high dollar mark."

Sidney spotted another group of men carrying electric saws and other construction equipment from a trailer into one of the uncompleted units. A couple of them smoked cigarettes and tossed live butts onto the ground. Sidney despised litterers.

She swung open the driver's door and stood in the street. The construction crew chatted among themselves. She recognized a few words from high school Spanish about tossing empty water bottles and cigarettes in the piles of dirt and rubbish and not giving a flip about it. Sidney wished she had taken upper-level Spanish between her pre-med courses, so she could yell objection to their vulgarity and sloppy work.

Forgetting about the ongoing call with Pritchard, Sidney decided to give it a try in garbled Spanish with a few choice words in English understood universally. She opened her mouth to scream her hatred to the construction workers for those who spoil the environment—even if they could not understand her. She gazed around, took a deep breath, and decided against the outburst, then lowered her voice. "Clean up your own mess, Sidney. Your family mess," she said softly.

A red stain erupted directly below her left scapula and spread in a starburst across the back of her white blouse. Sidney was thrown forward onto the side of the car. Her cell phone flew from her hand toward the street curb and bounced roughly toward the gutter drain. She screamed in pain and rolled across the side of the windshield onto the hood and onto her back. She stared up and over to the row of townhouses and into the sky. Another redbird flew over her. Could have been the same bird—likely not.

At the popping sound, one member of the construction crew glanced in Sidney's direction and rattled at a co-worker in Spanish. "What's with the white lady over there in the fancy car?"

Sidney struggled to turn her head in the direction of the construction crew. The pain in her back and chest burned in uncertainty of what had happened. She fought to take a breath and struggled to yell for help—but could only whisper, "Help me, somebody. Please."

The fierce banter among the men continued. They moved supplies and wheeled equipment around the site and ignored her.

Sidney struggled to lift her head a few inches off the hood to call out again. A second pop put another bullet to the side of her skull, smashing her head against the frame of the car. Blood and tissue splattered up the windshield and across the roof as her head exploded. More blood ran back under the body as it twisted and convulsed.

A figure in shadowy green clothing stalked the woman to the area across the street and traced her every movement from an opened window in the decayed, abandoned four-story building. When the target finally stilled after the second shot, the figure disassembled a long-range rifle and stuffed the pieces into a duffle bag.

Built in the 1920s, the Art Deco-style building had been home to the Bank of Central Mississippi. After the banking institution dissolved and the building failed to sell during a real estate slump, the vacant site unofficially welcomed the homeless and served as a place of business for drug dealers and prostitutes.

A long-time resident of the building spotted the shadowy figure as it ran down a fire escape to a vehicle left parked in the alley. She jumped from her window perch into a corner storage room once used to file away checking and savings account ledgers that now served as her home. She hid behind her shopping cart; salvaged sleeping bag and pillow, with large cardboard canopy; and stash of partially filled plastic food and beverage bottles.

When not soliciting cash from drivers stopped at red lights, the homeless woman's entertainment was watching the progress of the nearby construction crew. But today's monotony had been broken by the brown, four-door sedan she spotted follow the lady just before the bloody murder across the street.

Today had been an exciting day.

# Chapter 25

"Ellis Belmont, MD, here to see the Medical Examiner. I have been asked to make a positive identification." He dropped a business card on the desk.

The clerk at the reception desk of the State Medical Examiner's Office picked up the sturdy, embossed card, briefly took note of the name, and pulled up information on the computer in front of him.

"I've seen this sort of thing on television, not that I have much time for that." Before returning attention to the clerk, Belmont examined the austere reception area with its near floor-to-ceiling tinted glass windows and uncomfortable, generic-designed seating. "This is my first experience with this sort of thing. Could you please direct me where to go and could we push this along? My patients need me back at the clinic and hospital."

The clerk raised his eyes away from the screen. "Autopsy is required in most of the reportable deaths, such as this one. Yep, homicide falls under the violent death category."

"I would think so," Belmont said. "As to the time I will be required to complete this process?"

"The forensic pathologist has completed her notes." He clicked through a few other pages. "Postmortem was not invasive—external examination only, except for the routine toxicology screen. However, I need to warn you—"

"Warn me about what?" Belmont referred to his Rolex, the movement only to cement his impatience with the process. The current time did not even register with him.

The clerk continued to scan through the autopsy photos and noted that the victim's face should be recognizable to an observer even though a massive head wound was documented. "I've marked you in as here. One of the ME's assistants will be up shortly."

"I've been asked to leave my busy clinical practice and come down here to identify my sister's body. Again, how long could this take?"

"Are you Dr. Ellis Belmont?"

Belmont pivoted to the male voice behind him. The name on the police credentials was clear enough to read in a quick glance: *Key Martin, Chief of Police*. Another man, who came across about twenty years the chief's junior, stood behind and to the side of Martin. Gifted with lingering good vision, Belmont could at least read the designation *Detective* on his badge.

"Yes, and someone from your department summoned me down to this place. Are you the one who called me, or was it was one of your surrogates? Regardless, could you get these people to move this thing along?"

The clerk pushed back from the computer. The roller chair nearly collided with the counter behind him. He jerked open a drawer and produced a tall Starbucks cup with a plastic straw jutting out from the plastic lid over the top. "I'm due for my break now. I'm going to warm this thing up in the microwave. Employees only, by the way, in the break room."

He shoved the drawer closed. "And, Chief Martin, glad you're here, as always. I'm leaving this—this *drama*—with you."

"I'll walk back to the lab and see what's the hold up," Detective Thomas said and left Martin with Belmont.

"Sorry for your loss, Dr. Belmont," Key Martin said. "This is only a legal formality. Your sister, Dr. Sidney Eleanor Belmont, was ambushed, it seems. This was no random shooting."

"Ambushed?" Belmont continued to stare in the direction of the detective's exit. "Doesn't that seem rather extreme? People like us, I mean like the Belmont medical family, are targeted constantly for a lot of things." Belmont turned back to the chief. "However, not this."

"The ME is ready for you." A frail, pale young woman covered in a long white lab coat, sans make-up, and with auburn hair pulled back into a tight bun appeared in the lobby. The detective stood behind her, smiling. "Follow me, please. This way," she said.

"It's about time," Belmont said. "My afternoon at the clinic is nearly blown. Let's get on with it."

The pale girl led them down the hall to the pathology lab. Belmont trailed directly behind her as Martin and Thomas followed. The reception clerk waited in a hidden corner until the entourage disappeared then resumed his post at the desk.

"Unbelievable," the clerk said. "What a pompous ass."

The others were nearly to the path lab. "This place is so—sterile," Belmont said.

"Not like a fancy doctor's office, Doc?" Detective Thomas said.

Key Martin shot him a *less said, the better* look, and Thomas nodded *I got it*.

The pale girl stopped in front of a grey metal door and waved her name tag over a sensor. The door jerked open. Belmont, Martin, and Thomas followed her into the room. A lone body lay draped in a sheet on a metal table, the face covered. The girl motioned for Belmont to stand at one end of the table while she retrieved a clipboard and papers from a nearby counter. "The forensic pathologist has completed her report, and the ME has authorized me as his assistant to conduct this identification of the victim."

The pale girl waved Belmont closer to the body and began to lift the drape that covered the head area. Belmont stepped back.

"You okay, Doc?" Martin said. "Got to be different when it's flesh and blood."

"Is this Sidney Eleanor Belmont?" the assistant to the Medical Examiner asked. She gently dropped the white drape below the neck and clavicular area. The head rested on an opaque, spongy material that exposed only the forehead and facial area. Sidney's face appeared bloated.

Belmont had never seen his sister with a bloated face.

"I'm thankful her eyes are shut," he said. "I read the police report—the few seconds between the shots. She must have realized the situation."

"Is this Sidney Eleanor Belmont?" the pale girl repeated.

"Yes, it is. Yes, *she* is," Ellis Belmont answered. "Please cover up my sister as she was. This is difficult. Such a waste."

The Assistant ME raised the drape over the face and gently dropped it in place. The girl offered a weak parting of the lips, an attempted sympathetic smile, to Dr. Ellis Belmont and stepped to a nearby desk. She selected a pen from a drawer and began to complete paper forms in between typing information into a computer.

"Any idea who would shoot your sister?" Martin asked.

Belmont diverted attention from his empty study of the assistant. The girl was bone thin, her skin almost as pale as the long white lab coat she wore. Her black eyebrows—considered bushy even for a man—nearly met in the middle above her nasal bridge and forehead.

"Of course not. Who could do such a thing?" Belmont answered. "No way Sid could have gotten sideways with a patient. She never devoted enough time to any one of them."

"Anyone inside the practice itself? Any office employee or one of the other doctors have a beef with your sister?" Martin asked.

Belmont shrugged. "Not that I know of. Then again, you can ask around."

"Might just do that."

Belmont hesitated as though trying to recall the name. "Please remember—Chief Martin—the Belmont Clinic and Spa is a very busy place. The employees are on the clock, and the physicians do not like to be interrupted either."

"Got it," Thomas said. A weak smirk marred his stone expression.

"No one at your clinic did much hobnobbing around the office with Dr. Sidney Belmont?" Martin asked. "And no after-hours bunko or tennis or pickleball …"

Another shrug from Belmont.

"What about a significant other or others?" Martin asked.

"Married and divorced once and dated seldom, if ever."

"We've already searched—been—to her apartment," Detective Thomas interjected. "No family photos or snapshots with friends scattered about. And her social media accounts, more boring than mine." Another smirk from Thomas.

"Seems Dr. Sidney Belmont didn't have much of a social life outside of work." Martin stepped closer to Belmont, who straightened his posture in defense. "You know, Doc, I'm searching for a suspect or suspects. Let me ask again. You know anyone who would want to harm your sister?"

"I don't know of anyone, except with these women it's all about boyfriends— or, God forbid, girlfriends."

"You said she had no extracurriculars," Thomas said, and Martin nodded in agreement.

"What about any other business or financial problems?" Martin asked. "Anything there that could lead someone to target your sister?"

"No," Belmont answered without hesitation and moved away from Martin and Thomas.

The Assistant ME finished with the papers and the computer work and left the area.

"We tracked your sister's activities from earlier in the day using her phone," Thomas said, careful not to meet eye-to-eye with his chief. "She was pinged at a new karaoke club downtown on West Capitol Street the night before the murder. Place is called the Orleans Club. I talked with the manager. He remembered her: slight build, hair pulled back in a bun, dressed more upscale than most of the other patrons. Your sis won Best New Singer."

"That's preposterous!" Belmont jerked his head back, chin up, and tightened his posture. "Sidney would never have been caught dead in such a place."

Martin and Thomas both raised an eyebrow. Belmont glanced back at his sister's body covered with a sheet on the polished steel table. "I'm sorry. Bad choice of words."

Chief Martin took a deep breath and swallowed a grin. Detective Thomas again turned his face away from the chief's line of site.

"I know this is a difficult time for your family, Dr. Belmont. My detective here, as well as all the god-fearing citizens of the State of Mississippi, appreciate your taking the time to come down and identify your sister. Now, please get back to your patients."

"A karaoke club? I thought I knew Sidney. Guess I didn't," Belmont said.

"We have what we need for now." Martin motioned to Detective Thomas. "There is one more thing. We will need to talk to your brother, Dr. Miles Belmont."

"I'll come by your clinic tomorrow to chat with him," Thomas said. "The Chief will be tied up in court tomorrow. Bad, bad murder case." Thomas seemed to jot a note on his pad. "Hey, whaddayaknow? It's the gang shooting that went down on West Capitol."

"That's all the time I have for you today, gentlemen," Belmont said. He headed for the illuminated exit sign.

"You know how to leave the building, Doc?" Martin asked. "I can get that girl to show you out."

Belmont stumbled on the smooth concrete floor as though he had tripped on a dangling shoelace. He righted himself by grabbing the corner of another grey autopsy table then yanked his hand away as though his skin were singed. He wiped his palm against his suit jacket and headed toward the closed exit door. Without turning away from his escape, Belmont said, "Don't bother, Mr. Policemen." He paused before depressing the door handle and added, "You and the rest of the Jackson Police Department have a murderer—a real killer—to apprehend."

The sound of the heavy metal door banging shut behind Belmont reverberated throughout the autopsy lab.

"Seems the good doctor should have accepted the offer of an escort out of this place," Thomas said. "He headed to the right, not left, down the hall. He'll wind up at the hearse loading dock in a few minutes."

"I expect Belmont will figure it out," Martin said. "Don't think his type is much into accepting help—or suggestions."

The Assistant ME returned to the lab from a side door. "Left my backpack." She opened one of the lockers mounted on a wall opposite the sinks and autopsy table. "And hey, guys. Didn't mean to eavesdrop. The walls around this place are kinda thin. You know … leave it to the government."

She hung her lab coat in the locker and threw one of the backpack straps around her shoulder and worked into the other. Standing before Detective Thomas she said, "You got an address for that new club downtown? Me and my friends would dig that place."

"Sure thing," Thomas said. "I'll text it to you later."

The assistant lowered her bushy eyebrows in concerned disappointment and left out the same side door.

"Where'd you come up with the karaoke club?" Martin said.

"Didn't think it would hurt if we threw Belmont a line," Thomas said. "The guy's such a pompous, arrogant ass. How do you believe anybody like that?"

"Hard to say. But that girl with the eyebrows is gonna be pissed at you when she drives down West Capitol Street and there's no new club," Martin said.

# Chapter 26

Diana ripped open the paper packet of instant grits and poured the contents in a heated bowl of tap water fresh from the microwave. She replaced the bowl with four strips of bacon stretched out across a microwave-proof plate, covered the meat with a paper towel, and set the oven to three-and-a-half minutes.

"Mom? What are you doing?" Kelsey bounded down the stairs into the kitchen, fully dressed in her cheerleader outfit.

Diana admired the make-up. "Wow! Pep rally day brings out the best." She stirred the finely ground maize into the hot water and added a thin slice of butter. "Thought I'd be a regular mom today and make a real breakfast." The toaster sprang to life with two browned slices of raisin bread as the smell of sizzling bacon filled the kitchen. "Oops, I forgot the omelet."

She opened a freezer drawer, searched through the plastic packages, and removed one frozen omelet. "Here we go. An omelet in a minute or two. Go ahead and start on the grits and toast. The bacon will be ready in a few." Diana cut open the package and placed the frozen, processed egg product in a Pyrex dish, ready next for the microwave. She read again through the cooking instructions. "Kelsey, Sweetie, if you don't mind, please pour your own orange juice. It's in the fridge."

"Mom, I told you I had to get to school early." Kelsey found a package of sliced cinnamon and raisin bagels in the pantry, separated one into halves, and dropped each in the toaster. She pushed the lever, and the heating elements around the thick bread glowed red-orange. "This will be fine. I'm not that hungry anyway. Cheerleader sponsor wants us to run through our skit before first period. We had to change to new dance music yesterday. Principal didn't like a few of the lyrics."

"I didn't have any surgery scheduled for today, and my office nurse needed to come in an hour late. A program at her kid's school or something like that. So … I decided to make a homemade breakfast." Diana waved her hand around the kitchen as the timer in the microwave signaled ready-to-eat bacon. She opened the appliance door and removed four strips of sizzling bacon covered in grease-soaked paper towel and replaced them with the dish containing the frozen processed-egg omelet.

The bagels popped up brown out of the toaster. Kelsey grabbed them with a napkin. "I hate it, Mom, but this is all I have time for. Offer Brad breakfast?"

"He left for the hospital about an hour and a half ago."

Kelsey retrieved her bag and headed for the door to the garage. "I'll grab a Coke out of the back fridge in the mudroom. See ya, Mom. Love ya. And if you can make the pep rally this time, that would be awesome."

The door to the garage slammed shut, not far from the side door toward the rear of the house where Voncelle Wallace entered a few nights before.

The microwave chimed at the finish of the omelet. Diana studied the bacon, the toast, the grits, and the shrunken omelet. A short bottle of raspberry jam sat unopened on the counter, a gift from a patient from a Christmas-or-so ago. "Oh well, I tried."

She opened a drawer, grabbed a spoon, and sampled the grits. "Not hot enough and could've used more butter," Diana said. "Needs more salt."

Diana heard the doorbell from the side door and tossed the grits in the trash.

Voncelle Wallace stood outside under the overhang, visibly shaken. Diana opened the door. "Voncelle? You aren't at the office?"

She stepped past Diana into the house. "I heard about what happened to Garcia. I can't get my head around his getting shot."

Diana moved out of the way and followed Voncelle toward the kitchen.

"I figured it out while making rounds and listening to the scuttlebutt on the med-surg floor over the last couple of days," Voncelle said. "My first patient appointment isn't until 10:15, so I came by here first. Sorry to spoil your morning off."

"The police are keeping Garcia's shooting under wraps." Diana said.

"What do you know about the police?" Voncelle walked further into the kitchen, past the painting of an outdoor flower garden, a gift from Brad via one of the previous interior decorators. "Those med-surg nurses said it's all over the hospital about a gunshot victim that came in through the ED, shot at long range." Voncelle circled the kitchen island. "Shot at long range—same as Chuck. Hey, I smell breakfast. You got any coffee?"

"No, this morning was all about breakfast for my daughter. Kelsey's not ready for coffee. Besides, you already appear too jumpy for caffeine."

"Perhaps you're right." Voncelle leaned back against the edge of the Italian granite-covered island at the kitchen's center. She spotted the carton of orange juice outside the refrigerator and opened the adjacent cabinet. "I'll take a glass of OJ instead."

"Help yourself," Diana said.

Voncelle poured the glass full and took a long drink. Her hands no longer shook. "A couple of jiggers of vodka would put this juice over the top."

"Forgetting about your clinic patients this morning?"

"Wish I could. With Chuck gone, there's no hope of retiring anytime in the near future."

She finished the drink. "By the way, you didn't answer my question."

"I told you about the coffee."

"No, about the police," Voncelle said. "You said the police were keeping details about Garcia's shooting under wraps. What's that all about and how would you know what the police are doing?"

Diana moved to the sink and brushed and rinsed the dishes and cooking utensils in preparation for loading the dishwasher. "The housekeeper's off for a few more days. Brad took her gallbladder out last week and hasn't released her back to work—or filled in for her around here. My clinic starts at two, and I've got to hit the grocery on the way."

Voncelle stepped closer and grabbed the kitchen brush from Diana.

"Voncelle?" Diana said. "What is this?"

She released the brush and took a step back. "Diana, I need you to tell me why you know so much about police business."

Diana turned off the running water to the sink and faced her. Beads of perspiration lined the woman's forehead. "My husband's brother was murdered in an elevator of our clinic building; your former boss, Dr. John Haynes, threatened and wanted to take out my husband; and I was recently held at gunpoint after work in our clinic garage—and you ask how I know about the police?"

Voncelle seemed to relax, even offered a weak smile. "I shouldn't have been so direct. I admire all that you have accomplished—despite all that you've been through."

Diana loaded the last dish and cooking utensil into the dishwasher and retrieved her phone from the counter. "You said that Garcia was shot at long range, similar to Chuck."

"You already knew that, Diana. I can feel it. I'm no mind reader, but I've been around you enough to sense things. And my guess is that you know more than you're telling."

Diana looked at the digital display on the microwave. Voncelle had plenty of time to make her first patient appointment. "It's no secret that I have known the chief of police for several years, met him when he was a detective. Key Martin—Chief Martin—calls me from time to time about cases, mostly when they involve medical issues."

"I don't buy that, Diana. This thing with Chuck and Garcia, it's different. Brad was there when Chuck was killed and then I come over and tell you about Garcia stalking me and then suddenly Garcia is murdered too and—"

"What is it you want here?" Diana returned the remaining orange juice to the refrigerator along with the jelly and unused butter. She removed a towel from a drawer and wiped the island clean.

"I feel the world closing in on me, and I need a friend," Voncelle's fingers began to tremble again. "I could use lots of friends."

Diana wished Brad were again in the kitchen with them. "I know that Chief Martin and Detective Thomas came to see you after Chuck died. It's not surprising that police would question the wife of a murder victim. Everybody watches *Dateline*, don't they?"

"Come on, Diana. You know more about policework than what you see on TV. Plus, you're on a first name basis with the cops."

"*Thomas* is a surname," Diana sighed.

"What did Martin tell you about that day?" Voncelle's manner direct, her voice raised. Her hands still shook.

"I would like to help you. You are asking for a friend, and I'm trying to be that person. Still, if you have questions or anything that will help the police figure out who's doing this, who shot Chuck and Garcia, you need to talk to Chief Martin or Detective Thomas or anyone at the police department."

Voncelle walked back and forth across the kitchen. She ran her hands along the edge of the oven and microwave. She examined an empty flower vase by the sink, then selected one of the collection of cookbooks shelved on the opposite wall. Flipping through the breakfast and brunch recipes compiled by someone from the Mississippi Delta she said, "I'll ask again, and if you are my friend, you'll tell me. What have the police said about me? What did that Martin guy tell you about what they found or saw at my house?"

"This is really too much." Diana walked toward the exit from the kitchen into the rest of the house. "Let's talk later. I need to get dressed for work, and there are a few errands Kelsey needs me to run for her. There're always school projects and cheerleading or a birthday gift for one of her friends, so I should be—"

Voncelle stepped quickly behind her and reached for her arm.

Diana sensed the movement and jerked away. She turned around to face Voncelle. "Stop, Voncelle. Let's talk later."

"That won't work, Diana. I need to know. Do the police think I killed Chuck? They think I murdered Garcia too? I know they do. But how? How would I be able to pull that off?"

Diana envisioned the gun cabinet, missing from the library when Martin and Thomas visited the Wallace house. *What does this woman want from me? I can't ask her about the guns. I need to talk to Key Martin about this.*

Voncelle dropped the cookbook on an expensive cushioned chair near the door. "I haven't shot a gun since college."

Diana decided not to reveal she knew about the visit to the local shooting range.

"Then the shotguns, the rifles in the gun cabinet in your library. Those were yours?"

"I was on this girls' firearm league when I was in college. Requirement to graduate was three hours in some sort of sports activity. When I asked about women's golf or even tennis, my dad had other ideas. He thought his little girl might learn personal protection from a firearms course or even spark an interest in hunting. He never had a son. Besides, I heard most everyone who signed up for riflery made an *A*."

Diana nodded weakly. "Yeah, important in pre-med."

"I took the firearms course for the requirement and joined the long-range competition league for extra credit. My boyfriend would take me out to the practice range and work with me, and I got good at it."

"Chuck?"

"No, it was—"

"Your first husband?"

"No." Voncelle seemed puzzled. "I never told you I was married before Chuck."

"Oh. Someone mentioned that you lost your first husband. I don't remember who—and it was a while ago—when we were first getting to know each other."

"It was the boyfriend my senior year in college. The team went to state competition. My aim at target practice, even with my boyfriend's help, was so bad that the coach didn't even let me shoot, never put me on the roster for any events. Sent me to run errands during the competitions, like get the burgers or snacks."

Diana managed a smile. "Hope you still got an *A*."

"The word about the high grade was dead-on. The coach actually liked me because I took the brunt of the lousy shot jokes without any pushback," Voncelle said. "And was fast with the food and snacks."

Diana checked the time again. "I need to get changed." Voncelle reached for door, and Diana stepped closer. "I truly do want what's best for you. You've lost a husband, and everything I do is meant to help."

"Meant to help how?"

"I told Martin about the gun cabinet and the weapons—gone when he and the deputy went by your house."

Voncelle opened the door to the outside. "I inherited that gun collection from my father when he passed. I was still with my old surgery group, and Chuck didn't care anything about hunting. I kept the rifles on display to remember my dad—and added my Anscultz, my rifle from college."

"Did you move the guns to another part of the house?"

"I knew how bad it would look if I had all those firearms—after what happened to Chuck. I hid them under the bed in the master bedroom. I guess if your police friends had shown up with a search warrant, they would've found them."

Diana felt the back pocket of her jeans. No phone. *It's in the bedroom.* She took a few steps in that direction. "You said I'm buds with the police. Then it shouldn't surprise you that I might think—"

"Diana! You're such a goody-two-shoes. I know that the chief of police practically stalks you at the office."

"And if you must know, and Brad will agree, he's annoying. Except Martin gets the job done."

"Maybe you want to help him *get the job done*," Voncelle said, mocking Diana's voice. "Why don't you call your cop buddy and tell him where my rifles and other guns are. You can even use my phone. They can try to match ballistics to the one used to shoot Chuck and Garcia. See? I know TV too, Diana."

Diana ignored that. "You're already dressed for the day, Voncelle. I need to get ready. Remember? My errands and the office schedule? I'll be late." In a few steps Diana reached the junk drawer near the breakfast table. It ran the full length of a narrow cabinet below several shelves of china plates, cups, and saucers. Kelsey kept a mirror in the drawer. Sometimes she left a pair of scissors or a letter opener scattered among the drawer contents.

"Why are you afraid, Diana?"

"What?" Diana spun around to the question. She lowered the scissors below her waist, against her thigh. "What do you mean?"

"You're pale, Diana. And you're sweating." Voncelle lowered her eyes to the scissors and the tremor now in Diana's fingers. "And if you need a sharp object, most kitchens have knives in the drawers—you know, over by sink?"

Diana let out a deep breath and set the scissors on the breakfast table, then lowered her hands to her side.

"I've never seen you like this, and we've worked together on a lot of tough surgical cases. *Dr. Bratton, The Rock* one of the techs called you during a Whipple that nearly bled out. There've been other tough cases too."

"I guess I'm not sure why you're here, Voncelle. Please leave—now."

"I'll get out of your hair, but not before I make one thing clear."

Diana eyed the scissors as Voncelle continued.

"Sure, I know how to shoot a long-range rifle and was eventually good enough to make the first-string competition squad in college. I even qualified for regionals despite having a new coach who was a real ass and hated women on the team. He couldn't stand the fact that women could rack up higher marksman scores than men, like Margaret Murdock almost beating out a man for gold at the 1976 Olympics."

"This is too much," Diana said.

"I'd be a liar if I said I'm not good enough to take somebody out at long range. But any of those guys walking that night with Chuck and Brad could have done it. I know for a fact that several are deer hunters and good shooters. They bragged all the time about their trophy mounts. Chuck told me about it."

Diana walked to the door. "You've been through a lot. We all have. I suggest we take a break on this and—"

Voncelle pushed past her and pulled open the door. She turned back before stepping outside. "It's Martin and his cronies' job to find out what happened to my husband and to Garcia. They can come to me again if they want to talk. But if you and your buddy the chief want secrets, I can tell you a few."

# Chapter 27

Diana finished the afternoon clinic and picked up take-out on the way home. Brad had the same idea. She arrived with Thai chicken and pasta with spicy mayonnaise—Brad with three fully dressed hamburgers, jumbo fried onion rings, and French fries.

"I came prepared to feed Kelsey too," Brad said.

"She's at another cheerleader practice, and she's started to watch her waistline. Both of us made poor dinner choices," Diana said.

"What time is practice over?"

"In about an hour, and I'm running pickup carpool."

"So, before Kelsey gets home, it's either eat these rings before they get cold and hurry up and do what I had planned for dessert in the hot tub or put the food in the warmer and stay longer in the hot tub." Brad reached for Diana's thigh and rubbed it gently. "I'm thinking about dessert first."

Diana opened the container of chicken and pasta and got them each a plate. She remembered the tense moments with Voncelle earlier in the day. "The hot tub will have to wait, Brad. I'm starved." Diana scooped four large tablespoons from the container onto her plate. "You gonna go with the burger? I'll get you a beer, but I better stick with water."

Brad sighed and removed one of the hamburgers from the bag and place it in the center of his plate. He encircled it with fries and several onion rings.

"Not sure what's up with Voncelle Wallace," Diana said. "Definitely creeped me out this morning."

"At the office or in surgery? She's posted the worst cases lately." Brad took a plug out of his burger and engulfed almost half of his first extra-large onion ring.

"She came by the house."

"What's with her. I didn't even know she knew our address, then suddenly she's practically moving in and needs a key." He took another swipe at the hamburger, chased it with a guzzle of beer, then grabbed a handful of French fries for his plate. "These babies win out," he said and chewed several fries. "I should've picked up ranch dressing to dip 'em in."

"Voncelle admitted she knows how to shoot a rifle. Said she moved the guns out of the library to avoid suspicion."

"What did your boyfriend Key Martin say about that?" He squirted ketchup on his plate and smeared several fries in it. "Sure do wish we had that ranch."

"And Voncelle said any of those guys in that neighborhood walking group could have fired a gun like the one that killed Chuck."

"You're correct about that. All those guys hunt, probably learned how to shoot a rifle during Christmas break from kindergarten," Brad said. "You keeping Martin in the loop on this? He's never that far away."

"He'll show up sooner or later—and at the wrong time. I'll wait to tell him then."

Brad finished the burger, another onion ring, and pushed away the few remaining French fries. He glanced down toward his waist. "I gotta start exercising, walk with those guys again."

Diana continued to push the pasta around on her plate.

"You didn't eat anything," Brad said.

"Not hungry." Diana scraped her plate clean in the sink over the garbage disposal, ran the faucet, and flipped the switch. She turned around to Brad, still seated at the table. "I'm ready to distance myself from this."

"Don't worry. I'll be better." Brad jumped up and took care of his dirty plate and utensils. "And I'll do more than a walk in the neighborhood. I'll hit the gym."

Diana ran her hand up Brad's back, and he turned to her smile. "No, that's not what I meant." Diana gently backhanded Brad on the shoulder. "I'm ready to take a break from all this stuff with Key Martin."

"No argument there. It seems to me that Voncelle Wallace is in a bad place, and that doesn't shine a good light on our surgical practice."

"I need to concentrate on Kelsey and her school activities, and I've sensed more than once over the last few weeks that patients think I'm distracted in the office or on hospital rounds."

"I realize this has been too much on you," Brad said. "I need to help straighten out this thing with Voncelle."

"Voncelle Wallace is my responsibility. I brought her into the practice."

"And no one stopped you. Another warm body who could operate and answer a cell phone—every one of us wanted help with the call schedule. I'm going to Martin with this myself."

Diana reached to kiss Brad on the lips.

"Thanks to you," Brad said, "I know where his office is." He and Diana kissed again. "Now, what about the hot tub?"

"I ain't done nothing to get arrested. Nobody cares about that place."

Brad stood in the lobby of the Jackson Police Department waiting for a receptionist to finish a phone call and saw one of the officers lead a woman through the front entrance toward the back of the building. He recognized the man as the detective working with Key Martin. The woman wore a mismatched blouse and slacks set with grey sweater covered in snagged threads and dirty bright orange tennis shoes. Her stained, light blue baseball cap fell to the floor in the hassle.

"The first officer on the scene spotted you in the window, and we need your statement," Detective Thomas said and picked up the hat, returning it to her. "We need to know what you saw."

The woman halted and pulled away from Thomas, the two still in earshot of Brad. He pretended to study the sign-in sheet on the counter. "I told you that I keep to myself in my corner suite. That Mexican crew working across the street keeps to theirselves too and never bothers me when I come and go doing my rounds. My street don't get much traffic."

Brad smiled at the receptionist still on the phone. She mouthed, "Be with you in a sec. You want to take a seat?"

*No,* Brad responded with a soft shake of the head and picked up a brochure on how to correctly install infant car seats. He noticed the plant on the counter near the brochure display needed water. Its leaves drooped over the rim of the cheap, gaudily painted ceramic container.

Detective Thomas lowered his voice to a restrained tone. "Ma'am, could you follow me to the conference room, please, so we can talk in private?"

"Whatchu talking about? *Conference room?* I may be squatting in an empty building, but I know all about those rooms on cop shows where they grill the suspects—make 'em sweat." She straightened and extended her arms toward the detective, wrists up. "Go ahead. I've seen it. They cuff you to a cold, grey metal table for hours until an incredibly sexy guy with great hair comes in and threatens the gas chamber if you don't confess. And all these other cops, including female sluts with big boobs, check out the action through a two-way mirror, laughing it up and drinking coffee and eating doughnuts."

"Quiet down, please, ma'am," Thomas said.

"Yeah, I know all your ass-hole police tricks."

Brad swallowed hard, happy to see the show. Detective Thomas caught his eye and shook his head.

"Ma'am, I will arrest you for disorderly conduct if you don't quiet down." He glanced again at Brad and lowered his voice to a near whisper. "We searched the building across from the shooting and you ran from us."

"I ain't done nothing wrong!"

"You're wrong on that—trespassing for one." Thomas managed to move the now hysterical woman from the lobby into the hall toward the bowels of the building. His much louder voice trailed away. "Just tell us what you saw. That's all we ask."

Martin brushed past Thomas and the homeless woman as he entered the lobby. "Dr. Cummins, you're here alone? Can't deny I'm disappointed." He smiled and winked at the receptionist, a new one hired last week after a rowdy after-hours celebratory event retired the last one of twenty years.

"She's really busy at the moment with her daughter and taking care of all the patients. However, I gotta say, it's been a real show out here."

"It's a police station. What do you expect?"

Brad shrugged, *I guess you're right about that.* He folded the brochure and slid it inside a pants pocket.

"Come on back to my office, Dr. Cummins. I've got a few minutes before I need to talk to that lady my detective is dealing with. There's always a new case around here."

Brad acknowledged the goodbye from the receptionist and took Key Martin's lead from the lobby. "What's up with that woman with Detective Thomas? What'd she see?"

Martin motioned for Brad to take a seat in his office. "You docs live in your own world, I guess."

"What does that mean?" Brad settled into the chair. He remembered the hard, cold metal and the aroma of stale coffee.

"There's been another murder. It'll hit the TV news tonight. Probably already on the apps if you follow those things."

"Not like Diana," Brad said. "Hate to hear about another shooting. This city always ranks high on the media's national homicide list."

"This isn't a drive-by shooting of a hooker on a corner or a drug dealer pushed from a car outside a convenience store," Martin said. "A woman was shot at long range earlier today. No details released yet but considering the relationship I have with you and Dr. Bratton—Gee, I almost said *the missus*. What planet am I from?"

Brad offered a weak smile and decided not to answer.

"Word will probably get around tomorrow at the hospital, especially considering the victim. Don't they put on a big spread for you guys at breakfast?" Martin sorted a few paper files on his desk without opening any of them, a routine Brad remembered from his prior visit with Diana.

"Yes, there is a breakfast." He studied Martin fiddle with files. "What do you mean about the victim? Who was it?"

"It was one of the Belmont physicians—and a woman too. Dr. Sidney Belmont."

Brad took a deep breath. "What? How?"

"Long range rifle. Can't discuss too many details. Investigation is ongoing, and we're waiting on ballistics. Don't know if it will match other cases."

"As in Chuck Wallace?"

"You know, Doc, you're getting to be as good a sleuth as your missus. Hey, better not tell Dr. Bratton I said that."

"What about the woman the detective was bringing in through the lobby?"

"That lady witnessed the shooting and could have crossed paths with the guy. Guy—I keep saying *guy,* but who knows these days. The shooter likely took aim from the building where the lady resides under the radar. Thinks she saw the getaway vehicle."

Brad thought about calling Diana with the update about Sidney Belmont. *Cheerleading moms' meeting. First one she's made. Better not bother her.*

"Diana and I went over this before I came down. I'm not here to rat anybody out, but we may have information that could help."

Martin slid a pad out of a drawer and pulled a pen from his shirt pocket. "Go ahead. Shoot. Sorry, poor choice of words."

Brad tilted his head somewhat to the side. "Never seen you take notes before."

"New leaf. Go ahead."

"Chuck Wallace's wife, Voncelle—you know, she practices with us—confided that she was on a rifle team in college."

Martin assumed a blank stare, then scribbled notes.

"She admitted that she hid the collection of guns in her house after Diana showed up and before you and Detective Thomas visited her. She thought the rifles would draw attention."

"Why do you think Mrs.—I mean, Dr. Wallace—told you that?"

Brad hesitated. "I don't know. We, I mean Diana mostly, may have pressed Voncelle about what was going on. She has dropped by our house unannounced, at least twice, and they weren't social visits. Of course, she could have talked to us at the clinic."

"What did she want?"

"She seemed worried about the Garcia guy. Said he was making trouble for her."

Martin raised his head from the note pad. "What kind of trouble?"

"Everybody knew that Chuck Wallace was knee deep in a deal to sell the Belmonts' practice to an overseas financial outfit. Voncelle tells us that after Chuck was shot, Garcia shows up unannounced to her house wanting to see Chuck's business records and didn't take lightly to being told no. She showed us the bruise on her face."

"If Dr. Wallace felt threatened, why didn't she call me or Detective Thomas? We both left our cards. And then there's always 911."

"Dunno. Guess that's part of the reason I'm here. Voncelle showed up at our house, finding Diana alone—probably her intent."

"Garcia turns up dead, and she drops by for another visit," Martin said. "I suspect she regretted revealing he threatened her. Maybe she needed an alibi?"

"She should have kept her mouth shut," Brad said. His cell phone lit up with a text message, he assumed from the hospital.

```
I was elected Head Mother of the Cheer-
leader Squad.  📱
```

"I'm going to have to cut this meeting short, Martin. I'll need to be heading home. Family situation."

"Before you go, Dr. Cummins, can you spare a few more minutes?"

Brad sighed and sat back down. "Sure."

"You weren't aware of Sidney Belmont's murder until I told you, at least that's what you said."

"Hadn't heard anything about it. I'm too busy for pop-up news, and we don't work with those guys over at Belmont much. It's a shame about her death."

"And I didn't know about Dr. Wallace's connection to Garcia until you came by, Doc. You've helped a lot." Martin stopped jotting notes and dropped the paper pad into a drawer.

Brad stood again to leave. "One reason, the main reason, I came down to the station is that Diana and I need to move on from these police matters. You've got someone behind bars, accused of attacking her twice. And now two people we know have been murdered. I gotta admit, I've rolled my eyes over this ongoing crap. It's time to close it down."

Martin stood and managed the ankle boot the best he could, the thing scheduled to be tossed in a week or two. "If you and Dr. Bratton will work with me for a few more days, less than a week—no—let's make that two weeks, we can bring this deal to a close. We'll make sure Dr. Bratton is in no danger, and the person who's taking out people from rooftops around town is put away. What do you say, Dr. Cummins?"

Brad thought about his return to Jackson from overseas deployment as a trauma surgeon, his twin brother's murder that shortly followed, and his falling in love with the new surgeon Diana Bratton. "I'm in, Martin. And guess what. I'm holding you to that promise. Two weeks. That's all you got."

"It's a deal," Martin said.

"I'm going to call Diana and run this by her." When she did not answer her cell, Brad said, "I guess she's drowning her sorrows in a milkshake—better than a bottle of wine."

"Milkshake?"

"We'll be in touch, Martin." Brad left the police chief's office and headed for the lobby. A room to the left of the hall remained open. The woman dressed in mismatched clothes from earlier talked loudly to the two people sitting at the metal table opposite while a uniformed police officer stood at the door disinterested. He shut the door as Brad walked by.

# Chapter 28

The next morning, word of Sidney Belmont's murder dominated the local news. Social media lit up, and even a national television morning show mentioned it: no motive, no suspects, a tremendous tragedy that a healthcare provider was slaughtered in broad daylight.

"I wonder what Phoebe thinks about her former doctor getting shot. I hope she wasn't anywhere around that building. Chief Martin's on the prowl," Brad said, stepping away from the stationary bike in the exercise room located off the master bathroom. He left the television on.

"Glad you got that thing warmed up. I'm gonna take a spin, although I'm not feeling well. Still trying to get over yesterday's cheerleader moms' meeting," Diana said.

"You're going to do a great job. And for what it's worth, I'll help you."

Diana mounted the bike and started pumping her legs. "We'll watch YouTube videos together on how to bake cupcakes and homemade Oreo balls," she said. "I'm holding you to it."

Brad finished shaving and dropped his exercise shorts to step into the shower. "I'll join you in a minute," Diana called out. "I need a back rub. Maybe more than that."

A group text popped up from their clinic office manager. Diana reached for her phone and read the first of the message as she pushed her legs and feet forward but felt a cramp in her calf:

    Funeral services for Sidney Eleanor Bel-
    mont tomorrow at Church of the …

"Brad, we need to mark out of the office and go to this."

He opened the shower door and called out, "You say something? Come on in here, if you want to talk—or whatever."

Diana stopped the bike and stepped to the double shower built with separate controls on either end. She took off her exercise wear, slipped inside, and turned the knobs to her side of the shower. "You run your side too hot," she said.

Brad moved close behind her. "Hot? That's about right."

"Hold on a minute. We need to talk about Sidney Belmont's murder."

Brad ran the bath sponge from Diana's shoulders down the mid of her back and around to her front. "A shame. A shame for sure." He rested his chin on her shoulder and continued with the sponge against Diana's skin.

The hot water sprayed around and onto them.

"Did you and Key Martin talk about it? About Sidney's death?"

"He's trying to put a connection between Chuck, Voncelle, Garcia, and now Sidney Belmont."

Diana responded to Brad's pressure against her back. "Nice, but one question. Did Key, I mean *Martin*, know anything about the one-on-one between Voncelle and Garcia?"

"Not a clue," Brad answered. "I think I impressed the chief with our information. He's ready to slap a badge on me."

Diana turned around in the shower spray and pulled Brad close. She wrapped herself around him and pushed him against the tile wall. They braced themselves before nearly slipping in the warm, soapy water. "First, you'll need to put some clothes on before you get pinned with that badge. That is, after we follow up on this caper," she said.

Brad lifted Diana onto him. "I gave him two weeks to figure it out." He leaned back against the tile for support and spoke into her ear. "And I found a really neat brochure on the reception counter at the police station. I want that to talk to you about it."

Diana moaned.

"That starts the conversation," Brad said.

Miles Belmont followed the minister's remarks, his slim fitted, dark grey suit fresh from alternations at the men's shop near Old Canton Road. Miles stood at the podium in the funeral home, his sister's deep mahogany casket front and center of the room. Ellis's insistence, no demand, that he speak after Miles was not a problem, only a nonargumentative triviality. After all, Ellis was the oldest brother and remained the senior member of the Belmont clan.

The arrangement of yellow and pink roses interlaced with white snapdragons draped the center of his sister's closed casket. Someone at the funeral home, a paid consultant included in the family bereavement package, selected all of the flowers, and organized the funeral service. Miles flipped through the several-page printed program for the first time and stared at the photograph of his sister reproduced on the front cover. *Where did they even get that picture? She never looked that good.*

Despite the mortician's best efforts and a make-up artist from the local community theater, an opened casket remained out of the question. Though never much for fixing up, Sidney wouldn't have wanted to be seen that way. *The bullet really did a number on her.*

"Dr. Belmont?" The funeral home director emerged from behind the tight area off stage, an overweight man in an inexpensive black suit with thin white, parallel stripes up the legs and jacket. His imitation silk tie in a tight Windsor knot was dark purple with miniature white crucifixes scattered on the background. "Is everything to your liking? The arrangements as promised?"

Miles peeked around the curtain and out over the audience. Lined with illuminated stained-glass windows embedded in oak paneled walls, the chapel room assigned to the grieving Belmont family and their guests was only about half full. Fortunately, the mourners were scattered about the space to make the attendance appear respectable. Sidney Eleanor Belmont was never one to make friends outside her medical practice, or inside it for that matter. Miles recognized only a few employees in the audience and doubted many other attendees were patients.

*How many patients would come out to pay respects to a cold bitch*, he decided.

Two men in drab suits slipped in at the rear of the room to take seats side-by-side on the back row. The older of the two nodded cordially though absent-mindedly at the woman four seats over who seemed to ignore them. She had brilliant red hair, age probably somewhere in her sixties but looked early fifties due to an extensive history of good skin care.

"You're on in one minute," the funeral home director said. "There's a small mic on the podium. It's got fresh batteries. Speak directly into it. The special people out there are here to pay homage to your dear sister and will cling to every word." The director backed away and waved Miles onto the stage.

Miles stepped up to the microphone and returned a weak smile of acknowledgement to the sparse audience. In addition to that over the casket, florist flowers of white and yellow lilies and roses banked the banquet-style piece of mahogany furniture beneath the Christian cross at the side of the room. *Ellis spared no expense.*

He removed the prepared speech from inside his suit jacket and unfolded it. Authored by Sidney's secretary and printed in large font so he could skip the readers, the words paid homage to a brilliant woman brought down in her prime. Miles had wanted to add *brought down in a heinous crime*, then ruled out the dramatic. Sid's eulogy of *lifelong dedication to medical training and healing* would fill the aisle with tears and grow him a Pinocchio nose. He began the homage and stared at the audience, penetrating the eyes and soul of each person below him.

One of the other clinic secretaries wept in the front row as he spoke, rumor being she helped with the google search of tributes to the dearly departed and actually wrote his speech. Another woman Miles recognized as a Belmont family babysitter from about four decades ago sat near the secretarial speech writer and dabbed her eyes with a handkerchief.

"Childless," Miles continued, "Sid considered her patients her children, nurturing them through illness and through trying times. While the human body did not always respond to my dear sister's medical knowledge and skill, the soul accepted comfort in that Sidney Eleanor Belmont, MD, was doing all she could—bringing in the most talented consultants whenever needed and drawing on her number one rank at medical school class graduation."

Through the rear double doors, which remained open to the small lobby, Miles spotted Ellis staring at him. Ellis shook his head, grimaced, and shrugged in an *A little over the top with that one, don't ya think?* gesture and disappeared.

*You think you can do any better?* Miles thought and continued. He could hear Ellis off to the left and behind him quietly ascend the short section of steps to the stage. *Ellis will have his speech memorized or shoot from the hip. What an ass. I'll throw him a curve ball and ad lib.*

Miles paused a few seconds to improvise and cleared his throat, the short stall an added effort to show how emotion can overcome a speaker. He further slowed the pace of his speech. "No doubt our brother, our older brother Ellis Belmont, will share many fond memories of Sidney and me as his younger sister and brother, Sidney riding a bike with training wheels and me learning to drive. He may talk about our parents, both physicians themselves and proud of their three children. Mom and Dad had such high hopes."

The former babysitter nodded and glanced at her phone, presumably for the time.

"Those hopes achieved when their three offspring all became physicians, not all number one in the graduating class like Sid. The top ten for me and the top fifty for Ellis." The remark brought weak, almost embarrassed, chuckles scattered among the mourners. Miles sensed steam rise offstage. "Nevertheless, the three of us Belmont children have continued the dedicated healthcare mission of the Belmont Comprehensive Medicine Clinic established by our parents and added the Wellness Enhancement Spa, which—in another accolade to my departed sister—was her idea. In fact, I guess that's her progeny, the legacy Sidney Eleanor Belmont leaves. I will miss Sid dearly."

Miles gently rubbed the knuckle of his forefinger under his right eye. "I would like to introduce my brother, Dr. Ellis Belmont, who will say what I am sure are profound words. Ellis?"

Several in the audience fiddled briefly with the two-page folded program, including the old babysitter and the attractive older woman with red hair. They would take notice of the short reception with light refreshments scheduled to follow off the front lobby, an opportunity to visit with the family of the deceased.

Ellis Belmont spoke warmly of his sister, mentioning that she admirably filled his shoes as successor to area representative of the statewide medical organization, adding that he had also served as president of that organization and later national vice-president. Effortlessly, he worked into his talk Miles's shortcoming of lack of success in medical politics and spoke fifteen minutes longer than he.

At the reception, the lady with red hair and good skin stood next in line to great the Belmont brothers, nieces, nephews, and cousins on staff at the Belmont medical facility and spa as well as the several other cousins from Dallas who were not healthcare providers. The cousins had driven over with plans to continue their trip down to New Orleans for a short vacation. The lady sipped on water poured from a plastic bottle into a clear plastic cup. "Such a tragedy," she said to Dr. Ellis Belmont.

"I was a former patient of your sister. My name is Phoebe—"

The person behind her stood with an unruly child who picked the moment to tug away from the adult in charge and bump Phoebe's arm, interrupting her introduction and splashing water on Ellis's tie. Phoebe glared down in forced horror at the wet mark and then focused genuine annoyance at the boy.

"I am terribly, terribly sorry, ma'am. I couldn't get a babysitter—and I work at the office in billing—and I couldn't miss this and—"

"Never, never mind, Lindsey," Miles interjected. "It's only water. Ellis won't melt."

Lindsey pulled the boy away in admonishment. "Wait until we get home and I tell your father. I need this job and you have embarrassed me."

The boy and his mother disappeared around the corner to the amusement of Phoebe and the brothers Belmont.

"I was going to say that I visited your sister in your spa," Phoebe said, speaking to both men.

Ellis seemed to study Phoebe's face and figure with judicial discretion. "Well, I would say Sidney did a remarkable job," he said and inspected the line in anticipation of the next person to greet, an overweight man about five-six, the clinic's accountant.

Phoebe wanted to say more. Nevertheless, she overcame the urge to mention the facial and arm paralysis, the trip to the Emergency Department, and the physical therapy that followed—all due to the work of the dear and departed neurologist, Dr. Sidney Belmont. This was certainly no time to show disrespect for the dead. Nonetheless it had not been a waste of time. True curiosity about the Belmont clan brought her here.

"Toby, it's wonderful that you came," Ellis spoke ahead to the accountant, turning his head away from Phoebe. She stepped to the side and in front Miles, who extended his hand.

"Dr. Miles Belmont … nice of you to come by."

Phoebe considered her late mother and the manners she instilled. She questioned her decision to come to the funeral and her reasons to join the Belmont family for visitation. Phoebe pushed aside the manners.

*Sorry, Momma.* Phoebe smiled with beautiful straight teeth, then for only a few seconds twisted her face into contortion and dropped her shoulder and arm limp.

Miles backed away dismayed and near horrified, then dashed

forward as though the woman with red hair might need medical attention.

Before he could reach for her, Phoebe straightened up and chortled. "Don't you worry about it. Your sister didn't." Phoebe left the receiving line feeling Belmont's eyes stare a hole in the back of her head and said, "Sorry, Momma," under her breath this time. She purposefully rocked her right heel to the side in a show-off stumble, grabbed a sugar cookie from the refreshment table, and signed the attendance book on her way out the front door of the funeral home.

# Chapter 29

$B$rad gambled and won. He bet the men's walking group would continue to meet at the same time and location and reasoned that one deceased member getting shot from a rooftop would be no reason to disband an organization.

His only contact with the group had been the late Chuck Wallace, and he could barely remember the names of the other men much less have cell numbers. He did remember a Roger—*or was it Ralph, and a Peter—no, he goes by Pete—and some guy named Michael—no, Matt.* Others walked that night before Chuck's shooting halted the trek and Brad's opportunity to get to know anyone well.

Brad pulled up to the curb in front of the two-story house on the corner. He remembered the pick-up truck in the driveway, parked to the left to let the walking group member's wife and lady of the house in and out of the garage without inconvenience. An SUV pulled up behind Brad, and other vehicles were parked nearby along the street. Several men stood at the foot of the driveway talking. One studied his phone, the brisk neighborhood walking route to kick off in four minutes.

*Maybe one of these fellas had it out for Chuck. Maybe one of their wives is involved. Agreed: Diana and I need to get this crap behind us.* Brad raised the steering column for more space and reached to tighten a shoelace of one of the new pair of tennis shoes purchased for the night. A rap on the driver's window startled him into a strangle-tight knot. The man pointed to his Apple watch. Brad nodded and opened the door.

"Hey, just kidding about the watch. We got plenty of time before kick-off, a minute and a half!" said the guy Brad now clearly remembered as Pete. Brad stepped from his vehicle. "I'm Peter Mitchell. Most everybody calls me Pete."

Brad answered the offer of a handshake. "Sure, Pete, I remember. And I'm not late. That's one thing Chuck made clear."

The two men joined the others at the end of the driveway. "I'm surprised you came back after that night," Pete said. "We all took the rest of the week off after what happened to Chuck. We're back to full speed now. Aren't we, gentlemen!"

Other men welcomed Brad with handshakes and pats on the back as the caravan started, and Peter Mitchell moved ahead to the front of the line. Brad quickened his pace to blend in. Another one of the men moved in beside Brad. "Hey, name's Matt Batson. Glad to see you walking with us again."

"Sure. Glad to be back. Name's Brad."

"We all remember the doctor, Chuck's friend. Each one of us was worthless that night in helping you. I remember this one guy threw up over in a shrub when you started CPR."

"Wasn't much anybody could do. I got a pulse. That was about it."

Matt moved closer. "We didn't hear much about what happened after the ambulance showed up. That was a real shame."

Another man lined up to Brad's left. "It's *Brad*, isn't it?"

Brad nodded. "Y'all talking about the night Chuck was shot? Police ever figure out what happened? Haven't seen anything on the news."

"Ralph, here, knows all the detective shows and documentaries," Matt said. "Those JPD detectives ought to talk to Ralph. He's probably seen a TV episode where they solved a case like Chuck's."

"To change the subject, Brad, Matt thinks he's the jokester of the group—does Cajun accents and everything. A few jokes are good. Most are corny."

"You're the first to laugh, Ralphie Boy, every time," Matt said. "We'll have to let Dr. Brad judge for himself. Might have to tell the window story tonight, when we turn onto the next street."

"Can't wait," Brad said with a hint of sarcasm. All three snickered. A couple of seconds passed as they turned a corner and avoided a pothole in the street. "You follow a lot of crime dramas on TV, Ralph? What do you think happened with Chuck?"

"The perp is always the wife or the wife's boyfriend who wants the chap out of the picture. Same plot over and over," Ralph said. "They throw in a twist from time-to-time to keep the shows interesting. There was this one time when the wife buried the husband under the backyard firepit and married her boyfriend next to it and—"

Matt interrupted. "Brad wants to know what you think about Chuck. You joined the group about the time he did. Y'all hung out in the back most of the time."

"Sure," Ralph said. "At first Chuck seemed like most guys who join the group. There's a good mix of professions who walk at night. Lots of political or sports talk on these walks, not much about personal stuff. It's an hour or so in the evening when you can step away from the stresses of your own world."

"Sounds like a decent gig," Brad said.

Ralph waved his hand forward to the guys walking ahead of them. "We've got an understanding. You don't talk on your cell or text during a walk. In fact, most of the guys who live in the neighborhood don't even bring their phones. Chuck lived a few blocks over, outside of the gate, and seemed to always have his. He got calls a lot."

"Chuck got a call that night," Brad said. "He backed away and said he would meet up with us."

"Since the routes match the day of the week and we start on time, you can usually figure out where the group will be at a certain point," Ralph said. "It's easy to catch up."

"Not always the case," Matt interrupted again.

Brad turned his head toward Matt at the abruptness, barely missing the next pothole and avoiding a twisted ankle. "How's that?"

Matt hesitated. "Sometimes it rains? Or we get a late start."

"Bull crap," Ralph said. "You can set your watch."

"That's why Chuck said he could meet us up ahead," Brad said. "I guess he thought his time on the phone wouldn't be all that long." The three men walked in silence. Someone in the front row yelled that a deer was running out from a vacant, wooded lot to cross their path.

"Happens all the time," Matt said. "New residential and commercial construction pushes the wildlife up from the Pearl River."

"Better look out for a snake in the road too," Ralph said. "See 'em mostly in the spring."

Brad thought about the concept of a snake in the midst of the group.

"Any idea who called Chuck that night?" Matt asked.

"How would anybody know that? He dropped back with his phone and didn't say," Ralph said.

Brad wished he had planned the night better with Diana—or even with Key Martin—and established boundaries to the discussion or bullet points to cover. He shook his head clear. *This isn't a boring, routine patient interview. Try chatting with these boys. Put an end to this.*

"Believe or not, the police are working on it," Brad said. "And they're close to nailing who shot Chuck."

Matt's stride seemed to skip a step despite the smooth surface of this section of the route. "Really, man? How would you know anything like that? Nothing's been in the news."

"Who cares how Brad knows," Ralph said. "But I sure hope it's true."

Brad thought another moment. "My wife's got connections with the JPD. She talks to detectives. She knows stuff."

"When Chuck told us about you joining the group, he said your wife's a doctor too, a surgeon," Ralph said.

"She is. We're partners in a surgery practice. In fact, Chuck's widow works with us."

"Wow, no wonder you're into what happened to Chuck," Matt said.

"It's a lot to deal with, for sure." In the shadows of a streetlamp,

Brad noticed a curvy, thick dark object ahead of him and jumped back. Matt pulled a short flashlight from his pocket and pointed it at Brad's feet.

"Only a twisted stick," Matt said. "See?" He kicked the short, fallen branch from the tree near the curb back into the front lawn of the house they passed. "All this talk about somebody shooting from the top of one of these houses has made you kinda jumpy, Doc. Don't ya think?" Matt laughed and took another swipe at the small limb.

The three men realized they had fallen behind about twenty or thirty feet from the others and picked up their pace.

"Have y'all thought much about how Chuck was shot or from where the shooter was positioned?" Brad asked. "Even the news hasn't said much about what the police know."

"We don't need the news when we've got you with us, Dr. Brad," Matt said. "Do we, Ralph?"

"I hope they catch the ass who shot Chuck," Ralph said. The three picked up speed and caught up with the others. "Y'all think what happened to Chuck could ever happen again?"

"No way," Matt said.

Brad felt the laces to a tennis shoe loosen and slowed to tighten them. With the laces tighter, he stumbled to catch up.

"The shooter's still out there," Brad said, short of breath. "You men don't worry about a repeat? Even a copycat?"

Another walker trotted up to join the three men to form a line of four. "Wife booked us for a charity dinner tonight. Somehow, I got by with only cocktails and appetizers, and we slipped away before the buffet supper."

"Glad you got your priorities straight," Matt said and laughed.

"Justin, we wondered about you. 'Specially since you missed last night," Ralph said. "Thought maybe you had to babysit again."

"You know Brad here?" Matt asked.

Justin Horner smiled in Brad's direction. "Yeah, I was walking the night Chuck—died—and was useless to help with the CPR. I'm not much on medical stuff."

"Right. I remember," Brad said. "We got a heartbeat, and that was about all. The EMTs couldn't do much more."

"What do y'all think actually went down that night?" Justin asked.

Brad waited for an answer. Everyone remained quiet.

"And I guess y'all heard about the shooting near a construction site off Highland Colony somewhere," Justin said. "A woman was killed."

"Hey, Brad, that woman was a doctor too. Heard that on the morning news. Not many other details," Ralph said.

"You know who it was?" Matt asked. "Hope nobody you work with."

The conversation shifted as Brad hoped. He wanted these men to talk. "Name was Sidney Belmont. She isn't—wasn't—a surgeon, and from what I know, showed up to take care of patients, and that means a lot."

"I want my doctor to be there when I need 'em," Ralph said.

"Me too," Justin Harris said.

"There were three siblings who practice—or practiced—together. Two brothers are left with several extended family members also in the outfit," Brad said.

"My secretary went to the lady Belmont last month," Matt said. "Yeah, it was Belmont—Sidney. Secretary couldn't come back to the office for a week she was so messed up and had to work from home. That was a real pisser."

"For you or for her?" Justin asked. "She was probably happy not to see your mug for a few days."

All four men laughed, then Matt was quick to retort. "My secretary loves me. Brings me cookies and brownies. Makes my mom jealous. Wife could care less."

"Your wife's waiting for a big-dollar way out," Justin said to more laughter. "Same as mine."

Brad wanted to bring the discussion back to Chuck Wallace and tried to remember all that Diana had shared with him. The conversation drifted off among the three other men to secretaries who had come and gone through the years, never with a hint of envy from any of their wives. *Like to see what these boys would say about a few of the nurses I've run across.* Brad shook the thought away. *Now, what was the name of Diana's patient who told her she knew Chuck Wallace?*

"Hey, Brad. Mighty quiet over there," Matt said. "You still with us?"

"Oh, yeah. Counting the calories I'm burning up." Several steps ensued. *Roy ... Something.*

"Chuck Wallace had a friend from several years ago, like before he was married and lived in New Orleans. I know this because of what my wife told me. Name might have been Roy. He also moved to Jackson."

"Oh, man. That's that gotta be Roy Garnett," Ralph said. "Chuck invited him to walk a couple of times."

*The guy who got my number and thought he had appendicitis,* Brad remembered.

"Two bricks short of a load, that fella," Matt said. "Seems like it wasn't more than a couple of times till he finally drifted away. Can't say we were sad."

"I remember he talked a lot about his nephew," Justin said. "Asked advice, I remember, about how to handle him. Let's see, what was the issue?"

"He wanted to know if any of us knew a good psychologist or psychiatrist," Ralph said.

"For him?"

"No, for the poor nephew," Ralph answered.

*The nephew who attacked Diana.* "He ever bring the nephew on a walk?" Brad asked

"Think so," Justin answered. "Only one time."

"Don't remember that."

"I do. It was a small turn out, Matt. One of the few nights you've missed."

At Justin's remark, Ralph scanned the houses on both sides of the street. "I remember the nephew asking a bunch of questions about the houses in the neighborhood."

"What kind of questions?" Brad asked.

Ralph tilted his head to the side as they moved ahead. "Like: *What kind of people live in these houses. Who owns them? Are all the houses always occupied?* Stuff like that."

The group turned the corner onto the next street. "What'd you think about those questions. Sort of strange, maybe?" Brad's voice trailed off. From the distance, he studied the fateful area near the ditch and the curb of the street where Chuck Wallace fell. He envisioned the failed attempt at resuscitation that night with a sweaty Dr. Brad Cummins leading a pack of totally useless assistants. "I wish I—we—could have done more for Chuck," Brad said.

"If you got a pulse," Matt said. "Chuck had a chance then."

"Not much, I'm afraid," Brad said. "If you got close enough, you saw the blood. A lot of it."

"I remember it was a shot to the chest, not the head. On TV when they write in a head shot, the character is a goner. No way they'll make Season 2," Matt said.

"Who made you coroner?" Justin said. A couple of the walkers in the row ahead hooted and shot a grin back at the four.

"Matt is number one everywhere he goes," one of the men called back over his shoulder. "Just ask him."

The group passed the murder scene. Gone was the yellow and black crime scene tape that once encircled an area of the shallow drainage ditch and section of the adjoining driveway and street. Rain had since washed away the chalk outline of Chuck's body—the spot where he fell and was resuscitated. A woman in a bulky, dark housecoat and slippers wheeled her trash can to the curb, ignoring the men until they passed by. Garbage spilled from the top. Brad spotted her admire them from behind and smile.

*Old lady still got life in her.* Brad took a deep breath. *Back to the mission at hand.* "Garnett hasn't been back since Chuck died?" he asked.

"No. I would've been surprised if he'd showed up after Chuck was gone," Ralph said. "He stayed close to Chuck and didn't say much when he walked with us. The nosey nephew's the one who did most of the talking."

Brad felt his cell phone vibrate in the pocket of his athletic shorts. The text message was nothing urgent. He would call the hospital later.

"I spotted Garnett at Chuck's funeral," Justin said. "Sitting in the back, dressed in a beige suit and brown tie. The nephew wasn't with him."

During his follow-up appointment with Diana, as she had told Brad, Roy Garnett shared information about his New Orleans friendship with Chuck Wallace and Chuck's adulterous relationship with Voncelle. Brad did not consider sharing that information, a HIPPA violation, since it did not actually concern Garnett's medical or surgical care. He thought about Garnett's nephew holding Diana at gunpoint in her car and then grabbing her at the empty house across from where Chuck was shot.

*It's everyman for himself.*

"I believe Chuck and Garnett go way back. In fact, there's no question about it," Brad said.

The group was silent except for the sound of several brands of tennis shoes striking the pavement in a basic, uniform rhythm.

"Hey, man," Matt said. "It's great that you're out making this trail with us, getting healthy and all that. And it's a shame about what happened to Chuck. He was your friend, our friend too. But this is mostly a lighthearted group, and we got other things going on around here."

"Not sure what you mean," Brad said.

"It's like you're a detective or something, your wife too."

"That's coming down pretty strong, Matt," Justin said. "I don't think it's anything like that with Brad."

"I don't know. Buddy Brad's already let us know he and the wife are tight with JPD."

"What difference does that make? Brad and his wife are busy

doctors. People close to them have gotten messed up. I remember from the news that Brad's wife got held up at work—in her car."

*Diana wanted to keep the gun-to-her-head incident out of the news. No way that was gonna happen.* "Didn't mean to push too far, Matt. Just thought everybody would want to find out what really happened to Chuck."

"We already know what happened to Chuck," Matt said. "It's up to your buddies at JPD to figure out why. When it's all said and done, we come out on these walks to get away from having to figure it all out."

"I thought that talking about it might turn up more helpful information. Sorry if I was too much," Brad said.

"Find that Garnett guy. Pressure him for info. Leave us out of it."

"Hold on, Matt. We each got one vote out here, one lousy opinion," Ralph said," and my vote's with Brad. If I were invited to a party, to a baseball game, or to a neighborhood walk and my host was shot in the head at long range, I'd want to know what happened. I would want answers."

A clap of thunder heard in the distance over a cluster of pine trees knocked everyone off course for a few seconds.

"We better pick up speed before the rain hits," Justin said to more thunder. Lightning lit the sky. "Hate to admit it." He shook his head. "Matt could be right. Find Garnett and you might get answers."

# Chapter 30

Rain fell in hard sheets under the veil of more thunder. Lightning lit the sky toward the east in the direction of the Pearl River, framing the houses and the trees in the landscape along that side of the street against a deep, black background. "That's it, gents. See ya tomorrow night," Matt called out and peeled away from the group.

The men scattered in tangential directions, each on a deliberate path toward his own home or vehicle. Brad ran toward his SUV parked several blocks away, drenched.

Matt Batson cut through two or three backyards to reach his home in a minute or so. Rose bushes tore through his Spartan running pants when he jumped a low fence and outran an angry Siberian huskie imperious to the rain. Matt burst through his kitchen door, dripping wet.

"Home early, Matt? Guess the rain got ya. Your lovely wife left before the storm hit. She's out playing Mahjong."

Matt grabbed a kitchen towel from a drawer and wiped his face dry. His hair stuck up straight. He removed the wet quarter zip pullover and tossed it in a corner, leaving a dry-enough tee-shirt underneath. Next, he jerked open the refrigerator door and grabbed a beer.

"You're gonna have to leave. Things are getting too sticky," he said.

"Why, bro?"

Matt pulled a kitchen stool under him and moved in close. He took a long drag from the bottle. "Don't call me that, you ass. I'm not your brother."

Roy Garnett twirled the spoon in his bowl of cookies and cream ice cream. "Doesn't brother-in-law count for anything?"

"Only that my wife holds certain things over me. 'Be nice to my brother, Matt.' I hear that every night getting ready for bed," Matt said.

"From what I hear down the hall in my bedroom, even with the doors shut tight, you hold me in high esteem." Roy Garnett shoved a spoon full of ice cream into his mouth. Before he could swallow, he pushed in another.

Matt rammed his stool against Roy's. "I let you move in here only because my wife says you are family. God knows how your parents put up with the both of you. And up to a couple of weeks ago, I had no problem tolerating you."

"My sister's always been loyal to family," Roy said. "When our momma got dementia, she made sure she got to the doctor whenever—"

Matt pressed even closer to Roy, and Roy shut up. "This nephew. I know you let him in our house. I know you let him sleep here on the couch over there." He pointed to the short sofa in the keeping room off the kitchen and in front of the gas log fireplace. "Your nephew was gone when I got up. Left the blanket and pillow crumpled in a heap."

"The boy's never been much of a housekeeper," Roy said.

Matt knocked the ceramic bowl and spoon away from him in a sweeping thrust from his right arm and hand. The bowl miraculously landed in the kitchen sink, broken into several pieces. The spoon spun to a stop in the bottom of the basin. "Then I guess he's having trouble making his bed in the Hinds County Jail."

"Thank you. I was about finished with my ice cream."

"You can clean up that crap later," Matt said.

"You mentioned bail. Posted it this morning. Your sweet mother-in-law left him a nest egg for expenses," Roy said. "My mother, always the planner."

Matt guzzled the beer. "I bet Momma Garnett's leaping for joy in her grave over the use of what's left of her hard-earned teacher's pension," Matt said.

"Nephew never has been quite right in the head. Not in my opinion, at least. The judge should grant leniency."

"You know, Roy, you're full of it. More so every day."

"Any good lawyers in that treasured walking group of yours who could represent him? Enter an insanity plea?"

"I wouldn't curse any of my friends with a client like your and my wife's nephew," Matt said. "I could tell Dillon was looney the first time you brought him over to this house. Judge could see it that way. Depends on where the case lands."

Roy opened the freezer and served himself a fresh bowl of ice cream, this time birthday cake flavor. He ignored the mess in the sink. "Glad you see the case my way, bro."

Matt finished his beer and opened another. "Don't need to tell you again about dropping the *bro*. The lady surgeon your nephew assaulted—*twice*—her husband was with us tonight, asking questions."

"Dr. Diana Bratton is a nice person. In fact, I've been to her as a patient."

"She's tight with the police. I doubt she lets this case go. Neither will her husband."

Roy eased a heavy spoonful of hard ice cream between his lips, then popped his mouth open wide in surprise, his jaws extended to the hilt. "Gee, this stuff is freezing cold. Got my back molar good. Hurts like hell." He moved the ice cream around inside his mouth using his tongue and swallowed hard. "There, that's better."

"If I were you, I'd turn things over to the public defender unless Momma Garnett left behind a really fat bank account." Matt swallowed the beer and grabbed a bag of chips from the nearby pantry. He ripped open the top and tossed a corn chip into his mouth. "I do know one thing—Mr. and Mrs. Matt Batson ain't gonna lift a finger to buy the nephew's way out of this. Your sister and I had a long talk about it. She's got some girls' trips planned and wants to paint the bedroom and the living room. There's no extra cash around here," he said, chewing.

Using his spoon, Roy played with what was left of the ice cream in the bowl until it softened. "The account can handle it, and if not I might can help."

"That's sounding better."

"I feel a tiny pang of guilt now and then."

Matt washed down more corn chips with beer. "How so?"

"I mentioned that incident to him, the one that summer down on the sandbar when little sis and I were kids. Your wife was at a piano lesson."

"Oh, yeah. You saved her when she fell into the Pearl River. That's a bunch of—"

"No, there you're wrong. The river was low, and we were racing along the edge of the sandbar. I got ahead of her, stumbled, and she tripped over me. She was in the water before I knew what happened. I have to admit, the current wasn't much that time of year. Swimming out to get her wasn't all that difficult."

"You're several years older. You should have been able to get to her."

"I believe he saw it differently or heard the story in a kind of twisted way—as though I had been out to murder my sister and had a change of heart."

"I don't think my wife ever saw it that way. Or at least never shared that version with me. Gee, I married into a really screwed-up family." Matt finished his second beer. "There's a hurt on every pew, a minister once told me."

"I don't doubt that," Roy responded.

"There is something Brad Cummins told us tonight." Matt sneered. "You knew Chuck Wallace when he lived in New Orleans. He had an affair with one of Brad's partners while she practiced surgery down there. He married her after the first husband died."

"The poor guy was a resident or some kind of fellow in radiology at Ochsner. I shared that info with Dr. Bratton during an appointment—so much for doctor-patient confidentiality."

Matt stood from his stool and stared down at Roy. "You beginning to understand why I said this situation is getting too close?"

"One thing I do understand is that you're standing too close to me. Your beer-and-chips breath will for sure keep things quiet down the hall tonight."

"Cut the crap, Roy. Some ass shot one of the guys in my group from a rooftop, then your nephew gets arrested later near that same house pointing a weapon at Brad Cummins's wife—the lady surgeon who consults with JPD."

"Dillon told me what he told the police. That was all coincidence. He followed her there."

"And they believed him?" Matt said. "And get this—while walking I heard there's been another murder, a female doctor. Perp made sure the gal went down—no CPR needed. That makes two dead."

"What about ballistics with the female doctor? Same gun?"

"How would I know that? Ask Cummins or his wife."

Roy turned in the direction of the den, out from under the beer and corn chip breath. "You've got quite a collection of rifles in the display cabinet in the next room."

"What does that mean? Most everybody around here hunts and owns rifles and has at least one gun in the house. Some of my wife's friends are better shots than their husbands or boyfriends."

"You don't keep that gun cabinet locked."

"We don't have any kids left around here to mess with my guns. They're all grown," Matt said. "Besides, if we got robbed and the case was locked, the thugs would smash out the glass front."

"Don't worry. None of your weapons were missing."

"Thanks for the surveillance, Roy, and the update." Matt grabbed another beer. "And stay out of my business."

"The feeling's mutual, Matt." Roy slid off the stool and away from close quarters with his brother-in-law. "And I would slow down on the beer if I were you."

He rinsed out the second ice cream bowl in the sink, placed it and the spoon in the dishwasher, then picked up the pieces of the first bowl and dropped them in the kitchen trash. "Sis will appreciate my effort at housekeeping."

"I want you gone in the morning, Roy. I mean it. Think of an excuse without blaming me. I'm tired of you lurking around my house, getting in the way, listening to me having sex with my wife. I will be home from work tomorrow about five-thirty. You and your mess better be out of here."

# Chapter 31

$D$iana finished the spread sheet on her laptop. The snack assignments for the cheerleading moms were listed by date, practice location, person responsible, and number of servings required with an extra column for miscellaneous instructions. Although a lone dad had joined the moms' group, the name had not changed. At the recommendation of her predecessor, Diana assigned him to the easiest practice, the one scheduled in the school gym after regular working hours.

She put that task aside and accessed the patient file belonging to Chuck Wallace, understanding she might be flagged since Chuck Wallace was never her patient. Screw the hospital staff that monitors these things. She had to know.

Brad had a busy twenty-four call the day after Chuck was shot and did not have much time to follow his treatment once the ambulance arrived. Diana found the EMT records in the attachments file and scanned the medic's notes. Brad's CPR did regain a pulse, and Chuck survived the ambulance ride to make it to cardiothoracic surgery and a short admission to SICU, no more than four hours. She scanned the nursing documentation and noted that Voncelle had visited once with no record of how long she stayed.

*Regardless of visitors' hours, the front desk would have let Voncelle see her husband since she is a doctor. Likely let any wife in to visit under the circumstances.*

Diana found no record of Voncelle's leaving the ICU or how long she remained at bedside with her injured husband.

Her next search for Sidney Belmont could be another red flag. But then again, she was not altering the medical record. She expected to get a pass. *I'll take a box of fresh pastries by medical records tomorrow. Pick 'em up from that new place in Fondren.*

Most trauma like that seen with the Wallace and Belmont shootings, and Garcia for that matter, wound up at the medical center near downtown Jackson, although Metropolitan somehow received both. The first notes in the ED were morbidly descriptive about the physical condition of the corpse as were selected photographs. Nursing notes mentioned that several police officers hung around the Emergency Department.

Diana noted the full toxicology screens of both patients, a routine test in most trauma cases. Chuck's positive reading for alcohol was well below the legal limit. Sidney's results were pristine. Diana glanced around the well-familiar area of the Doctors' Lounge lined with the short bank of cubicles and computers and remained alone. She signed out of the computer and pushed away from the desk.

"I hope I'm not disturbing you."

Easy to startle since the evenings in the clinic garage and at the vacant house, Diana jumped in her chair. "Oh, no problem. I was deep into my medical records."

"Just taking a break from signing out path reports." Tall, slender, and bald (except for a semicircle of thin white hair at the crown of the scalp), the chief of the pathology department opened the refrigerator and removed a bottle of water. The flimsy, recyclable plastic container partially collapsed in his grasp as he twisted away the top, splashing water on his vest. He wiped against the spill with his free hand. "These thin bottles get skimpier and skimpier all the time. Where does this *all for the environment* push end?" He took a sip of what was left. "Oh, and again, I apologize for coming up behind you."

"No problem. I'm a little on edge these days."

"Better mind that caffeine! Too much is a killer." The pathologist took a place on the couch and started checking his phone.

"Thanks, I'll keep that in mind." Diana left the chair by the computer and grabbed a Coke Zero from the same refrigerator. She took a seat in a club chair opposite the couch and to the side from where the pathologist sat. "I know you're on a break. You mind if I pick your brain?"

"Anytime. You surgeons keep me in business. I'm at your beck and call." He lay the phone face down in his lap and took another drink from the skimpy water bottle, careful not to spill the rest.

"I should remember this from med school, and I know I could google it—but if you were going to kill someone—poison someone, perhaps—what could you use that wouldn't show up on a tox screen? A medication or chemical compound not routinely measured at autopsy."

The pathologist thought for a few seconds. "Well, the first thing that comes to mind is an easy one: potassium. You see that all the time on television, on those detective and murder mystery shows. Somebody pushes potassium chloride through an IV, and voila—instant cardiac arrhythmia. Since serum potassium levels increase after death, hyperkalemia is expected in the postmortem bloodwork, and potassium levels can often be used to estimate the time of death."

"So, elevated potassium levels as the cause of death could go undiagnosed," Diana said. The blood potassium levels in the lab reports of both Chuck Wallace and Sidney Belmont suggested nothing unusual. However, Belmont died on the scene. "Anything else?" she asked.

"There's always the ol' inject air into the intravenous tubing to mimic a pulmonary embolus. You see that a lot on TV dramas."

The pathologist chuckled, and Diana forced a polite smile. "I really do hate to interrupt your break, but can you think of anything not so overused?" she asked.

He took a deep breath and put the cell on the cushion bedside him. "Let's see. There's always Neo."

"Neo?"

"Neosynephrine or phenylephrine is often used by anesthesiologists to raise blood pressure. It would be kept on the anesthesia medication carts and readily available. It's a very potent agonist to produce vasoconstriction and must be used in the correct dosage. A little goes a long way, as they say."

"Phenylephrine is not routinely measured on a toxicology screen?" She remembered no mention of that compound in the reports.

"Phenylephrine or Neosynephrine is readily metabolized by the liver and quickly excreted in the urine. It works quick to raise blood pressure. Does its job and is gone in no time. I've never thought to somehow include it in a drug screen."

"So, if someone received an overdose of Neosynephrine—"

"Heart rate and cardiac output could acutely decrease in response to the jump in blood pressure, and it's all over for them. Used in appropriate dosages, Neo is safe for patients without pre-existing heart disease. If administered incorrectly, can lead to death."

"An MI or a stroke," Diana said. "Cardiac failure."

"Particularly if there is a history of cardiac arrhythmia, which often goes undiagnosed." A shrill chime burst from the pathologist's cell phone. "Oops, sorry about that. I keep the volume on this thing at max, getting harder and harder to hear these days. They need me in the lab to sign out path reports. Always, always busy it seems with all the gunshot wound victims of late."

He retrieved his phone, stood from the couch, and dropped the cell in his pants pocket. "Life moves forward, good and bad. We pathologists like it that way." He offered a polite good-bye wave, wiggling his fingers. "Please keep those specimens coming."

Diana smiled politely as the pathologist left the lounge, then circled back around to the OR. She grabbed a surgical cap and found the anesthesia tech, a diminutive, dark-skinned woman and longtime hospital employee, entering the double doors to the suite. Diana followed her to outside one of the operating rooms.

"Hey, Reba."

"Dr. Bratton, whatchu doin' back here at this time of day. The schedule's finished. You oughta be home with that handsome husband of yours. Don't you have a cute daughter too? If I were you, I'd make more babies."

Diana smiled nervously. "I was hoping you could help me."

"Anything, Dr. Bratton. And forgive my blabber mouth. I know you and Doc Cummins got it figured out."

"I hope we do," Diana said. She stepped with Reba to a rolling supply cart and into the operating room. "I've been curious about something."

Reba grunted and lifted a compact carton from the cart and slit open the top with a box cutter. She seemed to refer to her iPad and started to transfer bottles and cartridges from the box to the anesthesia supply cart. The cart stood to the left of the anesthesiologist captain's chair, in easy reach for administering medicine throughout a surgical case. The patient monitors and anesthesia dispensing equipment were to the side of the anesthesiologist's spot.

"Uhh … you're very busy, Reba. If you don't have time to talk now, I understand."

"Nonsense, you sweet thing. Tell me what you need."

*I'll need to do something nice for this woman.* Both women stood in the working confines of the anesthesiologist's space in the OR. Reba had moved a few pieces of small equipment out of the way to stock the supply cart. Reba was in total control of her world.

*How can I work this without sounding suspicious?* "We stay busy during a surgery case. Of course, we each have our jobs to do with the patient, but I wonder sometimes what the anesthesiologist or nurse anesthetist faces."

"You're the surgeon, Dr. Bratton, the big boss in the room. As long as they keep the patient asleep and wake 'em up when you're finished, then you're good." Reba tossed the empty carton into the nearest trash receptacle and picked up another. She slit it open before Diana could blink and emptied it before Diana's next breath.

"What about Neosynephrine? You ever stock that?"

"All the time," Reba answered. She seemed to consider what remained on her supply cart and found a smaller container. "Don't think they use much of that stuff. Sometimes the syringes and vials go bad, and I have to dispose of it." She lifted the cover to an empty drawer on the anesthesia cart. "This is where the Neo goes, and I stocked up about two weeks ago." She referred to her iPad. "Yep. Two weeks. Never seen the Neo go fast like this. I was out last week, and nobody filled in for me."

Reba restocked with what she had of the medication on her supply cart. "I don't have enough to fill this baby back up, and I'm not sure what I'm going to do about the other rooms. That girl that places the supply orders is goin' to have to step it up."

"I take it you don't usually see this much Neosynephrine missing when you restock anesthesia meds?"

"No, ma'am." Reba shut the drawer and again began to maneuver her stocking cart around the anesthesia equipment. She returned all equipment to its proper place.

"These supply carts are never locked, are they?" Diana asked. "In fact, is the OR Suite ever locked?"

"Not really," Reba answered, "as long as you've got your badge to swipe at the control to get in. A good while ago, I don't think you were even around yet, Dr. Bratton, they tried shutting down the badges at night to lock down the OR after some Fentanyl went missing."

Diana let out an exasperated sigh. "What a shame that things like that happen in a hospital."

"One night, I think around one or two a.m., the supervisor's override card wouldn't work and the door to the OR jammed."

"Bet that didn't turn out good," Diana said.

"No, ma'am. Emergency sent up this big car wreck, and they couldn't get into the OR."

Reba held up the hospital employee badge suspended from the left front pocket of her uniform. "They got a new system after that and no more jamming up. You know, everybody's always in such a rush and the doctors don't always have their ID badge pinned to their scrubs." Reba glanced down at Diana's missing badge as Diana put her right palm to her chest and frowned embarrassed. They both laughed. "So they keep the doors unlocked when the day shift is clocked in to make it easy on you busy doctors."

"Yes, I've never noticed them to be locked during the day. That could be a hassle."

"The night policy don't bother me, 'cause I ain't here after five. I gave up that night work a long time ago."

"I wish I could say that," Diana sighed. "Reba, I don't know how to thank you." *I'll bring her a Walmart gift card.*

"Never you mind, Dr. Bratton. It is nice that you care about the work other people have to do around here to keep this place open. That's really good of you."

"Thank you again. I know you have a lot of work left to do. I appreciate your time more than you could ever know."

Reba retrieved her iPad. "I'm gonna send that girl an email. She's gotta improve her inventory management and quit making my job so hard. I'm tired of these folks around here not doing their jobs and still wanting more money and time off and …"

Diana slipped away before the end of Reba's rant and returned to the computers in the Doctors' Lounge. Several hospitalists had taken up court inputting medication orders and progress notes, leaving only one computer free in the center of the swarm.

She slipped into the tight pack and logged in again to the EMR system. While no one acknowledged her, she still darted her eyes about in fear of discovery and re-entered Chuck Wallace's medical records. Rapidly as possible, she scanned the list of documents until she found the cause of death: Cardiac failure, post-operative complication following gunshot wound to the chest. Diana subtly glanced around again and took another study of the blood test results and recorded monitor readings. *Nothing about bleeding out, no sign of elevated cardiac enzymes and an MI. No record of a sudden spike in blood pressure. If he had suffered a stroke, would anyone have been surprised? An overweight guy his age?* "Chuck could've had acute cardiac arrhythmia, and they missed it."

"Pardon me. Were you speaking to me?" one of the physicians seated next to Diana said before sipping on her latte.

Diana realized she must have mumbled. "Oh, no. Uhh—I wasn't. Excuse me."

She shut down the computer, pushed away from the desk, and left the lounge for home.

Diana dropped her bag at the backdoor entrance to the kitchen, relieved that Voncelle Wallace did not greet her in the driveway or worse yet inside at the kitchen island ready to talk. "I'm going to have to confront that bitch about what I learned this afternoon," she said under her breath.

"I came downstairs to test out the pizza in the oven." Brad stood on the far side of the kitchen, wrapped in an oversized, white bath towel. "I picked the California margarita with extra cheese and thin crust. Easy choice—it was the one on top of the stack in the freezer."

Diana ran her eyes from his chiseled face and thick, wet hair to the tight towel and down to his calves, then back up, lingering an extra second or two at the snug towel. "Sounds and looks yummy, except aren't you too casual with Kelsey around?"

Brad returned the assessment, admiring her wrinkled, yet form-fitted, surgical scrubs filled out at the top and a bit snug at the waist. Her brunette hair fell out of place after a long day of operating and thankfully seeing many patients in the clinic. Diana's attempt at morning makeup was long-ago rubbed away except for the fake eyelashes someone talked her into. "Kelsey texted me. Said she tried you and got no answer. She's got a paper due and an after-school group help session with a creative writing class and should be home in half an hour. She suggested the pizza over frozen wings."

Diana took out her phone and saw the missed call. "Kelsey

seems to be balancing her schoolwork with all the other stuff she has going on. I'm proud of her."

"Me too," Brad said. He bent to peer inside the oven window at the pizza and grabbed at the towel to keep it from dropping. "I went walking tonight. We got hit with the storm—thus, an early shower." The towel slipped again. Brad caught it and wrapped it tighter.

"You better go get dressed and get out of that towel before Kelsey comes home to find more than toasty, thin pizza in the kitchen."

Brad gave her a lascivious wink, flashed Diana with an opening of the towel, and walked away to the bedroom. He grinned over his shoulder in suggestion.

"Later," she called out, "after we eat." Diana reassessed the pizza in the oven and grabbed a bag of mixed salad from the refrigerator. "And I want to fill you in on what I learned today."

"Me too," Brad said. "Oh, and by the way. We blew off Sidney Belmont's funeral late this afternoon. Should've at least sent our office manager."

# Chapter 32

Ellis Belmont left Miles to finish the paperwork at the funeral home—only fair since an emergency reading of Sidney's will named Miles Belmont executor of her estate. To keep the bookkeeping simple on her final arrangements, Miles used Sidney's personal credit card to settle-up with the mortuary's administrative office.

An hour after the service, he found Ellis relaxing in his office with feet propped on his desk. Both men remained dressed in immaculate suit and tie. "Most families would serve a big spread in the living room for the grieving friends and family members and anyone else who cared to drop by," Miles said. "Nonetheless, here you sit, big brother, taking it easy."

Ellis finished his scotch. He poured another from the half-filled Baccarat decanter of Johnnie Walker kept in the corner walnut cabinet and brought out on special occasions.

"And thank you, Sidney, for choosing cremation," Miles added. His eyes drifted to the ceiling. "We got to skip a graveside service and more flowers."

"I expect the clinic employees were disappointed about the no party plans," Ellis said. "Open bar, even wine and beer, would have cost a fortune—not to mention the catered pick-up food. Of course, we have the space, and there would have no need to trash one of our homes. In fact, the lobby in the main building can hold two hundred or more standing."

Miles selected his own crystal highball from the cabinet and poured. "This bereavement party of two is all we need," he said.

"Nonetheless, I'm surprised you didn't bring out the Glenfiddich or the Macallan to celebrate the late Sidney Eleanor Belmont."

"I quit keeping those bottles in the clinic when I caught one of the janitors enjoying a sample. Didn't even have the manners to use a glass."

Miles dropped into the leather sofa across from Ellis's desk. He swung his feet to the coffee table atop the sportsman's journals and the architectural design magazines. "Shame we had to ban smoking in the clinic. A good cigar would be a treat."

"Could open the window," Ellis said and gestured to the gold monogrammed box on his desk, shaking his head. "Too much trouble, and I'm trying to cut back."

Miles savored the scotch even though a much cheaper brand than he preferred. "Reading of the will this morning was a real eye-opener. Her leaving her ownership in the clinic to the children's hospital creates good PR—much better than to her cat as we thought. Our office manager will share sis's benevolence on social media."

"Your philanthropic spirit is touching, Miles. Splitting the rest of her estate between the two of us is certainly not a total bust." Ellis appeared to work the numbers in his head. "Her secretary asked for Sidney's cat, even though the poor thing is now penniless. *Meow, Me-oh-my.*"

Miles smiled and sipped his drink. "Of course, the exterior of Sid's Porsche is a godawful mess. The dealership says they can get it cleaned up for resale to an out-of-state buyer, good as new."

"Wonderful news," Ellis said.

"And with no trace of a woman's brains scattered across the hood," Miles added. "My words, not theirs."

"Did I hear rumor about a homeless, stinky busybody, a witness to our sister's death? A female squatter in the building?"

"I suppose, if the same detective in charge of the case—Detective Thomas, I believe—called you with the same report I got."

Ellis set his glass on a coaster and walked to the hall door to shut it. "I know that building. It was supposed to be vacant."

"It was. The corporate real estate agent told me that an assistant regularly inspects their properties, standard with listings."

"I can't say that I agree with your inquiry of the agent."

"Used a fake name," Miles said.

"Unless you called from a non-existent Jackson pay phone or used a burner, there's a record of the call, no matter the attempt at disguise."

"Touché, brother." Another sip of the drink, a long one. "I doubt the agent would put all that together. Besides, my little sister was murdered outside his listed property. Doubt he'll make trouble."

"Did you spot the woman when you were in the building?"

"Are you kidding? I was in and out there in less than five minutes," Miles answered.

"Should have done a room-to-room search to make sure you were alone."

"Come on, Ellis," Miles said. "Let's be practical. If we had hired a hitman, the outcome would likely have been the same. He could've missed spotting the bag lady too. And in case you haven't noticed, the police aren't too quick around here."

Both men drank. Miles refilled his glass. "Good thing you picked up on Pritchett, Malone, and Tudor. I wasted almost two hours in their parking lot in that crampy rental car waiting on Sid to finish meeting with them. Pritchard has always been such an ass. No one will play golf with him anymore, and he and his wife can never get up a table at dinner club."

"I did everything I could to get Sidney to go along with the sale. I thought once you were on board, she'd see it my—our—way. The promise of an extra five percent ownership didn't even do it," Ellis said. "Why was she so stubborn? This is best for all of us."

"She wanted to get another proposal," Miles said. "Nothing but a delay tactic. Sid was never good at making decisions."

"Three years ago, I tried to negotiate with Pritchard, and that fell flat. He brought nothing new to the table. A lot of money was involved, and I learned to be careful. Wallace seemed more practical, more resourceful. What happened to him was such a shame."

"You remind me of a sleezy gangster from an old movie," Miles said. "Right off the bat, Sid took a dislike to Chuck Wallace and the same for Garcia at a follow-up meeting. She was never going to be on board with any sale to GIE. Garcia's showing up to clean up only made things worse."

"Poor thing was never much of a businesswoman. And such a liability to the practice. Her medical malpractice cases will live on without her."

"Belmont Medical can still be sued for her latest screw-ups, even though she's dead. Not sure when that statute runs out. I'll give State Malpractice Medical Corp a call tomorrow. They might be relieved—no more unhappy and disfigured patients compliments of Sidney Belmont, MD."

Ellis referred to his Rolex. "Do us both a favor, won't you? Stay off the phone. Stop drawing attention."

"Give me credit for trying," Miles said. "How did I know someone else had it out for Sidney."

Ellis raised his glass. "You got me there. What do they call it on those crime shows—*modus operandi*?" Another check of the time. "See you later. I've got dinner plans at Walker's."

"Wallace and that Garcia guy were both shot long-range. My guess, Sidney too."

"All those riflery classes you took out in Rankin County went to waste."

"Glad I didn't bump into the mutual shooter," Miles said. "I left no prints, stayed out of the way of the bag lady, and got no chance to use my rifle." He finished the scotch and set the empty on the coffee table, ignoring the stack of coasters. "See you in clinic, Big Brother. When those redneck cops pin the murder on someone else, case closed."

Miles disappeared down the hall.

"Ingrate," Ellis said. He retrieved the empty high ball glass and used his bare hand to wipe the wet ring from the rich walnut surface of his expensive desk.

# Chapter 33

Voncelle found a surgical cap and shoe covers on the shelf outside the scrub sinks. She took a deep breath to recognize the first full day back at work and donned the disposable wear. The OR cases for this week at Metropolitan Hospital were rescheduled after her husband died. Time to get back in the saddle. The patients had waited long enough.

"Good to see you back at work, Dr. Wallace," Reba said. She rolled up with her anesthesia supply cart.

"Yeah, sure. Had to happen sooner or later," Voncelle said.

"I know it's hard. I lost my Billy five years ago. Still miss him. Heart attack."

Voncelle activated the running water in the scrub sink, peeled apart the wrapper to a soft scrub brush impregnated with surgical cleanser, and began to wash her hands and arms.

"I know the other doctors are glad to have you back."

"Hope so," Voncelle said.

"I know so." Reba stocked the paper towels in the dispenser in the hall. "Trying to help out."

"Super," Voncelle said.

"Don't you and Dr. Bratton work together? She's very nice."

"Yes, we do—and she is." Voncelle cleaned under the fingernails.

"Did Dr. Bratton found out all she needed to know the other day?"

"Needed to know … what?" Voncelle worked the light, red-tinted lather up both forearms and just beyond the elbows. "What did Dr. Bratton need to know?"

"She wanted to know about the Neo we stock in the anesthesia carts," Reba replied.

Voncelle dropped the used brush into the sink. "Neo? Neosynephrine? Why did Dr. Bratton want to know about that?"

"Dunno, 'cept she wanted to know what the anesthesia doctor had to do during her cases to take care of the patients. I thought it was nice that she cared about the work of the other doctors and included the CRNAs too."

"What did you tell her about Neo?" Voncelle rinsed her hands and arms in the warm water rushing from the sink faucet. She kept her eyes off Reba.

Reba snapped the cover to the paper towel dispenser back in place. "Funny thing was … a lot of Neo was missing from Room One." Reba gestured in that direction. "I found the other rooms about the same. The anesthesiologists must have had a busy couple of weeks since I last stocked my meds."

"I guess they did."

Reba seemed on the defense. "I don't skip rooms when I stock. I always do my job."

Voncelle finished the rinse and held her hands and arms in front and to the side of her face, preparing to enter the operating room.

"Yes, ma'am. I always do my job, and I told Dr. Bratton that."

Voncelle pushed open the door, activating the access lever with a shove from the hip. The nurses had completed the surgical prep and were ready for her.

"Will you tell Dr. Bratton that? That I always do my job?" Reba called out to Dr. Wallace as she entered Operating Room One.

"I sure will, Reba. I sure will," Voncelle said.

Martin scanned Thomas's report on the successful arrest of a home burglary suspect from last week. The perpetrator was picked up on a separate narcotics charge, and the one smudged fingerprint from the robbery scene proved to be a match.

"Great job, Detective. This culprit is probably good for a few other break-ins over the last several months. What about his friends?"

Thomas filled both coffee cups from the dispenser. "Like they say in those old cop shows, he's singing like a canary." Thomas poured and stirred in a packet or sugar and peeled away the top of a single pod of creamer. "I take both in my coffee. What about you?"

"Black, and I usually fix mine in my office when that damn machine isn't on the brink. Probably needs a rinse out." Martin laid the file on the JPD breakroom table and picked up the Wallace murder file next. "Nothing like paper notes," he said.

Thomas slurped the hot coffee. "We should have stayed for the refreshments after that Belmont service yesterday."

"Don't think they had any," Martin said. "Doubt we would have gotten much from the deceased's two brothers. They eulogized the woman like she was an angel. My guess is that with no kids those two guys stand to own more of the medical practice—unless she wrote them out of the will."

"She should have. They're both pricks, if you ask me."

"Don't need to ask. It's obvious," Martin said.

Both men laughed and slurped coffee.

"Ballistics report should be out tomorrow on the Wallace case. Interested to see what we find," Thomas said.

"Especially since we have multiple victims shot at long range in such a narrow window of time. That doesn't happen often."

"Not around here." The detective grabbed an unopened package of cookies from the counter and tore open one end. He removed two and ate both. "The first victim was married to a lady doctor and the second victim was a lady doctor. Unless the ballistics match up, I guess the similarity stops there for those two."

Martin flipped through the Belmont file. "Not so sure about that. Here's the GPS coordinates of Sidney Belmont's location the afternoon she was shot: *270 Highland Heights, Ridgeland.* That's a commercial address. Plug that into your phone."

The real estate equity firm of Pritchett, Malone, and Tudor,

Incorporated appeared on the screen of Detective Thomas's cell.

"We need to pay those folks a visit," Martin said.

"You sure you want to do that? I can get Robertson to go with me. Of course, I can go by myself."

"I can go. Better to work as a team," Martin said.

"You're chief of police and busy. You've got a lot of responsibility around this place. Administrative shit."

"Yeah, that's for sure. But—"

"It's that lady surgeon who's connected somehow to all these cases. I'm not saying that there's anything goin' on, Chief, but—you know."

"No. I don't know."

"You call her down here all the time. Go by her office all the time."

Key Martin glanced about the break room and into the hall. The two men were alone. "No, I don't."

Thomas ate another cookie. "Come on. You talked Dr. Bratton into getting up on that roof the night Dillion Garnett came after her again. What'd you say to her: *I want to get your take on the this*? She's a doctor, doggone it. Not a policeman," Thomas said. "I mean—a police person."

"We go way back to before I got chief. She helped bring down a few bad guys—before you even joined the force. Hell, Thomas, if I didn't know better, I'd say you're jealous."

Thomas laughed. "Chief, you're the boss. You lead the way the way on this."

"Gimme one of those." He reached for the opened bag. "Stale doesn't stop me from eating a cookie," Martin said, chewing. "And get somebody to order apple raisin next time. I never really liked chocolate chip."

"Sure thing. I'll make a note of it, sir. No question, you're  the boss."

"I consider you a friend, Thomas, and you got a good head on your shoulders—an ugly one, but a good one."

Both men chuckled and clinked the rims of their coffee cups in a toast.

"And it's true. Bureaucratic stuff is piling up all over my office. I ought to be down the hall weeding through it. That sure would make the mayor and city council happy."

"I know you wanna see these cases through, especially since your lady surgeon doctor friend seems to be what they call a common denominator. Don't get me wrong—not like she's committed a crime or anything like that—no way. Seems she's connected, though."

"Connected," Martin said. "You might say that. All within a matter of a few weeks, Diana Bratton gets assaulted twice with a gun, the hubby of one of the female surgeons she works with is shot, and now another doctor, a female, who works nearby is murdered—also shot at long range. The kicker is the female surgeon's dead hubby was doing a big financial deal with the female doctor who was shot." He sipped the coffee and frowned, then stared down into the cup as though the answer were at the bottom. "Then we got the visiting Spaniard who's in on the deal and turns up shot, then dies in the hospital after the surgeons patch him up. The doctors said he should have made it."

"How so?"

"Toxicology came up clean except for a reasonable amount of pain killers. No heart attack, no stroke, no blood clots in the lungs. The coroner ruled cause of death as assault with a deadly weapon."

"Too much coincidence, if you ask me." Thomas reached for the bag of cookies.

Martin pushed the bag to the other side of the breakroom table. "Don't do it man. You gotta pass your physical next month. If I'm going to slow down and let you detectives do all the leg work, I don't want to have to train new recruits if you get sidelined with a heart attack. In fact, I'd have to train three to do the work you do."

"That's a nice thing to say, Chief." Thomas rolled the top of the cookie bag closed and secured the entire bag with a large rubber band he found in the drawer under the coffee maker.

He tossed the bag inside a cabinet and closed the door.

"Let's check out the big real estate firm that Sidney Belmont visited the day she died and find out what she was up to."

"You gotta a plan. Now, what about all that mess in your office?"

"We'll do this one more thing together and close out this case—or cases. Then I'll bring in Detective Robertson as your partner and bow out on the day-to-day," Martin said. "Please keep me in the loop going forward with lots of reports."

"Got it, Chief. No problem," Detective Thomas said. "One thing, though. You remember the day we dropped by to see Wallace's widow without a search warrant?"

"She let us into Wallace's study. The wife called it the library."

"The library—the bookcase. We both flipped through a few of the books."

"I remember," Martin said. He rinsed his cup and set it in the bottom of the sink.

"I spotted a college yearbook, belonged to Mrs., I mean, *Doctor* Wallace."

"I saw that too." Martin picked up the file off the table and stuffed it under his arm. "You've got me thinking about the tornado in my office. I'm going to try to put a dent in it before we head over to the Pritchard firm and then call it a day."

"But get this. I opened the yearbook, and the pages fell open to the school activities section—a quarter page photograph of a college-age Dr. Wallace holding a trophy and a ribbon. She got an award."

"Congrats to her. What for?"

"Most improved marksmanship in Women's Riflery. Seems that the girls' college rifle club was a big deal."

# Chapter 34

"You're lucky the judge finally granted bail," Roy said.

"I figured you could float it yourself," the nephew said.

"Judge comes down hard on bad boys with two assault offenses, especially using a firearm."

"Shouldn't be an issue if you follow through with that lady doctor. What'd she say when you asked her to drop the charges?"

Roy unlocked his vehicle and slid into the driver's seat. He buckled up and started the engine before his nephew was fully seated in the car.

"Hey, Uncle Roy, hold on a minute." Dillon Garnett hurriedly fastened his seat belt and slammed the front passenger door shut. "I guess if I don't survive this ride home from jail, they void the bail bond? Is that how it works?

"Bondsman on Bailey Avenue will still want his money. By the way, the lady doctor's name is Dr. Bratton, Diana Bratton, and there's no way in hell she's going to drop any charges."

"You asked her, and she said *no?*"

Roy was silent as they pulled out of the county jail parking lot.

"You said you had another appointment with her, and you were gonna take care of it then."

"I am taking care of it."

"When is she going to drop the charges then? She's bosom buddies with the JPD Chief, or at least he'd like to think so. I could tell that night when they were on the roof. All she has to do is ask him—or tell him."

"I'm not sure who you got the extra thick skull from, Dillon, probably that ass my sister married and divorced twice." Roy turned at the next corner. "That' not the way this is going to end."

Dillon squirmed against the shoulder strap of his seat belt and ran his hand along the interior of the door as his body stiffened. "What'd you mean: *not the way?*"

"The judge is bound to go for it," Roy said. "An insanity defense."

"That's crazy, Uncle Roy."

"Yep, crazy. That's what we're talking about."

"I ain't no crackbrain." Dillon focused beyond the next intersection. "Go ahead and put me out up there. I can hitch a ride out of town with somebody waiting at these gas pumps. Get a ride to the bus station."

Roy slowed at the traffic ahead. The light changed to green before Dillon had opportunity to jump from the car. "I'm going to take the next turn, and we'll be on the interstate in no time. I'll be going a lot faster. I suggest you stay put."

"And I ain't pleading insanity to what I did to that other lady doctor." Dillon's head quivered. He ran his fingers from front-to-back across his scalp, leaving his thick blond hair to stand on end. "I knew exactly what I was doing. Did just what you asked."

Roy turned onto the interstate and quickly accelerated to seventy. *They won't pull me over unless I do seventy-five.*

"Your parents took you to therapy when you were a child, every Tuesday for forty-five minutes. I know because Sis talked about it. The therapist at the university was expensive, a real strain on two teacher salaries."

Dillon rubbed his temples and yelled, "Why are you telling me this?"

"No need to scream. On second thought, outbursts like that show anger, anxiety, and lack of self-control. That will play well before the judge. We might not have to practice as much as I thought."

"Practice?"

"I don't know how to get you out of this predicament any other way. They never figured out what you did to your mother in her trailer," Roy said.

Dillon was silent.

"Although, I bet the police could put this thing together. They study bullets."

"It's called ballistics," Dillon said. "Anybody who watches TV knows about ballistics—even from the newspaper, if anybody still reads that crap—like somebody your freaking age."

"You'd be surprised what someone my freaking age can do—or does."

"Whatever those stupid, asshole cops come up with on the ballistics doesn't matter."

"And why is that, Dillon?"

"The rifle I stole is at the bottom of the reservoir. They'll never find it."

"I hope you tossed it on the far side, away from the dam and spillway station where the security cameras are." The view from the exterior rearview mirror was clear, and Roy signaled to change lanes to get around a slower moving white Toyota.

"Don't worry about me, Uncle. I know how to stay under the radar."

"Considering I had to bail you out of prison, I don't have much faith in you, Dillon."

Roy took the next exit off Interstate 55 and in fifteen minutes turned onto a stretch of narrow two-lane asphalt, badly in need of resurfacing and bordered with skinny pine trees and scanty, ragged underbrush. Browned, dying, or already dead trees, a result of the recent late summer and fall drought and the unseasonably frigid winter weather that followed, broke the clusters of green needles. Roy took the gravel road ahead to the left.

In several miles they would reach the two hundred acres tucked away in northeast Madison County, Mississippi. Roy had inherited the isolated property from his father, Dillon's grandfather.

"The spotty to non-existent cell phone coverage out here should keep you from stirring up trouble, and the electricity goes in and out, mostly in. And believe it or not, the satellite dish picks up television on a good day—unless it rains," Roy said.

They pulled up to a closed, rusted metal gate mounted between sturdy wooden fence posts that dripped old creosote. The gate was secured to the left post with a rusted chain and padlock. Treacherous barbed wire, screaming of tetanus, composed the fence itself as it blended into the throng of vines and thicket of weeds extending in both directions. Thick fallen branches, long and short, littered the fence line.

An abandoned-appearing, single-wide trailer surrounded in overgrowth sat at the end of the graveled area well inside the fence and positioned to be invisible from the road. Its roof was heavily covered in several seasons of fallen pine straw.

"The place is stocked with plenty of canned and boxed food to last a few months. There's a fridge and an old freezer I used for deer meat. I put a lot of frozen pizzas and macaroni and cheese in there, even left a couple of gallons of ice cream. If you leave the top of it closed, everything inside should not ruin, even if you lose power for a few days."

"What the hell is this about, Uncle Roy?"

Roy reached into his front pants pocket for the keys to the gate and trailer. "I want you out of the picture for a while. You went overboard on that thing with the Belmont woman. And your trial for the stuff with Dr. Bratton is not for several months. I'll look in on you from time to time." He held up the key to the gate. "Wait here."

"You're full of bull crap. I ain't staying out here in this dump. You and that Wallace guy wanted Belmont out of the picture. No way she can vote *no* now!"

"That 'Wallace guy' was a friend, and since he's also 'out of the picture' I may not get any of the deal with those Spanish guys. The whole thing is likely to blow up in my face."

"We had a deal. I want my part."

"I'll know in a few days. A member of their board of directors has taken over for the Spanish outfit. Chuck used to refer to him as 'Rico.'"

"All I know is I ain't been paid nothing yet. No way I'm stayin' out here in the sticks for God knows how long. Take me back to my apartment in town."

"I let the lease go on that firetrap. Your greasy, stained furniture was a pile of nasty muck—worth nothing. I told the landlord to keep it, or better yet, burn it."

Dillon strained again at the seat belt, still in place. "You ain't got no right to do that. That was *my* place."

Roy opened the driver's door. "You have been paid. I covered your rent and utilities, and I tried to send a cleaning service over there several times. Struck out—no one would take the job." He gestured toward the house trailer. "At least there won't be much you can do to this place, except burn it down. And I would suggest that you not do that—or you'll be sleeping in a ditch." Roy stepped from the vehicle as Dillon unfastened his seatbelt. The skin around his abdominal hernia repair still pulled a little. "Wait here while I unlock the gate."

Dillon waited while his uncle fumbled with the chain and padlock. "Ha! The old asshole can't find the key." Dillon scowled and studied the area around the vehicle, spotting the fallen branches. "I told you I can handle things myself." He jumped from the car.

"Stay there, Dillon. I've nearly got it. Stay put."

The first branch Dillon picked up, about a foot long and the width of a baseball ball, fell apart in his grasp. Ants scattered about. "Shit!" Dillon shouted, glanced over at Roy, and covered his mouth.

"I said stay in the freakin' car!" Roy finally inserted the correct key and the lock released. He struggled to untangle the chain links from the vines and free the gate from the post unaware of Dillon's success with the second fallen branch, again about as thick as a baseball bat and as long—though rock solid this time.

Roy turned toward Dillon at the moment he lunged for him

and pounded Roy's head repeatedly with the hard piece of wood. Blood and pulverized skin and bone sprayed the front of Dillon's shirt as Roy fell limp into the fence. The gate popped loose. The body landed motionless, the minced face barely recognizable, Roy's legs and arms contorted. Blood oozed out into the gravel.

Dillon fished the car keys out of his uncle's pants pocket.

# Chapter 35

Voncelle stood in front of the framed art in the corner. Including the brushed gold frame, it covered a four-by-six foot area. Centered in the space and hung a tad below eye level, the piece painted and signed by an unfamiliar artist was a decent fill-in for the gun cabinet. "After Aaron died, Chuck bought me this atrocity in the French Quarter for my birthday."

On first glance, she could almost see a shadow of the gun cabinet against the wall. Voncelle turned to the window opposite and the curtains generally kept open. The paint around the replaced gun cabinet had faded barely enough to leave a faint outline. She grinned in satisfaction. "Only I can see that."

She removed the phone from her pocket and googled the name of the artist, then browsed through other examples of his work. This painting she and Chuck once owned together appeared in the gallery selection. Voncelle highlighted the post and the estimated current retail value of the piece appeared on the screen. "You're kidding. No way I would ever pay that now. Who would?"

Voncelle thought about the painting's original location—not where it hung in the apartment on the outskirts of the Garden District when she moved in with Chuck—but in the bedroom down the hall from this library.

"I wonder if those two nosey policemen went through my bedroom. How sick. Only Diana knows I hid the guns under the bed. And if those cops had opened the garage door, I would have heard the sensor chime." Voncelle considered the display cabinet, empty of the rifles and the revolver in the bottom drawer and left to rest against the wall in the vacant parking bay of the garage. She had already sold Chuck's car to a used auto dealer. "They would have asked me about the empty gun cabinet."

In case the police came back, Voncelle imagined other issues that could draw attention to an attempt to hide or disguise things around her house and came up with nothing. If they checked her purse, they would find the revolver; however, lots of women carry handguns these days. As far as the now blank bedroom wall, the curtains were kept drawn and the wallpaper had not faded around where the painting once hung. "A blank wall with nice wallpaper is all that's left."

Voncelle dropped the phone back into her pocket with the gallery website remaining on the screen. She retrieved her glass of chardonnay from the polished surface of Chuck's mahogany desk and had not bothered with a coaster. "Chuck would've had a fit if he'd seen that—such a neatness fanatic around the house, always doing the proper thing. I should never have told him how Aaron really died."

She sipped wine and let her mind drift to earlier in the day, in the OR with Reba.

"Diana's been snooping around behind me. Wonder what she thinks she'll find?"

Her college yearbooks were lined in the second section of the book cabinet near her, arranged in random order on the shelf. Voncelle smiled at the binding of the 1996 edition, the book protruding about an inch from the others. "I won that year."

It was nearly eleven, and she had surgery cases in the morning. She withdrew the book and tucked it under her arm. "I need to unwind. This will be a hoot on break tomorrow."

Voncelle's surgery schedule was completed by one o'clock the next day. She grabbed a sandwich and canned drink from a hospital vending machine and returned to her private office at the clinic. The 1996 yearbook waited on her desk. She left the office door to the hall open.

Voncelle popped the top to the Coke Zero, unwrapped the chicken salad sandwich, and tossed the tiny piece of aluminum and the plastic wrap in the corner trash can before opening to the *Sports and Activities* section. Still dressed in surgical scrubs, she propped her feet on her desk and flipped through the football, baseball, track, tennis, soccer, and volleyball photos until she reached riflery. The university program included a co-ed team as well as a women's divisional team. The future Voncelle Wallace with her Anschultz rifle posed proudly front and center in the photographs of both groups. Another action shot sampled her work standing at target practice. She remembered the male coach telling her to hold her breath, take aim, then exhale briefly before making the shot. Voncelle spotted herself in other pictures firing the rifle in prone and kneeling positions.

*Sitting to shoot was never a big thing*, she thought. "Although mastering prone sure came in handy," she mumbled. Her lips parted in a devilish grin as her eyes drifted up from the page.

Diana stood at her desk.

Voncelle slammed the book closed in surprise. It landed on her desk with the front cover facing up. She swung her legs to the floor. "Diana? I didn't hear you come in."

"Sorry, I didn't mean to startle you. I walked by and saw your office door open." Diana held a thin folder of papers in her hand. She stepped back to shut the door behind her and glanced down at Voncelle's reading. "Reminiscing?"

"Uh-huh." *Diana—the library—Chuck's desk.* The flashback overcame Voncelle, recalling the day Diana came by her house with food after Chuck's death and snooped down the hall as the police did later. Diana's reason was to use the restroom—the police made no excuse. Voncelle darted her eyes down at the yearbook. It had been out of place when she saw it yesterday in the bookcase. She glanced at her purse, left turned on its side on the top of her desk.

"Yes, I—try to cheer myself up the best I can these days with my husband gone. College life, wow, so very different. Not a care in the world."

"You said something about prone and handy when I walked in," Diana said to several seconds of silence.

"What I can do for you, Diana. Are those papers for me?"

Diana stepped closer, nearly pressing her thighs against the edge of Voncelle's desk. "A few days ago, you dropped by my kitchen again. You told me you moved the collection of rifles I saw in your library to the master bedroom. Hid them under the bed is what I remember."

"What I do with my own things in my own house is my business."

"You were hiding those weapons from the police," Diana said, tightening her expression in a mixture of amazed aggravation and puzzlement.

Voncelle pushed the yearbook to the side and stood, reaching for her purse. "You know that most if not all those men who walk in that group are gun owners. And not everybody showed up the night Chuck was shot—so call your policeman buddy and get him to inspect the list. I know that the guy named Matt keeps a roster. Chuck said he did. Find out who wasn't in the gang walking that night and raid their freaking house for rifles."

"If anyone needs to talk to the police, it's you." Diana gestured toward her with the folder. "I want to help you."

Voncelle sprang from her chair, pushing it toward the wall behind her. The chair hit hard against the credenza and knocked a lamp to the floor, shattering it. Several medical books on display fell from the piece of furniture onto the broken porcelain.

"What would help me is if you would mind your own business!" She stepped closer, face-to-face with Diana. Diana in turn straightened her posture to stand barely above eye level with Voncelle.

"You hid guns from the police," Diana said. "What else are you hiding?" She thrust the paper folder into Voncelle's chest. Voncelle had raised her hand as though expecting Diana to slap her face with the paperwork.

"I'm not hiding anything. Get out of my office, Diana." Voncelle grabbed Diana's arm, scattering the folder and its papers to the floor.

Diana backed away a few steps and retrieved one or two of the sheets.

"What in the hell is this?" Voncelle picked up one piece near her shoe. At the top of the page was printed *Surgical Supply Inventory – Anesthesia Department*. One of the columns indicated a dramatic drop in the available milliliter count of NeoSynephrine or phenylephrine.

"I know, Voncelle," Diana said. "I know what you did."

Voncelle spread her lips in an unnatural smile and stiffened her posture. She took a deep, forced breath. "What the hell are you talking about?"

"A person in housekeeping saw you slip into the OR area when you didn't have a case and had no reason to be there." Diana kept her composure and lied like Chief Martin had taught her—common practice when police question a suspect. "The person knew you shouldn't have been there and reported it. The Neo turned up missing a few hours later on inventory."

"Bull crap."

"It wouldn't take much over the recommended dose to induce a hypertensive stroke or a cardiac arrhythmia. Chuck survived your bullet. And you couldn't handle that a trophy winning, hotshot girl on the university rifle team could miss his heart or his head or whatever you planned to hit to drop him dead."

"I … uhh … I remember going into the OR Suite. I needed to borrow a couple of scrub brushes and towels to wash—my car and—"

"Don't even try Voncelle. A man named Roy Garnett told me he knew Chuck in New Orleans when the two of you started having an affair. You were married to a resident or radiology fellow at the time. You were unhappy."

"Lots of people have affairs. You probably started sleeping with Brad before his fiancée died."

"Your first husband, the guy in radiology, died unexpectedly in the hospital of a hypertensive stroke. How many other men have you knocked off?"

Voncelle shoved Diana away, knocking her to the floor, and grabbed the revolver from her purse. She pointed the gun at Diana, hesitated, then flew out the door into the waiting arms of Detective Thomas with Chief Martin by his side.

"Voncelle Wallace, you are under arrest for the murder of Charles Wallace." Thomas secured the gun and spun Voncelle around to apply hand cuffs, then finished administering the Miranda Rights. "Funny thing, Dr. Wallace. A nice judge approved a search warrant for your residence early this morning. We arrived at your house after you left for the hospital. Long day in surgery?"

"You had no authority to search my home."

"Odd you would say that. First off, Detective Thomas spotted the nice write-up about your riflery days in the college yearbook when we dropped by for a visit," Martin said. "We knew you were in university about that time and wanted to get to know you better, learn more about your background. Well, whaddayaknow?" Martin glanced inside Voncelle's office. "That yearbook is on your desk over there."

"I want a lawyer," Voncelle cried.

"And, second, you later told Dr. Bratton that you hid the rifles under your bed. Criminals share the strangest things. Don't they, Thomas."

"Yes, Chief," he nodded. "Stupid stuff. Oughta keep their mouths shut."

Diana walked up behind them, standing a couple of feet away. She massaged her stomach.

"Your partner there is the one to credit for putting this all together," Martin said. "When she told us about your first husband's death, we started to push ahead. We didn't want you to get busy with anything else."

"Because I know how to handle a rifle, doesn't mean I shot Chuck. And there's no way to trace the amount of phenylephrine in the body post-mortem."

"The ballistics on that Anschultz are matching up. Forensics put a rush on it. If we could make a match in the Belmont case too—wouldn't that be fun."

Two deputies walked up. "Y'all want us to take over?" one of them asked. "The patients in the waiting room up front are about to panic, asking loads of questions. A man and a couple of women are crying. Good thing you cleared the employees from this back area."

"It's your call, Chief," Thomas said.

"Sure guys. Take the good doctor in. Too bad she won't be able to wave goodbye to any of her patients."

"They'll need to find somebody else to operate on 'em, for sure," Thomas said.

"My lawyer will get me out of this," Voncelle grunted as the deputies led her down the hall. "I have money, lots of it. Chuck was hiding it from me and planned to rake in more." She lowered her head while the deputies paraded her through the full lobby. "And that creep, Garcia. He was no better!"

"You could have spared the practice embarrassment for the moment and taken her out the employee back entrance," Diana said to both Martin and Thomas as Brad walked up. She sat down in one of the office chairs.

"What's one more story in the news going to hurt? Just another murder, hold-up, or arrest at the Cummins-Bratton Surgical Clinic," Brad said. "And if anybody cares, I've been over at the hospital in surgery. I was next up after Voncelle's last case, and I guess I'll be doing her post-ops."

"I'm afraid I won't be much help filling in, Brad. I really don't feel well." With that, Diana stood from the chair and fell to the floor.

# Chapter 36

"I didn't know, and I don't think she did either. We never kept up with anything like that."

"Gross, Brad. It's no surprise. You guys are at it all the time," Kelsey said.

"And how would you know that, young lady?" Phoebe folded her arms across her chest.

"I'm not deaf, and the walls in our house are thin," Kelsey answered.

A lanky, but fit, man dressed in surgical scrubs entered the waiting room. He recognized Brad. "Diana is fine. No more bleeding. She and the baby are fine. Ultrasound says sixteen weeks."

Brad kept his eyes forward and shook his head before examining the opposite wall. A large piece of dense paper with a rumpled surface that passed for canvas hung framed in wide aluminum. It was splattered with a wide range of vivid colors and passed for artwork. "No, everybody, I'm not counting days. It's just I never thought this would happen, could happen."

"Older patients have healthy babies all the time," the obstetrician said.

"Diana wore herself out taking call at all hours of the night, treating all those sick patients, doing all that surgery. Of course, hanging around that police chief in all those dangerous predicaments hasn't helped," Phoebe said. She returned to her seat in the waiting room and picked up a magazine, more of a catalogue for a women's clothing outlet.

Phoebe continued. "Not to mention putting up with all those

lunatic cheerleader mothers. Did you know that Diana made out one of those spreadsheet things to keep up with snack assignments for cheer practice? And then, of course, she hasn't been eating healthy herself, never has." Her voice broke in concern.

Kelsey sat next to Phoebe and rested her head on a shoulder. "Mom's okay. The doctor said she's okay," Kelsey repeated.

"Diana's waking up. She was dehydrated," the obstetrician said. "I gave her some IV fluid and meds to relax the uterus."

"Contractions?" Brad turned away from the painting. "It's been a while since my OB rotation. I thought contractions came later."

"Irritability—uterine spasms—that's a better way to put it. The medication worked, and as expected made her drowsy. She's in the first room down the hall."

Brad entered the room first. Kelsey and Phoebe stood together inside the door. "Doctor says you and the baby are gonna be fine." He bent down and pecked her on the cheek.

"Yeah, lips wouldn't have been a good idea. My breath would kill roaches," Diana said.

Brad chuckled. "Boy, did that spoil the mood."

"No way. Your being in the mood all the time put me here." Diana grinned and lifted her arm, the one without the IV tubing, and stroked Brad's face. "You're tired, worried."

"I am. I was."

"I've never kept up with my dates, so I never suspected anything. I guess I should've taken better care of myself. That tussle with Voncelle Wallace didn't help much."

"Your doctor said everything is going to be fine," Brad said.

"Go ahead and try the lips, just a peck. I don't think you'll lose consciousness. I'm thrilled about the baby. I'm hoping for a Brad, Junior."

"I like how you're talking." The peck progressed into a lip lock.

"Looks like I'm the one who's gonna be sick now," Kelsey said, moving into the hall. "Come on, Aunt Phoebe, before they manage to turn Brad, Junior into twins."

The two left for the snack bar.

Brad lifted his head and smiled down at Diana. "I love you."

"I love you too. I know I've got to get better."

"Your buddy out there has prescribed bedrest until the baby comes, and that translates into sleeping alone."

"The doctor already laid down the law. We can cuddle a lot and take it from there," Diana said.

"*From there* interests me," Brad said.

Diana fiddled with the pliable plastic intravenous tubing. "I've been lying here, in and out of that Vistaril-induced stupor, thinking about a hamburger and fries in between trying to figure out what really went down with Voncelle Wallace."

Brad held Diana's free hand. "They got Voncelle. The bullet extracted from Chuck's chest matched her rifle. Her lawyer's going to try to claim that Chuck abused her, and she acted in sort of self-defense."

Diana released Brad's hand to reach for the cup of water by the bed. He handed it to her instead. She took a long sip and swallowed.

"While you were sleeping, Martin called to check on you and said that the final came in on the Belmont ballistics—not a match to Voncelle. But he thinks they will nail her for Garcia."

"We all know what Voncelle did," Diana said. "She had the skill to shoot her husband and Garcia and didn't try to hide it. And she was the second to last person to see Chuck Wallace alive. The hospital security camera recorded her leave a minute before the Nursing Assistant entered the ICU bay."

"The Neo would have worked in minutes," Brad said.

"The NA in ICU told Martin he was only making Foley catheter rounds and didn't want to invade Dr. Wallace's personal space with family," Diana said.

"If he hadn't been so nice and gone ahead and interrupted, he might have prevented a murder."

"My guess is that Voncelle wouldn't have stopped until Chuck was dead."

"Probably," Brad agreed. "And Martin said they're also gonna check the hospital security cameras around Garcia. Likely they'll see Voncelle pay a visit."

Diana drank more water and raised the plastic cup in a toast. "I guess this will be it for me for five or six months, longer if I breast feed."

Brad smiled and stroked her cheek again, then returned the cup to the table for her. "I'll follow suit. Wouldn't hurt to rest the liver. There is this one thing."

"What is that?"

"What would drive Voncelle Wallace to murder Chuck, and work so hard to do it? An affair, his life insurance, physical or emotional abuse?"

"I do remember something she said when she was arrested," Diana answered. "Something about Chuck and Garcia hiding money."

She moved her legs under the thin hospital sheets and blanket and flexed and extended her feet at the ankles. Brad put his hand on her abdomen.

"I'm fine, Brad." She placed her hand over his. "We're fine. There's no pain, and there's been no more bleeding. But I'm tired and need a nap."

Her OB physician tapped on the door and entered the room. "Your last set of labs came back good. I've ordered another sono for in the morning. If everything's normal and there're no changes, you're out of here tomorrow."

"That's great news," Diana and Brad said almost simultaneously.

"I'm headed home for the night. Wife says she cooked. See ya tomorrow." He waved a raised hand palm forward and backed out of the door as Brad walked toward the visitor chair in the corner.

"You're exhausted, Babe," Diana said. "Skip what's left of patient charting for the rest of the day and get some fresh air. Does that group meet tonight?"

"Yeah. I've got time to run by the house and change, then meet those guys."

"Those walks—funny—that's where most of this all started with

Chuck and Voncelle. Of course, Garnett and his nephew were enough to handle by themselves."

"That Garnett guy knew Chuck. One of the other guys mentioned that," Brad said. "I wonder if Garnett will show tonight."

# Chapter 37



*Six weeks earlier*

Voncelle Wallace lay stretched out on the couch in the Doctors' Lounge of Metropolitan Hospital. She tried the television remote but a documentary on reported sightings of alien ships in the Bermuda Triangle did not interest her, nor did the replays of *Law and Order*, the original *Match Game*, or *Bewitched*. A basketball playoff on a different channel and a soccer match on yet another did not draw her in either. "I wish administration would lose this satellite service and subscribe to decent cable."

"My sentiment exactly." The male voice from behind gave her start. Voncelle scrambled to sit up, knocking the blanket she brought from home to the floor.

"Hi, I didn't hear you come in. Guess the volume was too loud," she said.

"Merely passing through," Ellis Belmont said. "My team doesn't spend all that much time in here like the hospitalists do—that imported group paid for by the same low-budget hospital administration that also provides the skimpy television service."

"Yes, I see them hogging the computers. It's often hard to find a free one to do my own charting." Voncelle stood from the couch.

Belmont extended his hand. "Ellis Belmont, the Belmont Medical Clinic and Spa."

Voncelle muted the television and accepted the gesture with a firm grip. "I know your group. I worked with a couple of your GI guys."

"My, my," he said, ending the handshake. "Not like most of the Southern Belles around here."

"Raised in New Orleans," she said. "And not in the Garden District or in Audubon."

"And you're with the Cummins-Bratton Surgical Group. How's that going?"

Voncelle did not answer but instead thought back to the last time she pulled up her checking account on her phone. She kept a bank account for her own salary apart from the shared joint account with Chuck. Her new surgery practice with Brad and Diana and the others in the group had been slow to get off the ground. She felt all she did was cover for the other surgeons' patients while on call and assist with everyone else's cases.

Belmont tilted his head at the lack of response. "And any updates on John Haynes? I know it's been a big—shall we say, change?—for him to be incarcerated. Such a tragedy and such a waste." The tilted head turned to a disgusted shake.

Voncelle straightened her posture. "I'm loving my new practice. Getting busier and busier every day."

"Good to know." They remained alone in the room. "Please, please sit. I know you surgeons are always run ragged, always exhausted." Belmont waited until Voncelle stepped back toward the couch. He then took an upholstered chair opposite, settling in before Voncelle reached her seat.

"We have more in common than simply healing the sick," Belmont said.

"How so?" Voncelle wished for the solitude and stale television from before.

"Your spouse is Charles Wallace."

"You know Chuck?"

"Not personally, professionally. His firm is handling the potential sale of the Belmont Enterprise to an equity group, actually a foreign outfit—Spanish. Adds up to be a wonderful opportunity. Once-in-a-lifetime. Nearly every Belmont and associate is on board. My sister, Sidney, is—to say it mildly—somewhat hesitant. Nevertheless, she'll come around." He smiled in satisfaction.

"I don't keep up with any of Chuck's business affairs. It's enough for me to—"

"Well, you should. The man is likely to clean up on this one. If Hernado Garcia's outfit comes through on the sale, your husband's commission will be substantial, certainly nothing to sneeze at—impressive even to a successful surgeon like you."

"Who's Hernando Garcia?"

"Your husband has never mentioned him or this deal? Surprising," Belmont said. "Garcia heads a medical and surgical conglomerate overseas. Tragically, there is widespread, government-run socialized medicine outside the United States. However, that has not deterred Garcia International Enterprises from amassing a tremendous share in health futures in the overseas stock market."

Voncelle fought the urge to google the name and the company on her phone.

"Garcia hopes to extend his European and Asian reach into the more market- and consumer-driven USA. A tremendous amount of money remains to be made in healthcare."

A CRNA employed by the Anesthesia Department entered the lounge through a door around the corner nearer the restrooms and changing area. She jerked open the refrigerator and grabbed a canned drink and a bag of chips from a side counter. Belmont stared at her disapprovingly, and she left the room. The door shut loudly behind her.

Belmont leaned forward in a whisper: "If this deal goes through, you may be able to give Cummins and his wife your notice." He assessed the aging décor in the windowless hospital lounge, then stood to leave and jeered. "Imagine not being stuck up here, night after night, rotting in this place. There's a world out there, Dr. Voncelle Wallace. Time to live it."

She forced a smile of appreciation and studied her cell phone. Garcia International Enterprises appeared quickly in the search engine. Voncelle pulled up the website and scrolled through the listings and descriptions. Featured in flattering clothing and lighting was her husband, Charles Wallace, known to his friends and close business associates as *Chuck*. He stood in a group picture with two men identified in the photograph as Hernando Garcia and Federico Lorca-Pérez, principles of the investment firm. Much, if not all, of what that snooty Ellis Belmont said seemed correct. Garcia International Enterprises screamed impressive.

Voncelle shook her head, not sure if it should be out of aggravation or distrust. *Why hasn't Chuck told me about this?* She examined the sad lounge area thoroughly disparaged by Belmont.

*Is Chuck trying to surprise me?* She read on through the website. Lots of beautiful shots of Spain and the museum noted to be across the way from the corporate offices featuring new exhibits monthly. A spouse was mentioned in Hernando Garcia's biography—no spouse or partner for Pérez. Voncelle studied the woman's face and figure. *Not impressed with her, though.*

One of the Metropolitan hospitalists breezed in. She smiled curtly and absentmindedly to Dr. Wallace and accessed one of the computers, the furthest from Voncelle's spot on the couch. "That's what I thought. A negative culture," she cackled and left the area, leaving the computer to reset to standby in several minutes.

Voncelle sprang to the same computer and exited out of the Metropolitan EMR system. She accessed the internet through the hospital visitors' network and again pulled up the information on Garcia to read in greater detail. Mrs. Garcia was less attractive in the enlarged photo. "She works as an office administrative assistant. A secretary?" Hernando Garcia appeared even better close-up.

*Chuck's been holding out on this and why?*

Voncelle jotted down the contact number for Garcia International Enterprises and closed out of the site.

After escaping the life of a financially struggling resident and younger physician, she was not one to check bank or investment accounts often. Why would she? Monthly email confirmed deposit of her salary in her personal account, and the credit card payments for household and car expenses always went through on the joint account shared with Chuck. She also charged most of her clothing and other personal expenses to Chuck, since he never encouraged her to shop for herself, nor suggest they take a long weekend trip out of town or even go out to eat.

Voncelle located the app for their local bank on her phone and confirmed a healthy balance in that account. She paused a minute. Another person walked into the lounge and adjusted the channel and volume on the television. Voncelle ignored them. The computer cubicle was positioned in such a way that from the television viewing area no one could see her face or the computer monitor screen.

*I share with Chuck all the time. Tell him everything about what's going on at work: the patient load, how Brad and Diana treat me financially and professionally, what kind of mood my office nurse was in for the day.* She closed the bank app. *Dealing with those Belmont creeps. A big cash payout. Why did Chuck keep that from me?*

More investigative work on the desktop computer came next. *The name of our investment bank. The retirement money. What is it?*

She searched names of familiar investment firms until settling on American Worldwide for the People Bank. Voncelle went to the site, entered Chuck's personal email address to log in, and was faced with providing a password. She tried several with no luck. *Is there somebody in IT at the clinic who can get me in? Anybody I can trust?*

Then she remembered her phone. Against the advice of an in-the-know office nurse who told her she could get hacked by keeping a list of passwords on her cell, Voncelle stored them in her notes in a simple list—not in the software settings. She scrolled through until she found *AWFTPB*. She entered the password under the username and the account ledger populated the screen.

Deposits filled the credit column, most tagged to receipt of consultation payments from GIE. *That's Hernando Garcia's group.* The account balance popped up in bold black font in the upper left corner. "What the fah?!" she announced, easily audible over the television volume.

Brad Cummins voice startled her. "Voncelle, is that you over there. You say something?"

She raised slightly out of her chair and called out to Brad. "No, talking to myself. Can't believe how many delinquent charts I have to sign off on."

"I know. I heard those suits in hospital administration hired an overseas outfit to handle all that stuff and moved the medical records people offsite. All they do now is dump it back on us."

Voncelle settled back into the chair. She heard a change of channel, a different athletic event judging from the noisy crowd and chatty commentators. "Overseas—yes—seems that's where it's at."

A snapping shut of the refrigerator and a cabinet over the sink followed. Voncelle jumped to the ripping apart of a plastic food bag behind her. "You trying to balance your bank account?" Brad said, standing directly behind her. "I leave that crap to Diana and my accountant. Every time I try to call those numbers for help, I get somebody I can't understand."

Voncelle cowered over the information on monitor.

Brad popped several pieces of popcorn in his mouth. "This pre-packaged stuff is actually pretty tasty. Might eat the whole bag." He ate more and walked away, chewing. "Don't ask me to help with any of that banking stuff. Thank God for the bookkeeping girls we got over at the office and for Diana with our personal stuff. I'd be out on the curb, begging, or in jail."

Voncelle waited a few seconds for Brad to get settled. The channel changed again, and the volume increased. *Good.* She clicked on the memo section of each entry. Most indicated payment for hours of consultation services or negotiation work. One detailed travel reimbursement, and Voncelle noted the dates. "What? He told me that was a golf trip with the walking group."

She immediately regretted speaking aloud, but Brad could not have heard over the television. She closed down the computer and decided to make light of the interaction. "What are you doing here anyway, Brad? I'm the one on duty. I don't think it's for the free Mountain Dew and popcorn snacks."

"Got a call from a guy named Roy. Said he was one Diana's patients. She was already asleep after a bad call last night, so I didn't bother her with it. Not sure how he got my cell. Name does sound kinda familiar."

*Dammit. Chuck knows better than to give out a doctor's number.*

"He said he had abdominal pain, thought he might have appendicitis and wanted me to see him in the ED. He seemed legit." Brad took a long sip of the canned soda. "They're getting the OR ready now. I suspect an incarcerated hernia, not an appendix. Hope you don't mind if I go ahead and do the case."

Voncelle referred to the many texts and messages on her phone from the answering service, many left unanswered. "Sure no, problem."

"You seem plenty busy around here tonight," Brad said, "without having to deal with this guy too."

*Plenty busy? Yeah—busy getting swamped taking care of yours and Diana's whiny patients. That's why I'm busy.* She scanned the list on her phone and noted the missed text from a Roy Garnett with a follow-up reminder text from the answering service a few minutes later. Voncelle decided not to mention her oversight. She figured Garnett probably had high paying insurance. "Dammit. I missed out on that one," she cussed into the computer.

"Say something else, Von?"

A circulating room nurse from the OR stuck her head through the door. "Ready for you in three, Dr. Cummins," she said beaming, while ignoring Dr. Wallace.

"Headed your way." Brad rested what remained of the Mountain Dew on the center table in front of his chair and crumpled the empty popcorn bag in his hands. He tossed the bag in the trash and went with the nurse. "Catch ya later, Voncelle."

"Men—always taking advantage. Leaving me out while I do all the work." She studied the ledger of the investment bank account in more detail, referring to the memos and comparing the dates of other deposits and expenses against the notes linked to the calendar in her phone. No notes indicated any of Chuck's activities, confirming that she had been out of the loop with all of this except for the fabricated golf trip.

Shortly before signing out of the investment account, she spotted a voided entry with memo indicating that the deposit was meant as a corporate, not personal financial entry. "No telling what's in his business account."

Voncelle flipped back to the Garcia International Enterprises website and placed a call to Hernando Garcia. She continued to admire his photograph published on the internet and couldn't have cared less about the time zone difference.

Chuck Wallace circled until he located an empty spot in the patient visitor hospital parking lot. He strolled along the perimeter of the *physician only* section and scanned the vehicles for one belonging to Voncelle. "Good, no car. It's after ten, so she must be over at the clinic. I'll miss her inside."

Nevertheless, Chuck entered the hospital sheepishly. He glanced away from the obvious security cameras scattered about the lobby and located in the corridors as though Voncelle sat ready to catch him live at a bank of monitors in a dimly lit room somewhere.

The night before, Roy Garnett called Chuck in terrific abdominal pain and nausea. He shared he was a newly established patient with Dr. Bratton at Voncelle's surgery group and had not gotten a call back from the physician on call. "Don't know how much longer I can hold out," Roy had said. "Might have to show up at the ER. Throw myself to the wolves."

Knowing that Voncelle was on call and to keep his business with Roy Garnett under wraps, he decided to share Brad Cummins's cell with Roy since he did not have Diana's number. He told Roy: "Stretch the truth. Tell Dr. Cummins that you've been his wife's patient for a long time. He probably won't know you've only seen her the one time. Throw in that he and his wife are the best around, and you don't trust anybody else. Hell, he might even be flattered. Try to leave my name out of it and not offer how you got his number."

A groggy Roy Garnett reported earlier this morning by phone that his surgery went well and that he got his hernia fixed. "Doc said it looked like gangrene. Thing can go bad in a hurry, but we got it in the nick of time. He said something about sepsis. Man, I almost died!"

Aware of the over exaggeration, Chuck was thankful his longtime friend and now new business associate had survived. The nurse at the third-floor general surgery desk seemed busy and cranky and didn't bother to show Chuck the way when he asked for Roy's room number. He found the patient, nonetheless. Besides, he wanted to talk to Roy in private private and not attract attention.

"You think you can keep your nephew in line to help us out?" Chuck asked.

"He's good to go, as long as he stays on his meds." Roy continued to slur his words in what seemed like a successful attempt to put a thought together post-anesthesia and after taking narcotics.

"I need to keep him on retainer. This project with the Belmonts is hard sell to all the docs. The woman, name is Sidney, particularly muleheaded. I've met with her myself at least twice trying to convince her that Garcia's group is the way to go."

"The girl might need to be convinced," Roy said. "I'll talk to Dillon about it, and he can keep an eye on her. The kid might seem slow, but he's got a decent head on his shoulders—ugly, not much to gander at—but not a total imbecile."

# Chapter 38



*Present Day*

Diana sat at her office desk with her feet propped up and read through files on her laptop. "It's amazing how many reports mount up even if you're out of the office."

"I could have dropped the laptop by your house on the way home," Mallory said, "and by the way, no extra charge for watering this peace lily. All part of my job as office nurse." A patient sent Diana the potted plant on her desk after learning she had been hospitalized. Other plant and flower get-well-soon gifts were spread about the lobby and waiting area. "And another thing," Mallory raised her chin for emphasis, "your OB said bedrest. Doesn't that mean stay at home?"

"I took an Uber XL up here—a nice, new one—stretched my legs out on the back seat. Brad is going to take me home when he finishes clinic."

Mallory finished with the watering can, one of the old-fashioned, heavy metal ones, and held it to her side. She had brought it from home. It used to belong to her grandmother.

"I know you and Dr. Cummins are excited about the baby!"

"Yes, now that the shock has worn off. The bleeding and the contractions, or spasms, were a total scare. A lot of mixed emotions about it all, but I am very, very happy."

"What about your daughter?"

"Typical response from a teenage girl who has to fess up at school that her mother has sex."

Mallory giggled.

"Kelsey seems to be getting more enthusiastic about having a brother, even with the difference in ages, but I don't expect much help with diaper changes. Maybe she'll give a bottle or two." Both she and Mallory laughed. "My life is entirely different from when I was pregnant with Kelsey and took care of her as a newborn." Diana remembered the belt lashings from her ex-husband and his refusal to help with childcare while she was on night call as a surgery resident.

"How long will you be off work?"

"I hope my OB will let me come back at least to see patients in the clinic before the baby comes. I know a lot depends on the next few weeks." Diana detected a different show of concern on Mallory's face. "You have been a tremendous help to me over these last few years. I need you to still be around when I'm back up to full steam. We'll find plenty for you to do as a nurse while I'm out."

"I'll do anything around here to help," Mallory said. "You're wonderful, Dr. Bratton."

"Dr. Bratton says the same about me all the time. Don't you, Diana?" Brad appeared in the doorway, laughing. "My clinic finished early. You ready to go home?" Brad stepped into her office. "Hope you haven't over done it."

"A model patient, Dr. Cummins. Always," Mallory said.

"Let's go home. The couch and my bed await."

"I can either carry you or get a wheelchair," Brad said. He stepped closer and pulled Diana's chair back from the desk. "I'm not sure I ever carried you over the threshold. This is a chance to make up for lost time."

Mallory squealed when Brad lifted Diana out of the chair and carried her to the door in his arms. "Didn't I handle you like this when we stayed at the Ritz in New Orleans."

"I can't remember. What's more I try not to think about that crazy night and the sick nurse." She grinned at her own office nurse. "Long story, Mallory."

"Even if you did carry me over the threshold, it doesn't count, Brad. We weren't married yet, and I sure wasn't pregnant."

Still holding the empty metal watering can, Mallory joined Diana and Brad in the hall. "Let me get the elevator for you. You two are just too stinkin' cute."

The down control lit and the elevator to the parking garage arrived promptly. "See ya when I see ya," Diana called out as Brad carried her inside and the elevator doors began to close behind them. "Thanks again for all your help, Mallory."

"Oh, Dr. Bratton. Do you want to take your laptop home with you? I can run back and get it."

The elevator doors shut quickly to Diana's, "Yes."

About fifteen feet beyond the garage elevator, parking spots assigned to Diana and Brad were separated by the space once occupied by Brad's deceased twin brother, Brian. There were no plans to reassign the space.

Brad managed to fumble the fob to his new F-150 from his pocket and click open the doors. He settled Diana into the rear bench seat of the extended rear passenger compartment.

"Comfy?"

"Let me have your jacket." She removed his pen from the front pocket and wadded the jacket into a pillow. "There—perfect. Home, James."

"You two ain't going nowhere."

Brad froze to a gun at the back of his head and neck. "This whole shitty mess with my uncle and me started with all this medical business, and it's gonna end here. I've got his gun."

Diana sat up.

"Don't move," the man said.

"Yeah, Diana, stay put," Brad said.

"My uncle pulled me into all this crap."

Diana recognized Dillon Garnett. She forced composure. "Where is your uncle, Dillon? Let's call him. I've got my phone." She pointed to the front pocket of her slacks.

"I don't think he'll answer," Dillon said. "Unless it's from hell."

"What is it you want, man. Narcotics? We don't keep any of that around here."

"I know. I remember from the last time I met here with the lady doctor," Dillon chuckled. "That's not why I'm here this time."

"Why are you here then?" Diana asked. "Do you need money? My husband carries cash. Go ahead and show him, Brad."

"Don't move a freakin' muscle, you ass. Money is all you medical creeps care about. My uncle was trying to help a dude buy out a group of doctors around here. Now, see where that got him?"

"What dude? Who are you talking about?" Brad took a deep breath.

"Name was *Chuck*. My uncle knew him when they both lived in New Orleans. He moved up here after my mom died."

"You're talking about Chuck Wallace?" Diana said. "And your uncle has been a patient of mine. Roy …"

"Roy Garnett. And go ahead and cancel his next appointment. No doctor can help him now."

Brad stared at Diana: *Let me handle this.* "Fella, let's go back upstairs and talk this thing out."

*No, don't go,* Diana pleaded back with watery eyes. *Don't do it.*

"I'm not sure what your beef is with Dr. Bratton and me, but she's going to have a baby. I don't want to upset her."

"I don't care who I upset. I don't give a flip anymore."

Diana could see Brad's wheels turning before he said, "You're bound to need money if your uncle's not around to help and your mom has passed away. The office manager has a big safe upstairs, and I know the combination."

Dillon shifted his stance around Brad's chest to better see Diana. His arm appeared to grow tired of reaching to press his revolver into the neck of the much taller Brad. "I guess I could use money for gas and a motel room until I decide what to do next. I forgot to take Uncle Roy's wallet."

"You got a plan then," Brad said.

"Brad, be careful," Diana said with as much conviction as she could muster.

"Oh, don't worry. Dillon and I are on the same page. He needs a spot, a new crib, out-of-town to relocate ... like the beach ... or cabin in the mountains. He's been busy and needs to relax."

"Yeah, I need to relax."

"Okay, then," Brad said. "I'm going to turn around, and we'll walk to the elevator that's behind you.

"No, don't turn around." Dillon glanced over his shoulder at the elevator doors behind them. "Back-up slow, nice and easy. I'll push the button, and we'll step inside. No sudden movements."

"All right then. Whatever you say. You first."

"On a count of three," Dillon said. "And make sure you stay tight against the tip of my gun. You move quick and that baby won't see its daddy."

"Got it, boss," Brad said.

On *three* Dillon stepped back and Brad moved slowly with him, the gun tight against the nape of his neck. "Be careful now. Watch your step," Brad said.

When Diana spotted Dillon glance down at the concrete, she removed her phone from her pocket. She managed to slide the *SOS Emergency Call* bar to the right and ducked the phone out of site.

"I think I'm almost to the elevator," Dillon said.

Just as he reached for the control, the doors opened to Diana's plant-watering nurse from upstairs. At five-ten, Mallory's height was midway between Brad's six-two stature and the short guy she saw pointing a gun at him. She had planned to leave for the day after bringing Dr. Bratton's forgotten laptop to her and still held the heavy watering can in her right hand along with the laptop in her left. Mallory's purse hung over the opposite shoulder.

She dropped the laptop and swung the watering can down hard on the assailant. The man stumbled and lowered the gun. When he attempted to raise it, she struck again, much harder. The third blow splattered blood across the back of Brad's shirt sending the unfired revolver flying from a now unconscious Dillon Garnett to the concrete.

"Jesus, Dr. Cummins! Are you all right?" Mallory jerked her head toward the opened rear door of the truck. "And, Dr. Bratton?"

Police sirens could be heard in the distance. Diana cautiously worked her way out of the rear seat of the truck. "Boy, that was fast. I thought they'd call back first." She stood next to Brad. The nurse trembled.

"Yes, I'm fine," Diana said. "We both are, but I'm sorry you didn't have the lid to a toilet tank with you."

"Whhaaatttt?" Mallory said.

"It's a lot easier that way. One blow to the head of a crazy nurse at the Ritz does the trick."

Brad felt for Dillon's carotid pulse. It was present and the guy was breathing.

"I don't understand," Mallory said, still trembling.

"No need to. You, my hero, get paid overtime until I'm back in commission."

The police sirens grew louder as three cars appeared outside the entrance to the physicians' parking garage. Chief Key Martin and Detective Thomas ran forward, maneuvering around the non-raised boom gate.

"Martin, how'd y'all get here so fast? I only used my phone a couple of minutes ago."

"What? Brad asked. "You used your phone?'

"Your office manager called 911," Thomas answered.

"Our manager was out today, and the three of us were the last to leave the building for the afternoon," Diana said.

"The office manager happened to pull up the security camera feed offsite. Said she had a gut feeling. Guess she needs a raise," Martin said.

# Epilogue

Miles Belmont fished the paper tag from the depths of his pants pocket in preparation for the valet. The country club provided valet parking on Sundays and special events, like his wife's birthday party tonight—so special that Frances Belmont called it a night after the band's first encore performance and rode home with brother Ellis.

The raucous dance crowd had demanded more and the ten-piece band from Atlanta complied without question—all part of the contract that provided an extra thousand bucks for a second encore. Miles amazed even himself with his stamina on the dance floor as the band played on and an up-and-close, dancefloor invitation from the beautiful blonde lead singer drew him to the stage. Miles performed his best rendition of "Brick House" and "Y.M.C.A."-front and center.

*Thank God I had a blank check in my wallet,* Miles thought as his new white Porsche appeared under the porte cache. He presented the claim ticket with two folded one-dollar bills and slid into the driver's seat. The attendant nodded as he handed Dr. Belmont the keys, and Miles pulled the car away.

"Sure you shouldn't take an Uber? You stumbled a bit as you walked out of the club."

Startled, Miles jerked the sports car into the parking area near the tennis center. "Who in the hell are you? And what the freak are you doing in my car?"

"I saw the miserable tip you gave that old man. At least, I knew it was stingy from the look on his face." The Spanish accent was thick, the voice silky with a touch of professional polish.

"I'm calling the police." Miles grabbed his cell from his pants pocket.

"You do that and save me the trouble," the woman said. "But I really don't know what the police will do for either of us."

Miles turned to the back seat, the woman's face only half-illuminated by the parking lot lighting. "Who the hell are you, and how did you get into my car?"

"That fuddy duddy old man, the parking attendant, he will do anything for a twenty in American. I thought about making his night with a little touchy-feely below the waist, but I was afraid his ticker couldn't take it. I told him I was your girlfriend and wanted to surprise you with a nightcap in the backseat."

Miles stared at the woman—solid black hair, good skin, but too much mascara for his taste.

"I took my beloved Hernando, all that was left of him, and flew back to Spain. The funeral was stupendous … in the cathedral with the full choir. I will have to give the Americans credit. The mortuary did a wonderful job, repairing what the shooter did to him."

"I don't know what you are talking about." Miles renewed attention to his phone.

"Go ahead and call the authorities. I'm sure they will be interested in what the Belmont family has done."

*Hernando? Hernando Garcia?!* That day in the abandoned building flashed before him—the day when someone else shot Sidney before he could. *How could this woman know anything about that? Was she in the States?*

"Okay, I'm clueless," he responded. "Just what is it you think the Belmont family has done?"

"My poor husband was starstruck by you rich doctors. But I took some accounting courses, and I'm no fool. Hernando took your Mr. Wallace's financial records as gospel, despite my concern that he was being less than honest in pushing the sale through to our equity group. 'We need the Belmont Empire,' my Hernando said one night in bed."

"I'm sorry you lost your husband, but what does that have to do with me? My family is just as much a victim as you."

"Hernando was lured back to America, perhaps by his own ambitious desires, perhaps something else. I don't know. But I do know he was murdered, and all I have left is a lonely bed."

A text message from Frances lit up Miles's cell phone.

```
Where the hell are you? This is my damn
birthday!
```

"I don't know why you're here, but it's my wife's birthday. Get out of my car."

"My dear Hernando aimed for the sky. I think you realized he would uncover the truth, that the Belmonts are nothing but what you in the American South call *white trash*, maybe rich white trash, but slime, nonetheless. If you are not the ones who killed him, I think you know the bastard who did."

"Lady, or senorita—or whatever, I would tell you if I knew … honestly, I would. Anything to get you out of my freaking car. But I'm going to call the police if you don't get the hell away from me right now."

Lucinda slid to the door of the backseat behind Miles and popped it open. "I must return to Spain and try to save what is left of the Garcia company. Federico is demanding answers, financial answers. Perhaps, I can help him come out on top."

"Federico? Who the hell is Federico?"

Lucinda stepped out of the Porche and into the flickering light of the parking lot, leaving the door opened. "You will never be safe—you or your brother, Ellis. Yes, I know his name. I have seen and studied all of your pictures online. Your *medical empire*, as my wonderful husband called it, would have ruined Garcia International Enterprises had the sale gone through. Perhaps I should thank you."

Miles stretched into the backseat to shut the door.

Lucinda grabbed the door frame. "You go home to your rich wife, while I fly home to an empty house. No, I do not thank you."

Miles jerked the back door shut and gunned the Porsche. Lucinda watched him navigate clumsily through the parking lot, few cars remaining to be in danger of a collision.

"I will get answers. The Belmonts—or someone else—will pay. This I swear, Hernando."

# Acknowledgments

I would like to thank my advance readers for their tireless and constructive input used in completing this novel: Karen Cole, Betty (betsi) Bailey, Lottie Boggan, Lloyd Bourne, and Johnna Bickerstaff.

The research needed to complete *Rooftop* included topic conversations with Richard McNeel, Toni Upton, Bill Johnson, Harper Stone, Tim Cannon, and my family. In addition, I referenced this online article: icureach.com/ Author: Namareq Aldardeer, May 7, 2023, and Updated May 26, 2023: "Phenylephrine in Patients with Septic Shock."

I would also like to thank those who read and/or listen to my novels in the available formats and the booksellers and other vendors who make that possible. Hats off go to publisher Mike Parker and his staff at Wordcrafts Press for taking me on and for providing much encouragement. The book covers are always the best, and Mike is also a stellar editor.

Book clubs, civic organizations, libraries, conferences, and bookstores continue to ask me to speak about my novels and the craft of writing. Please keep the invitations and book signings coming. Online video events with author Darden North can also be arranged. It's easy to contact me through my website: *www.dardennorth.com* where readers can sign up for my email newsletter and get updates about new releases and events.

For those budding novelists interested in locating support or writing critique groups, I suggest they explore the availability of local writers' guild organizations such as the strong organization we have in Mississippi and consider participation in such online writing workshops as Writing Away Refuge or Pitch to Publish.

I'm looking forward to my next novel and thanks again for reading and supporting the craft.

~Darden North

# About the Author

Darden North's mystery and thriller novels have been awarded nationally, most notably an IPPY in Southern Fiction for *Points of Origin* and *Party Favors*. His other novels include *The 5 Manners of Death*, *Wiggle Room*, *Fresh Frozen*, and *House Call*.

North has served on writing panels or spoken at conferences including ThrillerFest, the Mississippi Book Festival, Killer Nashville, the 29th Natchez Literary and Cinema Celebration, Murder on the Menu, SIBA Thriller Panel, and Murder in the Magic City. He has been Chairman of the Board of the Mississippi Public Broadcasting Foundation and a member of the Editorial Board of the *Journal of the Mississippi State Medical Association*.

A native of the Mississippi Delta, North is a gynecologist and lives in Jackson with his wife Sally. They enjoy family, traveling, and outdoor activities.

Learn more at:

www.dardennorth.com